P A C I N O

CARLITO'S WAY

AL PACINO · SEAN PENN · PENELOPE ANN MILLER

UNIVERSAL PICTURES AND EPIC PRODUCTIONS PRESENT
A BREGMAN/BAER PRODUCTION • A BRIAN DE PALMA FILM • "CARLITO'S WAY"
MUSIC BY PATRICK DOYLE • EDITED BY BILL PANKOW • PRODUCTION DESIGNER RICHARD SYLBERT
DIRECTOR OF PHOTOGRAPHY STEPHEN H. BURUM, A.S.C.
EXECUTIVE PRODUCERS LOUIS A. STROLLER • ORTWIN FREYERMUTH
BASED ON THE NOVELS "CARLITO'S WAY" AND "AFTER HOURS" BY EDWIN TORRES • SCREENPLAY BY DAVID KOEPP
PRODUCED BY MARTIN BREGMAN • WILLI BAER • MICHAEL S. BREGMAN • DIRECTED BY BRIAN DE PALMA
A UNIVERSAL PICTURE
©1993 UNIVERSAL CITY STUDIOS, INC.

UNIVERSAL
AN MCA COMPANY

CARLITO'S WAY

EDWIN TORRES

AVON BOOKS ◆ NEW YORK

AVON BOOKS
A division of
The Hearst Corporation
1350 Avenue of the Americas
New York, New York 10019

Carlito's Way copyright © 1975 by Edwin Torres
After Hours copyright © 1979 by Edwin Torres
Cover art copyright © 1993 MCA Publishing Rights, a division of MCA, Inc. All rights reserved.
ISBN: 0-380-72287-9

First Avon Books Printing: November 1993
First Avon Books Printing of *Carlito's Way*: August 1982
First Avon Books Printing of *After Hours*: September 1982

AVON TRADEMARK REG. U.S. PAT. OFF. AND IN OTHER COUNTRIES, MARCA REGISTRADA, HECHO EN U.S.A.

Printed in the U.S.A.

RA 10 9 8 7 6 5 4 3 2 1

CARLITO'S WAY

To the memory of Orlando Cardona,
the best of the 107th Street bunch, killed in action,
February 4, 1951, Wonju, Korea

SOONER OF LATER, A THUG WILL TELL HIS TALE. WE ALL want to go on record. So let's hear it for all the hoods. The Jews out of Brownsville. The Blacks on Lenox Avenue. The Italians from Mulberry Street. Like that. Meanwhile, the Puerto Ricans been gettin' jammed since the forties and ain't nobody said nothin'. We been laid, relayed, and waylaid and nobody wants to hear about it. Well, I'm gonna lay it on you one time, for the record.

Who these people? Puerto Ricans. They come from an island a hundred long by thirty-five miles wide. They come in all sizes, colors, and shapes. They got a little of everybody. Heart like the Jews, soul like the Blacks, balls like the Italians. They hit New York in the 1940s, the wrong time. But like when is it right, when your face don't help, your accent ain't French, and your clothes don't fit? They hung in anyway—most of the tickets were one way. So they filed into the roach stables in Harlem and the South Bronx. They sat behind the sewing machines and stood behind the steam tables. In other words, they busted their ass, they went for the Dream. Most of them.

A handful couldn't handle the weight at the bottom of the totem pole. They wouldn't squat, couldn't bend. Had to take their shot. Them was the hodedores, hoodlums. Hard nose. And like the thugs from any group they went for the coin of the realm, head on.

I'm talking from the far shore looking back on thirty

years. At least I made it to the other side. Most of my crew got washed on the way. And if survivors don't talk about it, who's gonna know we was here, right? So here's how it went down for one P.R., me, Carlito Brigante.

1

I CAME ON THE SCENE IN THE 1930S. ME AND MY MOMS. Brigante Sr. had long since split back to Puerto Rico. Seem like we was in every furnished room in Spanish Harlem. Kind of hazy some of it now, but I can remember her draggin' me by the hand from place to place—the clinic on 106th Street, the home relief on 105th Street, the Pentecostal church on 107th Street. That was home base, the church. Kids used to call me a "hallelujah"— break my chops. My mom was in there every night bangin' on a tambourine with the rest of them. Sometimes they'd get a special *reverendo* who'd really turn them on. That's when the believers, *feligreses*, would start hoppin' and jumpin'— then they'd be faintin' on the floor and they'd wrap them in white sheets. I remember I didn't go for this part. I was close to my mom, it was just me and her.

I was comin' into my teens in the 1940s when they laid her out at Gonzalez's Funeral Home on 109th Street. Looked like she was into one of her faints, like she'd be all right. Wasn't like that. I ain't sayin' my way would have been any different if she'd been around. That's all you hear in the Joint—aw, man, I didn't have a chance. Bullshit. I was already a mean lil' fucker while my mom was alive, but I always respected women because of her.

Anyway, the court put me on to this jive uncle who come out of nowhere up in the Bronx. I got promoted from the basement to the sub-basement. No good. I cut out. Back down to Harlem. Sleepin' on the roof. Stayin' with friends.

7

Then the juvenile people put me in the Heckscher home near 104th Street. But I was always takin' off on them. I was still in my teens. World War II was over but they was warrin' in the streets. Kiddie gangs was goin' strong. The Puerto Ricans was boxed in. Irish on the south, Italians to the east, Blacks to the north and west. Wasn't none of that brotherhood jive in them days. Git that Po'Rican! We was catchin' hell.

The crazy part is me comin' up rumblin' against these groups as a kid—it should end up that the only two cats that was ever in my corner was Earl Bassey, a black dude, and Rocco Fabrizi, a wal-yo. Unbelievable. But I'm jumpin' ahead.

Lemme tell you about them rumbles. The wops said no spics could go east of Park Avenue. But there was only one swimming pool and that was the Jefferson on 112th Street off the East River. Like, man, you had to wade through Park, Lexington, Third, Second, First, Pleasant. Wall-to-wall guineas. The older guys be standing around in front of the stoops and stores, evil-eyeing us, everybody in his undershirt; the kids would be up on the roof with the garbage cans and in the basements with the bats and bicycle chains. Mostly busted heads, black eyes in those days. First into the street was always me, loved a swingout. That's when I first saw Rocco Fabrizi. He was running with a wop gang, the Redwings. One day we went down to the pool with about twenty or thirty P.R. guys—a hell of a rumble—and right up front is this guy, Rocco, swinging a stickball bat. Stuck in my mind, tough kid. We took a beating—their turf, too many guys. A while later we get the word that this Rocco is sneaking up on a roof with a Latin chick named Carmen—fine head—near Madison Avenue and 107th Street. The balls. He caught some beatin', but he stood up; the Lopez brothers wanted to throw him off the roof but I said enough. He remembered.

The spooks said no Ricans could go west of Fifth Avenue. So if they caught you in Central Park, shame on you. The Copiens, the Socialistics, the Bachelors, the Comanches— all bad motherfuckers—these were the gangs that started using hardware. Then the rumbles got mean—like if the

Copiens caught you, you knew they were going to stick you. Then the zip guns came out, metal tubes with door latches as firing pins set off by rubber bands—if the pin hit the .22 on the primer and the piece was held close to your head, you were in trouble. Lucky for a lot of diddy boppers it wasn't often. I once got caught by the Copiens in Central Park by the lake near 106th Street. Me and this black kid duked it out after he said, "Let me hold a quarter." I said, "Let yo' mammy hold it." We got it on, I was kicking him on the ground when his boys arrived on bikes—my blood was up; I said, "I'll take any one of you motherfuckers." "No, motherfucker, we gonna kill yo' ass," and they started pulling the rubber bands on the zip guns. So like I quit the scene, they chased me all the way to 110th Street. That was the last chase on me like that. I always carried a piece from then on. I wasn't about to take no shit. You step up, I'm gonna knock you down.

Summers were hotter in them days. No air conditioning—the asphalt could burn your sneakers. Took the bus up to Highbridge Pool in Washington Heights. The Irish jumped us in the locker room—we fought with the metal baskets. Know what the pool guard said? "You don't belong up here." No sooner we was on the bus back, we had to bail out the windows on to Amsterdam Avenue, a mob of micks was comin' through the door after us.

That same summer I got hit in the head with a roller skate by some spade in Central Park by the boats near 110th Street. Another time I got my neck all scraped up from a bicycle chain some eye-talian wrapped around me. We caught it from everybody. Don't get me wrong, we gave good as we got—but you remember your own lumps better. We was tryin' to melt into the pot but they wouldn't even let us in the swimming pool. *Hijos de puta*.

Irregardless, I was never a race man. Us P.R.'s are like that—maybe 'cause we come in so many shades. We always had a stray wop or Jew-boy and plenty of spades with our gangs. Anyway, I figure them beatings get you ready for later on—when you gotta get the money.

But the clubs wasn't always fightin'. There was a lot of stickball playing—we had the Devils, the CBCs, the Home

Reliefers (dig it), the Turbens (that's the way they spelled it), the Viceroys, the Zeniths, the Falcons, the Tropical Gents, the Royal Knights, the Boca Chica—these all claimed to be S.A.C.—social and ataletic club—ha.

Pimping was popular. Tony Navarro, the Cruz brothers, Bobby Roldan, all had whores. We looked up to these guys—big cars, always a ringside table at the Palladium; always clean, none of that zoot-suit shit—wingtip shoes, conservative-cut clothes. Imagine lookin' up to a pimp! Later on we wouldn't let one of them scumbag motherfuckers stand near us at the bar.

About that time *motherfucker* came into style—it came down from black Harlem in a game called "the dozens." Two cats would meet on the street and start playin' the dozens; one guy would say, "Ashes to ashes, dust to dust, your mother has a pussy like a Greyhound bus," and the other guy come back with, "The dozens ain't my game but the way I fuck your mother is a goddamn shame!" Rough on the mothers. From then on everything was motherfucker.

Mostly we stood around corners on Madison Avenue. Just like Middletown, U.S.A.—ha. The schools, Patrick Henry, Cooper—forget about it. No YMCA, no Boys' Club, no gym, raunchy houses, scummy streets. If you inclined to plea-cop, them streets contributed to the delinquency of a whole lot of minors. But who wants to hear that shit? Only plea I ever copped cost me three years in the slams. A man got to stand up. Take his shot.

Like when the junk started arrivin' about this time. And where did the wops first arrive it? Right on ol' 107th Street between Lexington and Third. A punk-ass kid I was, but I looked it over. I'm gonna ride the horse, or the horse gonna ride me? That was the question on a lot of them corners,'cause the junk was still a new scene in the forties. All the losers went for the spike and the dynamite high behind it. Only a skag high ain't but good the first few times out, then you hooked, all they gotta do is reel you in, by the crotch now, and squeeze till you cough up another five dollars for a bag. I seen the horse play with them junkies like a cat with a rubber mouse.

Age fourteen, I saw that. I said, uh-uh. Them's the

humped—I'm goin' with the humpers. The dealers had the pussy, the clothes, and the cars. That's what I wanted, in that order. The dope fiends had the sores, the scabs, the O.D.'s. Maybe that's what they wanted. Must be crazy— couldn't see it then, can't see it now.

I was thinkin' myself, among other things, half a pug in them days. I didn't really know the science of the game, but I was heavy-handed, with a lot of snap in my shoulder, so when I tagged a stud, he was hurtin'. So now I'm gonna go in the Gloves, this must have been round '48 or '49. With a little trainin' everybody said Carliot was a natural. I was gonna fight for the Police Athletic League. Ha. And who was the man there? Moran of the Twenty-third Precinct, my sworn enemy. "What, this fuckin' troublemaker on my squad?" So I ended up fightin' unattached. My trainin' was drinkin' wine and smokin' pot. One time I ran around the 106th Street lake in the park—finished up puffin' on a joint. Some program for a contender. Irregardless, I kicked some ass down in Sunnyside and Ridgewood, including a bad spook from the Salem-Crescent A.C. But then they busted my jaw in a street fight on 105th Street and I had to drop out of the tournament. What a laugh on Moran if I had gone all the way to Chicago. Him with his squad breakin' their ass runnin' around the reservoir every day.

Anyway, I'm too good-lookin' to be a pug. I'm gonna be a pimp. I'm runnin' round with these fly broads from 111th Street and Fifth Avenue. That's where all the whores were trickin' in them days. Whores galores. But I could take a knock-around broad but so long. I didn't go for that scene too tough. Pimp got to hate women. That sure wasn't me.

There was some nice chicks around but their mothers wouldn't let them out the house. Specially with *delincuentes* like me waitin' on the stoop. Them was not "free sex" days. Leave it to me to come up at the wrong time. The good girls held on to their cherry. And it was a big deal. If a broad dropped her drawers, right away she lost her rating—even to the scrounge who copped them; "I ain't gonna marry no broad what lost her cherry!"

I used to get laid in Central Park, but you had to have a long switchblade ready 'cause always some degenerate motherfucker would be sneakin' up on you and your girl from behind the bushes. I didn't mind a guy lee-gating (peeping), I used to do it myself, but these pre-verts would want to gang-bang your broad. I chased more than one around that park at night. One guy tried to hit me with a wooden Keep Off The Grass sign, which he pulled out the ground while he was running from my sticker. He missed, I didn't. Many a piece I missed out on, gettin' interrupted by this element.

I was a big pussy-hound. Ain't changed much either.

Was a big movie fan too. Knock-around kids was always in the movie house. No TV in them days. The Fox Star on 107th Street and Lexington Avenue was our show. There was some bad guinea racketeers in there. You had to go with a gang,'cause if the wops caught you alone on the balcony, you was a flyin' Po'Rican. I remember once they had a singin' contest on the stage on a Saturday. They was givin' ten dollars to the winner. I was there with a whole mob of guys smokin' pot in the balcony. I ran up on stage and sang "Bei Mir Bist Du Schön," which I sang as "My Dear Mr. Shane." I couldn't sing worth a damn, but you rated on applause and my people made the most racket. I won. Then I did "Playmate" and the dirty version of "La Cucaracha," which was my best number—they couldn't get me off the stage.

I was into being a musician too. This was 'cause I noticed they was gettin' all the fine women. Some ugly clown be shakin' maracas or a cowbell in front of a band and all the chippies be saying, oh, he's showbiz! Jive-ass bitches. Showbiz is the guy giving enemas to the elephants in the circus. Anyway, I got me a big conga drum out of the pawnshop and thought I was Chano Pozo, the great Cuban conga player used to work the skins for Dizzy Gillespie. Chano was the greatest. Bad too, big stud, used to be strongarm for the politicals in Havana. Came to Harlem, was bad there too. Somebody forgot how bad and blew him away. But he had some tough hands while he was around. My hands couldn't keep no beat, I was not about to be no great *conguero*. So be it. I'll get me that trim some other way.

Used to play at block parties—everybody in Harlem be there, dancin', drinkin', smokin','n fightin'. Had one on 107th Street, Copiens or Dragons came around—forget who—anyway, they started shooting pistols. My friend, Tato—"Carlito, they got me"—fell on his back under the lamppost. *Coño*, Tato, he's dead! No way, cap hit him on his belt buckle—didn't have a scratch. Just like in the movies. After that, I used to throw myself on the ground— "Tato, they got me!" I was a big ballbreaker as a kid.

But don't get me wrong, I used to do a lotta good things too. Although later on they never showed up in any of my probation reports. Like God forbid somebody abuse a buddy of mine. I'd travel for blocks to duke with a cat that would try to gorilla a friend—I tangle-assed with Sabu from 104th Street and Flash from 110th Street, bad motherfuckers in the first degree, and it wasn't even my beef. "This ain't witchoo, Carlito"—"Never mind, take to the street." That's the kind of guy I was. But sometimes could backfire on you. Like m'man Políto—went up to 113th Street to straighten a kid out for somebody. Políto told me he was a stringbean black kid. Skinny arms and legs. Políto was a regular lil' buzz saw. He said shee-it, I'll tear 'im up. Políto say that spook kid like to bust him everyway but loose. Later on he found out the kid was Sandy Saddler.

One time I had to rumble a deaf-mute guy. On me like white-on-rice. Couldn't get off on this guy. Whipped me. I had respect for the handicapped after that.

A lot of Hollywood names in Harlem at the time. We had Tarzans and Sabus and Cheyennes. I remember a guy used to call himself Naiyoka—like from Pago Pago. We had Cochise and we had Apache. Sometimes a name could cause a problem. Like Cheyenne from the Bronx would come down with ten or twelve guys to see Cheyenne from Harlem—"Who said your name was Cheyenne?"—"Not me, my name is Jacinto Quinones." I seen that one. Then you had a pimp name of Red Conk on account of he conked his hair red (hair was straight in them days one way or the other—Dixie Peach or Sulfur 8). We had a white guy named Negro, and we had a black guy named Indio. We had a lot of Louies—Louie the Jew (crazy Jew got killed in a stickup, spoke better Spanish than me), Louie Lump-Lump (had a funny-shaped head), Louie Push-Push (used to run fast). We had Tobacco, Chuleta, Machete, Frankie *La Cagona* (Frankie the Shitter).

How'd I exist on the street? Somtimes legit—like delivery boy on an ice truck, or a grocery, or a dry cleaner's. But mostly hustlin', thievin', break and entry—shootin' pool was my main stick. I used to catch merchant marines for a hundred, hundred-fifty dollars playin' nineball—this when I was fourteen or fifteen years old—always had good wrists. Then there was boostin' in department stores—and there was dice, cards, writin' numbers (single action) for Jakie Cooperman, one of the few Jew bookies left around. We had a little scare with Jakie once. Jakie used to book out of a candy store on 108th Street and Fifth Avenue—he was a degenerate gambler himself. Me and some other kids were hangin' around one night. This big black car pulled up with four rays of sunshine—older wops from the East 107th Street mob out of the Fox Star. Two stayed in the car, two came into the candy store. Skinny guy, Nino, he had half a button, cool head, he'd talk to you. The other guy, Buck, was a terror—looked like a buffalo, only bigger— and he used to carry a softball bat—was the bouncer at the Fox Star. God forbid he should catch you sneakin' in the side door. Buck stands by the door, Nino walks up to the counter and pulls an empty bag out of his coat (the two of them was wearin' black coats and black hats with the brim turned up—wops got this Al Capone shit down to a science). Anyway, the bag was a cement bag. Nino gives the bag to Moe, owner of the store—"This is for Jakie." Moe shit a milk shake right there. Then Nino turned to me and the rest of the kids—"Anybody here seen Jakie around?" No, not us, never happen. They split. We was shook up. Seems Jakie was into the shylocks for fifty thou. The wops said he ran away to the coast on them, but Jakie himself would have given you five hundred to one he was planted on Long Island. Wops was already leery about goin' up to Black Harlem. Not Buck (really Buccia)—he'd jump out of a car on 116th Street and Lenox Avenue bat in hand—"C'mere"—spook would run—one shot—lay 'im out. Buck didn't give a fuck. He went up in the mob later on. Stayed mean.

There was other guys like Buck around. *Abusadores*, we called them—abusers or ballbreakers. Uptown Harlem had one named Jenks, or Jinx. Bad nigger. Big—didn't fit through no door,'cept sideways. Take everybody off. Take your money, your welfare check, your watch, your dope—take a wheelchair, glass eye. Mean. When he was outa jail, people stayed home. Jinx had a pretty long run, then he tried to run a game on a friend of mine. Shakedown. So much per week 'cause I'm bad. My buddy was hardnose, so he had to deal with Jinx. Shot him in the legs—kept coming. Shot him in the chest—kept coming. Finally stopped Jinx with a bullet through his head. All this time Jinx was chasing him around the bar. My friend had to do time for this. Judge said, "Victim was unarmed"—that motherfucker was armed when he was unarmed. Some judges will say, "Why didn't you go to the police?" The fuckin' police only want to know you as one of two "de's"—de deceased or de defendant. In between—"Don't bother me, I got lotta paper work." If the judge took time to check out a "victim" like Jinx he'd give the defendant the Distinguished Bronze Cross, first degree. And if His Honor had to live in the same tenement with a Jinx or a Buck, he'd put the contract out hisself. Buck and Jinx—some neighbors we had.

Another source of likelihood for me was a first-class Murphy game I used to run up on 111th Street with the tricks looking for whores. Me and m'partner Colorado used pencil and paper (that would impress the Johns)—"Okay, write it down, eh, Chico? These two gentlemen, ten dollars a piece—that's twenty dollars. No rough stuff or fancy fuckin', boys; Lolita is only sixteen and just startin' out. I'll hold the money." Colorado would go upstairs, then he'd call down, "Lolita wants to see the money and the list first, Pancho." Wait right here, boys, she's very shy—I'll call you from upstairs. You could come back an hour later and they'd still be waiting with their hard-on. Lo-leeta, Lo-leeta, they'd be yodelin' in the canyon. Sometimes me and Colorado would fall down on the roof from laughing.

Them roofs was busy for us. Flyin' pigeons, flyin' kites,

flyin' dope. Somebody was always jumpin' off the roof too. Usually some Rican who couldn't cut it on the street. But the street got him anyway—unless he jumped in the backyard.

Anyway, I was a busy lil' snot in them days.

SOMETIMES MORAN THE COP WOULD GET A BUG UP HIS ASS and grab me or Colorado on the street and put us back in the Home. Maybe a kick in the ass and a few smacks in the face from a telephone book in the Twenty-third Precinct before he took us over. He wanted me to go over to another precinct to break chops—I said I was a citizen of this precinct and he couldn't deport me. To this day I don't pick up a phone that I don't say, "Moran of the Twenty-third Precinct." I used to do it then figuring the phones in the poolroom or the bar was tapped and Moran's name would get on some shoo-fly tape. He was a tough sombitch. One night, one of them traveling carnivals came to the lot on 108th Street and Madison Avenue. This guy Lucky ran out of luck in a fight with some marine tiger who cut him to pieces with a butcher knife. I remember him on his back on the ground trying to kick up at the guy. He never made it to the emergency table at the Flower Hospital. Moran was there with some photographers from *Life* magazine and he got a write-up with pictures and all. Lucky was a sharp dresser, used to be in the furnished rooms on 107th Street between Park and Madison. He didn't come out too good in the pictures though. Moran, believing his own publicity, became a worse ballbuster than ever.

Another ballbuster cop was Schula or Schuler, known as "Cara de Palo" (Woodface). He was a fat guy with glasses, but he could move, specially the time they threw the garbage can off the roof at him.

Baddest of the bad was Big Jeff from the "Mutt and Jeff" detective team from the Twenty-third. One was a little wop, Lil' Jeff, the other a big mick, Big Jeff; you couldn't call either one Mutt or they'd break yo' ass. When they'd pull up to the poolroom on 106th Street and Madison, everybody start walkin'. Nearly everybody. Legend says that one time they wanted everybody lined up against the wall in the poolroom—"All you Puerto Ricans up against the wall"—this smart guy wouldn't get up—"Me no Puerto Rican, me Cuban"—*wap!* "Same shit." None of that "move-along-boys" jive in them days.

Little Jeff give you sass, Big Jeff look around like he ain't even listening, but if you gave backlip—wap!—Big Jeff laid you out. I ain't seen nobody, in the ring or out, hit harder than him. Elbow close to body, leverage—lights out. Better you fell off a roof than he should land on you. Big Jeff finally got put out of commission by a little P.R. name of Augie Robles. Robles was a contract killer, one of the few we had around there. I mean this dude would travel to other states on hits. Around Harlem, he'd feed off the policy bankers. Like, "You know me, Augie Robles; you got a thousand for me by Saturday, okay?" Everybody was scared shit of him. Big Jeff and Augie finally got around to it on 112th Street. There must have been ten thousand people watching that shoot-out. Just like in *Scarface*. Big Jeff, as usual, was the first bull through the door. Imagine, Augie Robles, cornered, with four, count 'em, four pistols, waiting on you. Shee-it. The bulls killed Augie that night, but not before Big Jeff got his knee blown up with a dum-dum. They tried to do this gunfight in a jive movie, *Madigan*. Big Jeff make Madigan look like a faggot. He was bad. But he wasn't no flake artist. He let me walk away from one that wasn't my doing even though he could have laid it on me. Bulls ain't never been my bag—but here's to you, anyway, Big Jeff. You done the right thing.

The Ricans had some other hairy guys. Was a guy, Cabezon, sat down in a barber chair at Lino's on 107th Street off Madison—"Lino, cut my hair short today. Tonight I'm going to settle with a guy. No telling where I'm gonna go afterward." That's cold. He goed it too. Electric chair.

Then was a guy, Johnny Lata, had his face cut by a rival pimp, Tony Navarro. Lata kept a straight razor in a pan filled with onions and water so that when he got his revenge the scar on Tony's face would never heal. Lata did cut a forget-me-not on Tony's face, but the onion bit never checked out because Tony's liver gave out from too much coke not long after. Tony had in his stable of four the best lookin' whore in Harlem, a German war bride. When that *fenomeno* used to walk down the street I used to lay right down on the pavement—"Vee gates, fraulein"—but I was too broke to hit on her. When I think of all them fine women I didn't get nothin' of! Years later, after Tony died, I went to a party at Birdland and there she was with a spook band leader, one of the biggest in the country. Being broke never was no fun. I'll be dead or in jail, but I ain't ever gonna be broke. Believe that.

That's all I was ever interested in, makin' a dollar without hurtin' nobody. By my lights, I wasn't nasty or no troublemaker like them other motherfuckers around there; them guys was just burnin' up inside—the streets was battery acid to them. But the streets never whipped me that bad. I always saw the signs leading out—they was always painted green. Right this way, Mr. Brigante.

That guy Lino, the barber, used to worry about me. He was from the same mountain town in P.R. as my moms. They gonna kill you on the street, Carlito, they gonna lay you out in Gonzalez's Funeral before you're twenty-one. He wanted me to go to school like this guy on the block Wilfredo—imagine a grown man still going to school. Never learn nothin' out of no book. Keep your eyes and ears open, maybe read the *Daily News* to know who's gettin' locked up. If the smarts are there, you be all right—if they ain't, you can read books from shit to Shinnecock, ain't gonna help. Lino was a okay guy, used to bring me Baby Ruths when I was in the Home. He beat me to Gonzalez's. Here's to you, Lino—you done the best you could.

IN THE MATTERS OF RACE, THE PUERTO RICANS WAS AHEAD of their time in the forties. We accepted everybody. Nobody accepted us. Since black was not in style in them days, us P.R.'s declared ourselves white. We had a few variations but that didn't bother us none. The Cubans say, *El que no la tiene del Congo, la tiene del Carabalí.* Myself, I don't go for colored guys—but what about colored gals? This country can't do without them fine women—no kinda way. This country can make all them cars, toasters, ice boxes—goin' to the moon—meanwhile, it's still hung up on the race watzis. Bunch o' bullshit. If the rest of the country had listened to us it wouldn't be in the mess it is now. You take me for instance. I been light enough to sit in the front of a Jim Crow bus but dark enough to be worried about it. I been taken for spook, wop, and one faggot (used to come to the door jay-naked when I was delivering clothes for a cleaner) said I was Armenian. You're better off having a little bit of everything. That way you are what you have to be whenever you got to be. But who gives a shit, the main thing is to be good-lookin' so the broads will go for you.

Ricardo Montalban I ain't. But many a kitty has gone for me even when I didn't have big bread behind me. Believe that. It is true I spend all my time pursuin' good trim and, thank God, have a good rap. It is also true I have had knocked-out-lookin' broads. *Tremendos pollos.* White, black, tan, green,'n in b'tween (never had no Chinese broad). In other words, I have done all right with the fair sex. I got no squawks in that apartment.

Fact is, I got no beef about my first twenty years. Had me a hell of a time. Warts and all, the streets was my playground. Couldn't ground me down—not the bulls, not the thugs, not the landlord, not the welfare, not nobody. I ran all over them. Fact is when I was in the get-o I didn't even know I was there. I didn't even know how dee-prived I was or that I was one of the downtrotted—it was news to me when the socio workers told me about it. I was happy as a pig in shit.

I would say by and large and mainly Carlos Brigante, mainly known as Carlito, had a good time as a kid. The next twenty years is more tricky. In other words, in the 1950s I was mostly a criminal. I have to admit that. And I did a lot of time for it too. But then Earl Bassey wised me up and Rocco Fabrizi gave me a break into the heavy wood. So like the sixties was big time for me and I was less into bein' a thug and more like a class guy. But I'm runnin' ahead again.

OKAY, THE END OF THE FORTIES SAW ME INTO THE SLAMS at Elmira Reception Center, Elmira, New York. Thereafter known as "the El." First whiff of country air. Alma mater

for many a mope majorin' in thievery, roguery, lechery, and
mopery. Thirty-six-month bit I did. I had been on probation
for sticking a guy who'd busted my jaw with brass knuckles
made out of ashcan handles. Probation don't mean I didn't
have a few things going—burglaries, cars, like that. So like
I'm shooting dice on 105th Street off Madison Avenue on a
Saturday afternoon when this bad-ass named Chago grabs all
the money on the ground and says, "These dice are loaded.
You guys are robbing me; I'm taking the money," and he
pulls out the difference, size .38, so I say, "Motherfucker,
you ain't going nowhere with my bread."

"I'll kill you, Carlito."

"Kill me, *hijo de puta*, kill me—"

Everything is real quiet now except for Chago's
breathing—he ain't got no heart. I grab the piece,
bust him in the face with it; he falls down some
basement steps, and I grab a garbage can full of ashes
and throw it on him. That night I'm shooting nineball
in Ramon's parlor on 106th Street and Madison when
Mutt and Jeff from the two-three squad come in.

"Chago's over at the Flower Hospital. He's asking for
you, Carlito."

"Chago who? What right you—"

Smack. Right off my ear.

"Okay, let's go see him."

No lineup, no reading of rights—they even gave me
an admission. Times were rough. Judge put me away—
felonious assault, violation of probation. For Chago, they
shoulda give me a medal.

In the Joint, thirty-six months. Up there I meet a lot of
the boys, including Rocco Fabrizi, who was up for stealing
cars. He was tight with Earl Bassey. Earl was up there for
dealing in pot. I'd been hearing about him on the street in
Harlem, he was the war counselor of some click uptown on
Lenox Avenue. Earl was around our age but he was slick
beyond his years. He could see something coming around
the corner, like he'd say, "So-and-so is a faggot," and there
would be this big stud with tattoos and muscles blowing
everybody in the Joint. He knew things. I can't explain it;
he never went to school but he could read people in minutes.

His skin was black, but his eyes were like yellow, and when he put them on you everything was cool, like calm. Nothing went down without discussing it with Earl. Even the hacks would check out a beef with Earl.

Me and him got real tight when I started boxing again. Even in the street when I was smoking pot and drinking wine, my hands were quick and my wind wouldn't quit. Like I'd get inside a cat and hook to the body—I'd catch a few or be pushed off, but I'd get back inside—I'm swinging without stop—most guys couldn't stay with me. Earl had fought pro in the ring. He was my trainer, taught me how to hook to the head, how to finish a cat when you hurt him. I took a few guys out and my rep was made. Like Earl used to say, "Don't mess with Hoppy." Being Earl was smarter than me, I'd listen to him. He'd come on with, "Look here, Holmes, you got to dig yo'self—you gonna be on the street soon, forget about that okey-doke shit—gorilla-ing people, robbing pads—the shit is on, Briss, I got the word from Rocco—the junk is already here. And we is in—you think some guinea is going up to 125th and Lenox to deal with the niggers or to 111th and Fifth to deal with the spics? They gonna need distributors with brains and with heart—stand-up motherfuckers. I don't know about you, but I'm declaring myself in. These wops don't fuck around, bro—you got to play with their rules. Your word is your life—they make a meet, be there! This Mickey Mouse jive with the pussy and the coke and the booze don't mean nothin'. Got to be cool, stay clean. Make the move a few times a year—that's it. After a while, I'll have my own crew—then I'm gonna make my own world. I ain't gonna be a nigger all my life, pushing wooden Cadillacs on 37th Street—not Mrs. Bassey's boy. I'm going all the way—they got to kill me, Jack, kill me!"

"What about me, Earl, what about me?"

"You gonna be my man with the Ricans, Chappie—they ain't nothing but niggers turned inside out."

Rocco was from another garage—but a boss-type. Tall, lean, with light hair, he didn't look like no eye-talian to me. And he didn't give you the wise-guy jive. He was mobbed up with the Pleasant Avenue outfit. But his uncle was a

made-guy, a lieutenant with the Mulberry Street crew—a
heavy hitter—so like you knew that Rocco was marked. He
couldn't miss, he was a down cat, and he was connected.
Rocco didn't talk with no *dese* and *dose*; he spoke nice
and soft—like dignity—but he wasn't no punk. Word was
he had already iced some greaseball in the Bronx whose
bail had dropped too low. The only thing wrong with Rocco
was his love life; he had this thing for a P.R. chick, which
in those days was unheard of, so like his uncle kept him
in the boondocks—but I knew he'd work it out. Like I say,
he was a natural boss-type.

The three of us used to pal out. They'd rap and I'd
listen.

"Earl, I'm out of the doghouse, so I'll be moving
downtown—you know where to reach me. I'm not promising
you guys anything, but if I get a shot then I'm dealing you
in. We may connect once in a year, or even five years—
in the meantime I don't even know if you guys are alive.
We meet, we deal, good-bye. Now I'm not talking Harlem
shit, I'm talking kilos, up to ten thou a kilo. On my okay
you're going to get stuff on consignment at the beginning.
You cross me, I'm dead, because I'm responsible for you—
but you know you go right behind me. I'm moving up; you
guys can move with me or stay in the shithouse hustling
quarters."

"I'm your man, Rocco."

"Deal me in, Rocco."

It's hard to explain, but when you're doing time with a
man you can read him faster than when you're on the street.
He can't hide behind his rep or his clothes—shit like that
don't work inside. Inside, all you got is mostly yourself.
Like Earl used to say, yo' hole and yo' soul is buck neck-id
in the Joint. So that's how come three cats from different
alleys got close and stayed close for twenty years. The time
was ripe, was overdue—but that don't mean nothin' if the
right people ain't on the scene. Me and Earl was the right
people, and we was ready. We needed a break. Rocco—
Rocco had the inside rail from before, what with his uncle,
Dominick Cocozza, who was a boss. But he saw their thing
had to open up—open up or it was gonna bust open.

So he brought us in out of the rain. He didn't do it overnight,'specially for me; I was still a cowboy for years yet. But I knew he knew I was stand-up, and later than sooner he would cut me loose into the big bucks. Earl first, then me. Rocco was the icebreaker and he done the right thing. And it took balls, because there was fool wops that couldn't see it—no put grits, rice, and beans in the pasta. Prejudiced old fucks like Rocco's boss, Pete Amadeo (*maldita sea su madre*), who thought they could sit inside the one tent with a whole bunch of Indians like me and Earl runnin' around outside bare-ass in the cold. Not to forget the hole the feds was diggin' under the floor.

Sick—some of them guys is sick too. You take Amadeo— a/k/a Petey A. One night at the Copa—this is when Tom Jones was at his peak. All the wise guys 'n dolls was jammed in—place was hysteria. Broads throwin' their keys, their drawers even, at Jones. Pete says to this button-guy with him,

"He's a fuckin' nigger. All this noise over a fuckin' nigger."

"No, Pete, you got it wrong—he's English."

"I say he's a fuckin' nigger, awright?"

"Eh, yeah, you're right, Pete—lookit the way he dances."

We split from the El in the order we came in. First Rocco, then Earl, then me. I hit Harlem like Sonny hit Floyd.

2

THE FIFTIES CAME IN STRONG FOR ME. LIKE DANCE-CRAZY. The St. Nick's Arena, the Manhattan Center, the Caborojeño, Broadway Casino—seems like everybody was dancing their ass off. The tigers would go to the Cabo and the BC, the down P.R.'s would go to the Palladium. The Manhattan Center would be the place for Easter, maybe six bands followed by a riot where 3 or 4 guys would be thrown off the balcony. One Easter was maybe two hundred cats rumbling, tables crashing, bottles flying, and in the middle of this Noro Morales on the bandstand, "Pliz, we all Puerto Rican pipples, no fight. . . ." I laughed so hard I could hardly swing my chair.

The bands were hot—Machito, Puente, Rodriguez, Curbelo, Marcelino Guerra, they was all gigging.

The main joint was the Palladium on 53rd Street and Broadway; the owner was a Jew named Max, but if you looked around you knew he had friends. All the help was wops. The bouncers were somethin' else—real class. Like some *jíbaro* would throw a right hand; they'd catch his fist in midair, lift him off his feet, his little shoes kicking in the air, rush him to the back door parallel to the ground like a torpedo; a bouncer had the door ready—he's gone, head-first down a flight of concrete steps. The dancers wouldn't even break stride.

But the house wouldn't fuck with the wise-guys. We brought in the bread, drank J & B, had the sharp broads.

Lots of dressing in those days—dark suits, roll collars, skinny silk ties, short hair—dap as a Russian pimp. Fridays was our night. All the hustlers were there—103rd Street, 106th, 107th, 111th, 116th—Mario, Guajiro, Toñin, Cano. Everybody was cool—except maybe if the Viceroys and the Turbens was there on the same night. I would back out then because I was tight with both clicks and couldn't take sides when they'd get it on.

I always had my table with my own crew, Tato and Victor Lopez, Lalin, Monkey, Colorado—salty motherfuckers all. I was the main man. None of us was too smart then, but my hands were the best and in them days there was still duking with the fists, at least among the spics. We was small-timing in them days—thievery, nickel bags, and strong arm.

The broads were all over; we'd team up mostly with whores. Who else is going to snort coke with you in an after-hours joint or see you go for a yard when your bread is down? My old lady then was India from 113th Street; she was underage and her mother was going to lock me up, but after the kid was born we was okay. She was the most beautiful *mulata* uptown but she had this thing about being white—kept talking about the kid having good hair. P.R.'s used to make a big thing about hair in them days—this guy's got good hair, this guy bad, this guy suspicious hair. Me, I never gave a fuck—guess I was ahead of my time.

Mainly India was good people, but she was just a kid and very wacky. Like we'd be comin' out of a restaurant with some people and she'd jump on my back—"Carlito, carry me piggyback." 'Ey, I was already a mature cat—done time—respected. India's mother didn't go for me; I was a thug. Meanwhile, I know for a fact the old lady used to turn tricks in her day—had a fine body just like the daughter. All them "India" broads got fine bodies. Anyway, we didn't last long. The two of them and the baby, a girl, Prudencia (that was the grandmother's name), ended up in Florida with some Air Force guy India married. She had some shape, India did—like a guitar. You knew someday she was gonna turn into a bull fiddle, but in the meantime—some good strummin', Jack. Believe that.

Wednesdays was celebrity night at the Palladium—all

the showbiz and Jews doing cha-cha-cha-one-two-three, Marlon Brando sit in on conga (couldn't play to save his ass), out-of-town people—shit like that—all into Latin music. I say that put the spics on the map; we wasn't all behind them little glass panes at Horn & Hardart. Yeah, like a P.R. pot washer could dance up a storm at the Palladium and walk out some fine out-of-town fox. Yeah, the old P was all right. Had a hell of a run too. The forties, the fifties, right up to the early sixties. Then some lame was puffing on a joint one night, got next to a kitty and said she had to take a poke. In them days mari-gee-wana was a big deal. The broad blew up, ran downtown and put the squeal on the Palladium to her boss, an assistant D.A. name of Kuh who was already into being one of Hogan's main honchos. So now you got shoo-fly checking out the P and first thing down is a pimp name of Umberto beating up on two of his whores. And what does they see the house do? Throw the broads down the stairs and buy Umberto a drink. This is an outrage, say Mr. Kuh. And the great Palladium raid was on. 'Cept that by that time all the heavy people knew it was coming off—yeah, stool pigeons fly in both directions. So like, block all the exits, blow all the lights—"Everybody freeze!" By the time they got the lights back on, all the guns, knives, and dope was on the floor and the bulls was running around trying to match up whozis with whatzis. It was a jive raid but it blew the liquor license and the old P went under. Damn shame. Somebody always gotta mess up a good thing.

MIDWAY UP THE FIFTIES, EARL BASSEY SENT WORD HE wanted a meet with me. I'd run into Earl from time to time; I knew he was big in policy up in black Harlem. Sunday night at the Copa: I knew right away we was connected. So the wops are cutting loose; they been hogging it all to themselves—finally giving the natives a break. I got myself all dolled up and went down—big night at the Copa. The boys was all in their tiers, according to rank. Cigars, white-on-white, pinkie rings—the broads, roamin' noses, with hair teased like brillo. Every table like a little click, with the boss playing his crew like he had a baton—

he laughs, they laugh, he gets up, they get up.

"So I sez to him. . . ."

"*Madon'*, Fonso, you got some pair of balls. . . ."

"He's a fuckin' *cafone*. . . ."

I don't see a black face in the whole joint. I go back upstairs to the lounge and order a drink. I ain't there five minutes when there's a big commotion coming up from downstairs. This little blond guy is raising hell—he's got three or four guys with him, spitters all—the maitre d' is pleading, "Please Joey, please!"

"I wanna see this Jew cocksucker right here and now!"

This little Jew comes off the bar.

"What's the trouble, Joey?"

"What's the trouble? What kind of ratjoint is this that I got to sit in the back—I don't rate around here? Where's my respect?"

"Joey, please—there's been a mixup with the tables, we'll straighten it out—"

By this time, this Joey guy is stone-white in the face. He whips out an automatic and starts banging it on top of the bar—splinters flying—he's screaming, "I'm gonna shylock this joint, I am in—starting next week you're turning over to me—you hear, you Jew bastard?"

"Whatever you say, Joey, whatever you say." The Jew was cool, ice water. Sweat was coming down my spine; other people's beefs always scare me more than my own. I never seen such a show of *cojones*; there was a hundred guys frozen there—half of them had to be packing.

Then they were gone. About that time Earl came in—clean as always. He had with him a high-yaller chick that wouldn't quit. Uuwee!

I was still shook up. I told him this wop Joey, from Brooklyn, had terrorized the joint. Earl said, "He be bad as ten sacks of motherfuckers, but he ain't coming back next week; he's crazy, but he ain't that crazy."

This guy comes over and says to us, "You're Mr. Fabrizi's guests?" Well all right!

Rocco, you sombitch, I knew you was heavy in the mambo when I saw that table right down on the floor. Some mobbed-up Jew comedian was on the floor and every joke was played to some capo at ringside, like "Sonny this" and "Sonny that." I knew enough not to want to know who these guys were, but I was impressed—heavy, heavy.

About this time, slipping and sliding, Mr. Rocco Fabrizi. He looked like money—tiny cufflinks, tiny watch, shoulders just right on the suit. Rimless glasses in them days, warm smile—the guy could get to you.

"Did you marry her?"

"Yes, Charles, I am now a Puerto Rican by proxy."

We were bullshitting a while about upstate when Earl sent his broad upstairs.

"Let's hear the deal."

"Charles, there's a West Indian guy named Etienne uptown who's got a nice little policy bank going for many years. This guy is right next to Earl here. But lately we feel he's loosening up, getting old. Now there are some boys up there eyeballing old Etienne and they are ready to bite. What we need is somebody to prop old Etienne up for a while, keep the wolves at bay and then when things are ripe ease him out to pasture. Earl says you're the man."

"That's great and I can handle it, but why not take the old fart out right now?"

"No good; Etienne has run a good bank since the thirties. People trust him; you can't remove him overnight—this will be done our way."

"Whatever you guys say."

So now me and my boys were riding shotgun for old Etienne. We'd wake him up and put him to bed. He took a liking to me, and we'd rap in Spanish; he was a Haitian but he spoke Spanish, English, and French. That smart old geezer owned buildings, dry cleaning stores, groceries, you name it. But policy was his game—he was a genius at that. He knew all the dream books by heart, the Chinaman in the Daily News; he knew just when to lay off on certain numbers—it's like he would sense a heavy hit coming— like the plate numbers on a car in the newspaper or in a plane crash. He would start his own rumors about a special number being fixed for the controllers to hit—all his own bullshit—but he was always cooking; he'd stake people who needed money, helped a whole lot of people and he always paid his hits, no hedging. I learned a lot from him, old Etienne.

Right away I started earning my keep. The old man had the hots for some barmaid in the Heights in a joint called Carl's Corner. He dug that young poontang—even though at his age I knew he was shooting blanks. So like I was downtown in a bar when I get a call from this guy Snipe— "Carlito, they got Mr. Etienne in the back of a short in front of Carl's."

"Cops?"

"Club members, with a sawed-off shotgun in his face; they want twenty large right away."

"I'll be right there."

Maso the bartender loaned me this army .45, plus I had my own .32 Beretta automatic. I cocked both pieces and jumped in a cab. I got off at 149th and Broadway—they was double-parked in front of the joint, first in line facing uptown. I come from behind on the outside; I shove both automatics through the rear window, right in this guy's face—two spades, one shotgun, the old man between them.

"Make your move, motherfucker, make it—"

"Whoa, bro—"

"I'll splash your face all over this motherfuckin' car—"

"You right, man, you right."

The old man got out okay. But his nerves were bad after that. He said I was crazy, but it wasn't like that. I just didn't give a fuck; got a beef, jump out in front; you be first, you be best.

We checked Snipe out; he was wrong—set Etienne up. Somebody burnt some holes in his clothes. Later for Snipe.

About that time the old man started staying at home in St. Albans. That was all right with me. Good bread coming in. Everything copasetic. Too good to last. I started moving around more. Had me over twenty suits, three hundred a pop, from Leighton's, Cye Martin, and Kronfeld's. All my boys stayed clean; we'd run down to Atlantic City—Club Harlem, 500 Club—even Miami and Puerto Rico—we'd have parties with five or six broads snorting coke and doing tricks. I started going to the Copa regular; if I caught the show always a yard for the maitre d'—"Mr. Brigante, right this way." I was pal-ing around with a lot of wops from downtown and the west Bronx, younger guys like me, not the prejudiced old hoods. These kids would say I was half a wop with my name, which is Corsican—of which there's a lot in P.R. I'd think, maybe I'm gonna be the first made-guy P.R., and I'd say, "*Fangul*" and "Yer mudder's cunt" with the best of them. I shoulda known better.

Earl would come down when he had something to say to Rocco. Neither one of them would party as much as me. And they'd be down on me for fuckin' around so much. I'd listen,'cause I knew these cats was in my corner, but I couldn't see it. When you're highrollin' in the bread you're bound to be out there jumpin' come midnight every night. Rocco and Earl was businessmen, while-as I was a jive-ass party man. But I'd complain anyway.

"Rocco, gimme a break. Earl, here, be a doctor of numerology, like Etienne. But numbers ain't my game, Rocco. I ain't got the patience. Gimme a break."

"He wants to be the main skag man uptown, Rocco. He think he can fuck with the feds."

"Charles, you've been handed a ready-made, going concern. Etienne has the best runners in Harlem."

"Yeah, but I gotta work every day. Somebody's always trying to sneak in a late hit or change a number on us. Then you gotta be an administrator; then you got labor problems—what controller is humpin' what runner's wife. Rocco, I'm breakin' my ass."

"The money's good, right?"

"Slow comin'."

"What do you think, Earl?"

"Carlito's okay, Rocco. The bank's holdin' up."

"Okay, Mister Carlito. Next time I have an auction you may be invited."

"I'm ready, Rocco, I'm ready."

"Paint is very expensive, maybe ten thou for a bucket."

"Money is only an object, I'll get it. Got it, been there. Wadda you kiddin', I been waiting since we left the El, Rocco. Right, Earl?"

"I got no beef with the policy game, Carlito. Since Rocco got me on the pad, I been straight. Numbers is hard work, but it's clean. That don't mean I won't take a shot if I get a chance. Meantime I'm cool."

"Junk shakes you up, eh, Earl?"

"Earl is smart, Charles; he leaves well enough alone. He gets up early, he works hard, he sleeps nights. This other business is like Grand Prix racing. You have to keep your hands on the wheel at all times. You get the best engineers, the best mechanics, the best car, and they'll still run you into a wall. I don't recommend it to anybody. You're on a different level in that game—the air is very thin. You can choke on it."

"When did you ever know me to take a step back, Rocco?"

"It's not that, I don't want later on—"

"Rocco, I'm ready, gimme a break."

"Take care of things uptown, with Earl here; later on, we'll see."

Meanwhile, uptown some dudes is getting jealous—spics is like that. I'm tooling around in a big car with a fine kitty. Instead of saying one of the boys made it, no, they got to get mad; that jive Carlito, he ain't shit, when's the last time he took to the street with a cat—they wuz gonna try me out again. Mistake! It came down this way. I had me a fabulous Jewish chick name of Honey, a stone freak. A blonde, educated too—but she dug wise-guys. I'd play the Little Caesar shit for her and she loved it. She'd even come up to Harlem to meet me. One night she was waiting for me in this joint near 111th Street and Fifth Avenue. These three kiddie hoodlums came in, grabbed her fur coat right off her back.

"Tell Carlito that Chucho wants to see him; we'll hold your coat."

They were gone when I got there—lucky for me, since I didn't have no piece on me. The broad was all shook up. I told Guiso, the owner of the joint, "Tell Chucho I'll see him tomorrow night right here. I'm very embarrassed about my fiancee's coat—make sure he brings the coat; we'll work something out." Well all right. Step right up.

I dug the whole scene, that's my trouble. I coulda' had these punks taken out—no, I wanna do it myself; my blood was hot, got to be my hands.

It was after midnight, the three of them was in the joint facing the door, the fur coat thrown over a chair, I had a long leather coat on with a pistol in each pocket—automatics can jam, but they're faster. Only one way in or out to Guiso's diner, no back door. I come in the door smilin'—"*Ola*, Chucho"—then I started smoking with both pieces; Chucho said, "*Espera*, Carlito . . . ," that's as far as he got. We were going to talk all right. I killed him standing up. His partner, Nelson, took two in the chest—he had something on him, but he never got off. The third guy split out the door, taking tables with him; I chased him past the Park Palace into the park but he was movin', Jim!—he got away. I come back for the coat—some motherfucker had copped it. I come out and see Nelson crawling under a parked car—I bent down and put another cap in him—he screamed like a pussy. I quit the scene in a hurry.

Now I was in a real jackpot. Everything was fucked up. Why I got to be such a hothead? I blow town, get upstate around Newburgh. Earl, my man, come up to see me.

"Rocco be hot as a motherfucker about you, bro. He say you done blown the whole duke. He's right. That macho shit of yours shows you ain't no boss. Three street punks. You coulda skinned them cats twenty different ways without—"

"Had to be, Earl, it was coming—I just got off first. What's to be?"

"Cuba, Carlito."

"Cuba, what the hell I'm gonna do in Cuba?"

"Lay cool—you're driving down to Miami, then take the ferry to Havana. Rocco's sending a guy named Vinnie to pick you up; he'll have the other half of this dollar bill on him. Watch the speed limits driving down. When you get to Havana he'll connect you—you be there a while; when things calm down here, Rocco will send for you."

"Wait a minute, Earl, I got a self-defense case here. I can beat this in court—tell Rocco to get me Murray or Kleinman—"

"How you sound? That Nelson punk is alive, a material witness with $100,000 bail. Now how we know if he's gonna stand up? Gotta get that bail down, then we know what he's told the D.A. If push come to shove, we can wash him—but right now you need time, get it, time!"

"What about the other kids?"

"Chucho's underground; the third guy is still runnin' through the park—don't worry about them."

"Well then, we go to Cuba."

This guy Vinnie shows up next day, the dollar halves match, and we're off in a Caddie, and I mean off, this dude wouldn't sleep or talk—a driving sphinx. In twenty hours we're in north Florida. We're humming on an empty stretch of highway when there they were in the rearview mirror. Bulls. They pull us over.

Storm troops. Six-foot-two and twice as wide and as mean as they was wide. Wide-brimmed hats, pearl-handled revolvers—they must still be killing Indians around here.

"License and registration."

"Yes, sir," says Vinnie, showing his license. We're both out of the Caddie.

"Dagos, eh, drivin' a big Cadillac from the big city— where yo'all barrel-assing to?"

Oh shit.

"We're going to Miami, sir," says Vinnie—but the more you give the more they push.

"All you ginsos is comin' to Miami and Tampa—"

"I'm Spanish"—I'm hot.

"You ain't nothin' but a Cuban nigger—"

I threw a short right hand just below the breastbone—he went down on his ass, cowboy shit and all. He'd have shot me for sure but his partner stopped him. They handcuffed and slapped us around. Then they took us to a diner on the road; the cook took his apron off and come out as the fucking magistrate. The bulls told him what happened.

"Good Godalmighty damn, cain't decent folks be on our roads without gittin' run over with these heah big cars? Ah swear, it's a goddamn shame—an' now they wanna be assaulting peace officers. Couple of may-fia boys, eh? Wal, that don' cut no ice 'round heah; we'll put yo' ass on the chain gang, yo'all heah, the chain gang."

If he was trying to scare me, he sure as hell was succeeding—I was scared shitless.

"Yeah, you lil' ol' boys are in trouble—serious trouble. Now, whut kind of car was that? A Cadillac, eh? Lemme talk to the driver. Take this heah other boy out."

They took me to a back room. My ass was low—I'll be breaking rocks in a chain gang and if I'm lucky the warrant will come down on the N.Y. homicide.

After a while, Vinnie came to get me with the bulls; they drove us to a bus depot. Not a word was said. Then they put Vinnie and me on a bus headed for Miami.

"The man wanted the car?"

"Yeah."

"Man got the car?"

"Yeah." End of conversation.

3

HAVANA WAS REALLY JUMPING IN THOSE DAYS—BEST
town I was ever in. Tropicana, Montmartre, with chorus
lines of *mulatas* that put anything in N.Y. to shame. You
could party twenty-four hours a day—Olga Guillot, Benny
More, Rolando La Serie, they were all there. La Aragon,
Casino la Playa, Cascarita—gambling, pussy, coke—wide
open. Fidel sure fucked up a good thing.

The mob was into all the casinos and I was hanging
around the tables a lot. Pretty soon I teamed up with this
Cuban named Nacho Reyes. He was the bodyguard for a
senator and had connections all the way to the president.
The setup was different there; every politico had his own
crew working for him—like private little armies. Everybody
was robbing, but you had to be in the government, so at
election time things would get rough; murders were all right
as long as you had your rabbi—cops and robbers were all
mixed up. If your man was in you were a cop, uniform and
all—if not, you'd be a robber trying to get him in. Wild.

Nacho was a stone killer, he iced a guy when he was
sixteen years old and kept right on going. He had bullet
holes all over his body. I never saw him eat anything, but
he would snort coke day and night. With a piece in his
hand he was like a cat, a bad-ass. He said he had heard
about me in New York—that I had *cojones*. I learned a
lot from Nacho. One night we walked into this joint and
right away I could see it was a setup. The door was closed
behind us, the jukebox was loud—the bartender looked like

he was going to start crying. The hairs on the back of my neck said, "These motherfuckers are going to kill us."

Nacho saved our ass. He threw his arms around the bossman there—"*Mi hermano*, I have come to your house to have a drink with you as your guest; Carlito from New York, I have spoken to him about our Cuban hospitality. . . ."

Nacho ate crow but he saved our lives. After we left, he said, "Only a fool throws himself head first—when you are outgunned and your only exit is death, you compromise; *le comes el cerebro*, when the time is right, you strike—but you never hesitate. That is why I am alive and have buried a dozen men. The coke is in my nose but not my brain—"

I WAS IN CUBA FOR OVER A YEAR HAVING A HIGH OLD time. I was in a beach club, had a Cuban old lady—Earl would send me money when I needed it. My *Cubana* was a hooker, but she was a classy broad and moved in good circles. She spoke very refined Spanish and had elegant hands—I'd forget she was turnin' tricks. She'd tell me how great I was, how I wasn't cut out to be a knock-around guy. She was going to con a con man. Ha!

Then I got the word from Earl. Everything is set, come on home. *Adiós, Cubita la bella.*

I SURRENDERED TO THE D.A.'S OFFICE ACCOMPANIED BY my lawyer, Morris Steinhardt. They took me to the sixth floor, Homicide Bureau, for interrogation before arraignment. They got to be kidding. They questioned me in teams, the first team was threatening me, hooping and hollering; the second team was going to save me from the first, only I got to tell them the truth about the murder. Name and address, that's all they get.

I'm arraigned in Central Sessions that afternoon. Murder in the first degree; I could get the electric chair, Jesus! No bail, they hold me in the Tombs. Tombs is right—couldn't take a shower, place smells bad, food worse.

The word is that I am in good shape—all they got is a bus driver who says he saw me chasing a guy into the park with something in my hand but he's not sure what. Guiso's going to say he saw me around his joint that night but didn't see me at the time of the shooting and that he dove to the floor without looking as soon as he heard the first bang. The guns were never found and to add to the confusion, ballistics is going to show Chucho and Nelson were shot with different guns, like there was more than one guy shooting. They got no statement out of me since I come in with my lawyer. Earl tells me that Nelson is all right—he don't know who did what, all he knows he was shot. I don't go for this, I say wash Nelson, but Rocco says it will look bad, so I go along with them.

Meanwhile, I got troubles with my fuckin' lawyer. He's getting big bucks and he ain't doing shit. I got to lead him by the hand all the way. They are like these doctors who ask you what's wrong with you; if you know, what the hell you need them for? Shit. I break it all down for the lawyer—all the motions I want made—I want all the statements from all the witnesses, I want the ballistics reports, I want the autopsy report. I want the yellow sheets on all the prosecution witnesses, I want the case dismissed for lack of prosecution—the lawyer says that ain't got no merit 'cause I ran away. Ran away, shit, who ran away? I wasn't there, I just went to Cuba for a vacation—and if I was there I ran away from the same gang of guys that shot Chucho and Nelson, I ran for my life. This old con Walter, down from Dannemora on his own writ, told me what I had to do. He should know, he's been drawing writs for twenty years.

Me and Walter got together and wrote a summation for my case. Walter would sound off in the tank,

"Ladeez and genulmens of the ju-ree, yo'all is here to dee-termine iffen dis here boy be innercent or he be guilty. Now you got to know that this be important to the dee-fendant—now right away the Dee Ay gonna say that the case is important to the peoples too. Now what kind of nonsense is that? The peoples cain't go to jail, the peoples cain't go to the 'lectric chair, is only this here boy can go—so damn sho' more important to him! The judge he gonna tell you about reasonable doubts—ah say ain't no reason to doubt that this boy be innercent. Ain't no haps here, ain't even *per*haps. Now what went down here—I'm gonna tell yo'all.

"De deceased, may his soul rest in peace, he were a villain—he done been busted for everythin' in the book—assault, robbery, burglary, dope, and even unlawful entry on a young lady. He weren't nothin' but a dirty dawg. He was uptown—whut wuz he doin' uptown? I'll tell you whut—he was gorillaing peoples, mugging peoples—innercent hardwerking peoples like the defendant—that' whut he was doing. Ain't nobody gonna miss that mother—I'm gonna say it—that Chucho deserved killin'. That don't mean the defendant killed him, but he deserved it. Now the Dee Ay gonna say my man here killed Chucho. That be a dirty lie. Iffen he was there he didn't kill no Chucho, and ah ain't sayin' he was there—iffen he was there he was runnin' fo' dear life—they was shootin' goin' on in that joint—yessir, Chucho'll tell you that—whut's a man to do but run? Sheet, ah hear pop, pop, mah feet gonna run right out from under me. You people got to hip up that this weren't no Waldorf-Astoria, this were Harlem—it's mean out there. Now Guiso, he didn't see nuthin', he hit the dirt—I don't blame him, but you think iffen he saw who shot up his customers he wouldn' say? Damn right he would, but he ain't gonna lie—he don't know. Ballistics, what did they say? They didn't say nuthin' 'cept that they was two guns used—who was the defendant then? Wild Bill Hickok or Wyatt Herp with two guns? You gotta know there was a whole lot of guns there—and what about Chucho and Nelson, what was they packin'? It weren't no parcel post—and what about this third dude whut got away—where is he? where is he? That be the mystery here—why the Dee Ay don't bring him here, where he hidin', why he hidin'? Go to China, Dee Ay gonna find ya—go to Mangolia, Dee Ay gonna find ya—go to Spotsylvania, Dee Ay gonna find ya—meanwhile he cain't find this dude whut was seen runnin' in the park. That park ain't so big—he got to come out sometime—somebody's jiving.

"And the cops in this case—what did they tell you? That mah man come in under his own voluntary—yessuh, he come in under his own ree-cognizance—he was outa town on business a while when he heard the law was looking for him and he come right on in. Ain't no lammister here—he

here to face the charges. Les talk about this here Nelson—
you saw him slippin', slidin', and glidin' here, didn't you?
Ooweee—what a dirty dawg! Talk about stealin' a hot
stove, this turkey will steal the stove, the pots, the pans,
and the dirty underwear. It's a dirty shame the Dee Ay with
all his money got to bring in such a no-account witness—
ah gets sick in mah stomach thinking about that Nelson—
pardon me while I drink some water. That man would deal
in confederate money—a menace to chillun and society.

"You saw him up there on the stand sashaying around—
no shave, no tie—he ain't got no respect for this courtroom.
I'm gonna let you in on somethin'. You want to know who
the killer is, you really want to know who the killer is?
Don't look no further than that Nelson. There he be, brazen
as all git-out, with the mark of Cain on him, and he ain't
even got no tie on—whereupon look at mah man here—
clean, respetable, white shirt and tie. That ain't no killer
sitting there, thas' a Po' Rican there, and thas why he's
there. Everytime somethin' happen uptown the po-lice run
out and grab the first Po' Rican or nigro they can get their
hands on. Pre-judice is heah, yes it is.

"Ladeez and genulmens of the ju-ree, it come to me last
night when I was thinking what I am going to tell them
intelligent peoples on that ju-ree—yessuh, I do believe the
good Lord in his infinite wisdom, he done shot it down to
me as I lay there thinking, and here's whut I heard: this
here Nelson and Chucho had a shoot-out between them,
thas why each was shot with bullets from different guns;
they collapsed and a thief ran away with both guns. Why,
thas plain as can be. Now ah know ah ain't no Clarence
Darrence, but that don't mean ah ain't telling it like it is.
You gotta go in the ju-ree room and argue and you gotta
cut this man loose, cause he ain't hurt nobody! Now, the
law give the Dee Ay the last word—that ain't right, but
thas the law. But never mind whut he say, you remember
whut ah tol' yo'all, 'cause thas where it's at."

About that time I'd file in like I was the foreman of the
jury and ol' black Walter would say, "Mr. Foreman, has
the ju-ree reached a verdict yet?"

I'd say, "We have, Your Honor."

"And what is your verdict?"

I'd say, "Not guilty on all counts, and now we want to lock up all the lying motherfuckers the D.A. put on the stand." Had a lot of fun with Walter.

THE REAL THING WENT DOWN DIFFERENT. THE SOMBITCH lawyer Steinhardt didn't cross-examine Nelson right. On direct examination by the D.A., Nelson said he didn't see who it was that shot him and Chucho. That ain't good enough—he got to say no, that ain't the man; otherwise with the other shit thrown in I'm gonna get tagged. Now Nelson wants to do the right thing, but the D.A. has him scared. All Steinhardt has to do is lead him over the hurdles to "No, that ain't the man," but he don't know how to do it. First, he loves the sound of his own voice rolling all the *r*'s, then he don't never use two syllables where six will do. He wants to know about wind velocity, about one foot from the door and was the doorknob on the left or the right; did the guy put his left foot in front of his right or his right in front of his left? And every time Steinhardt gets an answer to his stupid-ass questions he looks at the jury like, "Aha!" Well, by the time Steinhardt got through with Nelson, whatever the D.A. left out Steinhardt filled in. So we ended up with Nelson saying "I don't know who," and I was in trouble. I couldn't get on the stand because of my record and all the shit they might bring out.

The jury hung up. I made bail then and went back to the street. I was just getting back into the groove when Steinhardt calls me up.

"Manslaughter in the first degree with a ceiling of five."

"A pound—that's too much, counselor."

"D.A. says he's got a line on that third guy you chased."

"He's bluffing."

"Maybe so, but you're in no position to take chances; this is a P-and-D murder rap—there can be no recommendation of mercy."

"Let me think about it."

What was there to think about? I copped. The night before I went in we had a big party at the Copa. All the boys were there. Everybody was stoned—nearly everybody.

Rocco pulled me aside—"Don't feel too bad about going in, Charles, it's only a couple of years. Keep your nose clean and when you come out you can get next to me. It's taken me a few years, but now I'm ready. This rule about the junk is not for me. The bosses are sitting on millions and they say, you no do-a this, you no do-a that—meanwhile they close the books and the soldiers have to drive trucks on the side to live.

"I've told them, there's a demand, there must be a supply—we step out, somebody else will step in. We can't afford that, matter of economics. All the soldiers in all the gambling and shylocking don't compare to what a few guys can do with junk. There's just no comparison. I was in Europe and my setup is complete over there. Over here I've had some trial runs with my boss—so far, okay; he turns his head away—except when I put the money in his hand, then he looks real hard. Of course, if anything happens, I'm dead—but that's all right—a little balls, a little brains, that's all you need. Why am I telling you this, Charles? Because I want you to go in knowing there's a big place waiting for you when you come out. You've stood up under some bad breaks and you've learned how to take orders—I want you by my side."

I was approaching my thirties, about time my train came in.

Upstate. I went first to Ossining, then to Green Haven. The whole neighborhood was up there. All junkies stealing to support their habit. Seemed like all of a sudden everyone was on junk. Got to be crazy, sticking that shit in their veins. Not crazy, just weak—and a bunch of them support one strong guy, that's the law of nature. Big fish eat a whole lot of little fish, and one lion eats twenty zebras. Everyone down on the pusher, but he don't push nobody, he only push the dope. He provides a service, that's all—somebody got to do it. Somebody wants something, somebody else gonna step out and get it for him—he got to be paid for that, that's the way it's always been. As for me, if they're gonna give me my druthers, I'd druther be a fucker than a fuckee.

In the Joint I always get in top shape; no coke, no pot, no pussy, so you work out. I always do good time—I don't go 'round whining about how I got framed again. I'm a *hodedor* and I'm paying some of my dues. If I'm dressing out of Leighton's and driving Caddies and Lincolns, there got to be a tab sometime; I got no time for these chumps crying about how they never had no chance 'cause their mammy was a whore or their daddy was a lush—who wants to hear that shit? You wanna be a hoodlum, be a pro; if you can't take the time, don't do the crime.

All these shrink and psycho mumbo-jumbo artists is making good money on these prison staffs and they don't know shit. This here's a capitalist country, ain't it? Which means supply-and-demand and dog-eat-dog. First is best and fuck the rest. I'll buy that, I'll compete—but on my terms. I'll go for the goodies, but I can't compete with my brains or family or education, so I do it with my balls. I'll take a shot where most people will step back. But if I come out the other side then I want a bigger cut of the pie—that's the dues the system got to pay. Ain't no mafia in China, but who wants to walk around in pajamas—see what I mean?

That's the kind of shit that goes down in the Joint—three years I had to hear it. Who got twenty whores and three Lincolns on the street? All the rice-and-beans pimps. And who's got the pipeline to the main man in France? All the nickel-and-dime bag-pushers. The criminal mind is a bitch. I don't want nothing to do with these scumbags; I know where I'm going and it don't include none of them. I'm with them but I ain't into them.

Then there's the sex problem in the Joint. When you're in, the worst skank you ever had becomes like a movie star. I've heard guys talk about streetwalkers as "the mother of my children" and "mi señora." Unbelievable. But a whole lot of suffering behind that shit too—I seen stone killers cry on a Christmas or New Year's, I seen a made-guy turn his head to a wall and will himself to death 'cause his old lady left him for another guy. Me, I don't give a fuck. I stay loose at all times, travel light—always been like that ever since I hit the street, age twelve. Then you got the faggots. Bad news. Once a guy starts on that you got to put him down—pretty soon you don't know who's the poger and who's the pogee.

And you get the legal faculty cons. Writing coram nobis and habeas corpses up the ass, arguing cases like they was Earl Warren. If you so slick, why you here, motherfucker? Get out my face.

Least, but not last, you got the stool pigeons. They go 'round dropping kites on everybody. Like:

Chief Judge
Court of Appeals
Federal Courthouse
Foley Square, New York

Your Honor:
 On April 1, 1918, at 8:43 A.M. I saw Joe Baciagalupe sell to Joe Abafangul a kilo of smack. I would be happy to testify about the herein incident. So far the five county D.A.'s, the U.S. Attorney, and the Attorney General have refused to act on my complaint. But I got something on them too. I know you ain't on the take so I'll expect to hear from you soon. All I'm asking is consideration on my fourth felony which I got a bum rap on account of a stool pigeon name of Joe Ugatz.

Your friend,
Louis Linguini

P.S. I'm sending a copy of this letter to your boss in Wash., D.C.

or

District Attorney
New York County
New York, New York

Your Honor:
 On July 4, 1902, my then lawyer, Oscar Meyer, gave to Det. McNulty of the 32 the sum of $500 to beat my case. Meanwhile I'm still here. This is an outrage and

I demand to be called as a witness. My time is your time.

> Sincerely,
> R.A. Fink

P.S. I'm sending a copy of this letter to Morris Nadjari.

WHEN A GUY GOES BAD, HE'S A RENEGADE, BECAUSE HE'S already lined up against society and now he's going against his own kind. He's in no-man's land—and like the guys in no-man's land, he's supposed to get killed. Unless he's ratting on the Latins or the Blacks—then if he survives the first twenty-four hours, he's all right; he can sit ringside at the Chateau Madrid or Smalls, 'cause the spooks and the spics can only stay mad twenty-four hours, then they forget—jive-ass. But the wops can stay mad a long time—one guy's supposed to have been done under ten years later when he got spotted as an extra in some flick—ten years he'd been cool on the West Coast. I heard of spitters going down to Honduras and Panama to ice a rat. Now that's staying mad! With the spics, if a stoolie moves from 111th Street to the Bronx he's out of the jurisdiction—jive-ass. That's why they all be in Lewisburg or Green Haven. Wise up, turkey.

If you been in the slams one time, you been in all of them, but if you're gonna survive in there, you got to be cool. Your rep gets there before you do, but you got to come in mean—mad as a motherfucker.

What you looking at, motherfucker?

You talkin' to a man, you motherless sombitch!

Don't fuck with me, I'll kill you!

Barking and growling—keep a stone face and a tight asshole—jump stink in a minute: they heard you was bad now you got to show 'em. What for? You slack up and they'll throw a mattress over your head. Ask some young blood from the sticks who goes upstate on some check forgery. I seen some had to have thirteen stitches in their asshole and I seen some jump off their rack with a towel wrapped around their neck 'cause some con was in love with them and they couldn't do nothin' about it—warden ain't gonna help you, hacks ain't gonna help you.

It can get nasty in there. Was a stool up there, black dude, rattin' his own people out. They caught him in the kitchen; couldn't hide the body. They cut him into little pieces, then they ground the pieces. There was a nigger in the salad that night. Nobody knowed the difference.

Then you got them little Gem blades that the guys hold in a handkerchief; don't let them corner you in the shower stall, you naked—splice you into spaghetti. That's regular, nobody say a word.

And don't be carryin' no bad habits over into the jailhouse. Had a thief stole an apple in the mess hall from the wrong guy. Guy put a wooden stake through his Adam's apple. I saw the thief spinnin' around trying to pull the stake out. He was all by himself. He didn't make it.

There's some rotten motherfuckers in there—I can take the food or the hacks, it's them criminals in there I can't stand. Like when you're short-timin', waitin' on your parole, the cons will provoke you to fight—make you blow your parole. Nasty people.

Yeah, Your Honor, check out that probation report real good—not all the kids you put in is ready for the Joint. Yeah, some of these lil' ol' boys you put in here is baby lambs and you put them in the same cage with a grizzly bear doing consecutive thirty-year bits. Rough in there, Your Honor—so like if you read the report in a hurry, read it again, 'cause you are fucking with a man's life. In America, God is dead; you the only one we got left, Your Honor—you a God. When you walk in we stand up, when you walk out we stand up. You say who lives and you say who dies—you got no boss and you can change the rules as the game goes along. So check out them lightweights good before you bury them. Now guys like me, you can deal with, 'cause I'll spit in your eye, Your Honor. I'll get to your D.A. or your cops or even to you. I may be on your hook but I'm slippin' and slidin' and one hitch and I'm gone—shit, I'll take you all on and I'll still come out on top!

I was all right in the Joint. My man Colorado was doing a deuce, and he had a little click waiting for me when I got up there. So like at chowtime Colorado is rappin' to the boys how bad I am—Carlito did this and Carlito did that. One dude, Zuzu, ain't impressed. "Aw, man, who wants to hear that shit?" Zuzu was bad, but he wasn't ready—hot soup bowl right into his face. Left hook, overhand right, then a couple kicks to the chest while he was down. Zuzu said we was only playing, but they gave me thirty days in the hole. Solder the door, motherfuckers, I don't need no bread, no water, no mail, no bed, no nothin'—Carlito is bad, ya hear, bad!

Back in population I stayed clean, worked out every day, did some reading, a lot of rapping. I seen guys go in can't read or write, come out talking Shakespeare. If you don't know nothin', the Joint is a great place—me, I had all my smarts long before.

THE WORD CAME DOWN. EARLY SIXTIES: THE GOVERNMENT was building the first big narco conspiracy cases—get them guineas, said Bobby, and they was got. Vito, Lilo, Big John, Chin, everybody went down. And the feds skinned the cats anyway they could—like with Vito—he only spoke to himself in the mirror in a Neapolitan dialect that not even an Italian could understand; meanwhile, the government has him dealing with a junkie P.R. from the Bronx—who they jiving? But like they cleaned Nelson up, gave him voice lessons, a good script, and the dude came on like James Cagney. Vito got fifteen—he must have loved P.R.'s after that.

The word came down hard on Tommy Dunphy. The cons was out in the yard. Spooks, wops, P.R.'s, everybody on their own turf. I was jivin' around with the Latinos, they was bangin' on the skins as usual, timbales, conga and bongos—like a regular fuckin' band. This wal-yo type come over to me. He looked like Marc Lawrence, pinched-in, pock-marked puss. Croaky voice—somebody once told me it's because of the water in Italy, but I think it's from always talkin' in a whisper, like when you scheme. Anyway he says,

"Carlito?"

"Known by that name."

"Rocco got somethin' for ya."

We split off from my click and walk across the yard.

"You're pals with Tommy Dunphy, right, Carlito?"

"Yeah, we're aces."

"He goes."

"*Coño!* Wait a while—what's this?"

"Wadda you want from me, details? I don't wanna know from nothin'. My people tell me to tell you Rocco said so-and-so. Check it out. You in or you out?"

"Okay, okay. But, Jesus, gimme a clue."

"Tommy and two other kids, brothers, handled a contract in Boston. The brothers got popped—they're giving Tommy up. The boss that ordered the hit says Tommy got to be taken out, save him the trouble of going wrong which is only a matter of time with the job busted open, *capisce?*"

"Je-sus, Tommy gotta be washed on a just-in-case."

"Wadda you want from me? I don't need this. I don't even work for Rocco or Petey A."

"All right. I'll take care of business."

"*Ciao.* 'Ey, Carlito, how can you stand that shit?"

"What choice I got? Rocco's my man."

"I don't mean that. I mean that racket from them fuckin' bongo players. Meeng!"

I was shook up—he was one of my main men, tough Irish kid from the West Side docks, good club fighter. We used to rap about being stand-up guys surrounded by rats. Bad news—I shoulda known then that I didn't fit in. But Rocco was counting on me, so I started scheming to get to Tommy—but I liked the guy, he was a down cat. So now I was sweating, kept putting the job off; some Mafioso I was gonna be. Lotta tough wops never get made 'cause they can't hurt people they ain't mad at. Ain't easy.

But got to be. Colorado had a shank he kept in a soap bar—piece of metal honed down. I caught Tommy on the ball field—caught him from behind, I didn't want to see his face—slit his throat from ear to ear; he fell on his back gagging on his own blood. I quit the scene without turning back, but I knew his eyes had to be asking Why? But he didn't go out. That night they brought a bunch of us into the hospital where he was laid out like Christ on the cross, pipes and tubes in and out of him. He was wheezing and gurgling terrible.

"Tommy, you can't make it—don't let them get away with it, you can still talk from the grave—we'll talk for you; you know you're dying—pick out the cock-sucker."

They brought us one by one to the side of the bed. He fixed his eyes on me like they was gonna pop out of his head.

"Tommy, for God's sake, just nod your head up and down—we know it's him; Tommy, you're a Christian lad— make your peace with God; don't let this bastard get away with this—give us a sign."

Tommy rolled his head—left, right, left, right. Negative. Captain Shea, there's your dyin' declaration. The rattling in his throat was getting fierce. I couldn't look at Tommy; I had tears in my eyes—fuckin' wops—my nerves were going—got to make a move.

"Shea, you Irish motherfucker, you trying to frame me."

Shea threw me a sucker right-hand which I caught on my chin—I laid down and let them carry me out. You almost had me that night, Shea, but you blew your cool.

That was a bad night—only time I ever doubted myself— what am I doing, where am I going? All that headshrinker jive that fucks a man up—start asking questions and they got you, they into your skull. No way, Carlito; don't let them get to your skull. You a natural-born hustler with iron balls—get the money and when they step up knock 'em down, that's all there is to it. If you start thinking and wording, then they got you, 'cause they can outthink you and outword you; then you rolling with their dice— like *society* and *humanity* and all them other *t's* that been trying to fuck you—no good. So you wronged a dude; how many times you been wronged? So he stood up—ain't he supposed to, he's a *hodedor*, ain't he? Get out my face.

In the morning I was all right. Tommy was all right, too—he recovered. Then he went back to court on some motion. They put up a big bail for him and gave him a big party.

"Tommy, there was a roundtable just before you come out and Mr. A said you done the right thing—so we're gonna move you up; you're gonna go back on the piers but with six runners turning over to you—no more unloading bananas, you stay clean. So tomorrow you run over to Leighton's, ask for Mel, tell him Mr. A sent you, get yourself five outfits—the works, look like a boss—*madon*—a donkey boss—Don Tomasino Dunferino—*uomo di onore*. Ha!"

They buried him in a lime pit. The suit had no labels but had to go for three yard easy.

Tommy, you went to your grave thinking, "That crazy Carlito tried to kill me—for no reason, spics are like that." You chump, if you had any smarts you'd have pieced it together, but they dry-humped you with a couple of quarters—you was a nickel-and-dime hustler, Tommy, but you was a good boy.

IN THE JOINT, YOU STAY UP-TO-DATE ON EVERYTHING— things you wouldn't know on the street you know right away inside. Whose old lady ain't putting the horns on who. Who's teamed up with who. What crew brought in fifty keys. Who is double-crossing who. Hoodlums gossip worse than whores.

Myself, I didn't want to know if one of my old ladies was cheating on me—'cause then you got to take an attitude, then where's your packages and your visits? So I told these mothers, don't be telling me nothin' about my women. But you gonna find out anyway—like somebody's old lady be visiting and you know she's tight with your broad. "Hey, how's my old lady doing?" Real whorelike, she'll bow her head and bite her lip—"Don't ask me, man, it ain't none of my business what she's doing." Yeah, you get the message. I told all my broads when I split, "You're on your own— don't be saying how you gonna wait and all that bullshit. I ain't waiting on you!" But they still come upstate to see you; they know you're short-timing and the bread is still there—jive bitches. Lots of them drive up to the Joint with their new stud wearing your clothes and driving your car. Kiss you right on the lips too—make you a cock-sucker by proxy. Me, when I go in I don't want to know from nothin'.

*   *   *

So, LIKE I PAID MY DUES TO SOCIETY AND AM READY to take my lawful place. Shee-it, now I'm really gonna double up, deal with both hands; got to catch up, make up for that lost time—that's what drives the penologists and parole guys nuts. The criminal mind, it is a bitch. "Yes, Mr. Dunleavy, I feel that I am ready to take my lawful place in society. I realize now that I've been trying to punish my mother for making me out of wedlock."

Or like, "The man been on m'neck all m'life, but ah know now y'caint beat the man head-on with a pistol in yo' hand—you got to get yo'self a gig, make that bread, then split on out the ghetto—and thas' what I'm gonna do."

Or like, "I believe, genulmens, that if you give me parole, I'll make good this time. The therapy sessions have shown me what I got is a ethnic identity problem—yeah, ethnic identity—in other words, my people are P.R.'s—but I'm born here in the city and I resent that and there's a crisis. Then I get guilt feelings 'cause I'm putting down my own people and that's another crisis—and like that. But that's all straightened out now; I found myself and I'm ready to get that job and work hard."

Bullshit. The cons are jiving the man, but the man is jiving the cons. We know what they want to hear. And if you ain't got the mental, there's always a con to feed you your lines, somebody got a paper on it; they got habeas corpses, coram nobis, appellate division, Court of Appeals, clemency, commutation, copulation—you name it, they got a brief on it. Full of shit most of the time, but just enough to keep you hanging when they get lucky. Around '61 the Mapp case came down—all the cons went ape, everybody writing papers, and the jailhouse lawyers were ridin' high talking all that jive about searching and seizing illegal evidence. The possession cases—dope and guns—started getting thrown out. Shit, everybody gonna get out 'cept me.

That cock-sucker Steinhardt of Four-Two-Oh Broadway railroaded me up here. Didn't I get searched and seized? Why didn't he make a motion to suppress me? Why did Mapp have to come after me? Why wasn't it Brigante? These are the questions I wrote to him. And I reported his ass to the bar association as uncompetent counsel. And I told them how I was innocent (which I believed myself by now) and that the goddamn lawyer had defrauded me into pleading guilty. I didn't know I pleaded guilty on account of I'm a P.R. and my English ain't that good and the day of the plea I was sick with a fever plus headaches plus the lawyer guaranteed me probation plus the probation report told a bunch of lies—I'll fix your Jew ass, Mr. Steinhardt.

But my writ wasn't worth a shit and they threw it out. That's me, always behind, *como los huevos del perro*. Everybody gets the word but me—everbody gets the edge but me—I got to do everything the hard way, never no break. Every favor I take I got to pay double. Uphill all the way—but I'll get even with all these motherfuckers. I'm going out of this Joint *embalao*. I'm gonna tear up that street.

4

So I DID THREE AND CHANGE. THE STREET, MAN, THE street. You still hit the bricks shaky, very shaky. Like you want to see people, but you don't want to. You got it all doped out in the Joint what you gonna do the first day you're out, the second, but when you come out, you like freeze up, like you're scared but you don't know of what. So you hang 'round your crib a lot, waiting for something to happen. Didn't take long.

My man, Earl Bassey—good looking out. Took care of my bank and my crew plus his own all the time I was in. Gave me a good accounting with books and all too. Over hundred thou—I like to fall through my asshole. When you're in the Joint, anybody holds five dollars for you is a miracle. Except some of the wops—there was one boss did a long bit in a dope pinch; when he come out his crew had made and saved for him close to a million dollars in cash—so what was their reward? He's still going around checking to see if they beat him out of anything. If so, shame on them. They shoulda iced him as soon as he come out and glommed the money—they take this mafia shit too serious.

But Earl is a special kind of guy. Like they say in Spanish, *servicial*—which is ready to help anytime, down for any action. Like if you need ten large right away, Earl was there, no questions asked. If you needed good advice, Earl was the man. If you was out of coke or needed some whores in a hurry, Earl could always come up with somethin'. And how many guys can you call at 5 A.M. and tell 'em, I'm in Baldy's after-hours joint and there's three Detroit pimps here I'm gonna waste so get yo' ass down here, and he be there in a minute with two pistols, no questions asked. Earl was the best.

Lot of people thought so too. While I was in the Joint, Earl was up to being one of the main guys in Harlem. He was into everything. Even real estate in St. Croix and St. Thomas. Mr. Bassey. Earl was good with figures and books and he wanted me back in the numbers with him, but I never had no head for accounting and shit. I was just biding my time 'til I got the word from Rocco, then I was gonna invest my hundred large in a big load of junk. That's where it was at. Ain't no money nowhere else. All them hoodlums out there, hijacking trucks, robbing hotels, cracking safes, ain't shit. One connection, one move—you the man; then you can laugh up your sleeve 'cause you got the secret. So I was cool.

Meanwhile, I had me some fun. Me and a few of my boys flew down to San Juan. I paid for everything. Gambled and partied every night—had a luxury suite. Champagne breakfasts, filet mignon, hundred-dollar hookers. By this time, I was a kind of boss—I enjoyed it, about time somebody catered to me. Like if we walked into a club, my boys would flank me; I sat down first, head of the table, first choice with the broads—and the party ain't over until I say so. Whatever the topic, I was the authority; sometimes I'd cross 'em up, reverse my field, then watch the boys jerk around to get back to my new angle. Shit, I was picking up the tabs, I'm entitled. *Capo di tutti capi.* Da'sa me. Ha!

One night we ran into Llanero. Llanero was a thug from 102nd Street in Harlem, gorilla people 'cause he had a bad face with a rip on it, but inside he was a faggot and the boys would kick his ass regular. He'd go somewhere he wasn't known like the West Side or the Bronx and he'd be bad. He was a beater. Like if you didn't make a bail right away he'd be the first one on the fire escape to rob your apartment or if you had a good card game going he'd find some outside kids to stick up the joint. Me he caught with some bad candy at a party years back—"*Coño*, Carlito, this coke is special

shit from the *altiplano* in Bolivia; only the chiefs snort
this shit"—and an old cornet player like me like to O.D.
I'd have killed the motherfucker but he was wily to find.
Then he went uptown to black Harlem with a big carton of
Central Park grass which he got off as Panama pot which
he had sprinkled on the top. Them niggers tracked him all
over the city, but when they caught up with him he talked
them out of it, talking on his knees in a garbage dump in
the Bronx with two pistols in his face. Llanero was tricky.
We was gonna have fun with Llanero.

My man Lalin said, "Llanero, Carlito wants you to join
us for dinner."

"I can't, Lalin, I got an appointment."

Loud and clear for all to hear. "Motherfucker, get yo'
ass over here and sit down," says me. This was a plush
restaurant in Old San Juan where the maitre d' cooks right
alongside you, but I didn't give a shit.

"Sit right here at the head of the table, Llanero, you look
terrific. Who you with here?"

"I'm with Santito Gil, Carlito; been here two years—
clean, no problems. I heard you was doing great, Carlito;
everybody in the Barrio always said, Carlito's going all the
way, he's—"

"Watcha mean, motherfucker, talking behind my back—
you some kind of stool pigeon? Who told you you could
talk about me?"

"You got it wrong, Carlito—"

"No, you pussy, you got it wrong. I got a napkin under
this table, and under that napkin there's a piece that says
I'm gonna blow your stomach out your back."

Ol' scarface Llanero turned green inside his tan.

"But you look terrific, Llanero, terrific. Let's see now,
them kicks you're wearing got to go for eighty dollars.
Take 'em off—I mean both of them, motherfucker. That's
it, cool-like. Hey, that watch, Llanero, got to be a Piaget—
let Colorado hold it a minute. Let's see the label on that
boss suit of yours—Louis Roth, California; I'll be damn,
you must be one of them executive cats. Tato, take the
jacket off him, throw it under the table. Lalin, bring the
maitre d' over here."

The maitre d' had caught the action and he was all shook up.

"Waiter, what kind of ratjoint is this that a man can sit around without no jacket?"

"*Señor*, I thought he had a jacket when he came in."

"Get his ass the hell out of my table."

Llanero was in such a hurry he forgot all his gear. We slapped skin all around on the running of our little murder game.

Early that morning the Rican police hit our suite. No warrant, no nothing. Llanero to Santito to the bulls—they pull that shit over there. They give us twenty-four hours. We left standby that afternoon. I don't ever want to be busted outside of home base; that's a world of trouble.

BACK TO THE APPLE. THE JUNKIES WERE COMING OUT of the woodwork by now—you'd see them on rooftops, fire escapes, in alleys—hauling TV sets, toasters, radios, clothes—you name it, they was selling. Grab your coat off a wall, your hat off your head—the junkies were scavenging; get off a one high, got to get movin' to the next one; busy stealing, scheming, conning—a junkie is a busy cat, always walking fast. Watch them on 100th or 117th Street—skanky, dirty, always in pairs like faggots, never no pussy; don't want to know about no pussy, just that spike. How they got that last bag, how they gonna score the next one—that's their rap, how they're conning the world.

"Dig, Jack, I tol' Moms, you got to gimme them five dollars you got stashed, she say no good, I jumped right out on the fire escape on the edge—I'll kill myself, I don't deserve to live, I'm making you suffer, Mom. She gimme the bread. Now Wednesday when she cashes her check you wait under the stairs. I'll play chickie on the stoop, dig? But don't hurt her."

There's got to be winners and there's got to be losers. They're the losers, that's all. So when one of these chumps O.D.s, everybody's saying, what a pity, such a young man; that's what the motherfucker wants—he wants that last high, going right up the roof of his head and keep going.

So what in hell is all the fuss about? They're scumbags. Get the money.

ABOUT THIS TIME ROCCO FABRIZI SENT FOR ME. JILLY'S. Class joint. Best piano in town. I just had Colorado with me.

"Only room at the bar, sir."

"It's okay, Mike, he's with my party."

There was five thousand years in the joint. Spitters. Rocco brought us to his table in the back—his crowd, no broads.

"You boys know Carlito, from uptown. Mr. A, I'd like you to meet Carlito."

Peter Amadeo, Rocco's boss, he's been around since they repealed Prohibition. He got three speeds—gun, knife, and the rope. Any beef or hassle come up, kill right away, then we discuss it later. He was made in the thirties, always seemed to be on the winning side in all the wars, a survivor. He come up the ladder but he ain't got no smarts, no class like Rocco. A crazy ginso with a horseshoe up his ass. Suspicious of his own mother.

"Wadda you crazy, Rocco? I got to meet people? I know too many people already—get them a table someplace else."

Real gentleman, Mr. A. I got hot but I didn't want to make more trouble for Rocco so I let it slide. Guinea motherfucker.

Rocco had them put a table for us right in the aisle. Bucket of champagne. He could see I was hot.

"The old man's very nervous, Carlito; he doesn't mean any harm, but he's got a thing about conspiracies—very nervous."

"Then maybe he ought to move over for you, Rocco."

"You're downtown now, Charles; don't fool around with that kind of talk."

"Okay, Rock, gimme the deal."

"Cubans—what do you know about Cubans?"

"The Cubans, they're here and in Miami, loads of them; what is there to know about them?"

"All right, Charles, I'll tell you. This is not a banana- or cattle-boat migration; these are doctors, lawyers, businessmen, the whole middle class—like the German Jews after the war."

"So?"

"So they're going to move fast, make their weight felt real quick-like."

"So?"

"So the hoodlums came with them. You've seen them hanging around the Latin joints down here and in Washington Heights. Light stuff feeling their way around now. But they're ex-cops and military people from the Batista and Prio governments. They're small-arms experts, they've all been in shoot-outs. They're also hungry; this is their last stop, and the pickings are easy. You get the picture now?"

"Yeah, Rocco."

"They're going to make their move. So we have to head them off at the pass, ease them in gradually. You take a few into your crew, this other guy will take some, like that. This way they won't come at us all at once. When they get greedy we'll have to kill a few but they'll be split up and all the rest will fall in line. I mean am I right or wrong?"

"You right, man, you right!"

"Things may get better because there's more than enough to go around and they're down in South America for the candy and in Europe for the real shit. I see all kinds of possibilities. Am I right or wrong?"

"The man is on, the man is on!"

"First off, you're taking a guy off my hands. They're sending him to me with his boys from Miami—yeah, your friend, Nacho Reyes; I need that crazy Cuban like a hole in the head, so I'm farming him out to you. You both eat rice and beans. Keep him under your wing, he's the main guy. If he goes along with the program, the rest will follow. Any Cubans give you trouble, send Nacho; I hear he's rough. As a matter of fact, some of my people will be using him from time to time for various—uh—house calls—ha!"

"*Carajo!* You gonna put this *verdugo* on me?"

"Look at that, you even talk the same language. Tell your man to get you your car, I'll walk you to the corner."

When we got to Eighth Avenue, Rocco said, "There's a car on its way over now—I'm forming a pot, ten guys, a hundred a piece."

"You running the deal?"

"Who else?"

"I'm in."

"Take this half of a dollar bill; Vinnie—you remember Vinnie—he'll have the other half on him; he'll be at your place Tuesday, have fifty ready for him—front money. Have the rest ready for Friday—C.O.D., I'm guaranteeing the shit."

"Rocco, you know what this means to me, I'll never let you down."

"I told you I'd give you a shot; it's a welcome-home present from your Uncle Cheech—'ey *afangul*, wadda you gonna kiss me on the cheek? Get uptown."

And the deal went down. Ten kilos I got. We had that shit in the street in no time. I was big-time. Imagine, me, Carlito, the main connection uptown. I knew I was bad, but I didn't know I was slick.

About this time I changed my image—conservative clothes, a pad on the East Side, a Lincoln. I even bought a discotheque downtown so I could get next to the young pussy that was down there—the help was robbing me but I didn't give a shit, it was just a toy. Funny the way the wise-guy can never make it in legit business because the square that covers for him will always rob him. Never fails. I guess it's like getting even. I used to like to stash into the joint with a big party. Champagne for everybody— make believe I was checking the receipts. "I don't want nobody in my joint with a piece"—law and order—when I think of the bread I've pissed away! Sometimes on a Saturday I'd jump up to Harlem in my Lincoln and play stickball in the street with the kids in my eighty-five-dollar slacks. Yeah, I was a big shot! Everybody said it, "*Carlito buena gente!*" Like if some P.R.'s was getting dispossessed or needed some funeral money, I'd see them go. Or if some dude come out of the slams or couldn't make a bail, I was always down. Like I wouldn't hog the bread—everybody with me went first-class. Especially my broads—you name it, good clothes, good jewelry, good coke.

Then the Cubans punched in. *Cubiches!* They sure shook up the hoodlums. Right away they was ringside at all the Latin joints drinking Chivas Regal and snorting. They call coke *perico* (parakeet) because it makes you talk all night. So they'd be in the after-hours joints until 10 or 11 A.M. Everybody had a pistol so it was Wild West stuff. A *pistola* they call a *fuca*—so when you mix *perico* and *fucas* you know you got trouble. People were getting killed. Ask the bulls from the two-eight, the three-oh, and the three-four— they thought a hurricane had hit Manhattan. The hoodlums were all shook up, everybody was packing; mostly the Cubans would fight among themselves but it was only a question of time.

Nacho Reyes: first night in New York we hit about ten joints—Liborio, Iberia, La Baracca, like that. He had put a group together in Miami, all hitters, all veterans of the Batista wars, all hungry. The Ricans quite naturally had to be the hosts.

Nacho's tongue was always thick from *perico*, which he snorted day and night, so when you talked he always got up close to your face—"*Mi hermano, mi consorte.*" If he wanted to get somethin' across to you he'd close his eyes in the middle of a sentence and leave his mouth open— so you'd be waiting. Before you knew it I was doing the same thing. "*Mi her-mano,*" crazy. His life was unreal. He'd killed four cops, two of Batista's and two of Castro's. His mortal enemy, Juanito Cuatro Vientos (Johnny Four Winds), had shot him five times in an ambush in Havana. They took him to the morgue where he came to on a slab. He got up off the slab naked with the five bulletholes and stumbled into the morgue attendant's office—scared the shit out of the guy.

When Nacho was a prisoner in Isla de Pinos, the Castro militia would take him to *paredón* each dawn, and the firing squad would shoot blanks at him. Bad for your nerves. He killed two Castro cops, stole a jeep, and sneaked into the Mexican embassy dressed like a Western Union guy. In

Mexico, he was working for the C.I.A. shooting Castro agents. Yeah, baby, we play rough, too. Nacho's boys was no slouches, either. They all been trained with the Rangers in the U.S. Army, in Florida and Guatemala, had jumped off at the Bay of Pigs and the Belgian Congo.

Nacho himself was not a hustler—he didn't racketeer. His business was his balls. In other words, if he heard that Rolando from Union City had made a score, he would drop in on him and hit him for five hundred or so. Or if maybe Mario from Miami was in town with a big bundle, Nacho would get next to him. No gorilla or stick-up shit, more like, "*Mi hermano*, I am short on funds to continue my fight against Castro and Communism; I know you want to give your share." Guys like Rolando and Mario were bad-asses and they really weren't afraid of Nacho, it's just that Nacho was like supported by all the Cuban wise-guys; so even though they weren't scared of him, they weren't ready to die any day of the week the way he was, and besides, if they had a problem of violence they could count on Nacho any time of the day or night no matter who or what was involved. It could be a beat—*tumbe*—for twenty thou or a piece of ass, all the same to Nacho.

Right away, he was trouble for me. That first night, we hit an after-hours place in the east sixties. Connected people own the joint. Hoodlums and whores all crowded together carrying on even though straight people are already getting up to go to work. Nacho says to his boys, "Manolito Matanzas!" Oops! *Qué pasa* with Manolito Matanzas? I see this tall skinny guy all dressed in white, in winter. "He is making his *santo*, I see; then this is a good time to blow him to hell."

"Wait a minute, Nacho, what's wrong with this guy?"

"He is an *hijo de puta* from Matanzas who was one of the jailers at Isla de Pinos. I told him that whenever I saw him, he would be mine. Tonight I keep my promise."

"Nacho, the people here are friends of mine, *Italianos*; we got to show respect."

"Fuck the *Italianos*, Manolito's time has come. But we

will give him a fair chance. Camaguey, give me your pistol; take the bullets out of the clip."

Camaguey took the bullets out of the clip, then slid the empty magazine back into the automatic and handed the gun to Nacho.

Nacho yelled from the bar to Manolito's table, "Manolito Mantanzas, you are a *maricon* and a *hijo de puta-echa pa'lante si eres hombre*."

The joint wasn't jumping anymore. Stand back. Matanzas was glue—he kept his hands on top of the table, but he wouldn't look up.

"Nacho Reyes, I do not have a gun on me, I am making my *santo* and I do not want any trouble."

"You made plenty trouble in Isla de Pinos when you had your gun and stick. You were an *abusador* but I told you then your time would come. Look at my face, *cabron!*"

"I do not have a gun."

"Then I will give you a gun, *maricon!*" And Nacho pulled out Camagueys's automatic and placed it out on Matanzas' table, all the time holding his own revolver in his right hand.

"*Agarra*, Manolito, *agarra!*"

"No, Nacho, I will not fight you with this gun. Give me the one in your hand; that's the one I want, you take this one."

Manolito was no fool.

With that, Nacho busted Matanzas across the face and head with the pistol butt until the blood ran all over the white suit. All hell broke loose now, chairs flying, women screaming. We quit the joint in a hurry. We drove down to another after-hours in the east twenties. We weren't there long when I got to feeling sick from all the shit I'd put in my nose—out of training, I guess. Nacho walked me outside to the street. All of a sudden, I see Manolito Matanzas running behind the parked cars across the street; he's got a carbine with a banana clip.

"Duck, Nacho!"

Pow, pow, pow—we're running but the carbine is plowing up the asphalt all around us—Nacho hits the ground, spins around, and empties his piece at Matanzas. By this time, Nacho's boys are down and shooting. Matanzas is down. "Look what you've done to me!" Last words. Later for Matanzas. Dump all the guns and let's get out of here.

Nacho was hit in the sole of his foot, blowing out the bones in his instep. Don't ask me how, but right there in his dingy hotel room, a Cuban doctor put wires in Nacho's foot, sewed him up, put a cast on the leg. Nacho stayed in the room a week, snorting coke. After a week he was getting around on crutches, no infection, no nothing. That cocaine will cure anything. Anybody else they would have had to cut the leg off at the thigh. Sombitch is indestructible. There was a roundtable about the brawl inside the east sixties spot but Rocco straightened it out.

The Cubans were all *santeros*. They believe in the saints. Saint Lazarus, Santa Barbara, like that. I been to Cuban homes where they'll have a special room for the saint. A plaster saint maybe five feet tall with a golden sword with real jewels in it and a velvet cape and a golden crown. Then they put food around the saint. They are sold on this stuff, can't tell them different. Then they got all kinds of hexes and voodoo. With big money being paid to the *santera* or *santero*. Like if a Cuban wants something real bad he promises to do his *santo* if he gets it. His *santo* might be giving up several thousand dollars, shaving his head bald, dressing only in white.

The Ricans got their hocus-pocus too—*espiritistas*, we call them. If they done a *trabajo* (a job) on you, you're in trouble, you're hexed—everything gets fucked up. The Latin hoodlums believe all that shit, so if they got a big deal cooking they get a job done, or if they been getting busted too often they get a job done to get the hex off them. I seen stone racketeers and killers going in for this shit. Me, I don't believe in nothin' but that dollar bill in my pocket—stay with the money, you be all right. You can be broke in China or Cuba where everybody is in the ditch, but how you gonna be broke and in the ditch here when you got them guys driving by you with Cadillacs splashing mud in your face? No way. Throw it all up in the air and see who comes up with what—I'll take my chances.

The Cubans were roaming around, looking for a soft spot. The cops were expecting an all-out war, but it never come off because there was more than enough to go around. Except for a few cowboys like Rocco, the wops were afraid of the junk, and the Ricans and the blacks never got connected overseas. But junk was king. So the Cubans filled the gap—with no money, no connections, no language, they set up on the East Coast, West Coast, Europe, South America. Unbelievable. They got heavy in no time. They had respect for the old pros like me, but once in a while they'd show their teeth.

Like there was this guy Rivas-Barcelo. He'd been a big shot in Cuba, minister of transportation under Prio; he sold the whole transportation stock in Havana and pocketed the money. Then when Batista came in, he was a boss in the secret police under Ventura. He'd walk into a precinct where they had some Castro suspects—"How come these men are still alive?" They wouldn't stay alive long. Stone killer but he always wore dark suits with vests and a homburg hat—with his gray hair, he looked like a judge. I liked to rap with him. He always spoke with a Castilian accent, and even if they was raunchy whores, he'd be bowing and pulling out chairs, "*señorita*" this and "*señorita*" that. He wore shades day and night but it didn't do any good, you could still see his eyes; you knew he would never hesitate. He brought his boys out of Cuba with him on one of the last boats to get out. Rivas paid the skipper in counterfeit money, but the skipper had the last laugh because he didn't know where he was going and they got lost all over the Gulf of Mexico. A couple of Rivas' boys couldn't cut it and had to be dumped to the sharks. The rest made it on account of Rivas kept them going when they about had it. They called him *Comandante*.

Rivas had some tough boys but one in particular, Roberto Palacios, was a very nasty kid, psycho-like. Palacios was around twenty-one years old but had been shooting people in Havana, Miami, and New York. He'd come into the joints and walk from one end of the bar to the other bad-eyeing everybody; then he'd go outside and come back to find out if somebody was saying something about him. He kept all the thugs on edge because you knew somebody had to kill him and you wondered if you was gonna be the lucky guy to lock with him. Rivas used to say he was a *buen muchacho* from a wealthy family who had lost everything. Then Rivas decided to aim the kid at us. One night I was at a joint near Amsterdam Avenue with my group and Rivas and his *bravos* had a table nearby. All of a sudden Palacios says to my man Victor Lopez, "You're sitting in my chair."

Victor don't take no shit nohow—"Fuck, you mean I got your chair?"

"You are lacking in respect for me, Victor."

"Wadda you crazy, man? Get out of here before I knock you on your ass."

"I am going to my car, meet me outside in ten minutes, bring something with you."

Palacios left. Rivas did not say a word to Palacios, instead he ordered a round of drinks for my table. "This is not our affair, Carlito, let these impetuous youngsters settle their differences; if we all go outside there might be a tragedy— Victor's blood is hot, let him go out."

So that's how it went down—one on one. When we got outside, Palacios was dead and Victor had three bullets in him. We got rid of both pistols before the Man came. I got to Victor first—"Not a word to the bulls, name and address, that's all—don't talk about no self-defense, don't say nothin', on advice of counsel!" They kept Victor at the Bellevue Prison Ward. I told his old lady, "You tell Victor that I am conducting his defense, he don't need no goddamn lawyers; the grand jury got to know that Victor acted in self-defense, and where is the piece for the possession charge? No case, the man got to walk."

The grand jury dismissed the case. Everybody uptown was saying how Carlito knew the law better than the lawyers. Goddamn right. After that I was giving out all kinds of legal decisions in all the joints. I missed my calling, shoulda been a judge. Will the party of the first part sit down so I can talk to that fine party of the second

part in my chambers? Or like I charge this jury that that cop
is a lying sombitch and you better come in with a verdict
of acquittal 'cause I'm going to dismiss the case anyhow.
Or I hereby order the D.A. committed for ninety days for
contempt of court for presenting such a shit-ass case. And
I hereby order the stool pigeon to the Elmira Reception
Center for an indeterminate sentence and suspend sentence
on the defendant. History-making decisions.

The Cubans livened things up and we had a lot of fun
with them. Nobody can party like them.

5

I HAD PLENTY OF BUCKS BUT ONLY FROM THE JUNK—
everything else I did lost money. And I was always angling
for schemes—like this middleweight who's knocking 'em
dead in the gym. When I'm promoting, every time he
steps in the ring he gets knocked on his ass. Then
there was this chanteuse who was gonna be another
Olga Guillot, cost me a bundle—had to get her an
apartment and everything. She couldn't sing worth a
damn; we'd spring her on the Cubans in Union City
and Hoboken with a big promotion—no dice. Seem like
dealing is all I'm good at, so be it.

Earl Bassey was married by now and he'd tell me, "You
got to get yo'self a good old lady and settle down. Look at
me, I got me a home on the Island, a wife and a kid. Come
Sunday I lay up like a respectable citizen. I'm putting it
all together and in a little while my lil' brother Reginald is
gonna have the whole thing and I'm retiring to St. Croix.
I got me the bread, what for I'm gonna wait 'til the Man
puts me back in striped pajamas? No good. You know I
ain't ever jived you, Carlos, I'm telling you in front—
the party's over. The Man be cooking up the conspiracies
again, but the sentences are gonna be a motherfucker—I
ain't jiving you, I got this from some big people. Get yo'
ass out now, bro, 'cause in a little while it gonna belong to
the government. That's the sermon for today."

"You right, Earl, I been thinking the same thing." Bullshit.
I always agree with what people tell me and it sounds good

at the time, but then I go my way anyway. But I didn't go for the bit about his kid brother Reggie. Now that was a bad nigger. Earl brought him up out of Philly where he was going to college. Earl had a blind spot for the kid. Reggie would strut around uptown with these two flunkies of his, dressed in some Fidel Castro overalls. Everything was "black" this and "black" that. When he first come up to New York, I was at the Baby Grand with some tan chick and he wanted to know what my white face was doing in the joint. Meanwhile, I knew he had a white bitch in the Village. The shit was straightened out but I knew he was trouble.

About this time I got hung on a broad bad. Her name was Leticia but I called her Tuta, like a nickname I give her. She reminded me of India in looks but she wasn't no *bollo-loco* like India, she was a clean girl. As a fact she was the first "good" girl I ever had. She was a very educated girl, been to high school and everything. I met her downtown in a joint I was eating at with my buddy. We noticed these two dolls at this table next to ours. So right away I sent them over a drink—no good, not interested. Then, like to made to order, some guy stoned comes over to their table and starts breaking chops. Right away, I jump up and grab the guy by the arm and pull him away.

I say, "Can I talk to you a minute, sir? I'm Detective Russo of the vice squad and I couldn't help but notice you were disturbing these young ladies. Now run along before you get yourself in trouble."

"Where'sh your identification?"

"After I show you my shield, I'm going to kick your ass through that plate-glass window."

He split. "Ladies, I'm sorry about this man disturbing you, I don't think he'll bother you anymore."

A while later, the waiter come over and said the ladies would accept our drink. Well all right!

She fell out when she saw my white Lincoln what I was rolling around in at the time. She didn't want me to drive her home but I insisted—then I found out why; she lived in the projects off 106th Street and Madison Avenue, a rose in spic Harlem. Them projects been low in income but high on beautiful girls. I got to hanging around the Gondolier and Sunlite bars on Madison and 104th to be near her. We snuck around a lot, I didn't want everybody to know I was going serious with a young thing. She was only nineteen. Like all Latin chicks, she loved to dance. She had me dancing at the Chateau Madrid, Corso's, the Ginza. I'd take her to the Garden to fights. I'd pick her up at her office and we'd go to dinner, like Forno's for Spanish or Sal Anthony's for Italian. Without realizing it, I got involved with the broad. It got so we had to see each other every day, and I wasn't even screwing her. I was worried about it, what the hell's going on here? Like, I wasn't myself; I don't talk on the phone for nobody—but her, we'd talk for hours. I wasn't snorting or even carrying a piece. Then I was thinking maybe I'm going to get married. Jesus. One day she talked me into meeting her family. Mistake. Her folks were all right—I came on with mucho *señora* and *señor*. But Tuta's older brother Sigfrido was there. And he wasn't buying no tickets off'n me. He looked at me like I was the devil himself. He had a grocery down the block and he knew my story from A to Z. This was a square who worked behind a counter sixteen hours a day—you know he was gonna love my ass. After he got through choking he called a family conference—I heard words like *delincuente, maton, droguero*—I eased out of the apartment. And even feeling relieved. This ain't my bag. But a few days later, Tuta got to me; she was crying and saying that she wanted to give me a chance to explain. I told her, "I have been in trouble before but that's because I was an orphan; I didn't have no family to look out for me like you, so I was always getting blamed for everything because I had no one to stick up for me. On account of my record I can't get a decent job, God knows I tried everything. So I turned to gambling and made a few dollars which I have invested in a bar—I lied to you when I told you I was in real estate because I knew you'd put me down for my past record. That's where it's at, Tuta. I've leveled with you—now you can believe in me or believe the goddamn lies and rumors these jealous Puerto Ricans are gonna tell you."

It was one of the best speeches I ever gave a broad and

she dug it. Meanwhile, she was eating sirloin steaks and drinking champagne and sitting ringside—that helped. She came my way. Now we really had to sneak around.

Came a long weekend and Tuta told her family she was going with her girl friends to the Spanish villas around Newburgh. We flew to Miami. *Qué* party! La Guillot, Manzanero were singing down there. Los Violines, Montmartre—the whole Cuban scene. Yeah, mother, I got to them drawers. Got my head bad too. I was really hung up on her. She knew she had me staggering behind her box. She demanded that we elope. I was groggy but not that groggy. I retaliated with, "I was married many years ago, as a minor, but I'm working on my divorce now. Then we'll get married right away." Ain't no rug can lie better than me.

It was fab'lous honeymoon without benefit of clergy. But now it was time to pay my dues. We arrived Tuesday night looking tanned 'n terrific. I drove her up to 104th Street to let her cross the street by herself. I waited on the corner until she was out of sight, then I decided to go into the Gondolier for a taste. Sigfrido came in from my right. I had no piece—the first one hit me flush on the chest; I tried to grab him, but he put two more in my stomach. The guys from the Gondolier came running out. "Carlito's dead," "They killed Carlito," people yelling. And I was going out. I was freezing, maybe I'm dead already. I couldn't see, but I could hear voices. I wanted to get up but couldn't move. I remembered other guys dying on the streets of Harlem wanting to get up as if you couldn't die standing up. The bulls—"Wait for an ambulance," "Some dope pusher named Carlito, I know him," "Sure punched his ticket."

Then Cheo from the Gondolier said, "Don't wait for no fucking ambulance—don't leave him there—what about my fucking license? Carry him to the Flower Hospital— it's only a block away." Cheo saved my ass.

I was dying for two weeks, especially around early dawn I'd really fade, but I kept coming back. Them doctors like to croak me, but I survived just for spite. Like the bullet in my chest, they couldn't find it. It's still in there—I don't bother him, he don't bother me. In the evening, everybody would come in to see me, everybody but Tuta. They told me she and her whole family had checked out that same night. Figured I'd have the brother killed. No way. You know that chump had to be sore, peddling *bacalao* and *plátanos* in a store the size of a closet. And me with my pimp-car running off with his sister. Shit, he was smoking. Me, I ain't no grudgeholder—if I had caught the dude early on, I'd a put a hurtin' on him, but later on—what the hell? Fact is, Sigfrido did me a favor—I felt better every day, like I took a weight off. Always felt that way when I shook off a broad—don't have to account to nobody—stay loose—if I'm busted don't have to worry she's cheating on you. My line of work, man only supposed to worry about one thing: staying out the Joint. Anything else is superfluid.

The bulls from the two-three was up to see me regular. First time I was a complainant.

"They was three muggers, hofficer. Mean, too. Didn't give me a chance to hand over my money. A man cannot walk in the streets 'cause Lindsay has tied your hands—a regular ghetto here in the two-three, I'm moving up to Simpson Street where a man is safe."

"You always been a wise cock-sucker, Carlito—that's why they perforated your ass. Listen, if it was up to me they coulda buried you, but we got these reports and we gotta have a description of the assailants—now quit fucking around!"

"Well, your honor, the assailants looked colored, but they might have been dark Italians or even that other group you got around here. In the dark, *todos los gatos son negros*. Don't get mad at me, officer, all I saw was bang, bang, bang. I wouldn't want to make no mistake, I know what it is to be framed by your house."

"Aw, you wise—!"

"Don't mess with Hoppy, pres, I'm a sick man." Man, would I break their hole!

Last time I heard, Tuta got married down in P.R. I dug her, I can't deny it, but my way is still best. Loose. But *un clavo saca otro*, and pretty soon I was cruising around with this bandit from Brooklyn. Uweee, you devil. I got back into the groove real quick-like. They was robbing me in my disco joint but I was getting plenty of pussy out of there.

The horse was riding high. But getting harder to come by. What with the government and the stool pigeons a lot of heavyweights was getting put away. The heat was on something fierce. But all the better for the guys that really knew what's happening. That's money, baby, money. Be a fool to walk away from that. Myself, I'm down for the action anytime, and I don't want to hear this ol' bullshit about the little kids in the schoolyard. The only ones dealing with the little kids is the little kids themselves, and if people want to get high, that's their lookout. Shit, if they ain't on junk, they'll be on wine or some other shit. They can't cope—shame on them. I'm short-timing in this world and any way I get by is okay with me. I only know one way—my way, like the song. Frank'll tell you.

About that time, Rocco had a baptismal affair for his new baby boy at his house out on the north shore. Me and Earl drove over to pay our respects. Reggie came too—seem like Rocco told Earl to bring his kid brother, Reggie, along. With Earl pulling out I guess Rocco wants to make sure Reggie can step in without no hitch. It was an afternoon affair on Rocco's big lawn, catered, very nice. There was some heavy people there, including Rocco's uncle, Dominick Cocozza. Cocozza ranked Amadeo, so for the first time I seen Amadeo not acting like an animal. Cocozza would talk and Amadeo would "Yeah, Dom" and "Right, Dom." Amadeo told Cocozza what a great guy Rocco was and what a great moneymaker he was for the outfit. He also said he had his son Paul moved in two houses down so that some of Rocco's smarts could rub off on Paul. Everybody was drinking and feeling pretty good. Cocozza told Earl, "My nephew's told me what a great help you been to him uptown, that your word is good. A man's word must be sacred. Not like these punks and stool pigeons coming up. *Combinazione*, that's the ticket, we work together; you make money, we make money. Let's drink to that." Everybody was drinking except Amadeo and Reggie.

Rocco pulled me over to a corner. "You remember Sixto Davila?"

"Yeah, Rock, quarter-key man from the Bronx, up in Prospect. He was at the El when we was there."

"Right. While you were away we tried to help him—he was always crying, gimme a break, Rocco, so I gave him a break—a heavy number. He dealt the goodies, but being a garbage can he showed his hand on the first deal—glommed the money and he took off to Europe. I didn't say anything because Petey A gets excited and I made up the money. Now I don't believe in hurting a guy over money, most of the time you're getting off cheap. But I have a man in Madrid and this Sixto has gotten to him and he's giving my man a big play. I say Sixto is a beater and a beater is the next thing to a rat. I say he's stooling for Interpol."

"Which does what for me?"

"You're going to Spain, Carlito!"

"I ain't no hit man, Rocco, why not Nacho?"

"A Cuban has trouble getting in and out; and besides, this is not a cowboy job. You get next to him, get his guard down; the hit will come from somewhere else. This is important, Charles."

"Whatever you say, Rocco."

"Vinnie will be around to see you tomorrow with the details."

Almost didn't make that trip. Got pinched—me and this guy, Chángui—and while I was on a mission for mercy, mind you. My ol' buddy Lino, the barber, was dyin' in the Mount Sinai—doctors said he was terminal. I used to see him regular, he didn't want for nothin'. Lino had looked out for me when I was a kid. Anyway, he asks me for a favor. Seem his son, Felino Jr., known as Junior (no fuckin' good), was doin' a lot of scratchin' and eatin' a lot of jelly rolls. Lino was suspectin' he was on junk. Now I follow the golden rule about mindin' m'own business, but what the hell—I owed Lino. So me and this guy Chángui go lookin' for Junior. We find out that he was scorin' out of a Bickford's on 145th Street and Broadway. He didn't wanna come out the joint, so we dragged him outside, put him against a building, and give him a few smacks. Then we tried to reason with him. I told him if his father was a barber without no schoolin' he could be a doctor if he had some schoolin'; he said he was in a trade school, Machine and Metal Trades on 96th Street. Wise cock-sucker. Then be a fuckin' dentist, and I gave him another rap. I read him the riot law—if I find out you're using hard shit I'm gonna pull your tongue out yo'ass, etc.

About this time, four detectives come out of an unmarked car with their cannons out. *Puñeta*. Me and Chángui get tossed up against the wall. They chased Junior. They got our pistols and they got eight yard I had in my pocket. This is after 4 A.M.,'cause the crowd from the Caborojeño Club upstairs had already let out. The bulls take me and Chángui down to Riverside Park. Ain't no precinct in there, so I know we gonna settle out of court. Moldy-puss was the main bull of the four, he said,

"Watcha names, punks?"

"I'm Inspector Moran, this is Lieutenant Chángui."

"I'll bust your ass, Brigante. I know you—what the hell are you doin' this far up in a cheap shakedown?"

"We were just tryin' to straighten the kid out for his father."

"Oh, I see, juvenile aid work, eh? Your ass. We gotcha for assault and possession of loaded guns. How do you like them onions?"

"The kid won't sign no complaint, and this was an illegal search—we weren't committin' no crime. Bust won't stick."

"You fuckin' hump—we went to question you, you stumbled, fell against me. I felt the bulge on your hip. Gotcha. Right, guys?"

I know when I'm in an over-the-weight match.

"Officer, that eight hundred ain't mine. S'pose we split down the middle. That'll give you guys a hundred a piece, right? Everybody wins."

"Wrong. You are a cheap cock-sucker, Brigante; you're lucky you're dealin' with me. Beat it."

They kept the guns too. Mother-hoppers. I got back to Lino next day and told him what he wanted to hear, that the kid was only sniffin', not skin-poppin', and that he was straightened out. The kid was straight like a fishhook. Can't do nothin' with a *tecato*. Lalin's kid brother, Narciso—forty-dollar-a-day habit—jab himself in the cock and in the neck. Once, Lalin knocked his teeth out—didn't do no good. From the whole army of junkies marchin' around Harlem I ain't seen but two guys walk away from the spike.

It didn't matter Lino none—them doctors finally terminaled him. *Adiós, buena gente, descanse en paz.*

I would have gone for the funeral, but he had insurance. I put some bread on Lino's widow, Doña Mercedes. It didn't take Junior long to put Doña Mercedes in the box next to Lino. I cried at that funeral; she was a lady.

Don't look at me. I never put no needle in nobody's arm. How many Juniors have I tried to straighten out? Shit, I'm just gettin' by myself. Plenty bites been taken outa my ass—lucky I got a rhino hide and a concrete skull. Else my ass would be grass now too.

6

V*IVA* E*SPAÑA*! M*ADRID*, A CLASS TOWN. R*IGHT AWAY* I liked it. Clean, big boulevards. Everybody's a square, no angling. Almost everybody; Don Jorge Betancourt, Rocco's man, came by my hotel the first night I was in town. An older guy, European-type cat—like a headwaiter, very dignified, with a heavy theta sound I had to get used to. I never heard that kind of Spanish in the Barrio. But we got to rapping pretty good. I told him this had to be wham-bam-thank you Ma'm because I had to get back to New York. We put on a terrific feed that night, then we went bouncing around the *tablaos*. Fantastic looking heads—Gypsies. This might be fun. Second joint we hit we run into Sixto. The joint was shaped like a cave, with a lot of Gypsies singing and dancing. Don Jorge spotted him first—"He is here, on the left near the stage; his man is with him." Sure enough, there was Sixto Davila yelling "*Olé tu madre*" with the best of them like a regular *Gallego*—jive Puerto Rican. We were cool, didn't look his way. Sure enough, a bucket of champagne arrived, compliments of *el señor* in the corner. He come over. I threw my arms around him. "Sixto, my man! You look terrific, put on some good weight. The hell you doing in Spain, I thought you was in the Joint?"

"I been moving around a lot, Carlito. I got bored of New York and P.R Figure I'd check the scene over here."

Jorge said, "So you know Carlito well, Sixto? Well, Carlito, you are now better recommended. I have much

affection for Sixto, a man of *condiciones* and respect—
perhaps we can be friends."

I picked it up. "Don Jorge, Sixto will tell you that I am
a man of honor and when I give my word that is my life—
no es así, Sixto?"

"The man don't lie, Don Jorge; you can count on Carlito
Brigante, anytime—I back him up hundred per cent."

You stool-pigeon motherfucker.

Don Jorge went to rap with some people there so I leaned
over to Sixto—"*Mi hermano*, I won't forget this—you don't
know what this means to me. I need this connection bad; a
guy in the Joint put me on to Don Jorge—he got to give
me a break, this may be my last chance to make it after
all those years I suffered in the can."

I put on like my crying face, like uptight. Sixto bit
good—"Don't worry, Carlito, the old dude is in my pocket;
he will deal with you—what the hell are friends for? After
all the shit we been through together! How long since you
been out on the street?"

"Just a few days, ain't had a chance to see nobody.
Wanted to hook up with this man right away. I want nothing
to do with them motherfuckers from before; they all let me
down when I was in the Joint—fuck 'em."

"That's what I say, Carlito—fuck 'em where they
breathe."

Well all right. So me and Sixto got tight—had to be, he
was lonely for New York. So we partied for days, me not
acting too flush so Sixto was thinking I was hungry for
bread. After a couple of days we sprung the trap.

"Look, Sixto, while the old man is in the john, let me
level with you fast. I ain't got no bread, I'm here to rip
off this Jorge faggot. I got a line on some big bucks he
got stashed away plus a meet he's got on the border this
weekend for two hundred keys. Sixto, this is the maximum
shot we ever gonna have. I need your help, Sixto."

"*Coño*, Carlito, *coño!*"

"We can't talk here, this old motherfucker has spies all
over Madrid. Tomorrow I'm driving out to Franco's tomb,
El Valle de los Caidos, near Segovia."

"I know where it is."

"I'll meet you there at 3 P.M. and we can scheme in private. Cool it, here he comes. 3 P.M.—come alone and make sure you're not tailed."

That morning, Vinnie and his man Lucien showed up at my room. Lucien was a demolitions guy from North Africa, knew his stuff.

"Okay, Vinnie, I'll follow your car out to the tomb. We'll both park in the lot by 2 P.M. Make sure we're there first—he'll show early to check out the scene, he's a suspicious and jumpy sombitch. I'll go out and put my arm around him—I'll take him up to the top of the cross. Slap the bomb on his car but give it a half hour. After I'm upstairs fifteen minutes you and Lucien come up—he'll get suspicious right away, think it's a setup—he'll run. Give him five minutes to get down to his car; ten minutes he's driving down the mountain—boom. Later for Sixto. Got the picture, Vin?"

"Uhuh."

"Some pair you are; Lucien can't talk English and you are a goddamn mute."

"What's to talk, Carlito? We know the way out there and we got the firecracker—you just point him out. One thing—what makes you so sure he'll run when he sees me and Lucien?"

"You kidding? One look at your guinea puss and this fuckin' A-rab of yours and he'll bolt like a rabbit—I know my man."

Next day, we drove out on schedule. Not ten minutes after we pulled into the parking area Sixto arrived. A beater is always on time. If a guy is right he don't rush because he's sure, but a schemer can't afford no delay, so he's always on time. You don't read these things in no book, you just got to develop the vibes. Trouble is too many guys get wasted before they hip up. Shame on them.

It was a cold fall day, sun was shining. No one around hardly. "Sixto, my man, you're early, I like that—I can't stand these cats that ain't never on time. Let's go to the top together." We took the elevator up, just me and Sixto. The elevator shaft cuts right through the heart of the mountain, clear up to the peak. There they built like a giant platform, and on top of this a stone cross 450 feet high. They've cut men riding on animals out of stone at each of the four corners of the platform. But each figure maybe sixty feet high. Cannot be believed what Spanish sweat has worked here. Forget about the Pyramids, the Valley of the Fallen is the maximum. A hell of a monument to Spanish blood. I wonder if it covers the Spanish blood spilling in the hallways and alleys of Harlem, if it got room for the Latins O.D.ing on the rooftops of the South Bronx. Something happened to my people since they come across the water.

It's cold on top of that mountain and the wind blows strong. If you look straight up at the cross with the clouds blowing over it, you get dizzy, like the cross is swaying and gonna fall on top of you. Not to be believed.

"There's no one around, Carlito."

"Oh, yeah, Sixto. I wanted to get together with you on this business I told you about last night, but early this morning some people got to me with a bad report about you—now I ain't saying I believe it, Sixto. You know me, I always like to give a man a chance to explain."

"Is this from the wops, Carlito?"

"Yeah, like you beat them—"

"That money was coming to me, they was humping me on the deal—you'd have done the same thing."

"Including me being a rat, Sixto?"

His eyes popped, so I knew he'd seen Vinnie and Lucien. He was gone. We waited a while. Everything was real quiet, just the wind blowing up there like on the roof of the world. Boom. Later for Sixto.

Before I left, Don Jorge came to me with, "Carlito, I have been much impressed with your *hombría*; perhaps we can work together directly. I mean, we are Latinos, why need you work behind these people?" Right away, I knew Mr. Petey Amadeo was in the junk business. I recognized Amadeo's handwriting right away. Check. Double-check. Triple-check. Cross. Double-cross. Triple-cross. I knew Don Jorge was in bed with Amadeo. And the *cornuto* is Rocco. Amadeo's got Rocco taking all the weight what goes with being a dope pusher—meanwhile he's clean to all including Rocco. All the time Don Jorge got to report to Amadeo.

"No, *mil gracias*, Don Jorge, but I could never go it alone and I am grateful that they should give me this chance."

"Your loyalty is touching, I commend you for it. *Adiós*."

So Amadeo is looking for an excuse to have me washed. And first dollar Rocco steals, Don Jorge will rat him out and Amadeo will have him. Amadeo can't cook up deals to make money like Rocco and he ain't read no books, but he is a crafty motherfucker. That's why he been attending other people's funerals since the thirties. These fuckin' wops, they ain't satisfied with loading the dice, they got to stick you up after the game too. I'm over my head. I'm getting out; I'm gonna tell Rocco as soon as I get back.

7

I GOT BACK TO NEW YORK. BUT I DIDN'T SAY NOTHIN'
to Rocco about Don Jorge and Amadeo. In the life, a
man cannot be involved with words, like who said what
about who—for sure you'll be in the middle. In other
words, you can rat out a ratter but you can't rat out a
double-crosser. Some fuckin' business. I started partying
like crazy again. Rivas *el Comandante* had run into a crew
of teenage boldykes, so we was renting hotel suites, feeding
the dykes coke, and watching the show. That Rivas was
a stone degenerate but he sure could dig up some freaky
broads.

About this time Reggie started hanging out with me. Earl
told me, "I want my bro out them goddamn dungarees—I
tol' him, how you gonna command respect? Lookin' like a
reject from the janitor's union. I tol' him he got to move
around, not just in Harlem, get to deal all around, we're
black and proud of it but that don't mean we got to beat
our chest all the time, it ain't cool, and it sound like you
don't believe it yo'self. I tol' him that I am leaving for
good and if he want to be the main man he got to clean
himself up—and iffen he don't, then I'm just gonna pass
him up for somebody—like Carlito."

"Thanks a million, Earl, you got some sense of humor."

"I don't get out much anymore, Carlito, I been busy
getting everythin' together—you on the street all the time,
take Reginald under your wing once in a while, show him

the Latin action, like that. If he gonna be a boss he got to get rounded out, y'dig?"

"I dig."

Reggie. Fuckin' pain in the ass. He was a good-looking cat so we'd have a good time at my discotheque—a lot of the fay chicks would go for his revolutionary bullshit, and if that was the program I'd come on with "Right on" and "Off the pig" good as Reggie. Shit, anyway I get that pussy is all right with me. But then the dude started to lay heavy on me, like *caerme pesao*.

Reggie come on with, "You and my brother Earl are two of a kind—social parasites with no awareness of the revolutionary changes taking place around you. The Third World is on the march and you guys are going around hustling your own people. You and Earl are obsolete—there will be no hustlers in the new world. If you don't join the ranks of the oppressed then you'll be put up against the wall with the rest of them. You have no education, but that's no longer an excuse."

Always throwing that education shit in my face. "You're full of shit, Reggie. O-pressed, my ass, you been sucking Earl's titty all your life. He's the one that put you through school. Had you driving cars since you sixteen, dressed you sharp as a pimp, took care of business. Now you puttin' him down. I know what's got your head bad—I ain't so stupid, I know about Fanon and the Battle of Algiers and all that shit; I got the word from a brother in the Joint. You gonna kick over the man by shooting a few cops in the head? You crazy, that's what—they gonna bury you so fuckin' quick and nobody gonna even know you was a hero. What the fuck you care about the o-pressed? Take care of business; look out for number one—one way or the other there'll always be hustlers."

Earl, Earl, shoulda told you about your crazy brother, but I kept my mouth shut like usual and carried this cross around. One night, me and Reggie closed up my joint and then went over to this after-hours joint downtown Manhattan. Nearly all greaseballs that night. I was stoned, otherwise I'd never have gone there with this fuckin' Reggie. We was sitting at a table when we get a round of drinks from a table with around eight wise-guys. Valerio Mitri—a made-guy, underboss to Rocco's uncle, Dominick Cocozza—and company. Reggie says real loud, "We don't want no fucking drinks, take them back." Before I could say anything, Val Mitri came over. "I know you don't know me but I know your brother Earl."

"I'm getting sick and tired of hearing about my brother Earl—as far as I'm concerned he's a fuckin' Uncle Tom."

Val looked at me. I was stoned, what could I say, I smiled. This Reggie motherfucker is going to get me killed. Val went back and sat down at his table. Right away the joint is cleared out—my head was fogged—but I knew I had to do something. I stumbled over to Val's table. "Val, the kid don't mean no harm, he's high." Val's main gorilla, Buck, said, "We ain't mad, Carlito, these things happen." He stuck his hand out. Like a chump, I put my hand out. I was in a vise, couldn't move. Another gorilla grabbed me around the neck; I couldn't budge. But behind me I could hear feet like thrashing on the floor and I heard Reggie in a croak—"Carlito, Carlito"—I screamed, "Val, Val Mitri—Earl Bassey was breaking bread with Cocozza a few days ago—you know how much Rocco thinks of Earl— you know you have to kill me too—what are you going to say at the sitdown—that you killed his brother because he refused a drink? Think, Val, you ain't crazy, think!"

I got to him. He said, "*Basta.*" I heard puking; I knew it was Reggie. Jesus, his tongue must be strung out like a necktie.

"Get the shine out of here, Carlito—Buck ain't put hands on him yet." Buck. Buccia was a psycho, killed people with his bare hands, bit off noses; he weighed three hundred pounds but could jump over a bar like a fuckin' Doberman. I'd seen him in the east Harlem days. I was sobering up fast. "Val, you're doing the right thing, I'll get him out." Reggie was out—he had puke all over him. I dragged and carried him down the stairs. When I got him to the street, he come to, and what does he say? "Get your fucking hands off me, I can walk."

"You do just that, Reggie, take a fuckin' walk; you and me is parting ways."

He took off. I stood by the doorway of the joint trying

to clear my head in the night air. Val came down with his crew. All of a sudden, Reggie came tearing around the corner in his car; he braked in front of the joint and started yelling, "Fuck all you guinea motherfuckers and fuck you, too, Carlito, you spic cock-sucker." Then he was gone.

I couldn't talk. Val said, "You see, Carlito, we give him a break, now we got trouble, on account of you sticking up for him. You see, you see!"

Yeah, I saw all right.

I didn't see Earl for a while after that. I didn't want to hassle with him over Reggie, I didn't want to tell him that Reggie had a watcha-call-it, complex, about him. I had Reggie figured—Earl is a man, a boss, uptown or downtown, where Reggie is a shitass and he knows it. Reggie don't want to be Earl's bro, he wants to be a big shot—dig me standing on my own two feet. Yeah, but you got athlete's feet, bro. He's going to do somethin' crazy, then jump into his grave—but let's not be in the hole with him, Earl, when he pulls the zipper up over hisself.

Earl called me. We met at Frank's Restaurant on 125th Street. He looked great, we rapped about old times. Then he told me, "Rocco gave me the word what Reggie did downtown—I know you went all the way for him, Carlito, even though he don't deserve it."

"He's your brother, Earl."

"I sent him back home, him and his two punks. He can't cut it—the slot is too big for him, he gags on it. The power is too much for him—I knew it in front but like he's my bro and I was hoping. Now I got to worry about these niggers robbing me when I ain't around."

"Reggie would have robbed you, Earl."

"I know that. I figure Lloyd is the man to run my thing. What do you think?"

"That's the man. Good business mind and bad on the street. But he's a gentleman moving around people; I dug him—he got style—good spender—rap with anybody—that's your man."

"What about you, Carlito?"

"Me? Shit, you crazy, Earl. I can't deal with them digits every day—bad numbers, runners robbing you, all that bookkeeping every day—I'd go crazy. Nah, that ain't my stick."

"Well, how about fronting for me? Lloyd can do the figures."

"That time is long gone, Earl. I'd have to kill me a spook every day. Look around you right here, some brother'll be bad-eyeing me. No good, you and me come up at a different time—these guys today don't want to hear that shit. I don't blame them. But Lloyd got to know that I'm with him a hundred percent; when they come to lean on him—and you know they got to try—he won't have to look around; I'll be there."

"I know that, Chas, I also know you boys'll be making your twice-yearly soon. Hip up, turkey, Uncle Sam wants you, and you gonna train in Atlanta, say twenty years."

"How you sound, colored boy?"

"I ain't jiving, Carlito, the handwriting's on the toilet wall. They ain't gonna let you out. Are you blind? These dudes is putting people on the moon; do you think they can't put the junk boys out of business? Where is your mental?"

"You know me, Earl; clean, baby, clean."

"You always was a crazy Po'Rican—I'm splitting for good soon, you know where to reach me in Saint Croix. If you ever need a job reference or somethin' that's where I'm at. Now get out my face."

And Earl was gone—and with a bundle. Was it possible for a hustler to make it and not pay his dues? I mean I heard about dudes running big joints like hotels and class restaurants in Miami and Vegas who made their bread racketeering but I never knew one close up. But here was Earl scuffling alongside me for twenty years—did time, been stabbed, been shot—come through all that and come out the other side with big bucks and retire clean. Unreal. Maybe that's the ticket for me too? Who you jiving? Shit, can't even be out of New York two weeks I go crazy. Some people get down on somethin' they want to go to the mountains or the woods—not me. I jump in my short—up the highway to 96th Street, then I cut through Harlem—junkies, whores, noise, fightin', garbage, fire escapes—

that's me, that's reality. That's how I charge up again—clear my head, dig myself.

You ain't going nowhere, Carlito. You got people depending on you to live, people looking up to you, and like when you walk into a joint—no noise, cool, but everybody knows you're there. Carlito, *un bravo*. Right now, that's all there is. I don't understand living in the future—like Earl, doing this to get ready for that—who knows what's waiting on the corner? Could be an elephant gonna step on your back or a bullet up yo' ass. Stay loose, Carlito.

I don't put nothing in writing and the phone company has put more people in jail than cops, so I figured I'd heard the last of Earl. Lloyd Simpkins was a serious cat, I knew he could keep the thing together for Earl. Then Rocco sent for me. We met at a joint near La Guardia. First he gimme the good news—told me to get ready, that some big shipment was coming in and Vinnie would be around to see me. Then he gimme the bad news. "Something very bad is happening, Carlito. Someone put the snatch on Petey Amadeo's kid, Paul. They had him for two days. The old man put up a hundred thousand to get him back."

"What?"

"That's not the half of it. They were spades. Amadeo is a bug by nature but now he's going around biting himself—he brought in some old Sicilian who is supposed to keep a guy alive on a meat hook for days. And he sent for Nacho Reyes to come up from Miami. He doesn't want anyone to know. He wants to grab everybody at the same time."

"He's got a line on the guys, Rocco?"

"Yeah, the way I hear it—and I'm not supposed to know anything about this—but you're involved and I don't want you or Earl hurt—"

"What the hell you talking about?"

"Mr. A figures like this: his kid was snatched in front of his house; he'd just moved in—the only people that knew this were the people at my kid's christening. Now who was there? All wops except two spades and you—so he had Reggie checked out and Reggie fits right in with his two boys from Philly, Alfonso Lee and a guy called Shad."

"Well, that's his three right there."

"You don't know his mind, Charles. He figures Earl masterminded the whole scheme and since you're his boy, you're in on it too, and if you're not, then you go anyway so you won't get mad about Earl being taken out."

"Jesus Christ!"

"He's going to sweep all the pieces off the board."

"Hold the fuckin' phone! Rocco, what are we gonna do?"

"This Reggie and his two punks have to be buried—then we have a roundtable on you and Earl."

"Your uncle can do it, Rocco?"

"My uncle can do it, Carlito. The question is will he let us off the hook? Besides, my uncle is a very sick man."

"Us, Rocco?"

"Yeah, I'm in the jackpot too. Amadeo hates my guts—for many reasons. I've come up with a ready-made hook in my uncle. I've tried to use some finesse and my brains. I've tried to open up for the new groups, the Latins and the Blacks. Amadeo can't see this, he's a terrorist—with him it's kill and kill again. His solution to everything is a hit. So this beef now about his kid being snatched, when all are dead and buried he's going to blame the whole mess on me—I'm the one who opened up to the spics and niggers, I'm the one who is breaking with tradition—I'll be hit."

"That motherfucker! Let's whack him out first, Rocco—he bleeds! Then we check out."

"Use your head, Carlito; for once think with your head instead of your balls. Where would I go, where would I hide, some banana republic? I'll ride it out right here, and if not, so be it."

"Yeah, guess you're right, Rocco. Only the Cubans can run away—one place is as good as another to them. But if a P.R. jumps bail in Brooklyn, he runs away to the Bronx, and if a wop is deported he goes crazy. There's nothin' shakin' outside the U.S.A. You right."

"This is the way we'll deal: you will get to Nacho and his crew right away; you will con him that you got a good line on Reggie and that you're expecting word any minute—that will keep him off your back a while. After Reggie is iced, Nacho will double back for you, but you'll be ready. By that time, my uncle can step in."

AND THAT'S THE WAY WE DEALT THE HAND. I COLLECTED all of my boys, including some who was like retired. Got all the hardware together and called for a meet with Nacho. He showed up in Harlem with two carloads of crazy Cubans (most of them dead now). They had pistols, sawed-off shotguns, and even hand grenades. All veterans from the Cuban shoot-outs, these kids didn't give a shit about nothin'. But my boys was all bad gangbusters too. There was no cause to rumble; I wanted to show Nacho I was talking from muscle, then I'd jive him Cuban-style. "*Mi hermano, mi par' na Nacho.* We must work together. We are after the three *niches* too. I know you're ready to do up Harlem and Bedford-Stuy to find them, but that ain't into nothin'. You can blow up all the black after-hours joints and you ain't gonna find them—you don't know what Reggie looks like, your *pistoleros* don't even speak English. *Ten calma,* Nacho, I'm expecting word any day now—I spread big bucks around with the *chibas,* then we grab all three. *Como te cae,* eh—you get first crack since you're the *echao pa'lante.*" He dug it.

Then I got to Lloyd. "What the fuck I care if Reggie ripped off a couple of wops, Carlito? Ain't no skin off my ass."

"I'm gonna tell you one time, Lloyd, and you will believe me. The wops say me and Earl put Reggie up to the snatch. You're gonna say Earl ain't here. But when Earl hears they're gonna kill his brother he's gonna be here, and it's gonna be a bad motherfucker—won't be no tendin' to business. You and your boys gonna have to be in a war, and when the dust settles maybe Earl won't want to leave again and you got to get out that chair you're so comfortable in— and over who? Reggie? I know you'd piss on his grave in a minute, Lloyd. You gonna bleed over that motherfucker Reggie? You better give him up, Lloyd, he is a dead-ass, don't let's get weighed down with him. And what about me, Lloyd? When they come for me you know I got to tell them where Earl is; they got a guy put you on a meat hook for days—you think they ain't gonna go down there and get Earl? There's only one way, Lloyd, and that's me coming up with Reggie in front: that'll show 'em that me and Earl was clean, that Reggie is an outlaw. You can find Reggie, Lloyd, you the only one can do this thing."

"What is Earl gonna say when he finds out I gave up his brother?"

"He's not gonna find out, Lloyd, no way—Nacho's got the contract. Since when you dealin' with the Cubans? You think I want Earl to know I put Reggie in the soup?"

"You comin' on too strong, Carlito, I need time to think."

"I'm thinking maybe you see both Reggie and Earl getting washed behind this thing and you walk away with all the fig newtons. If that's what you're thinking, Lloyd, I'll blow your motherfuckin' head off right here. Don't fuck with me, Lloyd; my balls is in the wringer and you turning the handle."

"I'll see what I can do."

"Do it, brother."

Alfonso and Shad were grabbed in Newark. Nacho and his boys delivered them to Amadeo on Long Island. Nacho told me this old Italian guy hung them on meat hooks in a walk-in freezer. Nacho said it was the worst scene he'd ever. From Nacho I believe it. Lloyd found out where these were for me and I gave them to Nacho, but Lee and Shad didn't know where Reggie was. Lloyd couldn't come up with Reggie and Reggie had the money—all of it. A week went by, no Reggie. The Cubans were running round the clock.

That Saturday morning I was closing up my disco joint when in walked Nacho and two of his goons, Camaguey and Paniagua. I was bullshitting Nacho about how I was expecting word on Reggie any day now when in came a kid ran errands for me, Squeaky. "Carlito, I just left the Village Gate with my girl—I saw him walking down to Houston Street, going in a building near the corner with some blonde chick."

"Why didn't you stay there and call up?"

"You always say never to talk on the phone, Carlito."

Nacho, who ain't supposed to understand English, said,

"*El negro, eh? Vamos!*" I didn't go for moving with these three *Cubiches* alone but I had no choice. We barrel-assed down to that corner, parked, and waited. Everybody was packing—Nacho even had a silencer on his piece. We stood until daybreak, then this blonde came out the corner building. I jumped out of the car, waving my wallet like I had a shield—"Young lady, I'm Detective Velez from the safe-and-loft squad. We have that second floor under surveillance; were you stopped by my uniform man?"

"No sir, I came down from the third floor. I didn't see anyone."

"Okay, miss, sorry. You better hurry along—this is not a very nice neighborhood."

I got back in the car. "He's on the third floor—I'm sure that broad was with him." We waited until she was out of sight, then we piled out. In the hallway, Nacho started giving orders—"Camaguey, you cover the entrance to the building—Paniagua, you keep going up to the roof—Carlito and I will hit the apartments." Me and Nacho got to the third floor which was the top floor, the front pad was quiet so we eased to the back apartment—voices. I put my head down on the floor by the door—Reggie. The door was an old plank with a snap lock—I knew the kind from my B-and-E days, we hit the door together—wham! She come right off the hinges.

Reggie and Earl. They was sitting on a couch, one bulb overhead—a real skanky crash pad. "Freeze, motherfuckers." Me and Nacho was both crouched like shooters no sooner we hit that door. "Carlito, don't let him kill us," Earl yelled, his eyes on Nacho. "*Aguarda*, Nacho," I cooled Nacho, "You're supposed to deliver him alive." Earl said, "Let me explain—" "Too late, Earl, lights out. You cooked up this snatch—and of all people, Amadeo's kid—knowing that you was leaving me and Rocco holding the bag—you knew these wops would cut us into little pieces. Reggie's a crazy nigger but you was always my man—how could you jap us like this, Earl?"

"You done fucked with m'dignity now, so kill me right here or hear me out."

"Cop your plea, Earl—*aguarda*, Nacho."

"I ain't copping no plea, motherfucker—I'm gonna tell you where it's at. The kid did it by himself with his two punks. I knew nothin' from nothin'—you gonna put me in a class with these crazy kids? Think, Carlito, is that me, is that my style? You think I'm out of my fuckin' mind? I been in Saint Croix. Reginald finally got to me yesterday, I flew in last night—look at the flight ticket in my pocket."

"*Qué pasa*, Carlito, *qué pasa?*" Nacho was getting annoyed. "*Espera*, Nacho. Earl, you my brother, the only one I ever had. I want to believe you—but Reggie got to go."

"Earl, they gonna put me on a meat hook"—Reggie was sweating bullets.

"You a fuck-up, but you my kid brother—you know you got to take me too, Carlito. Make your move, I'll understand."

"Earl, tell me what to do—you always tell me what I gotta do!" I was uptight.

"You got to off this dude alongside you and then we all split to the islands."

"No good, Earl, they're outside too—"

Then Reggie rolled the dice. He jumped and grabbed under a pillow of the couch—he got to pull the piece out—phft, phft—he took two in the back of the head splashing red right up in the air. Earl came straight for Nacho like a crazy man, screaming, "My brother, my brother!" Nacho smoked again—Earl stumbled in his tracks, then went down on his face right at our feet. Nacho pointed his piece at Earl's head—then, without even knowing why, I put my pistol to Nacho's temple.

"You know I will blow the top of your brains out, Nacho."

"*Es un moyete.*"

"*Es mi hermano*, Nacho—I owe him too much."

"*Estás loco*, Carlito."

"I'll take my chances—you leave now, there's been noise here; take the car and beat it before the bulls get here. Take Paniagua and Camaguey."

"*Los Italianos*—"

"You contracted for three, you delivered three—case closed. If they find out about Earl being here today, that's my worry, they all look alike to you. Why should you and I kill each other over these fuckin' Italianos? Let me do it my way."

Paniagua and Camaguey appeared at the door. They said, "Nacho, people opening doors, the *camarónes* will be here any minute. *Vamos a echar un pie.*"

Nacho picked up his shells from the floor.

"*Vamos andando*," he said; as he got to the door he turned smiling at me. "I could kill you now but I do not choose to—your loyalty to your friend is a rare thing in this business. I am impressed—but it will get you killed. At your funeral I will say, he was a loyal friend, crazy, but loyal. *Adiós*, Carlito."

"*Adiós*, Nacho."

And they split. I got Earl to Beekman Hospital in a taxi. He was hit in the stomach and in bad pain but he could hear me. "Give me your wallet, Earl, don't have no identification on you—tell them your name is Johnson, Earl Johnson. I'll keep tabs on you that way while you're in the hospital—nobody will know you were in New York—then you can hop a plane home."

"My brother, Carlito—"

"Forget about him, Earl, he's gone. He was bad news from the get go—everybody told you—and he had a bad attitude for you; he was gritty but he was greedy and he'd of got us all killed. You did more than enough for him, mark it paid—you got your family to think about."

I carried him to the door of the emergency entrance. "This far as I go, Earl. There may be cops in there. I don't want no static now—you was drinking, you ended up in the Village, you was mugged, had your wallet taken, you put up a fight and got shot, got it?"

"Thanks, ol' buddy."

"I'll have a broad down here to visit you, whatever you need. Catch you later."

Never seen either of them cats again. Earl made it back to Saint Croix and got out of all the shit. You entitled, Earl. Nacho finally ran out of luck. He got whacked out in Miami. Nacho was in a joint, coked to the gills—this young kid who Nacho hardly knew came in complaining to Nacho that his girl had been abused. Nacho went out to the parking lot and these thugs shot him in the head. Didn't even know who he was and didn't care. Jesus, Nacho Reyes—unbelievable.

8

I TOOK A PLANE TO PUERTO RICO. JUST TO GET AWAY from all the hassle and shooting going on in New York. I heard Prohibition was a bitch, but the dope rumbles sure has buried a lot of people in my time. I got a small room in a guest house in Isla Verde, stayed out of the fancy hotels and late-night joints. I wanted to rest up and I wasn't carrying no piece and didn't want to run into no half-bad-ass looking for a rep. So I just lay around the beaches—no shave, just a pair of shorts—my head got together. Then I teamed up with this fox from Ohio. She was a schoolteacher and into the hippie scene but she was a knocked-out-looking broad—blonde hair, green eyes. Here was me, with no diamond pinkie ring and walkin' around in my drawers and sneakers, making time with this doll. This new scene was really somethin'. I guess I was born too early—all this protest shit can't be all bad if it's made all these freaky heads available.

Her name was Gail or Gale. She was a real American type—anglowasp bit—but she was all shook up about Vietnam and the poor and worried about the lettuce and the grapes in California and all that bullshit—unbelievable—but looking as good as she was I went right along. I told her I was with the poverty program in New York and doing a lot of work on my own time with the Lords and with spade gangs, and I'd rap about commitment and orientation like a welfare dude. We flew to Saint Thomas, then we chartered a boat and just bummed around. Beef, Trunk, Drake's Anchorage,

Virgin Gorda—all the islands for a couple of weeks. A Hollywood scene starring me and Gail. She smoked grass and I'd smoke a joint with her, but I told her I was against all drugs and that she should put that scene behind her on account of dope was a drag on the revolution. Lordy.

I was in love—again. She was into music. I got her some of the Sinatra ballad albums and we'd get high and goof behind them—she was young but Frank can talk to anybody. "My Way" is Paul Anka's song for Sinatra; on a night when we was real cozy anchored off Saint John's we got to rapping about favorite songs and I told Gail this song has a special message for me and if she could dig the song, she could dig me—the moon was out and we went into a great clinch. *Qué* party!

I put in a call to New York and got the word that everything was okay by Rocco, come home right away. Me and Gail flew back to San Juan—I bought her an outfit all in white—she had a heavy tan. When she got all dolled up to go out that night she looked like a movie star. Like to fall out when I saw her. I ain't a profane cat, but I had to say, "Thank you God, for them fine chibs." Of course, I was clean m'self. You must be doing somethin' right, Carlito, here you are pushing your forties, nearly everybody is in jail or been wasted, and here is you still out there with a young thing on your arm. You devil! It was our last night. We caught the show at the Tropicoro. Damn if it wasn't Paul Anka hisself. We had to be at ringside although it cost me a yard. He sang our song, we drank champagne, held hands—shit, ain't no more after this. Like Gail would say, groovy.

After the show, we wandered into the casino; gambling is not my bag but Gail wanted to shoot a hand. Bad news. No sooner I walked into the casino Cesar come over to us. Cesar was an old Harlem boy—he'd been a knock-around guy as a kid but he'd been straight for years, been working as a croupier in P.R. and now was an assistant manager in the casino. He'd made it the hard way and I gave him a lot of credit.

"Carlito, I'm in trouble. I need your help. Walberto and Monchin—you know them, from the 103rd Street crowd—

been running a murder game on me. I won't okay their credit—they are beaters—so last night they got real heavy on me, tried to gorilla me with a piece. I can't deal with these motherfuckers, Carlito—you know my job here. Can you straighten them out for me? I hate to bother you but I got a family now."

He's worried about his family—who's worried about me? Jesus! What am I, the fuckin' Red Cross?

"Okay, Cesar, I'll hang around awhile; maybe I can talk some sense to these guys."

Gail had a funny look on her face. I guess she got the picture real quick-like—the money, the clothes on me now, the wise-guy talk.

I told her, "Wait in the lobby for me, Gail. If anything happens, you don't know me—don't get involved. Otherwise, I'll be with you in a little while." She split and I hung around the crap table.

In walked Walberto and Monchin. Walberto was white and Monchin was black, so people would laugh when they said they was brothers, but they was really cousins. They were all duded up in tuxedos and patent leather so they must have made a score in New York. Never seen one without the other—two lightweights, but Monchin was sneaky fast and would hurt you. Walberto was the slicker of the two but he was jive. If you got to him Monchin would go along.

"*Ola*, Carlito—wha's happening, my man! Monchin, dig who's here—Carlito."

"I got a beef with you, Walberto, let's go to the back of the room."

The three of us went to a back corner of the casino—place was crowded but nobody was paying us any mind.

"*Qué pasa, mi hermano?* Monchin and me always been tight with you, Carlito, why you sounding us?"

I was rapping to Walberto but I had my eye on Monchin, who probably had the piece.

"Cesar is my man in P.R.—now you gonna come here from out of town to gorilla my man here. You crazy? Don't you know there are heavy people into this casino—and you gonna come in here with a rice-and-beans shakedown? Back off, motherfucker, and tell your brother not to be bad-eyeing

me, because if he makes a move you gonna get the first shot
in the face and my people here will take care of the rest—
okay?"

"*Coño*, Carlito, I'm surprised that you should say that
about us—me and Monchin always look out for Cesar—
he's one of the boys. I'm surprised—right, Monchin?"

"Yeah, Berto, Cesar's our boy."

"Then it must be a misunderstanding. Come here, Cesar.
Cesar, the boys say it is a misunderstanding, a breakdown
in the communication; they didn't mean no harm, they
ain't gonna bother you. However, Cesar, if you see the
boys around town in any joint you send them a bottle
right away—do the right thing, okay?"

I shoulda been a diplomat. That's me, always trying
to straighten things out without nobody getting hurt and
everybody making a dollar. But what do I get, a bum rep as
a troublemaker, that's what they say about me. Fuck 'em.

My girl was waiting in the lobby.

"I left, Charley, but I came back."

"Why?"

"Charley, you've been playing a part for me and it wasn't
necessary. I don't like to be made a fool of."

"Listen, Gail, what am I supposed to tell you, that I'm
a hoodlum? What's the point? I didn't ask you where you
came from or where you're going. I'm only interested in
the Gail standing in front of me; I couldn't care less what
you did in Lawrence, Ohio."

"Lorain, Charley—Lorain, Ohio."

"That's what I said, Lorain, Ohio. Yeah, I consorted
with known criminals—uh—bad guys—when I was a kid,
but that's in the past—in the new world that don't mean
nothin'. As far as me being in the socio bag, Gail, I ain't
jiving you, I been helping people in the ghetto—why, just
the other day, this cat got stabbed on 111th Street, I took
him to the hospital even though the seats in my Lincoln
got full of blood—that's typical of me. Like a good-will
ambassador—here tonight a working man was being abused
by these two thugs, I intervened and prevented a problem.
People don't give you credit for things like that. I can't
believe that you'd walk out on me without giving me a

chance to explain what it's like to come up in a jungle."

These socio broads always go heavy for that shit about the jungle. I had to pull out all the stoppers—I wasn't gonna forfeit my last piece on my last night, looking good as she was. Gawd, she was a doll.

"Charley, we have Puerto Ricans in Lorain; I know what your people have to go through. Look, let's forget it—let's just have some fun."

Well all right. And fun we had. She had me dancing to rock music at the Hunca Munca, then we danced at the El Chico, then we hit Armando's, Danny's, the Wine Cellar, drunk on one another—gonna play the string out. Don't know if it was the booze or what but Gail was getting misty-eyed and wouldn't let go of me.

"Charley, what about us? Is there any chance something can come of us? I don't know whether it's the beauty of these islands or what, but I've never felt this way before. Will I ever see you again?"

You know I was stoned because I got noble and didn't put down no spiel—I leveled with her, guess I had a feeling for her I didn't realize.

"I don't know, Gail. I'm into some bad scenes. My life ain't tropical beaches and sunny skies—in the city it's different, it's asphalt and gray and busted windows—I'm different. I move around a lot, get into hassles. You ain't ready for that, and because I go for you, I'm telling you in front. Believe me, if I had anything to offer you, I'd never let you go. But I know myself—I get restless, I'd hurt you. I'm poison, Gail—don't get mixed up with me."

We was both cryin' in our champagne. It was great. Then we went to her hotel room and had each other for breakfast, lunch, and dinner. *Qué jéva!*

That evening she went with me to the airport. I didn't want her to, she insisted. I told her to stay in the cab and go back to the hotel, but she got out. I got a flight on standby. We had a few minutes just holding hands in the middle of the terminal, not saying anything. Then I could see the tears.

"Let go, Gail. It's for the best."

Those pretty green eyes were flooding now. I was wishing

I could say something to her, for her. Like my life is a garbage can, I'm a street fighter, a dope pusher, even been a pimp— get away, girl, don't get into my mess, I ain't gonna be around long. But I said, "Tell you what, baby, write down your home address and telephone, I'll get in touch with you next week after I've taken care of some business. Then I'll fly out to see you or I'll have you fly into New York and you can stay with me—we'll give it a try, how's that?"

"You mean it, Charley?"

"Have I ever lied to you?" I lied.

She wrote her address down on a piece of paper and pressed it into my hand—all this fuss over a mug like me. Unbelievable.

My plane was leaving. "Okay, Gail, no more tears, you're gonna have me crying—now you turn around and start walking, you got a great wiggle. That's the first thing I dug about you—c'mon, lemme see you wiggle away."

I watched her all the way to the end of the terminal until she was gone. Then I let the paper out of my hand onto the ground.

Adiós, rubia. I got on the plane dragging my ass low. I didn't know why but that night my way didn't seem so hot. Like I was unsure of myself, my way of life—bad vibes, man, bad vibes. I shoulda listened. And like always when things is so bad they can't get worse—wha' happen? They get worse.

9

So THEY HAD THEIR SITDOWN OVER THE REGGIE AF-
fair. Rocco was my mouthpiece. The joint was Messina's
Restaurant in guinea Brooklyn around Bath Beach, Graves-
end Bay. The jukebox was playing "Mala Femina" so right
away I knew I was in trouble. Me and Rocco sat at the
bar.

"Don't be nervous, Carlito, they're not going to shoot
anyone at a roundtable—this is neutral ground, like a
court-martial in the army."

"I ain't in the army, Rocco."

"Neither am I, and that's part of our trouble."

"Wadda you mean, Rock?"

"I mean I've not been made. I never went for this protocol
shit. My only interest was making money; I don't want to be
a tough guy talking about this hit and that hit. And I've made
more money for the outfit than all of them put together, so
I've been independent and walked away from this made-guy
business—and now I'm in trouble."

"Wadda you mean, Rock?" Jesus Christ!

"I mean Uncle Dom is dying, cancer. Amadeo is acting
boss—this guy Mario Battaglia is like an underboss; my
rabbi is fading, Charles, and for the first time I need rank—
everybody is getting promoted except me."

"Wadda you give a shit about this captain-and-general
shit, Rocco? Make the money."

"They'll whack me out, Carlito. Mr. A cannot stand my
guts; he knows I've been going around him to Uncle Dom

for years. When my uncle goes, I'm in trouble."

"These people got to be crazy, with the money you've made for them!"

"That's the only thing I got going for me."

"Well, you got me and my guns going for you."

"I know that, Carlito, but it's not that simple."

I'd never seen Rocco so down. Then that fucking "Mala Femina" playing—that's got to be the background music on all the F.B.I. tapes. I was shook up. Then to improve things around this time in stashes Mr. Petey A and his traveling kangaroo court of the ugliest spitters I ever did see. Two gorillas in front, two flanking Amadeo, and two bringing up the rear. They marched straight through the bar into a back room. Everybody in the joint was examining their glass all of a sudden like a freeze—the little wop scared the shit out of everybody, including me. *Madonna!*

Then Cocozza came in with Valerio Mitri, Buccia, and this guy Battaglia. Yea, team!—'til I got a look at Uncle Dom—a dead man—his skull was coming out through his skin, he couldn't have weighed a hundred pounds. His voice was a croak, "Hello, Rocco—I see you got your Spanish friend here. *Como está*, Carlo?"

"Okay, Mr. Cocozza, okay—glad to see you."

The back room had a long table with a short table crossing it at the end like a *T*. There were three chairs at the short table; they were empty when we came into the room, everybody was sitting at the long table. I said, "What about bugs, Rocco?"

"Don't worry, we got a guy checked it out this afternoon."

"If I had m'druthers, we'd be out in the bay talking underwater—these guys look like conspiracies all by themselves. Jeez!"

Then these three old guys walked in. Everybody got up—me too. What is this jive? The pope, the three kings— what am I doing here? Dom Cocozza and Amadeo was kissing and embracing with the King Cole trio; they were rapping in Sicilian—"*Pietro*," "*Domenico*," "*Don Cesare*." *Don Fangula*, sez me. The three wise men sat down at the small table facing us. Reminded me of my first bust down in the old special sessions. The guy in the middle was an active boss—old, gray on top, but dap in the dark suit with a shoulder fit that had to go for three yard. It took him five minutes to take off his hat, gloves, and topcoat—with everybody standing up. Everything he had on seemed cut from the same material. This guy had to be a general, for low.

Cesare Mazzone, also known as Chick Mason. All these Italians was Irish prizefighters in the thirties. The two old guys flanking Mazzone—Mustache Petes—had the shirt buttoned to the top but no tie—rumpled black suits and puffing on guinea stinkers. They was old dons, but their faces said Don't fuck with me.

I ain't ever felt good inside a courtroom. Mazzone opened up sounding like Wallace Beery with a sore throat.

"Awright, wad is the beef here, wad's the problem here? Lemme hear from Pete first."

Pete Amadeo. Short, squat, dark with like nappy hair. Maybe some club members swam across from Africa to Sicily way back when. He had a bad-news face, the kind you ain't gonna stop and ask Where's the Woolworth Building? Stays mad. Maybe he's right—he stayed alive through a whole lot of wars.

"The beef is that I'm out one hundred large. Three niggers put the snatch on my boy Paulie, and I had to buy him back. One of them was Earl Bassey's brother, Reggie, and he got the line on Paulie from the time he came to Rocco's house with Earl and with this mutt Carlito, here."

Rocco grabbed my arm—steam was coming out my ears.

Cocozza stepped up. You could hardly hear him but everybody listened. Ol' Dom was very respected. He made his bones in Sicily as a kid—when he came here in the twenties he was already a man of respect. He'd whacked out his share but he was known to have a cool head and a good rap. Dom said,

"Good evening, Don Cesare, Don Peppino, Don Nicola. Before we get into what happened with the money, I think I ought to say that this kid Carlito is here on his own hook—nobody brought him here. He came because Rocco asked him to, because he's doing the right thing. I admit he's a Spanish kid, but he can't help that—he's trying to do the right thing. I don't think we should kick off this meet by insulting him, Pete."

Pete said, "Everybody knows I got all the respect in the world for you, Dom, but you got the wrong slant on this thing; your nephew Rocco has sold you on the niggers and the spics and that's crazy. This thing of ours been doing okay without these people. Why do we have to do business with them? Why do we have to open up for them? You give them a break—what happens? They put the snatch on you. I say freeze them out—anybody gets out of line, whack him out right on his front stoop. And you listen to Rocco, Dom, and yet twice he's been asked in and twice he's walked away—is that the right thing? I mean, am I right or wrong?"

I could see Cocozza got hot—his face got white, his eyes got small—but his voice come up strong; you could see old Dom was a man of *cojones* in his day.

"Pietro Amadeo, when you talk about my kid nephew you talk about me. If a man ain't ready to be made, he ain't ready—that don't mean he can't do a good job. You know Rocco is the best man in your whole fucking crew—maybe he ain't out there waving his pistol at waiters like some of the young punks you got right in this room—he's using his brain and making money, that's what he's doing. Half of these tough guys you give them a contract and they shit in their pants. I know what Rocco can do because I've sent him myself. And you, Pete, have you forgotten what I am to you that you don't give me respect? I'll go out in the fucking alley with you right now and we can kill each other."

Pete got shook up here.

"No, Dom, I didn't mean I got no respect—"

Chick butted in here.

"Take it easy, Dom, you know Pete says things, but he don't mean no harm."

But Dom was hot. Go get 'im!

"No, I've had it up to here with your bad mouth, Pete. I took you off a cattle boat with holes in your pants—I put you behind one of my trucks and bought you your first suit. You forgot that, huh, Pete? And the time of the Castellammarese you went with Joe the Boss. You bet on the wrong horse that time, right, Pete? Who got you out of town when Maranzano said you was to be hit? Who got the okay from Charley Lucky so you could come back? *Cretino*—you owe me your life—and I should live to hear you insult my family—you scumbag!"

I was scared shitless by now. These wops are crazy. What am I doing here?

I could see Pete was stunned. Everybody was very nervous by now. Even the two old dons had stopped sucking on their stogies.

Chick Mason said, "Take it easy, Dom, take it easy—we ain't gonna get nowhere talking about old beefs. What's the story about Pete's money, Dom? That's what we gotta straighten out."

"All right, Cesare, the story is, yeah, Reggie Bassey and two black punks snatched Paulie, but they was all hit right away, and the Spanish kid came up with them. Are we gonna blame Carlito and Earl Bassey for what three crazy punks did? You know how these kids are today, Cesare—you can't talk to them. Look at some of our kids—good Italian blood being lost right here in Brooklyn in crazy cowboy shit, and even stool pigeons. I mean these kids got no respect nohow.

"Now, we gonna blame Rocco too because he got friends with the Blacks and the Spanish? Cesare, we got to move with the times—the holy Church stays on top, right? Why the Church stay on top? Because the pope and the cardinals they see the handwriting on the wall. Times change, they change—make a cardinal here, one there. Move with the times. We gotta do the same. You do not fight history, you learn from it. We can live with these new groups—we can make money with them. These younger guys can't, but you and me, Cesare, we remember when we was the niggers here. I mean, am I right or wrong?"

Chick and the two dons went into a huddle. Then Chick said, "I wanna hear from this Spanish kid."

Oh shit. I almost said Yes, your honor.

"Right here, Mr. Mason," says me.

"Where's the money?"

"I don't know. The first two, Fonso and Shad, said Reggie had it all. Nacho and me had to waste Reggie quick—he went out on us before we could find out where the money was. It couldn't be helped, he was shooting at us like crazy."

"Where's Earl Bassey?"

"I don't know that either, Mr. Mason. Earl took off long before this happened. I think he was worried about the feds and he wanted to retire and get away from it all—you know, one of them numbers."

"Don't give me that nigger talk; you ain't no nigger— that's the trouble with you spics, you don't know what you are. Some of them even look like Chinese, so help me. Now you listen to me, Carlo—I don't believe a fuckin' thing you're sayin', but we're gonna let it slide because we can't prove different right now. But we'll check it out and if you come up wrong we'll stick your head in a bucket of acid, *capisce*?"

"I got you, Mr. Mason."

"Now tell me the truth, if you knew where Bassey was would you tell us?"

"No, I wouldn't."

"Well, at least you ain't no stool pigeon. Dom, here's how it's gonna be: Rocco stays in business but he owes Pete the money. Pete, you'll apologize to Dom for hurting his feelings. Dom, you'll go along with Pete—what the hell, you guys go back too far to fall out over a couple of shines. Rocco, you listen to Pete—don't go running to your Uncle Dom over every little shit. And you, you fuckin' Puerto Rican—you watch your ass, don't try to be a smart guy. Awright, enough of this bullshit. Bring me the cook over here, I wanna put in a special order of calamari for everybody."

They put on a feed that was out of sight. They may be crazy but they sure eat good. Then they started telling war stories about who had to shoot his brother, his mother— how the mob wasn't the same, the new kids were a bunch of faggots, like that. The party broke up late; me and Rocco were leaving together when over comes Mario Battaglia, big smile—"Rocco, I wuz wid you all the way—put it there, Carlito, I heard you was a stand-up guy and now I believe it."

Me and Rocco shook hands with Battaglia. He was a made-guy with a lot of balls—Pete liked him and he was moving up fast in the outfit. Then he said, "Listen, Rocco, I want in on that next order of yours coming in but you don't have to say nothin' to Pete about it." Me and Rocco were surprised but Rocco said, "Okay, Mario, you're in." Me, I didn't say nothin', I know I didn't say nothin'.

Rocco drove me to midtown where my car was. "Talk about a kangaroo court, Rocco—that's a hell of a legal system you guys got."

Rocco laughed—"You got a fair trial, didn't you?"

"Listen, Rocco, they didn't give me my rights and that fuckin' judge, Chick Mason, he'll shoot you first then find you guilty later. Unbelievable."

We drove awhile, then Rocco said, "The whole thing's falling apart, Carlito."

"Wadda you mean, Rock?"

"I mean the mob is falling apart. These guys like Chick, my uncle, they're dinosaurs. When they go, there won't be anyone to replace them."

"But there's always someone who'll take a shot, Rock."

"It's not the same; the new kids aren't as hungry, for obvious reasons—they're in school, they got jobs—a wise-guy is made on the streets catching hell. He can't learn his trade in suburbia. Then there's the government with the bugs. The electronics have knocked the jock off us. You can't talk anywhere, we're all paranoid—there's guys don't want to be bosses, imagine, for fear of the heat. Then the feds are on our ass twenty-four hours a day—they put a team on you, put you to bed, get up with you, follow you into the restaurants, the fights, the bars, checking your tabs, checking your kids in school. They got a bug into Sonny's house while they were laying the foundation, they got a bug into Patriarca's office. Then you got stool pigeons inside the mob—Vinnie Teresa in New England, Joe Cago right here in New York."

"How could that be, Rock?"

"A lot of reasons—some of the bosses have been too greedy, sitting on top of millions—meanwhile the soldiers are starving. New attitudes—every man for himself, no loyalty. This country will corrupt anything, even the mafia."

"Wadda you gonna do?"

"What am I going to do, Charles? What can I do? I've got both feet over the edge of the roof now, there's no turning back. I'm going straight down—maybe I'll grab a clothesline here and there but that won't hold me. Can't run, can't hide, so just keep going till I break my neck. Maybe you should have let those guys throw me off the roof on 107th Street."

"Your ass! If I know you, you probably would have landed on a pile of twenties and walked away with the bread."

Rocco snorting and getting high. I didn't like it but like fuck it. That's my main trouble. I don't worry enough. I always get the right vibes, the knot in the gut, the chill in the back of the neck, just like anybody else, but the trouble with me is I don't stop, I wanna come out the other side anyway. I see the stop sign and I wanna press on the pedal. Like when I was a kid I'd race a bike through the tunnel on Park Avenue against the light or I'd hang from the roof with one hand. And didn't need no audience. I been my own spectator like there was two of us—watcha gonna do next, Carlito? That kind of scene. But I ain't crazy and I ain't got no death wish. That kind of bullshit pisses me off. The shrinks always give you that, you wanna be punished, you wanna be caught—garbage. Who the hell wants to go to jail? You really gotta be crazy. They don't understand that the hustler's got confidence. That's the key, confidence. The hustler's got the confidence he can pull it off, he's coming out the other side okay. When he's up on a roof looking at apartments he's confident no cop is gonna put a bullet up his ass when he's on the fire-escape. And he's confident no cop or the owner is gonna stop him when he's carrying a twenty-one-inch Motorola down the street in broad daylight. And he's confident he can walk through Kennedy Airport with a kilo strapped to his back.

Ain't nobody more surprised than a hustler when he's popped. Damn, what's going on here, how did this happen? The shrinks has been conned—been psyched by the clients. Ha, the dope pusher's got it all doped out. I am the master of this field too. Many is the time in the Joint that I have worked out a man's legal problem and then I have gotten to his skull and "That's where your head is at" and the dude has gotten shook up—"Damn, Carlito, how'd you do it? That's it, that's where my head is at." The public don't know it, but there's plenty heavy thinkers in the Joint and there ain't no better place for heavy rapping and thinking, except that most of them are only worried about their own writs and briefs. The government ought to start up a think tank in the Joint—I'll bet they come up strong. Yeah, a think-tank tank.

10

WELL, NOW WE'RE GETTING DOWN TO MY LAST conspiracy. I was busy fixing up my discotheque, trying to make it like a joint from the speakeasy days—Bonnie and Clyde jazz. What with all the straights dressing up like Al Capone, I figured this was the ticket. I got a lot of ideas about things like that. Anyway, Rocco's man Vinnie dropped by one night. In all the years I known Vinnie, I never got his last name. The bulls never believe you, but in the life you can know a guy for twenty years and never know his last name. And if he's a wop, God forbid you should ask—automatically you're a stoolie. Funny. Anyway, Vinnie walks in, points to the john, and says, "Let's go for a blow." I got mad at this—I did not allow no snorting in my joint. Fuckin' people got no consideration for a man's living. "Vinnie, you know I'm very strict about my rule, let's go round the block." So we went for a walk around the block. Good candy too. The sphinx speaks, "Get your money together, then double it—yeah, double it. It's already left—should be here by Friday, Saturday— I'll be around. Fifties and hundreds."

"Wait a minute, Vinnie. Double—that's long bread— way out—I don't know if I can make it—"

"That's your lookout. You in or you out?"

"Okay, I'm in—I'll get it together."

"Saturday."

"You got it. That's good snort, Vin, you got some more?"

"See ya."

Two hundred thou. That means the pot is two mill. That means two hundred keys. Must be coming over in a trailer truck. Good God almighty damn, biggest move I ever heard of—you know I'm dealing myself in. The government declares war, all the pushers run for their holes—meanwhile the panic sets in, the price goes up, up, up. Then the real hustlers grab hold and make the real scores.

I'm scuffling around all week getting my money together. Friday, the *France* docked. Well all right. But Saturday, no Vinnie; Sunday, no Vinnie. I knew we were in trouble, I knew it in front, but I hung in anyway. That's when the hustler pays his dues, when he don't know how he's gonna get zapped—he knows the rug pulled out from under but he don't know how or where or who. That is a bitch, when you're waiting. You know the feds are out there scheming, but you don't know who they got, or what they got, or who's talking, or whether they been staked out next door for a month. But you know yo' ass is up for grabs. You know it, motherfucker.

I ain't left the house for two days. Monday night I can't sit no more. I go to my discotheque—I was calling it Bonnie 'n Clyde; it was really shaping up with live music and everything. Around 3 A.M., the phone rang behind the bar. "Carlito, for you." It was Rocco. "Close up and wait for me." Click. Jesus Christ! Maybe the wops got him and I'm gonna be hit. I chased everybody out the joint. Then I ran down to the basement and got a sawed-off shotgun and a Walther PPK automatic I had behind a vent. I put the piece under the cash register and the shotgun at the far end of the bar—the way I was going if I had to make a fast exit. Better call uptown for some of my people. Hold the phone—maybe the feds got Rocco and they're coming for me, and me with all this hardware. I must be out to lunch in my skull. I ran downstairs and hid all the artillery again. By now I was in a cold sweat—like I said, it's a bitch when you don't know what's coming off. But Rocco would never give me up—what happened to Vinnie? All the lights were out; I sat behind the bar and poured myself a stiff shot.

Car lights outside, then I heard Rocco—"Carlito, open up."
So be it.

He was all fucked up. I never seen Rocco this way—
scuffed, no shave, all shook up. "Trouble, Carlito, trouble."

"Jesus Christ, Rocco, what's up?"

"The shit is down in a station wagon under the highway—
been there since Friday."

"So what happened?"

"This French kid, Marcel, drove it off the ship; Vinnie
got in with him—they got as far as Canal Street to go to
the tunnel. Then they bailed out. Vinnie got to a phone—
he said where he left the car and that they'd been made by
the feds. The two of them have disappeared, but there's no
arrest."

"So what the fuck is going on, Rocco?"

"Battaglia got to me tonight. He says his two hundred
large came from Amadeo and that I have to account for it
plus the hundred from the Reggie mess. But that money is
already gone with my own three hundred as front money.
I put up five hundred thou!"

"But where's Vinnie—he's gotta account."

"Battaglia said don't worry about Vinnie, I'm responsible
for Amadeo's money. My uncle is in a coma since last
week—he's going out for sure, they know it. Can you
believe this?"

"We're in trouble, we're in trouble."

"I'm ruined, Carlito. I have to account for their three
hundred and I've blown my own three hundred. I'm dead,
Carlito, I'm dead."

Rocco slumped on a stool. The joint was pitch-black but
I could see he ain't slept for days. He was at the end of
the line.

"What'll we do, Carlito, what'll we do?"

The brains have failed, now comes time for the balls!

"We gotta get that car."

"Are you crazy? The feds are waiting."

"Vinnie may have panicked, Rocco, and even if the feds
made the car—if a good driver gets the jump on them he
can get away. You remember that guy, Bobby Iggione?"

"Yeah, Bobby Higgins—they were waiting and he still got away—that was in the fifties."

"I'm down."

"You're crazy, Charles."

"You got a suggestion, Rocco?"

"I'm wasted."

"Okay. First, we'll take a dry run in my car, shoot past the station wagon, check out the scene—then we double back in your car. Wait a minute, Rocco, how am I going to get the car going? Got no time to be crossing wires."

"I got a duplicate set of the keys when the money went down."

"Well all reet! We'll come barrel-assing down, you brake, I'll roll out—you take off south, I'll cut east on Canal. I know the area like my hand. I'll run them sombitches into the ground—they won't catch me."

"But—"

"Ain't no butts here 'cept ours, what we is trying to save, Rock. If Amadeo says you gotta go, how far behind am I gonna be? I say roll the dice."

"You're on."

I felt better already. Waiting around is a drag, but once you make up your mind what's to be, it's easy. Action is where I'm at.

IT WAS AROUND 4 A.M., NO MOON—LIKE THE P.R.'S SAY, darker than a poor man's hopes. We drove both our cars to 23rd Street near the Hudson River. Then Rocco parked his car and got in with me. I drove south under the West Side Highway. We were moving downtown on West Street when on our left we passed the Federal House of Detention. Of all the buildings in the world to see tonight, we gotta see the fuckin' federal jailhouse. "*Madon*," said Rocco. "*Bendito*," said me. We were approaching Canal Street—I was clocking lights so the red light would catch us on Canal Street. We caught the light. There it was under the overpass, second car down, facing east. A Volkswagen bus. Four hundred pounds, eighty million fuckin' dollars in those side panels. The sweat was coming down my back into my ass.

Not a livin' ass in sight, stone quiet, nothing moved. That means there's forty agents around here. The light turned green—we went down to Chambers, made a left, went east a few blocks, then back up to 23rd Street where Rocco's car was.

Nobody on our tail. Ha. We got into Rocco's four-door Caddie. He was driving, I was in the back laying on the floor, facing the left door. Rocco said, "Bobby Higgins crashed into the cars, drove all over sidewalks—you ready for that, Carlito?" "No I'm down here on the floor knocking off a piece of tail. C'mon, Rocco!"

"You know what they told Bobby Higgins?"

"What?"

"The feds can only put you in jail, but you know what we're gonna do—that's what they told him."

"So he went, right?"

"Yeah, he had to, but you're not in the same jackpot, Carlito."

"The hell I ain't, Rocco! Amadeo's got a double-decker coffin ready for the two of us. Now listen, no sense trying to sneak up on them—you barrel-ass, hit your brake when my rear door is on a line with the driver's side of the bus— I'll dive into the street and roll right up to the door of the bus and jump in. Do me one thing, Rocco—jump out of your car for a second, stand up, then jump back in and drive like hell, make a lot of noise. They'll think you came for the junk, got cold feet, and took off. They'll come after you like gangbusters."

"Meanwhile, you'll tippy-toe out with the bus, right?"

"Sounds terrific, don't it, Rocco?"

"You're out of your mind."

We came back down on West Street. I had the door cracked.

Rocco said, "We're coming to Canal Street, I'm stepping on the gas—get ready!"

He slammed on the brakes—I dove out to the street with the keys in my hand. I heard Rocco yelling, then he took off. All hell broke loose, like the Fourth of July—lights, whistles, sirens, cars screeching and braking, gunfire. Don't ask me how, but I got into the bus and got it started. *La puta madre*—let's roll. I shot across West Street right into a garage on the corner of Canal. At least three cars came running out right at me. I cut left hard, bounced off a gas pump, then with my foot on the floorboard I cut east on Canal. The agents' cars were swarming all over me by the dozens—we was banging and crashing all over. They was hitting me from the back and the side like fuckin' kamikaze. But I still had the four wheels down on the ground, still running east on Canal; then I saw a helicopter coming at me when I was getting near the entrance to the Holland Tunnel. Blam! They blew my windows out—the bus jumped in the air, but I kept going. The chopper was bumping me with the pontoons trying to tip me over. *Madre puta*! Canal Street is wide open—I need a roof. On Varick Street I made a hard right, jumped a sidewalk, and went through a space in the wall of the exit ramp of the Holland Tunnel. Wrong way— fuck it! I was out of my skull—I barreled into the tunnel with the cars coming out. Move over, I'm coming on. I was bouncing off the walls of the tunnel, gas pedal going through the floor. Almost out the outer end. Then I saw it. They backed a fuckin' truck sideways into the tunnel. That ain't gonna stop me, I'm coming out the other side! Then I saw the guy in the Hawaiian shirt. I hit my brake and turned the wheel hard left. Too late. I hit the truck like an artillery shell. There was an explosion—I flew out the door, bounced off the tunnel railing, and fell on the highway. Look like the whole fuckin' tunnel was on fire. I couldn't move, seemed like every bone was broken. *Puñeta*, is this the end of Carlito? Nothing like that. The *federicos* dragged me out. The vehicles were still popping, metal was flying all over—a real torch job. And the snow was all melted. I was laughing through my ribs, but I was laughing. Exhibit One coming up, a roasted marshmallow—they can roll it in front of the jury. Maybe it wasn't such a crazy ride. Then I passed out. I woke up in Beekman Hospital handcuffed to the bed with two agents on me twenty-four hours a day. Concussion, busted ribs, no big thing.

Next stop, 427 West Street, Federal House of Detention. I'd passed it on my way down twice. It's a Joint but it's a country club compared to the Tombs. They took me in front of the U.S. magistrate in Foley Square. I couldn't get hold of a lawyer so this Legal Aid kid spoke up for me— "Mr. Brigante has deep roots in the community." That's for sure. "I admit Mr. Brigante has a substantial criminal record." Admit shit, my record ain't bad compared to a real criminal and I ain't messed with the federal government before. "Mr. Brigante is enveloped in a presumption of innocence, notwithstanding the gravity of the charges." The wops would have enveloped me in a gravity all right if I hadn't gone to get that junk—besides, the ice cream is melted so how's a dope pinch gonna stick? The lawyer did such a great job they only fixed a half-million-dollar bail. Five hundred thou for a cat like me, an American citizen, a lifelong resident of New York. That ain't right. Where the fuck am I gonna go, Patagonia? I do the crime, I do the time—I ain't no fuckin' Bolivian with white socks on; I'm here and I'm gonna stay here, but I got to be on the streets so I can wind up my affairs like them white-collar boys do. Right away these lawyers fuck you up. Damned if dealing with lawyers ain't the worse part of being a hustler.

So they put me in maximum security at West Street. Guess who my neighbor was? Rocco Fabrizi, formerly with the firm of U.S. Mafia. "Damn, Rocco, how far did you get?"

"I don't think I got to the next corner. I told them, you're making a big mistake. I hear you were A.J. Foyt going through the tunnel."

"I might have made it, but I thought about this guy I saw on the Jersey Turnpike years ago and I hit my brake and cut—otherwise I'd have hit the truck full speed."

"What guy are you talking about?"

"Some guy wearing a Hawaiian shirt—this was many years ago—he was going a hundred miles an hour on the Jersey Turnpike the wrong way. They couldn't stop him so they put a firetruck across the highway. He hit it full clip—he and his sports car went through and up. I saw him hanging on top of the ladder; he was wearing one of them shirts, what was left of him. Cop said the guy had lost his girl. When I saw the truck in the tunnel, that's what came to my mind like twenty years later—crazy, right?"

"Listen, Carlito, I'm surprised you got as far as you did. Bobby Higgins didn't have a helicopter on top of him. It was in all the papers."

"Guess I'm only the second-best wheel man around."

"Cut the bullshit, Charles, I know you stuck your neck out for me—I won't forget it."

"Don't get sloppy on me, Rocco."

"Your ass!"

So I took it easy for a few days—sacked out a lot, watched television—like I say, I do good time, don't go around cryin' and wailin'. But real quick-like, the party was over. Rocco had the word, they brought Amadeo into West Street together with four of his crew. Holy shit, this fuckin' guy in here! *Maldita sea la madre*.

"Yeah, Carlito, Mr. A himself, and Mickey Connors, Joe Cass, Petey Pumps, and Larry Bennet."

"I don't know any of them guys, Rocco—sounds like an Irish basketball team to me."

"Nah, they're all wops, spitters. Petey A's main guys except for Joe Bats."

"Joe who?"

"Battaglia—he's not here and not expected. I'm more worried about his not being here than I am about Amadeo being here."

"I thought Battaglia was some kind of lieutenant."

"Doesn't mean a thing, Carlito, this is a new mob."

Next day, all seven of us were brought down to the Federal Courthouse on Foley Square. We were all bunched together downstairs in the detention pens waiting to be brought up to the courtroom. Petey A sat by himself in a corner of the tank. His four thugs stood between him and the rest of the guys in the tank, including me and Rocco. Amadeo had that hit-in-the-face-with-a-bag-of-nickels look on his puss. Nobody was talking, not even to Rocco. I felt a bad chill and it wasn't the thermostat. Problems, Carlito, problems.

They took us upstairs to a courtroom on the third floor and arraigned us before a federal judge. The clerk called out the names on the indictment: Peter Amadeo, Michael Coniglia, Peter Pompano, Joseph Castaldi, Ilario Benetti,

Rocco Fabrizi, Charles Brigante. What am I doing here with these criminals? They look right out of Elliot Ness. I gotta get a severance right away. That's what I get for not keeping to my own kind. Between the mau mau uptown and the mafia downtown I'm in a sandwich. You try to do the right thing and you get screwed, blued, and tatooed. No way, *salvese él que pueda*.

We all got bail reset at half a million apiece. Mother-hoppers. And it turned out I had the worst record of all seven of us. Ain't this a blip, a clean-cut-looking guy like me with a worse record than all these *bandidos*. Shows the kind of lawyers I've had. Then this faggoty D.A., or U.S. Attorney they call him, kept calling me a murderer. I said, "I demand to be heard—this is an outcry being committed here against me, Your Honor. This D.A. don't know me or what he's talking about. I ain't been found guilty of no murder—I pleaded in that case because my lawyer pulled the wool over my eyes, and I've already reported him to the bar association. This attack is not founded and I protest, as a matter of fact I refuse to proceed no further in these proceedings." The Legal Aid said, "Please, Mr. Brigante, keep quiet." I told him, "What are they gonna do, give me thirty days?"

I always rap good in the courtroom—the other guys in my case were struck dumb. Not me. The judge got hot and started yelling. Then he told me and Rocco we had to get our own lawyers. Then they read the indictment. Must have been twenty counts—conspiracies with people I never heard of and possession of junk I never heard of. A frame-up. They claimed they salvaged ten kilos from my wreck. No good. That shit was all cooked—this must be from their private stock. Another frame-up. The Legal Aid kid said that I was the manager-bartender of the Bonnie 'n Clyde discotheque in midtown—so what did this *cabron* of a government D.A. say? "The Bonnie 'n Clyde is a notorious gathering place for narcotics peddlers, organized crime figures, and assorted undesirable and criminal elements, Your Honor. The government has had the place under surveillance and we know Mr. Brigante, who is the owner, to use it as a shield for his real sordid business."

Yer mudder's cunt, I thought, but I said, "Gawd, Your Honor, this is a slander—if I am the owner, why don't I appear on the license? As a matter of fact, I am there to help the owner keep out the bad element. Mr. Caraballo, the owner, don't cater to no riff-raff, and he gimme a break on account I can't get a job nowhere else on account of my record—and I ain't gonna sit still for his place being put down."

The judge got hot again—"Mr. Brigante, your impetuosity is getting to be a problem here. I do not want any more outbursts from you. You will refrain from such conduct. You have an attorney by your side—consult him."

"Your Honor, Guido versus Wainwright says I got a right to counsel of my own choosing and he ain't my choosing."

"That is not what the case stands for. But what are you waiting for? You've had ample time to get yourself a lawyer. This case will be moved for trial with the utmost celerity and dispatch. I want that understood by defendants and their attorneys."

Everybody said Yes, Your Honor—except me. I said, "Your Honor, being dispatched is what I'm worried about. I'm like a man sick-to-dying looking for the right doctor; it ain't easy."

"I agree, without wishing to prejudge the case, that your affliction might be termed terminal in this instance. I am according all defendants thirty days to prepare their motions. Mr. Scott, it is my understanding that this matter is to be referred to Judge Rossi. Is that correct?"

"Yes, Your Honor."

"Very good. All motions will be directed to Judge Rossi. Remand the defendants."

Mr. Wesley Scott, the government prosecutor. What a pain in the ass! An anglo with a last name for a first name is automatically a prick. Ugh, did he break cajuns in this case. Mr. Ass-ley Scott wearing bow ties and Coca Cola bottles for eyeglasses. Look like that guy from TV— Wally Peepers. He was sharp—he had a wheelbarrow full of papers, but he could pull them out when he needed them. He had all the exhibits down pat. If you asked him what time he's going to lunch he'd hand you a memorandum of law. He was wound up tighter than the pope's dick. No sense of humor. I knew he was a bad-news cat right away.

The marshals took us back down to the tank to wait for the bus to West Street. I could see I made a big hit with the boys. Fuck 'em. I'm fighting for my life. Am I supposed to stand there and take a third strike? Not me, I'm taking my cut.

Amadeo speaks. "Rocco, your Uncle Dom is dead, You're off his titty, Rocco, you're on your own. He had *coglioni*, your uncle did—may he rest in peace. But you, you're different, Rocco—you ain't a Cocozza, you're a Fabrizi. You ain't direct—you go around, you scheme, you grease your way into one ear then you connive your way out the other. All the time smiling. I know guys like you all my life—you topple buildings, bring everything down with your goddamned schemes. But I've seen it right away, thank God, and as soon as I've run into one like you, *finito subito*! I saw it in your pink face and blond hair twenty years ago, like you was better than me—I'm a greaseball. But I stepped back out of respect to your Uncle Dom, God rest his soul, and this is my reward—that I should be sucked into a junk conspiracy when God knows I'd kill every dope peddler in America. *Che infamia*!"

Rocco winced. "Give me a chance, Pete—I don't know how they mixed you up in this thing; we know you're clean."

"Who's the we?"

"Me and Carlito here."

"There ain't nobody next to you, Rocco. I never heard that spic's name, never seen him, I don't know who he is. You heard him upstairs? He's a maniac, you know that."

That got me. "Who the fuck you think you're talking to, Amadeo? It ain't my fault you're in here."

"Carlito, take it easy."

Amadeo wouldn't look at me—he kept staring at Rocco. "Rocco, I ain't mobbed up. I don't have to take this shit, I don't care how many ginsos he's got in here."

Amadeo said, "Rocco, how's your wife and kids?"

Rocco got white.

"And give my regards to Vinnie."

So they hit Vinnie. That figures. That means me and Rocco are overdue already. *Hijo de puta.*

We went back to West Street. Then conferences up the ass. Must have been twenty lawyers in the case at one time or another. I myself went through four lawyers. I wanted Steinhardt, but he was still mad at me from the time I ratted him out to the bar association. Grudgeholder. Then I settled on this young kid, David Kleinfeld—he was a good appeal man, very sharp on the case law—when we was on the motions. We moved for discovery, inspection of the grand jury minutes, bills of particulars, severance, suppression of the evidence—shit, we even moved to get the junk back. I moved to get me moved out of West Street. I coulda told them in front how far we was getting with all these papers flying around. As if Uncle Sam was gonna let us plead guilty with an explanation and mail in the fine.

Judge Gaetano Rossi: a high Italian—Milanese, they told me. A former U.S. prosecutor himself. He was always in a hurry. "What's your point?" "Go on to the next question." "You already asked that, next question." "Motion denied" was his favorite expression. If you had to move your bowels, he'd say, "Motion denied." We were in great shape. These ethnic guys are worse than the wasps; they say, "I made it, why can't you?" They don't want to hear about life in the ghetto—they been there and back. Don't get mad at me, Judge, I ain't no Italian.

I let this kid Dave Kleinfeld handle the preliminary garbage. I was saving myself for the jury. With my rap, I'm a natural. Then I get a caller. It ain't bad enough I gotta worry about the case and Amadeo having me whacked out, I gotta worry about a visitor. I was sacked out when the hack says to me, "Brigante, you got a visitor." Who the hell would want to visit me now? I don't want no visitors, you feel worse when they leave. They took me down to the visiting room, you talk from behind a glass partition into a phone. Phone has got to be tapped. It was Gail. Unbelievable.

"What are you doing here, Gail? You crazy?"

"It was all over the newspapers and TV, Charley."

"Yeah, I had a lot of offers."

"I had to visit some people in New York and I—"

"Don't bullshit me, Gail."

"You never wrote or called me. I guess I'm making a fool of myself, Charley."

What could I say? She was a beautiful girl—I reached out for her hand and had to settle for the glass partition. That brought me around real quick-like.

"You don't know what you're doing, baby. These people are crazy. They'll put you in a conspiracy. Aiding and abetting, anything. Just knowing me can hurt you—they'll check you out, embarrass you. I can't allow that."

"I love you, Charley. I can't help it."

"Cut out that kind of talk, Gail, you trying to drive me up the wall? I'm in a pine box already, all they got left to do is pour the dirt on me. And you want to talk about moonlight and roses."

She was crying already.

"You been crying since you met me, Gail."

"Charley, all those horrible things they said about you in the newspapers—"

"Every word was true and they don't know the half of it—I'm a stone degenerate."

"But Charley, narcotics are destroying people."

"I can't worry about people, Gail, I never could. That's what makes me different—I can't feel that far. I care about you or someone I know, but when you talk about people— faces—it don't mean nothin' to me; they're not real. I don't even think about them, much less worry. Don't try to understand that—you can't."

"What can I do, Charley? Can I help in any way?"

I ran a murder game on her.

"Yeah, get on a plane and go home. You're screwing me up worse—I got to concentrate in preparing my defense, I can't be having no distractions. That hearts-and-flowers jive was all right on the islands but it's over—don't try to rehash it over here. Look around you, look where we are. You playing some kind of caseworker bit with me, Gail, that's all it is—you're doing missionary work but the devil got to me long ago. You know what I did with that address you gave me? I threw it away, that's what I did. Okay?"

I wanted to crash my skull through the partition. I got up and walked out of the room.

When I think back at that scene now it reads like Warner Brothers with Gail as Ida Lupino and me as Herman Brix (a/k/a Bruce Bennett). The bad guy is really a good guy, so he has to play the bad guy to let the chick off the hook when she can't let go. And maybe the bulls got us trapped up in the high Sierras and yeah, we got a little dog too. I seen it twenty times in the flicks.

But I wasn't laughing that night. Me, who always sleep like a champ, looking at the ceiling and swallowing lumps in my throat. Then the fantasy shit—me and Gail living on a boat on a marina off Fajardo, P.R., or Saint Thomas. Sailing down the chain of islands to Venezuela—all the trimmings, golden sun, blue skies, clear air, and me and my *rubia* goddess screwing on the forward deck. I jumped right out of my fuckin' rack. Get a hold on yo'self, motherfucker, ten minutes with this fox and I'm halfway to being a stool pigeon. Maybe they let her in for that reason. They're slick, nothing like a pussy to soften you up. Then your own skull starts to chip away—she needs me, I need her, we got a right to be happy, we'll get away together and start a clean life, get a job, do the right thing—they deserve it, they let me down, they double-crossed me, they ain't bailed me out, they ain't taking care of business, they ratted me out, they're criminals anyway. And you're in the government bag. Gail, you cunt, you gonna destroy me. I made it through the night, I was okay in the morning.

BUT THAT WAS JUST A LEFT JAB. THE GOVERNMENT CAUGHT me with a flush right-hand right after that. "Brigante, you're wanted in the office, right away." They were waiting for me in the cubicle where the lawyers rap. Narco bulls. Two white, one black—but they all look alike. The old guy, gray hair, "Mr. Brigante, we're from the B.N.D.D., as you probably know and we—"

"I got nothing to say to you guys."

"Wait a minute, Mr. Brigante, what we say to you may determine what happens to the rest of your life. Hear us out. Your future depends on it. I'll be frank, we need your cooperation. We know they used you as a patsy, a fall guy. They probably threatened you to make you drive the car. No doubt your being a Puerto Rican made you expendable. Let the spic take the rap—they're scum anyway. They're going to let you hold the bag, Mr. Brigante. You're not a mob guy; you don't owe them a thing. You don't necessarily have to be a witness, just talk to us—you help us, we'll help you. You'll be afforded complete protection. It's not like before; we have special appropriations and facilities for this now. You'll be in a special institution with all the comforts—you can have your family with you, you'll lack for nothing. You don't have to give us your answer now, just think about it. We'll be back to see you next week."

"Don't bother, I won't be here."

"What? What do you mean you won't be here?"

"I just got the word from my lawyer. The government's dismissing the case against me—it was all a case of mistaken identity. I'm suing for false arrest."

"You out of your fucking mind?" Mr. Gray blew his cool.

"No, you out of your fuckin' mind comin' in here with that okey-doke play of yours. Now don't bother me no more."

End of the roundtable. I stood by the door waiting to go back to the tank. The black narco came over—"You're making a mistake, Carlito," real soft-like.

"That was high gear, now you're coming in low, right?"

"You got it wrong, bro—that was low before, I'm coming on strong. I ain't no fed, I'm a city cop. Here's where it's at. This pow-wow right here is news inside already. You're half a stoolie now. You won't see me again so no point telling your lawyer, but they'll be sending for you regular, here and to Foley Square. Even if you got nothing to say. The boys know when you got to go to court; any other time is suspect. Then we'll cut the word loose on the street Carlito is a stool. You better come on in, bro, you gonna need a friend. Take a look at some of them eye-talian faces when you get inside. Later."

Yeah, I was in great shape at West Street. Amadeo and his people weren't talking to me or even to Rocco, not even to cuss Rocco out for being in my corner. That means they're gonna whack him out, too. I felt bad for Rocco— one of his kids was in college, the publicity had hurt the kid. That's why I'm always loose—can't be worried about nobody else. Carmen, Rocco's wife, was into West Street regular. She was a great broad, it was a goddamn shame. We been at West Street a couple of months when Rocco came up from a visit with his wife. His shirt was torn— I could see he'd been in a fight. I got shook up, thinking Petey A had made a move. "What happened, Rocco?"

"I had to deck some degenerate down in the visiting room."

"What?"

"I'm talking with Carmen, when I look, this broad next to Carmen has her tit out and this guy next to me is jacking off—I broke his hole—cock-sucker—right in front of my wife he's beating his meat."

That's what happens when you got guys locked up and they ain't gettin' no trim. Then we had a guy wanted to see a pussy—he was a boss, had bread, so he put up a hundred dollars for anybody to get his old lady to show her snatch in the visiting room. I know guys was there, this ain't no bullshit. The broad was there in a short skirt with no drawers; when the guard wasn't looking—zip— she flashed her box, now you see it, now you don't—like the guy in the raincoat in the subway. The Joint makes a degenerate out of a man. Although I gotta admit some of the guys got a head start on the street.

WE WAS GETTING READY FOR THE TRIAL. I WAS DOING A lot of heavy thinking on what my trial strategy was gonna be. My lawyer, Dave Kleinfeld, was a good kid but jerky. I used to call him Mickey Rooney 'cause he looked like him, a little stump-jumper maybe five-two with fat mod ties. He didn't have the dignity or the class my old lawyer Steinhardt had. That old bird Steinhardt would stand in front of a jury over six feet tall, like a Prussian colonel. He'd have these funny glasses without no frames that he'd hitch up on top of his nose. Then he'd take them off and start polishing them with a big handkerchief. "The crown never loses a case. . . ." The jury was dry-humped from the giddy-ap. He was always talking about the "immortal" what's-his-face, like the "immortal Lord Coke" or the "immortal Bard." It's a goddamn shame he's such a sorehead and I gotta go to bat with Mickey Rooney. *Pero no hay mal que bien no traiga,* because Steinhardt wouldn't wanna do things my way, but this mini-lawyer gonna do what I tell him. We gonna run this trial my way. I will be heard, believe that, wops or no wops. So now here's me, working out the knotty problems of a heavy case when Rocco delivers some bad news.

"They got the scissors out of the barbershop—the contract is down; it's to be one of your own people, a Cuban or P.R., that's all I got—watch your ass, Carlito."

Now I'm seein' red rats. Mother's twat, just when I gotta concentrate on my case I gotta worry about a pair of scissors in my chest. I could snap up and get sent to the federal bughouse in Springfield, Missouri, or I could refuse to come out of my cell. But I decided to grab the bull by the balls—I yelled out like a crazy man all over maximum security, "I know there's a motherfuckin' Latino in here with a pair of scissors for me. Well, I'm waiting for you, *maricón*, whoever you are, but have two sacks with you, one to bring and one to take back. *Hijo de puta, me cago en tu madre,*" etc. You can't beat Spanish for cursing. Everybody said Carlito's gone crazy but somebody got the message—the hacks found the scissors two days later and they weren't in my back. If I ever had a son, his name would have been Rocco. Would have been funny, a Puerto Rican kid named Rocco, but that's how I felt about the guy. He was a man.

11

ALL THE SHADOWBOXING AND GYM-FIGHTING WAS OVER. We was all going in the main arena in the main event. Trial, baby, trial. A heavy mother going down, ain't nobody in Foley Square to pay traffic tickets. There was so many lawyers they was stumbling all over one another, bunch of hooples. They had scads of papers and thick folders, meanwhile they didn't know what the hell they were doing. The only one with a good rap was Albert Freidman, Mickey Connors' lawyer. He used a lot of fancy words and would ask for side-bar conferences every five minutes, but he was the pilot fish and the rest would go along with him. Right away I told Mickey Rooney, "Be cool, low-key—don't mix me up with these gangsters; I'm here on the fly, like caught up in the web on a hummer—you make that clear to the jury. You supposed to get me a severance; you screwed that up. And where's my Spanish interpreter?"

"I told you, Carlito, that is ridiculous; you were born in New York and you've lived here for forty years—how could you not speak English?"

"So what? I been forced to live in the ghetto, ain't I? A man could live his whole life in the Twenty-third Precinct and never speak no English. You gotta keep me apart from these criminals one way or another."

The jury panel filed in. Ugh, what a bunch. Look to me like they all worked in the post office, had friends in law enforcement, and had been victims of crime. Yeah, we were in great shape. The lawyers was making a big fuss about what kind of jury was needed. The Irish is all cops, the Jews is getting mugged by the dope addicts, the Blacks ain't gonna favor no white defendants dealing dope in the ghetto. They ain't no Latinos in the jury panel. What do we got to get them? An Eskimo jury? Goddamn lawyers. Then they're all psychiatrists—this juror walks with a gimp, he's mad at the world—this juror looks like a fag, he might go for me or Rocco—this juror sounds like a boss, he could take over the jury, but in whose favor? Like that. Well, after all this noise about the jury we ended up with the hanginest bunch of mothers in history. Lucky they didn't convict the bailiff and the marshals, too.

So now we got the jury picked. Mr. Ass-ley Scott starts his opening. Good Godalmighty damn, I ain't never heard so many lies and slander. *Calumnia*! Then he started talking about deals I never heard of and shit that was brought in when I wasn't even on the street. "A sinister conspiracy encompassing far-off places and persons all intertwined in varying degrees of complicity and participation with one avowed purpose—to bring in the white death to our borders." I told little Dave, "You better have somethin' good to answer that bunch of bullshit." Then I heard Scott mention about a Jorge Betancourt being picked up by Interpol in Europe and the international combine that had been smashed that supplied 99.9 percent of the junk coming into America. Shee-it. Amadeo like to vault six feet in the air. The jury saw this and said, "Hmm. . . ." I said to myself, no matter what lies they say about you, be cool, be blasé, like Shit, is that all you got against me? 'Tain't nothin'. Then after winding through all this jive he got to me, like least but not last.

"In the presence of an army of agents and a helicopter, this brigand, Brigante, took possession of the vehicle which contained two hundred kilograms of heroin. And then, with this contingent of law-enforcement officers in his van, he took off with the vehicle. A more bold and audacious flight has never been recorded. The chase was climaxed by Brigante driving into the Holland Tunnel the wrong way where he crashed into an oncoming vehicle. The resultant fire destroyed much of the contraband, but we will introduce into evidence at a later time—subject, of course, to His Honor's ruling—a full ten kilograms of this most dangerous drug which was salvaged. This seizure marks the culmination of an investigation the development of which has taken years. I will, in my presentation, put together for you all the parts, piece by piece. The mosaic will be complete at the end, I promise you."

Scott sat down behind his mountain of papers, books, and exhibits. He had a new air in front of the jury, did ol' Ass-ley, he wasn't going around glaring and staring anymore. Now, with the jury digging him, he was very amiable, like he was walking on soft-boiled eggs. In other words, Hey, folks, I'm a nice guy, I ain't gonna hurt nobody if they don't deserve it—I wouldn't kid you. If a juror wanted to see an exhibit he'd float through the air to bring it over. And he'd be smiling at them, and bowing and scraping when they would file into the courtroom. Another dry-humper, just like Steinhardt—they're all in the same bag.

I says to Mickey Rooney, "I want a dynamite opening, Dave."

"We're going to waive the opening, Carlito."

"You crazy, Dave? The best offense is a good defense, or some shit like that. Now you jump off first, you be best."

"You don't understand, Carlito. The opening is to state what we're going to prove. What are we going to prove? We don't come in until the tail end of this case, I say we lay low, out of sight, out of mind, until we hear the evidence—then we formulate our attack. Why should we reveal our hand to the U.S. Attorney?"

"Now, hold the phone, counselor, you ain't talkin' to no Eighth Avenue pimp here. I been around courtrooms all my life—I was in trials when you was still suckin' hind titty. I been in the old magistrates' courts, the special sessions, the general sessions, the criminal court, the supreme court—shit, I had a paternity case in the family court. And I near always been a winner, in spite of my lawyers. So don't be sounding me about what you is or you ain't gonna do. You're gonna do it my way, that's where it's at, y'dig?"

"I dig, Carlito, and you better get yourself another lawyer.

I've had it with your bullshit; I can't take any more of it."

"What a nerve—consider yourself discharged, *ab initio!*"

"Aba who?"

"You got the message, buzz off!"

Dave called for a side-bar conference and told Judge Rossi that me and him was at an impact or somethin' like that. Ol' Gaetano got all shook up. He crooked his eyebrows at me, like, I knew you'd be trouble, you cock-sucker. Then he excused the jury.

"Stand up, Mr. Brigante. Let us get something straight at the outset. I do not tolerate any undue delays in my courtroom. There will be no dalliances here of any variety. I am well aware that disruptive tactics may be on your mind. If they are, dismiss them, for I shall deal summarily with you. Now this trial is going to proceed in orderly fashion and I will suffer no nonsense. Do I make myself clear?"

"Yes, Your Honor, you sure do. And I couldn't agree with you more."

"I have been apprised that you are a somewhat impetuous individual. So I am warning you I will tolerate no outbursts from you."

"Your Honor, I'm surprised that you been apprised of that. That ain't me. I got all the respect in the world for this court, as God is my witness. But I've fired my lawyer."

"What nonsense is this?"

"I don't want Mr. Kleinfeld, he's uncompetent. And furthermore he has lost confidence in me."

"In you?"

"Yeah, in me."

"But this is preposterous. This trial has commenced. Mr. Kleinfeld is your lawyer. Bring in the jury."

"Wait a minute, Your Honor. I'm ready to proceed, but without Kleinfeld. I will be my own lawyer."

"Does this man have a record of mental illness, Mr. Scott?"

"Not that I know of, Your Honor."

"I ain't crazy, Your Honor. I got a right to a lawyer of my own choosing and I choose me. That's the Guido case."

"The who? This is absurd. All right, Mr. Brigante, you

will act as your own attorney. Mr. Kleinfeld, you will continue to sit by Mr. Brigante's side to assist him in any legal question that might arise and you shall be prepared at all times to resume your original role as lawyer for the defendant, should he decide to desist from his, er, irregular conduct. Am I understood by all?"

"Yes sir."

"Proceed to bring in the jury."

I ALWAYS KNEW I'D GET THERE. CARLITO BRIGANTE, MEMber of the bar. Ha.

So the trial went ahead. They had everything. Scott tracked the junk from Don Jorge Betancourt to Canada, New York, and Florida. Undercover narcs, customs agents, Interpol cops, motel clerks, hotel clerks, all kinds of people Scott put on the stand. I didn't hear my name mentioned yet, but I'd jump up and object regularly.

"What is the nature of your objection, Mr. Brigante?"

"I'm objecting to my being on trial here when my name ain't been mentioned and I ain't never seen none of these witnesses."

"Objection overruled. Sit down, please."

And like, "I object to all this noise about Jorge Betancourt when he ain't even here. I got a right to face my accusers."

"This is taken subject to connection. Please sit down."

And, "I object to all this gas about Canada—I ain't been north of Green Haven. This is deflammatory and prejudiced to me—I object."

And my favorite, "I object on the grounds it is unrelevant, unmaterial, and unconsequential." I loved to say that one. Used to drive ol' Guy up the wall.

"Mr. Brigante, will you please refrain from these exclamations in the presence of the jury? This is uncalled for. Consult your attorney."

"That's me, Judge." Wow, would he get hot! Ol' prissypants, Scott, would have a pained look on his puss like he been goosed with an umbrella.

"This is inexcusable, Your Honor. Mr. Brigante is deliberately thwarting the continuity of my train of thought.

It is a shameful attempt to thwart the orderly presentation of the evidence."

I really got out of line that time. I said, "I object to all this talk about twat in the presence of the jury." That did it. The judge ordered a recess for the day and had a shrink check me out at West Street.

Through all this, Amadeo would have daily conferences like he was a field marshal. Mickey, Petey Pumps, Joe Cass, Larry, and even Rocco had to sit still for his speeches. He scared the shit out of all the lawyers. "I'm paying big money, you bunch of scumbags, meanwhile you're sitting on your asses and let this one *figlio di putana*, Scott, do all the talking. I got a family, I got businesses, I pay taxes—I gotta hear this *bastardo* ruin my good name with this talk of junk. I'll break your ass you don't do something." His lawyer, Jacobs, had to be the most underpaid lawyer out. But Pete wouldn't look at me—I knew he thought I was crazy. Fuck 'im.

By now, I was getting bored with all the yin-yang. Just when I was losing interest, Scott played his trump. Mario Battaglia also known as Joe Bats. I remember like now. The marshall opened the door behind the jury box and there he stood, all 260 pounds of him. Joe Bats—I heard stories he offed people with his bare hands. The bosses had their eye on him when he was sixteen. He could rip the gates on store fronts when he was a kiddie burglar with his mitts, didn't need no crowbar. Didn't take long before he was mobbed up. He didn't disappoint them—they could aim him in any direction, all six-four of him. He took two bullets meant for a boss, and he still put the shooter through a plate-glass window, and then he kicked the guy to death. They don't come no tougher than Joe Bats. He was a pig-fucker but he was bad. But like having balls in front of a gun or a knife got nothing to do with having the balls to do time. That's another scene, baby. Believe that. And then a lot of guys with heart ain't got no smarts, so then the bulls outfox them, put them in a bind, and then turn them around.

Scott was carrying on like the MC in a lounge act, like here he is, the one and only made-guy canary in captivity. *Madre mia.* Amadeo said, "I'll drink his blood, I'll eat his liver—" Jesus Christ! All hell broke loose, the marshals had to grab the boys. Talk about blowtops, they were screamin' and cursin'. There was a recess, the judge threatened to put them all in straitjackets and gag them. I was cool, the jury could see that. Then I made my objections. "I demand a mistrial, Your Honor. This commotion just now has hurt my case. The jury is gonna visit with me the sins of other people, namely these guys."

"Motion denied—do you think you can exploit a disorder of your making?"

"It ain't of my makin', I'm an innocent bystander. And I object because all this ruckus has messed up my continuity, like Mr. Scott would say."

"Objection overruled. Proceed with your questioning of the witness, Mr. Scott. The jury is instructed to disregard the disturbance before and to draw no conclusions from it."

Ain't this a bitch. King Kong could appear at the window and some judge will say, "The jury will disregard that."

Well, Battaglia put the zinger on all the troops. He buried them all, one by one, all the time looking up in the air. He said he gave Rocco two hundred thousand dollars of Amadeo's money for the last order and they had discussed what the junk would be worth. Amadeo screamed, "Mario, how could you do this to me, how could you lie like this?" Then he bit his own hand and turned purple. We had another recess. Then Battaglia put the wood to me—he talked about the sitdown out on the Bath Beach, how I had been there with Rocco and how he had discussed the two hundred thousand for the junk with me and Rocco. I jumped up. "I object. I plead surprise, Your Honor!"

"What do you mean, surprise?"

"I'm surprised this man is testifying against me—I have never talked to him in my life."

"You will have ample time to cross-examine him. Your objection is noted. Please refrain from these unnecessary outbursts."

Then Battaglia went into heavy details, really loading it in. How he had discussed the arrival of the *France* with Rocco. How Betancourt's go-fer, Marcel Boucher, was with Rocco's man Vincent Fusaro at a garage on

West 44th Street. Vinnie Fusaro was to be in work clothes, chewing on a toothpick, and with a work cap on backwards. Once Fusaro was in the bus, they was to match up halves of a dollar bill. Then they was to drive to a motel in Jersey where Rocco had some guys waiting. The jury ate it up. We were in trouble. Al Friedman did a good job on cross, I gotta admit. He brought Joe Bats up from his kid days on Thompson Street through all his collars. There was assaults with iron bars, assault with a hatchet, assault with an ice pick, with sawed-off shotgun, with a pistol, hijacking, extortion—the dude was a crime wave all by himself. A terrible record. I was shocked that such a hoodlum was walking around the streets.

Friedman: "Mr. Battaglia, you have criminal matters outstanding now right in this jurisdiction, do you not?"

Battaglia: "Mr. Scott says you ain't suppose to axe me about dem tings, I ain't convicted."

Judge Rossi: "I determine what questions are to be answered, Mr. Battaglia. You will please answer the question."

Friedman: "And what is the nature of the charges pending against you, Mr. Battaglia?"

Judge Rossi: "Mr. Friedman, I try to afford counsel the widest latitude on cross-examination, but I believe you are now straying far afield into collateral matters."

Friedman: "Quite so, Your Honor—I shall endeavor to hew to the prescribed limits more carefully. May we have a side-bar conference, Your Honor?"

Ugh. All this Alfonso-and-Gaston jive gets me sick.

Friedman: "Mr. Battaglia, you are expecting consideration from the government in exchange for your cooperation in this case, is that not a fact?"

Battaglia: "That ain't why I'm here. Mr. Cronin told me the truth about the dope racket and I seen the light. Now I'm trying to do the right thing to make up. I don't need no break—they ain't got nuttin' on me."

Friedman: "Mr. Cronin is the agent in charge of this case, is that correct, Mr. Battaglia?"

Battaglia: "You got it, counselor."

Joe Bats had a tan. Had to be in La Tuna, Texas—the

stool-pigeon farm. But he started to lose it as the legal fleagles had him under cross for close to a week. Judge Rossi was hot. I never seen a guy in such a hurry—he must sleep with his clothes on. I said I got to have my shot at Joe Bats. Even my fellow lawyers was yellin' at me that they had covered all the ground.

Friedman: "Mr. Brigante, you're opening up a Pandora's box."

Me: "I ain't worried about her box, I'm worried about my ass."

Jacobs: "Brigante, you're irritating the judge and the jury; you're repetitious and redundant."

Me: "Listen, Jacobs, I'm the one that's being double-jeopardied here."

Friedman: "I was unaware that you had been tried before on the same matter, Mr. Brigante."

Me: "Don't be a wise guy, Al, you know what I mean. What do I give a shit about being redundering? I'm worried about going to jail. Now lemme do it my way."

So they trotted Battaglia out again special for me. He looked like the Swedish Angel with a tie on.

Me: "They call you Joe Bats, right?"

Joe B: "Yeah, short for my name, Battaglia."

Me: "It ain't 'cause you been battin' people on the head with tire irons, right?"

Joe B: "Do I have to put up with this abuse, Your Honor? He ain't even a lawyer, I mean, am I right or wrong?"

Judge Rossi: "Mr. Brigante, please limit your questions to the issues in the case."

I tried to do an Al Friedman: "I shall endeavor in the utmost extreme, Your Honor," and I bowed.

Me again: "Now, Mr. Joe Bats, you say you saw me at Messina's Restaurant in Brooklyn, right?"

"Right."

"What I was wearing?"

"The hell I know what you was wearin'. The nerve of this scurve!"

Me: "Would Your Honor please apprise Joe Bats not to use profanity in the eyes of the jury?"

Judge Rossi: "Mr. Battaglia, please refrain from the use

of any profane language. Answer the question if you can."

Joe B: "You was wearin' a suit—yeah, a dark suit and a tie."

Me: "Ugh, what a goddamn liar. I was wearin' a knit sport outfit with no tie."

Mr. Scott, blowing smoke-rings out his ass: "Your Honor, this is an outrage; this is a travesty. If Mr. Brigante wants to testify he will get his chance later."

Me: "Aha—I demand a mistrial—the D.A. can't talk about me going on the stand in front of the jury—but I agree that what Joe Bats is doing here is an outrage."

Judge: "Motion denied. You will not make statements, you will put questions to the witness, Mr. Brigante. I warn you, I am approaching the limits of my patience with your contumacious behavior. I will not tolerate it. Put your next question."

Me again: "What song was they playin' when you saw me at Messina's?"

Joe B: "That's easy—'Mala Femina'."

Me: "Who singin'?"

Joe B: "Al Martino, I tink."

Me: "Ha! Wrong again—Jerry Vale."

The judge called a recess. Then he told me my cross-examination was over, that he ain't gonna allow no more questions from me. Just when I had Joe Bats on the ropes!

"In the words of Mr. Scott, this is an outrage, Your Honor, this is breaking my chain, this is a drag. I have harpooned the witness lyin' like a rug. And in the middle of my job I'm being cut off. I'm moving for a mistrial, for a severance, and for a reduction in my bail. And I want it in the records."

Judge: "Everything being said here is on the record, to my great distress, Mr. Brigante. Your motions are denied and your cross-examination of the witness is terminated. Call your next witness, Mr. Scott."

The agents marched up and down the stand, a slew of them. Goddamn feds don't look like feds no more—some of them look like zonked-out freaks, long hair, pocketbooks. Unbelievable. Finally, Scott got the junk into evidence. Bad news—once a jury locks on a live exhibit you in trouble. Words are just words, but a pistol is a pistol—they can see it, they can touch it. Same with the junk—they know that ain't pancake flour, they can see it. I figure I'm behind on points, but with a dynamite summation in the last round, I can pull it out. Sugar Ray did it with Randy Turpin, so did Marciano with Ezzard Charles. When you been stunned, when you reelin' and the canvas is spinnin', that's when you separate the men from the pussy. I saw Muhammad Ali go it with Frazier—cost me eight hundred to get ringside, worth every penny. The dude was hurt bad in the eleventh, but he showboated his way out like 'tweren't nothin'—then in the fifteenth, Ali saw it coming, he leaned back to get away, and he's the only pug ever been able to do that, but Frazier was off his feet and he threw the hook high enough. Left hook with all the shoulder behind it—I knew it was a home-run ball, Ali's feet flew out from under him. Splat on his ass. No jukin', no jivin' now, no playin' 'possum, you all by your lonesome on the seat of yo' ass. Where you at, colored boy? Brain don't do you no good now, only your heart. Ali showed them that night—the man got heart. If you ain't got that, you ain't into nothin'.

The main man in that department of all time was Rocky Marciano. He had every handicap—short, around five-ten; light, 188 pounds; no jab; no speed; and at the beginning, no left hook—he was not a good defensive fighter and to cap it, a bleeder. Of course he had a great cut man, Whitey Bimstein, and Charley Goldman, a great trainer, taught him to shorten up his shots and develop a left hook. The rest Rocky did all by himself, from inside—his great heart got past all these hurdles. Nobody will ever come close to the Rock. I saw him not long before he got killed in the plane crash. It was at the Copa at a Tom Jones show. I don't go around makin' a big deal out of celebrities, but that night I felt like going over and telling him what a great champ he was. I wish I had. I was at the Garden after he got killed. They rapped the gong ten times for him, only time he was counted out—me and a couple of tough-guys with me got sloppy for a few seconds there. Yeah, we cry too. I'm just like anybody else—I don't beat up on old ladies or kick a guy on crutches, ain't no tail and horns on me. The only difference between me and the average guy is that I don't follow no rules put down by somebody else. I gotta do things my way—don't matter what the cost, and it's been heavy—I gotta go my way. I always thought I coulda been a good duker but people would tell me, You a pretty boy, supposed to be a pimp. Yeah, they gave you great advice in those days.

We're down to the wire and we're neck and neck. You know whose neck. Summation, the last roll of the dice. My associate counselors did their thing rapping long and hard, mostly long. It ain't easy to get up and sell them stone faces. I didn't listen too close, I was working on my summation— I wrote it all down, then I shitcanned it. This got to be done on the feet from the top of the head, otherwise it ain't gonna have no punch. I watched them laywers rattlin' papers—that jury is gone in a minute. No way, you're shooting from the hip, Carlito.

"Your Honor, Mr. Scott, gentlemen of the jury: I know you're wondering, Who does he think he is summing up his own case, and with all these brilliant lawyers here? Where his head at? Well, I'll tell you, I'm here because I believe in me even though everybody else don't: But nobody, no lawyer in the world knows better than me what happened here. And I'm gonna tell you about it and I have the confidence that you gentlemen of the jury will believe me when I tell you how this thing went down. But first, let's get the prelims out of the way before we start the main event. From the get go let me tell you I'm against dope one hundred percent—it's a sickness that's gotta be wiped out, we all agree on that. Of course, Mr. Scott is gonna tell you he don't have to tell you how terrible dope is, then he's gonna take a half hour telling you anyway. But let's not get carried away, let's don't get hysteria about it where we're blinded and can't see the bushes for the forest. That's right, let us keep a cool head, like you promised to do when you was first picked out.

"Remember what you promised the lawyers? That you was gonna consider only what comes off that chair right there, right? Well, let's see what come off that witness chair. I'll tell you what come off—Joe Bats, also known as Mario Battaglia. If you believe him I'll plead guilty right here and now. Joe Bats—when he come through that door, I thought it was Rondo Hatton. It's bad enough he come on like Primo Carnera, he's gotta have a piece of pipe in his hand, or maybe a hatchet. How'd you like to have him as your friendly bill collector? Or maybe you honk a horn at him and he come over and rip the door off your car. You heard his record—talk about safe streets—is any street safe with a torpedo like that on it? That's their main-event boy, Battlin' Joe Bats, manager Scott, and trainer Cronin. They're betting everything on him. Are you gonna buy that? Are you gonna pick up anything put down by Joe Bats? I don't believe it. I believe you're gonna say Joe Bats come out of the black lagoon and no amount of Brillo is gonna clean him up. Anybody go along with that villain, shame on them. Check him out, does he have a motive to lie? You better believe it. But what does Cronin's protégé Joe Bats say? He says he now know the truth about dope and he was trying to do the right thing! If there's a God in heaven, and I believe there is, the plaster on the ceiling shoulda fell on Joe Bats' head—the lights shoulda blown out. And then you saw him with me. You heard his profanity. Then he couldn't remember what I was wearing, but he could give you tiny details about things that happened long before. Joe Bats is a kewpie doll wound up by Scott—you pull the string, he goes bla-bla, wa-wa, but get him off the script for one question and he gets the apple right away. This is a put-up job of the high water. So much for that lyin' dog, Joe B. May God forgive him, for he knows not what he done.

"So what really happened in this case? I can only tell you about what happened to me in this case. I got nothing to do with these other people. Any resemblance is purely coincidental. I'm a Puerto Rican and I stay with my own kind. I got no truck with people of other national origin and, er, customs. That ain't my lookout. But I can tell you I was drunk that night and wound up on Canal Street I don't know how. I saw this bus and half-stoned I decided to go for a joyride—next thing I know these crazy hippies are banging into the car—I thought they was hot-rodders or muggers, I panicked and cracked up the bus, and—"

Scott: "Your Honor, I must inject myself—"

Me: "Wadda you mean, inject yourself? I resent that kind of remark in this kind of case."

Scott: "Your Honor, Mr. Brigante is, in effect, testifying in his own summation to matters not in the record. He cannot do this, he did not testify during the trial—"

"Aha! There it is again, Judge. Mistrial."

"Mr. Brigante, I have granted you wide latitude in your summation out of deference to your position as a layman. However, I cannot permit you to inject, er, infuse matters that have not been testified to. You cannot have it both ways. You assumed a certain tactical position; you are bound by it. Now continue with your summation."

Me, continuing: "Where was I before I was interrupted? Oh yeah, about me stealin' the bus—well, I can't go into that, you heard Scott. But I say let it all hang out. I know what you're thinking. Why didn't this Puerto Rican take the stand? By law, you ain't supposed to think about that, but I ain't hiding behind no technicalities. I'm gonna tell you. It's because Mr. Scott here would start hoopin' and hollerin' about my prior record to make me look bad. It's an old D.A.'s trick—so what if he got nothin' to do with this case, let's get him on his past record. But I been looking at you people and I said, Carlito, these people is not about to get the wool pulled over their eyeballs by this D.A., so I'll lay it out for you—yeah, I been in trouble but never for no dope, mostly fightin' for survival in the ghetto that's my record. I am a victim of circumstances. I was in the wrong place at the wrong time. Mr. Scott takes that little circumstance, works it backwards through Joe Bats, and makes a big circumstance out of it, like he was lookin' in a telescope. Now that's a terrible thing, circumstances, they have put away a whole lot of people behind circumstances. To me, that's a dirty word. Why, when something happens uptown, everybody quits the scene and no witnesses? Because people are afraid of circumstances, they know about them. Like a guy is stretched out stone cold on the pavement, you best not be there when the Man shows up, because that's the time the shooter will drop the pistol at your feet. And you with a record, you know you're going to be talkin' uphill when they get you in the squadroom.

"Circumstances. You're riding the subway to work with both hands on the *Daily News*, a fine fox has got her back to you, some degenerate will lean over past you and give her the dead hand—when she turns around who's gonna get the pocketbook in the face? Circumstances. They look one way, but they're the other. They can bury an innocent man. I know Scott's gonna talk about the total and the parts and one brick on top of the other. Well, I say Scott's house can't get no building-code permit because the foundation is rotten, that being Joe Bats. And the plumbing and wiring ain't no good either—you saw them federal agents. Unbelievable. That our government gotta hire these hippie guys with long hair and messy clothes. What an example for our youth! That don't command no respect. Yeah, Scott is a builder, all right, a builder of Fox Street tenements with termites in the woodwork and rusty fire escapes. He's asking you to destroy men's lives. I don't have to tell you what a conviction in this means. But what are the tools he's given you? What are the pieces in the jigsaw? They don't fit, they don't jibe, because they're made out of Joe Bats and you know what he's made of. You can't go by Where there's smoke there's fire. You gotta be sure when you dealin' with people's lives. Can you say Joe Bats didn't cook this up to save himself? You know he'll kill and maim—you don't think he'll lie? You don't think maybe he conned Mr. Scott here? You know there's people that see a conspiracy when two bedbugs cross a mattress. A guy like Joe B can play on that. That's the kind of guy Scott wants to strap on you. I don't envy you. Well all right, I've had my say. I may have been clumsy, I may have been the lawyer with the fool for a client, but I went the only way I know—my way. If my speech was rough, I apologize—I was on the street when I shoulda been in school. I wanna thank you for listening to me. I know, whatever you decide, you did your best. God bless you."

Try and read them faces. The lawyers start in. The foreman is with us, it's plain on his face. Number 4 juror was smiling—he's going along with us. Number 7 juror was disgusted by these hippie-type agents. Numbers 8 and 9 jurors are fighting, you can see that—they'll be deadlocked for sure. Etc.

Bullshit. Everybody got tagged on every count. Thirty days for investigation and sentence. *Finita la commedia.*

I was worried about Rocco after that. He didn't want to eat, didn't want to clean up, didn't want to do anything. He was doing bad time.

"I'm not gonna make it, Carlito."

"Wadda you mean, Rocco? You got a lot going for you."

"I'm tired, I want out."

"Rocco, you got bread, you can put together a dynamite appeal, knock the jock off these sombitches—there was error like crazy in the trial."

"You're too much, Carlito, you never say die. I wish I was like you. But they're going to close the door on me. Wops don't make parole—right away they stamp us O.C. or mafia. My life is over. It's okay, I got no squawks."

"Don't talk like that—what about Carmen and the kids?"

"They'll be taken care of."

"What about me, Rocco? Don't you give a shit about what happens to me? You know I depend on you for the smarts—who's gonna give me the right scoop now?"

"You'll be okay. You got a talent for survival—c'mon, don't get sloppy on me. You're supposed to be a tough guy."

"You ain't gonna hurt yourself, are you, Rocco?"

"Get off that kick, will you, Carlito? For Christ's sake. Hey, tell me about that thirteenth round with Walcott and Marciano."

Rocco hung himself the week before sentence. He used his shirt. Let's just say it was the worst news I ever got and I been in a lotta hassles and seen a lotta good boys go out. But Rocco was like an older brother to me—I'd have given my life for him. I ain't no hack fighter, but when they wouldn't let me attend his funeral I went bananas. He was the best guy on the street ever was. Always had class, even as a kid back at the El with me and Earl.

12

AND NOW THE END IS NEAR. . . . FRANK'S SONG FOR THE wise-guys. My way, yeah, I did it my way. Regrets, I've had a few—ha! Thirty years, the man said. The streets'll be buzzin' tonight—Simpson Street, Fox Street, 117th Street, 111th Street, all the Rican hustlers—"Carlito got thirty years, that mother, had a ton of bread, why he so greedy, fuck 'im!" Yeah, your own kind always gives you a break. Judge Rossi made a big spiel about me being a cancer: "You, Charles Brigante, are a malignant tumor in the soft underbelly of our society. The influx of heroin for which you and your co-conspirators are responsible has caused untold suffering and anguish. The toll in human life is incalculable. And yet you stand there in the full flush of your arrogance, swaggering about as you did throughout the entire trial. No contrition, no repentance from you, Brigante. . . ."

Bla, bla, bla—repentance, you goddamn right, I'm goin' to jail for thirty years. Mr. Assistant U.S. Attorney Scott smirking—he swear his ass weigh a ton. As if he could lose in that kangaroo court—they was playin' with marked cards, loaded dice, and tilted tables, real sportin'-like. Shit—any fool could have won this case for the government. Ladeez and gentlemen of the ju-ree, we done caught this jive Po'Rican with two hundred keys of horse worth eighty million on the street, but he didn't know it was in the car. Shee-it, ain't no big deal.

"Does the defendant wish to address the court before sentence?"

"Yes, Your Honor. I swear to God I did not know anything about what was in that car. I know how my people have suffered with the drugs and I won't have nothing to do with it. But like, I come up in Harlem at the wrong time and I been keeping bad company, so that's how come I'm in trouble— bad people around me—I'm trying to do the right thing, but it's hard to turn your back on people you know all your life. So like these agents cook up this conspiracy—maybe something bad went down, but it ain't like these agents and stool pigeons—eh—informers told it. That Battaglia, he lied. I swear to God I ain't never dealt with this man. I know Your Honor's Italian and I don't mean no offense, but these Italian guys, these other defendants wouldn't have nothing to do with a Puerto Rican like me—no way—the jury was crazy to believe that. This is guilt by association like the lawyers said. And the probation department of this court. All they want to talk about is my record—what kind of justice is that? They want to talk about twenty-five years ago—why we got to talk about that? Let's talk about this case, not about no unlawful entry or lousy assault case skatey-eight years ago. A man had to have a record in those days, the Ricans was not in style—wasn't no social workers out there worried about you. The bulls outa the two-three and two-five precincts had one hand on your throat and one foot up your butt—they didn't answer to nobody in them days—if you got popped, wrong or right, shame on you. How many times I got stomped right there in the bathroom of the two-three on 104th Street or got my head shoved in the toilet bowl? It was rough out there— weren't none of this Miranda jive. So like if a dude had heart and got himself a rep, every time something happened the man would be on you. So that's how come I got a record. I don't know none of these Italians and I didn't get no fair trial. I demand a new trial! That's all I got to say."

BACK TO WEST STREET MAX FOR A COUPLE OF WEEKS, then Lewisburg or Atlanta. Let's see now, thirty years, I'm forty-two—I'll come before the board in ten years,

they'll say no dice—motherfuckers—yeah, I'll do twenty—
I'll be sixty-two. Fuck it, the kid always stands up—I'm
going into the yard lookin' every motherfucker in the eye—
never ratted nobody out. The wops are mad at me because
I was my own lawyer—fuck 'em, it was my ass. And the
stool pigeon, a wop! Ain't this a bitch—all this bullshit
about the outfit and the stool turns out to be a made-guy.
Ha! What a joke on Amadeo when they opened the door
behind the witness chair and in came Battaglia. The big
guy like to fall through his own asshole. Mr. Amadeo, Mr.
A, Mr. Mohair, Mr. White-on-White—up yours. Me being
the only spic right away I was wrong. All those months in
West Street, not one look, not one word—sidge talk with
his crew was all. Me, I'm out, I'm a niggerican, but when
the shit had to be moved from the pier, nobody wanted
to get near the car—the spic was the only one with the
heart. Then when the shit hit the fan, I'm a garbage can—
all the spitters close ranks and the Rican is out; he ain't
family, he's the weak link. Fuck you, Mr. Petey A—I stood
up—like a chump—even when you had the scissors stolen
from the barbershop to put through my chest. The contract
never went down—Rocco saw to that. Rocco, m'main man.
Good-bye, ol' buddy.

Good-bye to a lot of things, Carlito. Good-bye to flyin'
to Panama to catch a fight. Good-bye to ringside at the
Copa. Good-bye to Sinatra at the Fontainebleu. Good-bye
to the lounges in Vegas. Good-bye to the dolls of San Juan.
Good-bye to all that.

Well, de judge had the last laugh. He slapped thirty
years on me like I was a common criminal, same as the
other guys. He had to know I was light stuff compared to
them thugs. He figured I was trying to break his chops—
maybe I just knew I was sinking and wanted to go down
smokin'. I don't know, half the things I do I don't know
why I do them. Figurin' things out is a pain in the ass. I
just act most of the time.

LEWISBURG IS A HOTEL COMPARED TO ATLANTA SO I HOPE *I get sent to Lewisburg. Hope they don't send Amadeo there. He'll have me whacked out for sure. But then again I might get lucky. There's this Peruvian guy down there who got a big connection. But then again I ain't ever liked the coke business. That means South America and I ain't ever liked dealin' with them people. There ain't no gangsters down there. You got to deal with businessmen, diplomats, squares like that. You know they ain't gonna stand up. And anyway, there ain't ever been no real money in the candy trade.*

Maybe the horse is dead. Like Earl used to say, the feds has killed the golden horse, and all the riders gonna get splattered. Bullshit. Had me a hell of a time. We had a twenty-year run, figure—better'n Prohibition. Maybe the party's over and the junk scene played out. Maybe.

Best racket ever was. Nobody rode it better'n me. Can't make no racehorse out of a jackass, well I'm the versa vice—I'm a Derby winner, irregardless they sprung me out of a garbage lot outa 113th Street. Right from the jump I said, "Carlito, you ain't stayin' here."

Right off the git-go everybody knew I was class. So like what, a cat with heart is gonna gig in some shoulder-pad factory? Scoffin' pimp steaks off a pushcart? Summerin' on the fire-escape? That's cool for some fools, but I was mad like a motherfucker in the 1940s. The Ricans was into nothin' in them days. Wasn't no Mobilization this or

*Poverty that. Wasn't nothin' but the landlord with his foot
on your neck. Wasn't no way a P.R. could get indoors to
rob like everybody else. Had to get his on the street where
the man could see him. And don't tell me that Horatio
Falger faggot shit. Don't wanna hear it. Wasn't born to
press my nose against no candy-store window—I'm comin'
through the fucking window. How you gonna be broke in
the U.S.A. with all them goodies out there? I seen them in
sneakers in the snow pushing racks in the garment center—
got to be crazy. Meanwhile, money is walking on a rug on
the sidewalk with the doorman holding an umbrella over
his head till he gets in the limousine. Hey, motherfucker,
slide your window down—lemme in on it, what's the secret?
Jiveass, grab hold with your hands, stuff it in your pockets.
Get the money—anyway you get it is okay. If you sick, it'll
make you well—can't be broke if you got it. That's what
goes on in this country. Climb up on a long pole, look
down on the U.S.A.—wadda you gonna see? You gonna see
the slick ones going after the chicklets and the jiveass will
be dumbfounderin' around. I seen that right away when I
was a kid in Spanish Harlem. And I went for the bullseye,
express train. Had to make a couple local stops. But that's
all right.*

*That's all this last bust is, a local stop. Battaglia's a
renegade, ain't he? So you know he got to renege on the
government. I can hear him from here. Where's my house,
where's my car? I ain't gettin' no protection. They'll fall
out and when Joe Bats gets mad enough he'll spin around
again and turn on them. Which'll mean a new trial for me,
y'dig?*

Shit, I'll be on the street in no time.

Glossary

abusador: a bully.
Agárra!: reach! draw your gun.
Aguarda: Hold on!

B and E: break and entry.
bacalao: codfish.
beater: a swindler.
blow away, blow up: shoot dead.
bollo-loco: a crazy broad.
boostin': shop-lifting.
buena gente: good people.
bulls: cops.
busted: arrested.
button: another word for made-guy. When a mob associate
is elevated to membership, he is referred to as a button, as
in "he's got a button." While on the fringe of membership,
he can be referred to as "half a button."

cabron: cuckold; a guy whose woman is cheating on
him.
caer pesao: to lay heavy, to be a drag.
camarónes: police; camarón is the Spanish word for
shrimp.
candy: cocaine.
cap: bullet.
chiba: stool pigeon.
chibs: buttocks (f.).

click: crew or gang, clique.
coglioni: balls (Italian).
cojones: balls (Spanish).
como los huevos del perro: like the balls on a dog.
connected: part of a gang, protected.
coño: sex organs (f.); also, often used as exclamation.
contract: (1) murder assignment; (2) a case in court which is "fixed."
cornuto: cuckold (Italian).
cowboy: (v.) to shoot or kill spontaneously, without proper planning. (n.) a reckless guy having no discipline.
Cubiche: Cuban.

delincuente: a hoodlum.
doing a deuce: doing two years in prison.
down cat: a good guy.
droguero: a drug-peddler.

echa pa'lante: to move forward, from expression *echar para adelante*, which means to go forward.
el que no la tiene del Congo, la tiene del Carabalí: if you're not from one African tribe, you're from another.
el echao pa'lante: the boldest, (lit. he who first goes forward).
embalao: like a bullet; from Spanish word *bala*, meaning bullet.
Espera!: Wait!

fenomeno: phenomenon.
figlio di puttana: son of a whore (Italian).
flake: to frame.

Gallego: native of Galicia, Spain.
garage: "he's from another garage"; he's from another world.
Guido: Gideon vs. Wainwright, 1963. United States Supreme Court decision requiring that defendants have legal counsel at all stages of criminal proceedings.
ginso: Italian.
git-go: the beginning.

give up: to squeal, to inform.
glom: to steal.
gorilla (verb):   to intimidate, bully, push around.
gui: boss (Italian).

Hatton, Rondo: a bit player in the movies, known for
     playing ugly brutes, e.g. "The Creeper" in Sherlock
     Holmes films.
heavy hitter: boss, person of authority, one who carries
     a lot of weight.
hermano: brother, blood brother.
hijo de puta: son of a whore.
hit: n. a kill; v. to kill.
hit the bricks: to come out of jail.
hodedor: hoodlum. Phonetic spelling of Spanish idiomatic
     expression, *jodedor*, an extension of the verb *joder*, which
     means to foul up or mess up.
hombría: manhood.

ice: (v) to kill.

jackpot: trouble.
jeva: girl.
jíbaro: Puerto Rican hillbilly, dude.
joint, a: marijuana cigarette.
Joint, the: jail.
jump stink: to fight.
juntos pero no revueltos: lit., together but not scrambled
     (as in eggs). This expression is used to denote a
     relationship of alliance or association without loss of
     individual identity or freedom of action.

key: kilogram (2.2 pounds).
kicks: shoes.

large: a thousand.
Later for (as in "Later for Snipe"):   He's dead; that's
     the end of him.
le comes el cerebro: (lit. you eat his brains) to outsmart,
     to outfox.

lee-gate: act as Peeping Tom. From Spanish slang expression *ligando*.

made-guy: initiated mafioso. After years of association with the mob or syndicate, a candidate will be sponsored for membership. He must be of Italian descent. The initiation rites include having "made his bones," which usually entails an assassination. Once his worth is established to the satisfaction of his sponsor and the presiding bosses, the candidate is "made." Thereafter, he is a "made-guy," with all the attendant privileges.

maldito sea la madre: a curse on your mother.

Mapp case: Mapp vs. Ohio, 1961. United States Supreme Court decision that required all state prosecutions to exclude illegally obtained evidence.

maricón: faggot, homosexual.

maton: killer.

me cago en tu madre: I shit on your mother.

Miranda: Miranda vs. Arizona, 1966. United States Supreme Court decision requiring that an arrested person be warned prior to any questioning that he has the right to remain silent, that anything he says can be used against him in a court of law, that he has the right to the presence of an attorney, and that if he cannot afford an attorney, one will be appointed for him prior to any questioning if he so desires.

mope: stupid person; mopery is stupidity.

moyete: a negro.

niche: a negro.

O.C.: organized crime.

P. and D.: premeditated and deliberated murder.

paint: narcotics (word *paint* used as verbal camouflage).

paredón: the wall used by the firing squad, as in Castro executions.

par'na: partner.

pero no hay mal que bien no traiga: There is no ill wind that does not bring some good.

pinch: arrest.

plátanos: plantains, a banana-like fruit grown in tropical zones.

popped: arrested.

pound: a five year jail sentence.

Puñeta: jerk-off.

Qué pasa?:   What's happening? What's going on?

rabbi: protector, guardian angel.

rubia: blonde girl.

sálvese él que pueda: save yourself if you can.

shoo-fly: police internal investigators, cops spying on corrupt cops.

short: a short is any automobile, from a Maserati to an old Chevy.

short-timing: serving a short jail sentence.

sidge: Sicilian.

smack: heroin; a/k/a. horse, skag, junk, shit, stuff.

snort: cocaine.

spike: hypodermic needle used to inject heroin.

spitter: hoodlum; a/k/a. wise-guy, knock-around guy.

spook: a negro.

stand-up guy: a man of integrity, one who would never inform on another.

stone killer: (1) cold-blooded assassin; (2) superlative, as in "That's a stone killer suit."

tecato: heroin addict; from Sp. slang word for heroin, *tecata*.

Tiger: a Puerto Rican newcomer to the U.S. Term originated from a ship, the *Marine Tiger*, which brought many Puerto Ricans to the U.S.

thou: a thousand.

todos los gatos son negros: all cats are black.

tremendos pollos: good looking girls; lit., tremendous chicks.

trim: slang word for female sex organs, as in "get me some trim," "some good trim."

tumbe: a swindle, a beat. Taken from Spanish verb, *tumbar*, to knock down.

two-eight (three-oh, three-four): 28th, 30th, and 34th Precincts in Manhattan.

un clavo saca a otro: one nail removes another.

uomo di onore: a man of honor (Italian).

upstate: prison.

Vamos andando: Let's go.

vamos a echar un pie: to flee (lit. to shake a foot).

verdugo: executioner.

wal-yo: Italian.

wash: to kill.

wise-guy: hoodlum.

yard: a hundred dollars; "go for a yard" means to cost a hundred dollars.

After
Hours

For TUTA

1

THE BURNT ALMOND FINISH OF THE LINCOLN CONTInental gleamed as the vehicle sped northward on the Henry Hudson Parkway. The four occupants rode in silence, impervious to the clear blue of the afternoon sky. The car veered gracefully along a ramp and headed west across the George Washington Bridge toward the rusted cliffs of the Jersey Palisades.

They sped south through Fort Lee along Palisades Avenue until they braked gently to a stop in front of a small house. Two small white concrete lions flanked the entranceway to the modest brick structure. One of the men in the back, dressed in a gray suit, slid from the backseat to stand motionless on the sidewalk. Behind the round, steel-rimmed glasses, his eyes constricted in the midday sun. A massively thick, younger man, wearing sunglasses, emerged from the car, shaking his arms and legs, rubbing his gloved hands, and swiveling his neck inside his tight-fitting leather jacket. His movements subsided and he leaned against the rear fender of the Lincoln, head bowed, as if examining an object on the sidewalk.

The man in the gray suit stood rooted, staring intently at the house. The front door opened. A short, white-haired man in a dark suit and tie stepped out and walked toward the waiting men. The motor of the car was started up as the old man reached the sidewalk.

"They sent you, huh, Zack?" he said quietly.

Zack shrugged, then bobbed his head, the sun glistening

off his metal-framed glasses. The old man's gaze turned from Zack to the two men still seated in the front seat of the car, then came to rest on the young man leaning against the fender, who promptly stood erect and stretched his gloves tautly across the knuckles. He would not meet the older man's glare. The old man's long jaw was clamped as he uttered, "Punk."

"Mr. Petrone, please," Zack said.

The old man pointed his finger at Zack, then swept a horizontal line the length of the car.

"*Sons of fifty-cent whores—all of you!*" Nicola Petrone shouted, his forehead glowing red under the white of his hairline.

Zack extended his arms outward, then folded them as he brought the tips of his fingers to rest on his chest.

"Meeng!" he said. "Wadda you want from me? Ya think I wanna be here? I got respect, Mr. Petrone. But I'm just a soldier. I got nothin' to say about these things—this was between you and Tony Tee. Bosses, remember? You came up tails. We gotta do what we gotta do, awright?"

"Maybe you gotta do it right here," Petrone said, his tone suddenly low and measured.

"Nicky, for chrissake, she's lookin' out the window," Zack cautioned.

Nicky Petrone turned to face his house. At a second-floor window a woman stood behind a frilled curtain. Petrone stepped quickly to the car.

"Let's go," he said.

METROPOLITAN CORRECTION CENTER (IN OTHER WORDS, the new federal can on Park Row, lower Manhattan) beat the hell outa their former rat joint, Federal House of Detention, on West Street. They got us in blue jumpsuits and Korean sneakers, like Chinese acrobats instead of convicts. And, I gotta admit, the MCC is a fancy building with a lot of electronic gadgets and gismos. The visiting room had these glass walls and thick carpets. It ain't Jilly's, but after doin' a pound in Atlanta and Lewisburg, you're grateful for small favors, babe. I was waitin' on my lawyer, David Kleinfeld, so I got off to the side of the room into a plastic chair and checked out the population.

There was inmates, lawyers, even a couple of wives or girlfriends, all bunched and hunched around tables with their big secret. I got my own troubles. Tiny window behind me. The Apple is out there, worms and warts don't matter, after five years I'll settle for a small slice.

I seen him right away. Guiseppe Castaldi. Joe Cass. Guy had aged twenty years in five. Musta done hard time. Unusual for a regular mob-guy. He was one of six Mafia ghees in my conspiracy trial in 1970. Meanwhile, I had never heard him speak. Know he had steaks on a hot plate and a silk robe in Atlanta. Know he would stand in the ghinny corner of the yard with his boss, Pete Amadeo, the two of them, fist-faced and polyps-throated, like they was Sicilian "dons" checkin' their olive groves outside of Palermo. They play this *capo* bit to the hilt, even in the joint. They was out there sellin' dope and stranglin' people with clothes hangers, but like—"'ey, respet. Keepa you distance." Amadeo, specially, was all heart. Let him hear that a "mom and pop" candy store on Thompson or Carmine Street put in a cigarette machine and *Che cosa!* *"Signora, cinque soldi,* on every pack, *per me,* capische?" He's a millionaire, he needs the money, right? But he figures, "That's how they start, a nickle here, a dime there. It's a crack in the glass, could spread out. Everybody in line, *subito.*" He was a janitor's dog with a bone in his mouth. Him and the wops really gave me a bad rap on that conspiracy pop. The stool pigeon was a made-guy belong to Petey A, meanwhile, me, the house Puerto Rican, who kept my mouth shut and took my weight like a man, for me, they had a pair of scissors to put through my chest. Maricónes. Judge Rossi gave me equal time with the "Don Cheeches," thirty years apiece. He parceled them out like they was samples.

Almost didn't make it in Atlanta. First time I was in the yard, Pete Amadeo aimed a finger at me.

"It was your people put me in here!"

My fault, imagine. Like the Italian priest said, "Fucka me? Fucka you!"

Atlanta was bad heat for me, no PRs hardly, only crackers, spooks, and wal-yo. Whack you out for a carton of smokes. M'man, Zusu, who done ten winters in the cold wing of Dannemora, finally got iced in Atlanta. In the teevee room, spike went right through the back of his chair. They carried him out like that, nailed to the chair. Me and Zusu had our differences (he was a lowlife), but to see the dude upholstered like that didn't do me no world o' good. In other words, hindmost was a dead mother fucker. So I said to myself, "Oh yeah? Get off early here, Carlito."

First one out was some country nigger sweepin' with a broom and gave me sass ("Move, turkey") while I was in my rack. I had this honed-down mop handle under my blanket. That jig was quick, I missed him turnin' the corner on the tier by inches. They never coulda zippered him up if I'd have caught him. Another time, in the shower, this greaseball (look like Carmen Basilio after the Robinson fight) come givin' me the "mal di occhio." I took a Gem blade from under my tongue and stuck it in a bar of soap. The chump started singin' Figaro.

On top of all my troubles the hacks wanted me to work. I'm in the joint 'cause I don't wanna work and I'm gonna work in the joint? Never fails. They're crazy. But as usual, they said I was crazy!

Dave Kleinfeld saved the day, he got me transferred to Lewisburg. Plenty rice-and-beans pistoleros here. With a li'l backup maybe I can do my stint. Only thirty years. Maybe piss on Petey A's grave too. Yeah, Dave's takin' care of business for me. At first I had him down as a Mickey Mouse lawyer. He's a "media-pinta" and funny lookin' but he's grown big the last few years. All the connected guys been usin' him. Quite naturally, he picked up a lotta points with my case. I mean, he can't be no slouch to reverse a thirty-year-sentence conviction, but I did a whole lotta the spadework for Kleinfeld. That's right. You know I got the motivation, one. And two, I got the time. Three, they got more lawbooks in Lewisburg than in the courthouse, and four, I been writin' to all the clerks in the court for information, and even to Judge Rossi (whether he likes it or not). In other words, Dave is gettin' credit on the street for work that I'm doin', plus the prestige of representin' a former heavy hitter, which I was. I got the newspaper clippin's to prove it.

But that's cool,'cause Dave is workin' mostly on the arm now, since at the present time I am in a financial state of insoluble. But that is only a temporary disturbance. Lemme get on the street. A fuckin' roto-rooter will I be. Dave and me, home free.

The last week in June, Kleinfeld was comin' to see me and I went up to the visitors' cage to wait on him.

Looks like the MCC is gonna be the jump-off for more than just me. Imagine, puttin' a hoodlum like Joe Cass in the street again, a regulation Mafia-ooney!

Joe was there talkin' to one of the lawyers from our trial, forgot his name. They was talkin' good news, that was plain. The lawyer got up and took the elevator down. Joe Cass got as far as the door of the visiting room, then he spun around and came straight toward me. He'd clocked me early.

"Mind if I sit down?" he said. Had one of them hardwater voices. They all got them. Comes with the button.

"Your dime."

"Brigante. Charles Brigante. Rocco always called you Carlito."

"Yeah, that's me."

"Remember me?"

"The face, not the voice. You never said a word through the whole trial."

I didn't mention his name. They like that. He sat down. We lit cigarettes.

"You look good, kid," he said.

I'm forty-five years old. I let it slide. I wanted to hear what he had to say. Him and Pete Amadeo were cousins, Sicilians, from Catania. Rocco used to say, to a Roman or a Milanese, they weren't Italians, they were Africans. As a matter of fact, Joe Cass, with his short height, small, dark features and kinky hair, looked like a lot of PRs I know. That would go over big with him. Ha.

"You never hurt nobody, Brigante."

"That's what I tried to tell him five years ago at West Street."

"Pete's dead."

Now we can use his name. See, protocol.

"May he rest in peace," I said, makin' the sign of the cross.

Mother fucker should be condemned to walk through hell wearin' gasoline drawers, forever.

"Passed away, two weeks ago, the strain of the appeal was too much."

"He was a very excitable guy."

"The man had a lotta responsibility, Brigante. You're only on the street, you don't know what it's like for guys like him. Lotta, lotta headaches . . . . God rest his soul in heaven."

I thought we was gonna do the rosary beads for that rat bastard. But I just shrugged and looked up at the ceilin' to see if I could make Pete out on his way to heaven.

"Brigante. Where'd you get that name? Goombah?"

"Nah. Strictly PR. But the name is Corsican. Lot of them settled in Puerto Rico."

"How do you like that. We had some Corsicans down in Atlanta. *Molto forte*. Stand-up guys. Like you, Brigante."

"Thanks."

Who don't like to be stroked? We were comin' to the end of the riddle.

"Pete gave you a hard time. No question about it."

"Well, he had a lotta responsibility."

"Right. But that's in the past. We're gonna hit the street, so we gotta take care of new business, right, Brigante?"

"Right."

"Awright. I'm puttin' a few things together. Some people from Atlanta, down in Colombia now. Corsicans, but they speak Spanish. You can fit in down there. Help us, help yourself. You got some bad breaks, you stood up, I wanna give you a shot. Pete's gone. What the fuck, I ain't prejudiced."

"Thanks loads."

Bullshit. First time they bagged me was their fault. Next time be my fault. Ain't gonna be no next time.

"We're takin' it all back. The niggers spoiled the whole thing. Chick, Nicky, Tony Tee, everybody's givin' the okay. We're in again."

"Sounds good."

Bullshit. Colombia means coke. Never liked the candy trade. No new tricks, I'm an old dog.

"I'm with Chick Mason. The bar on Prince Street—ask for Dom the waiter, blond kid."

"He's the waiter in the joint?"

"Naw. Just ask for Dom the waiter. Period."

"Gotcha."

"Or Messina's. Y'know, Bath Beach. Where they had the roundtable on you, ha. Remember?"

"Treasure it always."

"So you had some bad breaks. That's in the past. Now you're gonna make some money, huh, Brigante?"

Oo-gotz.

"Beautiful, who do I ask for?"

"Ask for Zip."

"Zip?"

"Yeah, just Zip."

"Oh. Okay."

"If worst comes to worst, go up to 116th Street and Pleasant Avenue. Ask one of the kids for Minghee."

"Minghee. Right."

"What's my name?"

"Eh . . . Joe?"

"You got a good memory, Brigante. Joe, that's my name. We'll be in touch. By the way, this lawyer of yours has worked a few miracles. We're all ridin' out of here on his back. My lawyer, Jacobs, tries to snow me, but I know it was Kleinfeld broke that wiretap."

"I spotted Dave Kleinfeld in the sixties when he had a storefront in Harlem. I told the boys he was goin' all the way."

"Yeah, huh? That's why you used Steinhardt on your homicide case and fired Kleinfeld durin' our trial?"

Bail bondsman eyes he had, I gotta admit, in the mob they know. What the CIA don't know, the Ma-fee-aye-a long forgot. They keep tabs on you, even when I was a crazy kid in east Harlem, they kept score on everybody. This guy use, this guy deep-six, like that.

"Nobody's perfect," I said.

Joe Cass got up.

"He's here. See ya," he said.

Dave Kleinfeld stepped out of the elevator behind the glass partition and was talkin' to the guard in the waiting area. He was very natty, all decked out in blue. That's the color he favored since he come into the money. No more bushy mop, now look like he conked it, perma-press, like a Jewish Cab Calloway. Guy had changed his act total. Can't fault him, he's gettin' the big clients, the big fees (includin' some I referred to him). See-saw, he went up, I went down. Wasn't always that way. In the 1960s I was knockin' 'em dead. Bug bucks, big broads, big cars. Uptown, downtown, Carlito Brigante was heavy duty. I'd total a Caddie against a highway pillar on 96th Street in the morning and be drivin' a new Lincoln around 111th Street by evening. Party at my house? You'd have five hundred dollars worth of candy in your snotlocker before you sat down. Trim? Man, them broads was fallin' all over me. Ask anybody who the main stud out there was. Dave Kleinfeld, meanwhile, was on the balls of his bearin's. Had a storefront law office near 112th Street and Fifth Avenue. He was teamed up with a shyster name of Woodrow Wilson Cohen who used to cop drawers off Fifth Avenue whores for his fee, right on top of his desk (after he'd gone through their pocketbook). Dave was down from Yale in them days, wanted to be a criminal lawyer, so he set up shop where the criminals was at. He wasn't there a hot month when I had to bail him out. Outa the fire hydrant. He came up 111th Street in his jalopy with the windows down and stuck. "Boys" had the pump on. "Go ahead, Counselor, we'll keep the water down till you pass." Splash, like to drown Dave in his car. Ballsy li'l fucker. He came out with a piece of pipe in his hand to do battle. Boys had him halfway down a manhole when I intervened to prevent his bloodshed. We got tight socially, after. He liked to party, blow coke, but that's as far as it went. When it came down to business, I was not goin' downtown with no storefront hustler. I was into Steinhardt and Friedman for the heavy cases. Me and my people wanted the downtown lawyers that them big ghinny boys used. Big office, plush carpets. What the hell did I know? I thought my ass weighed a ton. I was a junior button guy. Yeah, out of a Cracker Jack box. Dog days came down, thirty years' worth. And worse than jail, broke. Me, who always pays my way (plus a lotta other people's), hat in hand, "Dave, gimme a break, save me," and so on. The humiliation a man gotta go through in the joint. They downslope you on the edge of a cliff, the skids are greased, and everybody's goin' in the opposite direction. Not a hand in sight. "Carlito who? Who he?" My buddies . . . Be nice goin' up, they say, 'cause sure as shit gonna meet 'em goin' down. Amen.

Kleinfeld walked into the visiting room, leaned against the glass door and stared at me, heavy-pussed. Oh shit. Then he locked his raised fist and gimme a big smile. Goin' home, bubbie, beat them thirty years! I jumped up to grab him.

"My man, Dave."

"Get your suit ready. We go before Judge Rossi tomorrow. They're not re-presenting the case. The government threw in the towel. Battaglia's disappeared, the tapes are suppressed." He grinned. "You're going to walk, Carlito. How does it feel?"

How does it feel? Like Ronald Colman fallin' through the Hollywood snow into Shangri-La. Or Victor McLaglen stumblin' into the Garden of Allah after five years in the desert (no water). That's how. Could be a pile of burned bricks on Morris Avenue. Could be a pigeon coop on a Harlem rooftop. It's the street, babe. The sun will come out, tomorrow.

So that's how come I ended up in Foley Square before the same judge who banged me thirty years (shy by twenty-five). You'd think I was gettin' away with murder the way he carried on. Like it was personal between me and him. Finally he asked me if I had learned anything. I musta been a lawyer in the other life, because I can't resist puttin' down a spiel in the courthouse. I gave Judge Rossi both barrels (with all due respect, of course).

"Your honor, with all due respect, past and present, and without further to-do, let me insure this court that I am through walking on the wild side. I been sick with the social ills known in the ghetto. But my time in Atlanta and Lewisburg has not been in vain. I been cured. I been born again, like the Watergaters. And not in thirty years, like your honor said, but in five years. Like I had cancer, but I took a heavy dose of penicillin in the form of the Jaycees, and the educational courses, and the chaplain, and lest I forget, mighty god, without which no case gets tossed.

"I know your honor didn't want to nol-pros this case no-how. Now with the witness recantin', not with the illegal tapes, not with the bad sealing, not with nothin'. Not even with the U.S. Attorney sayin' he couldn't try the case again. And I had Brown versus Illinois, and I had Robeerio and the One Lung rule goin' for me—with all the fruit from the poisonous trees and all like that—like my lawyer, Dave Kleinfeld right here, been telling you for years. And I want to thank the Second Circuit for reversing you—"

"Your honor." Kleinfeld cut me off here. "Please excuse my client. Mr. Brigante is understandably excited at being vindicated."

The judge got blue in the face. "There has been no vindication here, or absolution, or benediction, or anything else here, Counselor. Just an incredible convergence of circumstances, which you have exploited on behalf of your client. Appellate bodies do not see and hear witnesses. But it is intemperate of me to comment on the decision of the Second Circuit. I have abided by it. It now devolves upon me the painful duty of unleashing upon society this convicted assassin and purveyor of narcotics, Charles Brigante—" Judge Rossi said.

"Not convicted on no dope," I cut in.

"Shut up, Carlito," Kleinfeld said. "Once again, your honor, thank you for your patience and forbearance—"

"Call the next case."

Quittin' time.

2

DAVID KLEINFELD'S OFFICE WINDOWS OVERLOOKED THE southwest corner of Central Park. The desk, mounted on a platform to secure the high ground for the attorney, was the width of the window. The early afternoon sun glinted off Kleinfeld's heavily lacquered hair into the eyes of the two black men seated in front of him.

"You brought my retainer, Tyrone?" Kleinfeld gently queried.

Tyrone James reached out his hand. His companion pressed into it a tightly rubber-banded packet of bills. James placed it on the desk. Kleinfeld snapped the bands off and quickly sorted the cash into seven rows of one-hundred-dollar bills, stacked ten high.

"There are only seven here, Mr. James," Kleinfeld announced, his eyes focused somewhere above Tyrone James's head.

"This is jus' to git off, Mr. Kleinfeld."

"I told you ten."

"Yeah, but I'm a li'l up tight right now, y'understand, Mr. Kleinfeld."

Kleinfeld quickly reassembled the bills into one packet, rewound the rubber bands around it, and slid the money across the desk to James.

"I said ten."

Their eyes met and held. James broke it off with a smile, extending his arm toward his companion.

"Bunny," he said.

167

Bunny placed a second, smaller bundle in James's hand, who tossed it on the desk. James stood up, yawned as he arched his back. Bunny also rose from his chair. He was six feet, four inches.

"Money don't mean nothin' these days," he said.

There was a short burst of laughter from Kleinfeld and James as they shook hands.

"Ten A.M., Part A," Kleinfeld said.

"I'm worried about this one, Counselor. I'll be there," James said, turning to leave. A buzzer sounded. Kleinfeld spoke into the intercom.

"Diane, I told you I was accepting no calls—oh, Mr. Brown, put him on."

Kleinfeld exclaimed a long "what?" that wrinkled his face and bared his teeth. James led Bunny out of the office into the hallway. The two men regarded each other as they rode the elevator down.

"Whatcha think, Buns?"

"That Jew-boy's packed tight," Bunny said, clenching his fist, "he got his troubles."

"Y'see. Now you got me worried about my money. Shit, who ain't got troubles? He's the guy suppose to pull all the rabbits out, all the big people usin' him. I seen him in Stubby's trial. The dude got it all in his head."

Back in his office Kleinfeld had his head in a washbasin. He tasted an acidy saliva. His throat burned as he spat repeatedly into the sink. Eyes tearing, he stared at the water rushing down the drain from the open faucets. He splashed cold water on his face, then he straightened up, facing a mirror.

I can see it already in your face, Dave—you're dead. Look at your face.

Kleinfeld took a paper towel and slowly dried his face and hands.

Nicky Petrone. So quick he's dead. Hard to believe. They killed him like he was a nobody.

With quivering hands Kleinfeld tightened the knot of his tie and patted his hair.

Now they'll come for me. For me!

Kleinfeld stepped out of the bathroom and strode rapidly

to his desk. He depressed the switch and spoke into the intercom.

"Diane, bring me the folder on Charles Brigante—yeah, the crazy one, Carlito."

SO HERE'S ME BACK ON THE STREET. WITH THE GRASS EATERS, punks, and stool pigeons. That's all that's left out here. Man might as well be in the joint for all that's out here. No money either. Gone city. Goddamn Alderman and Herlickman fucked this country up! Where did the money go? A man cannot take care of business. Only junk comin' in is with the chinks and niggers, behind them spook Air Force sergeants from Nam. And the coke is with them "cholos" from Colombia and Argentina. So the Ricans ain't got shit. I mean what's left,'cause my crew is all been wasted or doin' time. Fuckin' wasteland out here. Fuckin' Republicans.

I was hurtin' for bread. Bad. Couple of guys gave me a few parties, trying to trade off my old rep. Ham sandwich. Didn't even collect ten thou. Some kid brought me a wardrobe. Another Bronx guy got me a car. Big deal. I cold-eyed all these mother fuckers. Buncha punks. They made some Mickey Mouse bucks while I was doing time, now they suppose to be somebody. They're scared of me, though nobody knows what I'm gonna do. Not even me.

Maybe open up an after-hours in Harlem. But bringing in all the Bronx and Brooklyn crowd. Nobody knows I'm broke. They'll come 'round. Once I got them under a roof, I'll rope them all in.

Me, like a chump, right away I'm doin' favors. This guy, Guajiro, asked me to ride shotgun on a coke deal on 100th Street, West Side. As a rule I don't trust Cubans, but Guajiro grew up with the Barrio crowd, one of the boys, so I went along with him. Light backup. Just a favor. We pulled east on Broadway into the block. Skank street. Backroom of a barber shop, color it dingy, like the greasy, nappy-headed Dominicans around the miniature pool table. There was four of them. Right away I checked out windows with bars, a bathroom door, and one bulb overhead. Didn't go for it nohow. Shows to go you, when a man of "tabla" like Guajiro got to score behind a scene like this. Them's the conditions we face in these hard times.

"Hola, Quisqueya," says Guajiro.

Big, gap-toothed smile of surprise, like we wasn't clocked before we came in the door, comes up from the pool table.

"Guajiro, mi hermano," Quisqueya says loud, with both arms extended. They embraced like they just come back from a war. Mi parna, mi hermano, mi socio, etc. Meanwhile the other three guys never took their eyes off the table. So.

When I get a message like that, my aerial goes up. Could hear the chalk dust landin' on the floor. A .357 Dan Wesson Magnum in an elastic band around my crotch said, Ready, Jack.

"Tienes el dinero, hermanito?" asks Quisqueya, his hands holdin' Guajiro's shoulders.

"Tienes el material?" is Guajiro's answer.

"Como no, hermanito," says Quisqueya, his head back laughin' but his hands still on Guajiro.

I'm hawkin' the three guys at the pool table, but all I see is cue sticks. Never no mind, I'm stayin' with Dan Wesson, nickel-plated.

"Como no, hermanito," says Guajiro as he grabs Quisqueya's wrists.

That's what saved me. When Guajiro's hands went up, I turned right. The shooter bust out the bathroom door and shot Guajiro in the neck, behind the ear. Guajiro spun around draggin' Quisqueya with him. They got between me and the shooter, who kept shootin'. That's all I needed. I threw myself backwards and pulled my piece out. I fired at the pool table to my left first. I musta blown it up 'cause splinters was flyin'. Somebody screamed for his mother. I'm rollin' all over the floor. The shooter, a little fucker, got clear of Guajiro and Quisqueya. I think he'd gone through his five shots (he had a snub nose) because he just stood there. I blew his chest out with two or three quick shots, then still firin', I scrambled over him into the bathroom. My back burned as I crawled into a stall. They kept shootin', but there was no light in the john and they wasn't about to charge into the dark.

"Maricónes! I'm all reloaded. Come on in," I shouted.

Zilch I had reloaded. I was out of bullets. Everything got quiet. Could hear a rat piss on cotton. I'm stretched out on piss and cold tiles.

I yelled again. "Mother fuckers, get ready. We all gonna die here,'cause I'm comin' out. Se va' joder to'el mundo!"

Bang. They blew the light out, then a stampede of feet makin' for the outside door. All clear. I felt a sting across my back like I'd been whipped. The bulls will be here, make your move. I crawled out on all fours. Wait awhile. Guajiro brought a bundle with him. Ain't gonna do him no good. Lit a match. Inner suit pocket. Okay. Let's go. Seventeen big ones. This is typical. Guajiro goes down to close a deal—wham, he gets offed. Ain't no more racketeers, just a bunch of muggers rippin' each other off. I don't need this. The street is too hot (está que chilla!). Time to get off, Carlito, while you still upright.

3

Brigante was awed by the splendor of Kleinfeld's large office. In fact, it was a melange of Spanish furniture, Revolutionary War metalwork, and assorted nautical apparatus. A ship's sextant, compass, and steering wheel; charts, nets, even a stuffed marlin. A glass case contained a display of conches, star and shellfish. On the walls several paintings were hung. They depicted ships, boats, seascapes. A guy could get seasick here, Carlos Brigante thought. The cluster of shiny metal and burnished leather glimmered in the late afternoon sun. Brigante studied an immense globe fully three feet in diameter, which turned on what appeared to be golden hinges mounted on a solid mahogany and leather base.

"Each red pin represents my associate in that city. London, Paris, Rome, Geneva. I'm going international," Kleinfeld said to Brigante.

Brigante settled into a low-slung chair.

"Got a guy that polishes your leather?"

"Got a guy for everything," Kleinfeld answered. "What do you have on?—it's gorgeous."

"A li'l Piatelli, a li'l Giorgio Armani, things is so bad, so 'mala hora, buena cara.' "

"Bad times, good front, right?"

"Very good, Dave. You haven't forgotten."

"I practice with Diane, my secretary, she's Puerto Rican, you know."

"I get heat flushes when I look at her, gimme a break, I

172

been in the joint almost five years. Hey, I ain't out of line.
I mean you and her ain't—"

"No, Carlito, she's married."

"He's doin' time."

Kleinfeld smiled.

"All checked out, eh?"

"Dave, Dave, what is not known in the joint, cannot be
known."

"Whatever that means."

"I mean the best brains are in the joint. We have Hoffa
down there, and Bobby Baker. Big people. You find out
everything."

"That's why they're in the joint, because they're so
smart?"

"No, no, they wise up in the joint. I mean—you take
Alderman or Herlickman, down in Allenwood or wherever.
When they come out, y' hear, they will be ready to run the
country."

Kleinfeld stood up behind the desk, nodding his head
to Brigante's words, anticipating a change of subject matter. To no avail. Brigante accentuated with his forefinger,
undeterred.

"I tell you, if those guys had done their time before
Watergate, there wouldn't be no Watergate, because they
would have told Nixon, 'Are you crazy, you burn those
tapes or all our asses will burn slowly in the wind.' "

"Saw it all on television, eh? 'Time frames' and all."

"Was the biggest thing in Lewisburg. When a guy like
me is locked up, his brain grows. Read this guy from the
Gulag, I can't pronounce his name—"

"Solzhenitsyn."

"That's the guy. Guy did a dime—in the labor camps,
froze his ass. But he was thinkin', schemin', all the little
parts, all the little cells were growing. So now he's sprung,
but he brung his brain with him and he's gonna bring down
that whole country. Unless the KBG puts a hit on him."

"KGB," Kleinfeld corrected, adding, "I didn't realize that
you were a political prisoner. Here I thought you were a
common criminal."

"I'm serious. I'm heavy into all that shit."

"It's clear you've become a man of scholarship."

"I am a changed guy. Never thought it would happen to me. Ready for the pasture, but still horny. Diane Vargas. Just her name gives me a hard-on."

"How's your back, Carlito?"

Brigante paused, then smiled as he rubbed his back.

"Your set got a big antenna, huh?"

Kleinfeld laughed.

"What did you hear?"

"That you were lucky, as usual. One dead on your side and one dead and one wounded on theirs. I also heard you scooped up all the chips on the table."

"For instance."

"Like fifty large."

"Mother-fuckin' liars. Guajiro had five thousand on him. Anything you hear from the street divide it by ten."

"I thought you said it was the great teacher."

"Lotta bullshit too."

"Got a job for you."

"Where?"

"Right here, in my office."

"Doing what?"

"General office work, eh, take messages, you know."

"You mean bodyguard."

"Well, kind of."

"I didn't do too good by Guajiro."

"In the totality of the circumstances, you performed admirably."

"You know, I always wanted to be a lawyer."

"Now is your chance. I'll give you five hundred a week, off the books. I know you snort more than that in one week but—"

"It's not the bread—"

"You owe me, Carlito," Kleinfeld said, raising his voice.

"I owe you for the appeal, and you will get paid."

Kleinfeld sat down. "I'm in trouble," he said, his voice dropping.

"I'm going partners in an after-hours joint over in the seventies. I won't have time—"

"Do you even want to know?"

"I heard a few things in the joint."

"What did you hear?"

"I heard you beat a few guys, I heard you gave some guarantees and didn't deliver, things like that."

Kleinfeld stood up, his face reddening.

"Things like that. Goddamned liars. I never gave you a guarantee, but I delivered for you, Carlito Brigante," he shouted.

"Hey, don't get your balls in an uproar. You done square business with me, I'm with you."

"You'll help me?"

"I'll help you," Brigante said as Kleinfeld settled back in his chair, his exasperation ebbing.

"I know them?" Brigante asked.

"No."

"Spooks?"

"No."

"Wops?"

Kleinfeld nodded his head.

"Connected high?"

Kleinfeld motioned again. Brigante whistled a low tune as neither spoke for close to a minute.

"You want to tell me about it now . . . hey?"

"Just watch any white guys that come in here for a while, until I straighten things out."

"What do you think, they can't send you a spade or a Latino?"

"Watch everybody, everybody," Kleinfeld said, his voice rising in pitch.

"Awright awready, take it easy. Jesus."

"Stick with me a couple of weeks. It'll all be straightened out. Maybe we can cancel the fee you owe me."

"You will be paid, Counselor. No favors, a favor can kill you faster than a bullet. Please. I gotta go. I'll send Pachanga around to take you home."

"Pachanga? That's the guy who was around for your hearings. He's shorter than I am, and he doesn't even speak English."

"That's my backup man. He'll go all the way with you, believe me."

"Well, if you say so."

"Call you at home later."

THE JOINT WAS CALLED THE LATIN REFORM AND PROGRESS Social Club on West 79th Street. It was a brownstone— with a regular casino upstairs and like a nightclub on the second floor. Never no last call. They kick off when the regular joints close. I trillied on in 'bout three A.M. Lookin' clean. Monday night, I figure I'd catch the business on a slow night. When you're buyin', you want to see them on the down side. But there was a whole lot of people. Maybe Saso, slick, puffed up a crowd for me. Square-shaped bar with two pair o' low-cut pretty titties behind it. The bottles was in racks overhead and everytime one of them reaches up, I'm looking for a boob to slip out under an armpit. One was Latin, Clorox dye job, more chicken than chick. The other head looked like a short Pam Grier, yaller gal, New York sirloin. There was a whole lot of spinnin' lights, glass and metal fake walls, pink smoke—a regular flyin' saucer with a sound system to blow you away. People sittin' on pillows, cushions, and chairs around tables. Big crowd on the floor lined up in rows. They was goin' up and down, sideways, round and round, nobody touchin'. Boogeyin'. Never fails, no sooner I get over on some new dance, I go in the slams, when I come out they're doin' a different one. But there was plenty of money on top of the bar, plenty broads, things was hummin'. Ol' Saso had hisself activity in the bullpen. But I knew whatever he won down there, he's lose upstairs. Saso was a card freak. Action bring reaction, true of any man. So he needed money. Ha. Everybody knew I had a big stash left over from my big dope days. Ha. I was broke like a mother fucker.

Here come big Saso, ol' 105th Street boy, now a "community" dude in the Bronx. He was into every "poverty" scam up there. I sure missed the boat on them rackets.

"Charles, Charles Brigante—"

He gimme that Charles business from when we went to Patrick Henry Junior High.

"Howya doin', Saso?"

Saso wrapped me in a hug.

"Charles, you're a sight for sore eyes. Thank God you're safe."

This is the way he always talked. Right in the middle of all the shit and Harlem. I always thought he was talkin' on the radio. See here, you guys. Big two-hundred-pounder, glasses, tie, tropical suit rumpled up like Pat O'Brien in one of them Panama Canal movies. Degenerate schemer, scammer, and gambler.

"Everybody calls me Ron, Charles, you know, from Reinaldo."

I nodded. I could see him at the "Board" meeting, Ron Reinaldo, a voice from the community, who will pull no punches. Jive-ass poverty pimp.

"So whatcha got for me, Saso?"

"Stephanie! Rorita! Anything this gentleman wants—on the house."

The barmaids checked me out heavy. I'm sipping Château-neuf-du-Pape. I'm wearing a wide-open off-yellow silk shirt, an Ultrasuede Halston jacket, with matching suede loafers. I'm lookin' like money, but the best kind, casual, loosey-goosey. Next best thing to havin' it.

I got Saso salivatin' like a Russian dog, he must be up to his asshole in markers. Probably over a hundred large.

Saso gimme the ol' "sincere" eyes.

"Charles, this place needs your experienced hand around here."

Rolls them *r*'s around so much that when he finish a sentence, his lips are still sticking out. Yar, yar. I hate that because when I'm around people, I start talkin' like them. Can't help it.

"I remember your old Bonnie-and-Clyde watering hole—"

"Saso, let's not be bringin' up spilled milk."

"Of course, Charles. Everybody calls me Ron now. Eh— dammit to hell, let's talk turkey."

"How much you in?"

"Fifty or sixty—"

"That means over a hundred. You don't change, Saso. Who to? Wops?"

"Twenty-five will quiet them for now. You will come in for a quarter share."

"Pachanga will bring you twenty cash tomorrow. We'll be full partners."

"What are you doing to me?"

"What am I doin'? I'm savin' your life, Saso. It's either Fat Anthony or Scooze, right? Either way you'll be in the trunk of a car on the Belt Parkway. Maybe weeks before they find you, like DeeDee, right?"

"What time tomorrow?"

"About this time. Shake, partner."

About this time the li'l black freak that was behind the bar looped around and come alongside Saso.

"Ah gotta leave, Ronnie," she said.

"What are you talking about, Steffie, you just started to work. The bar's jammed, are you crazy?"

"It's Alonzo. He's high and he's on his way up here. Ah don' want no trouble. He will hurt me. Don' care where it is."

Saso got all out of shape.

"You see what I have to put up with?"

"Qué pasa, Saso?"

"Alonzo used to be Stephanie's boyfriend—"

"In other words, she chased him, but he don't go for it. What is he, square or knockaround, miss?"

In other words, she was a fox with big jugs. Therefore, I don't mind my business. She's lookin' me up and down, so Saso says, "It's all right, Steffie, Carlito's my new partner."

"Alonzo's a bad nigger pimp. He wants me trickin' on Eighth Avenue next to that snow bitch o' his—"

"You too fine be doin' that," I cut in.

"Damn straight. Fine as I am, I'm lookin' for somebody lookin' out for me."

She said this laughin' and spinnin' full around, hands on hips, showin' them fine chibs. Shit, I'll kill that Negro.

Wasn't but ten minutes, ol' Alonzo come tire squealin' in front of the club. Me and the two bouncers was checkin' him from inside the door downstairs. Big player's Cadillac, Michigan license plate, and here he come, skinny six-feet-three spook, dressed like José Greco, with sequins all over, specially on his platform shoes. Heah, heah! I could hear his mind:

Nigger-bitch be playin' with me. Ah'm go do her up one time. She gonna know who the man is. Bitch must be crazy.

I'm behind the door. He come in all bad. I pressed Dan against his cheek, pushin' the long barrel 'til his mouth was wide open, then I cocked the big flat hammer back. His eyes got very white.

"Gimme your wallet," I told him. One of the bouncers pulled his wallet out. Popcorn pimp, he didn't have fifty dollars.

"Take the money and give him back his wallet."

The bouncers kept going through his pockets. They came up with a Derringer, double shot.

"Lift up his pants," I said.

He had a converted 007 knife in his sock.

"Okay, Alonzo from Detroit. The chick belongs to the club. If you ever, but if you ever come around here again, you die. Y'hear, mother fucker?"

He was on tiptoes now, the Magnum was lifting him. One of the bouncers said, "Let's fuck him up, put him in the trunk, and drive him off the pier. Ain't far."

Alonzo didn't go for this.

"Don't do that, man, don't do that," he said. Very quiet m'man was talkin'. It was plain the coke in his head was all played out. He didn't want nobody gettin' excited. We ran a game on him awhile and then we let him go.

I was surprised at myself. Any other time, that pimp would have bled. Gettin' old, that's what. Hesitatin' and delayin' and second-chancin'. No good. The street is watchin'. Kindness is always taken for weakness. Uh-oh, the joint got to Carlito, he's flaky, slacked out, a used-to-be bad. Now you blew position, now to get back to the rail you overact to the first guy round the curve, you kill him and blow your cool altogether. The street don't wait on nobody. She is a jealous mother. One slip and she will claim you. P.S.—didn't get to Steffie's drawers either, she was making it with one

of the waiters, Rudy. She was a real satin doll out of
Jock's and Wells's, uptown Harlem. Kinda broad get
you killed, wouldn't bother her none. Rudy had his work
cut out.

4

DAVID KLEINFELD ROLLED HIS MERCEDES-BENZ SLOWLY down the basement of Ben's Garage on Worth Street, pulling into a stall near the garage office. He came out of the vehicle carrying a suede attaché case and two square-cut pieces of cardboard. The cardboard pieces he hung on the door handles.

"We do all the parking here, Dave. We ain't gonna bang your doors," the attendant chided.

"Yeah, I know," Kleinfeld said as he hurried up the ramp to the sidewalk. He walked west to Centre Street and entered the New York State Building. A custom-made navy blue suit hung snugly on his slight frame. A powder blue spread-collar shirt and solid-colored dark tie completed the ensemble. He owned a dozen of each. No business day ever found him in a different outfit.

He stepped out of the elevator on the fifth floor; his elevator-heeled Chelsea Cobbler shoes clacked loudly down a long corridor leading to a complex of offices. The sign on the receptionist's window read, District Attorney, Special Narcotics Court. The woman slid open a glass panel.

"Attorney Kleinfeld. I have an appointment with the district attorney," he said.

"Mr. Haynes is expecting you," she responded.

She pressed a buzzer and the door was opened by a burly, dark-haired man in sports clothes.

"I'm Detective Frank Rizzo, Counselor. The boss is waiting."

There was a wary exchange of glances between the two men before Kleinfeld followed Rizzo to the private office of Mitchell Haynes, District Attorney, Special Narcotics Court for the City of New York.

The Spartan austerity of the room proclaimed the agency's rank in the prosecutorial scale of succession. Bottom rung. Its budgetary survival clung by a cuticle. All the funds were two buildings south, at the United States Attorney's office.

Haynes, a large black man, ex-police officer, rose from his desk, his hand extended. They shook hands.

"Mitch Haynes. I think we've met, Mr. Kleinfeld. This is my chief assistant, Bill Rutledge. Detectives Frank Rizzo and Leo Donnelly I believe you know."

Kleinfeld strode past the detectives to shake hands with Rutledge. This placed him alongside Haynes's desk. Haynes motioned Kleinfeld to a seat. Kleinfeld regarded Haynes for a second, then gestured with his head at the two detectives behind him.

Haynes said, "You two guys go check out that file we were talking about. I'll see you later. Thanks for the coffee."

The detectives left, closing the door behind them. Rutledge opened the coffee containers and the three men sipped in silence. Rutledge sallied forth.

"You're going to turn Black Bart around for us, Mr. Kleinfeld?"

"I think I can persuade him that he has no other alternative."

"The last time you had a client that turned informant, you withdrew from the case and made a big hullabaloo that jeopardized our case. You came dangerously close to obstruction—"

"Mr. Rutledge, every case is unique. In this instance I am convinced that the best interests of my client, Bart Saunders, lie in cooperation." Kleinfeld leaned forward, his dark eyes shifting to Haynes as he added, "Of course, I expected the utmost secrecy from your office, Mr. Haynes."

"Of course," Haynes said, nodding vigorously.

"Of course," Rutledge said.

There was a lull as Haynes placed his container on the desk. Rutledge followed suit. Kleinfeld tilted his head back, draining his cup.

"Good coffee," said Kleinfeld.

They waited as Kleinfeld methodically replaced the container top and inserted it in a paper bag on the desk. He patted the corners of his mouth with a paper napkin as he scanned the room.

"It's a disgrace how this office has been relegated to second-class citizenship by the powers that be. Really," Kleinfeld said.

Rutledge raised his hand. "Mr. Kleinfeld, Mr. Haynes has another appointment, could we—?"

Haynes interrupted.

"Dammit, Bill, he's right. Let's face it, this is a shithouse. The feds have all the goddamn money. We should talk about it, let people know what's going on. All we can buy are nickle bags. No wonder 117th Street is wide open. It's not just the niggers that are dying now, so there's a big clamor. But what tools do they give us, I ask you, Bill, what tools do they give us?"

"None, Mitch, none," the redheaded Rutledge responded.

Kleinfeld, his brow furrowed with concern, nodded in serious assent. There was a pause as they contemplated Haynes, momentarily lost in his ruminations over the deplorable state of law enforcement.

"May I, Mitch?" Rutledge inquired.

"Go ahead," Haynes said, leaning back in his chair.

"Dave, can I call you Dave, I mean—?"

"Of course," Kleinfeld said.

"Bill, get the cigars, will you?" Haynes said. Rutledge brought down a box of cigars from the top file cabinet. All three men lit up and puffed amicably. Feet propped on his desk, Haynes said, "Swag. Czechoslovakian Cuban. Only way to put in a contract with me, a good cigar."

Kleinfeld laughed the loudest, but the air of bonhomie and cigar smoke was beginning to stifle him.

"Dave," Rutledge started again, "we're really not interested in Bart anymore. He's got his fifteen to life. Who can he give us? I mean, really? Couple of flyweights out of Jock's or Small's? He was just a middleweight himself. Black Bart is yesterday's news."

"I'm listening."

"I'll be frank, Mr. Haynes is looking for bigger fish—ghinnies—" Rutledge's eye caught the scowl of Haynes's face, "I mean, Italians, Mafioso."

"Quite frankly, I've been trying to get away from the organized-crime type of client. Primarily, at my father's behest. I'm doing a lot of *pro bono* work, representing minority causes, that sort of thing," Kleinfeld said.

"Josh Kleinfeld's your father, right?" Haynes asked. "Hell of a judge. One of the best we have in Criminal Court. Send him my regards."

"Thank you, Mr. Haynes. He's told me so many wonderful things about you, about the old days in the DA's office and—"

Rutledge interrupted Kleinfeld with a gesture and addressed Haynes. "Mitch, you have that meeting. We better finish up."

"Oh, yeah. Go ahead."

"Like I was saying," Rutledge continued, "we're interested in major distributors or people who can hook up to them."

"For instance?"

"Charles Brigante. Carlito."

"He's on the balls of his ass."

"He's been with the biggest."

"He's Puerto Rican."

"A Puerto Rican, Nelson Cantellops, shot down Vito Genovese for the feds, remember?" Rutledge pressed.

Kleinfeld turned toward Haynes.

"I came here to see you about Bart Saunders."

"Dave, we appreciate your coming here and being upfront with us, believe me. It's just that United States versus Brigante made the front page of the *Law Journal*. It's been cited everywhere. You wrote a remarkable brief."

"It took me years to get that reversal."

"Hell of a win nonetheless, two hundred kilos of heroin. Peter Amadeo, Coniglia, Joe Cass—"

"I only represented Brigante."

"He was in with all those biggies. We're very much interested in this individual." Haynes rose to his feet and lumbered around the desk to stand looming over the seated Kleinfeld. Like a stone edifice. Resting a ponderous hand on Kleinfeld's shoulder, he said, "Dave, help us and we'll help you."

"Who says I need any help?"

"You're here, aren't you, Kleinfeld?" Rutledge said.

Kleinfeld got up from his chair slowly.

"I don't want this man around if I ever come to see you again, Mr. Haynes," he said.

"Bill doesn't mean any harm, but we can talk under whatever circumstances you're most comfortable."

"I have to leave."

"I'll walk you down the hall. Stay here, Bill, you bug people."

Haynes's hand rested on Kleinfeld's shoulder as he escorted him down the hallway toward the elevator bank.

Haynes returned to his office to find a smiling, ebullient Rutledge perched on the desk.

"He'll be back."

"I know. I think he knows about old man Petrone and Nuncio."

"Of course. What do you think, he's got religion all of a sudden?"

"How much does he know? That's the question."

"Enough to scare him shitless. Probably knows more than we do. Any lawyer standing in the rotunda of the courthouse knows more than we do."

"Kleinfeld knows about the property clerk switch. He was Nicola Petrone's lawyer and Nicky Junior's too. He weaves in and out of the whole case. And he engineered the Nuncio murder."

"First Junior, now old man Petrone's disappeared. Tony Tee is in. Even the cops got burned. The case is jinxed. Kleinfeld's overdue. If we turn him around, he can open up a lot of coffins, Mitch."

"Let's not get overanxious. Kleinfeld is a fox."

"Yeah, the little fuck. Patent leather kid."

"Dixie Peach," Haynes said and the two of them joined in the laughter.

"Did he tell you anything about Brigante when you went out? He's got Carlito Brigante hanging around his office now. Bodyguard."

"Some deal Kleinfeld probably reneged on. Needs a shooter around. No, he didn't tell me anything about Brigante. Not yet." Haynes winced as he tasted the dregs of cold coffee in the Styrofoam cup.

"Carlito Brigante is an old pro. He could really make some cases for us."

"Bet your ass. He was a big action guy. One of the few PRs mobbed up with the Italians. You know that's not easy."

"He moved a ton of junk in the sixties," Haynes agreed.

"When Brigante was caught, he was sitting on two hundred kilos. Went in with Amadeo, Castaldi, and assorted super biggies. Carlito was connected. Is connected. You saw that report that Castaldi and Brigante got chummy at the MCC before they came out."

"Yeah, Joe Cass. Amadeo's dead, Tony Tee's dying in jail. So Joe Cass is the boss, by default."

"Wrong. By directive—of Cesare Massone."

"Chick Mason?" Rutledge glanced up.

"Yeah, he's the real don. Castaldi is just the street boss."

"They're like a fucking army, Mitch. We come and go. They stay."

"I know. Musical chairs. We put one in and another comes out. Gets discouraging. . . ."

Haynes sat in the chair behind the desk and puffed on his cigar.

"What I go through every year for the crumbs they give us." Haynes shook his head dejectedly.

"And we have a tougher statute than the feds do," Rutledge added.

"We just don't have the money, goddamnit."

"It's not your fault. You go to Washington, you go on TV. You do a hell of a job."

Haynes shrugged. "What good did I do? The goddamn Turks are replanting the crops. This job *sucks*," Haynes said loudly as he crushed his cigar stub in an ashtray.

Rutledge remained silent.

After a while Haynes said, "I can't understand how Josh Kleinfeld could have a son like this David character, up to his armpits in swindles."

"Why is he so good to us?" said Rutledge. "Why didn't he go to the feds? They'd put an umbrella over him, and we'd never be able to touch him. Why doesn't he make cases for them?"

"He knows we're hard up for big cases here. Figures we'll be easier to manipulate. We'll owe him, ergo, quash Nuncio and Petrone."

"A murder conspiracy? He's got big balls."

"He's a juggler, but we'll nail him, Bill, don't worry."

"Yeah, he's panicked. That's obvious."

"I feel bad for Josh Kleinfeld. I respect that little man. I knew him when I was an assistant DA with Hogan, just breaking in. There were some wild contracts out. You had cops taking money standing on toilets seats in the courthouse. No one got next to Judge Joshua Kleinfeld, though. He used to brown-bag down from the Bronx in the subway. He must be close to retirement. This will kill him."

Rutledge stood up. "Way it goes, Mitch. I'll see you later."

"Make yourself scarce in the morning."

"He's coming back already?"

"What do you think?"

SO HERE'S ME IN THE CLUB AND I'M PISSED OFF. FUCKIN' Saso's upstairs gamblin' with my money. I'm broke, but like usual when a man comes out of the joint, I ain't sure about nothin','cept that nothin's goin' right. I cannot get into Diane's drawers down at the office. I cannot get into Steffie's drawers behind the bar. (Rorita I don't go for— pa' viejo yo, no joda!) All I need is for a dog to piss on my leg. Plus a dependent named Pachanga. Short and squat, like he grew up under a safe. I knew him on the street in the stickball days, but he was never part of my click. Cat couldn't even speak no English. And he forgot his Spanish. So he ended up a mute. Well, almost. He was down in

Lewisburg, but he came out before me, so he ran me a few errands while Kleinfeld was finishin' up the appeal. Now he's stuck like a leech. Can't shake him off. Thinks I'm gonna make him rich. I'm a big-timer. Ha. Since he's with me in the club, he thinks he's a boss or at least maître d', so he goes around in a black suit, one of them old skinny ties, white socks, and them pointy shoes with Cuban heels like George Raft used to wear. Damn! Two things he can do, dance and fight his ass off. So, with the shortage of volunteers he ended up as my backup man.

Yeah, that's what I was into. Bein' alone. No more boys. All the people I came up with is long burned, whacked out, and buried. Wasteland out there. But I'm still standin'. Unbelievable. I don't like none of the new crew. Buncha punks and stool pigeons. The men is in, doin' their time. All these young bloods, they think they bad, they think they sayin' somethin'. They ain't shit. They ain't sayin' nothin'. And I have told them. I have put my finger in all their faces. You all a buncha punks. I been to Europe. Where you been? I made hundreds of thousands. You got a hundred dollars in your pocket you think you somebody. I have been with connected people, made people. Who you been with? Mickey Mouse mother fuckers! I have told them. But my rep goes way back and they're scared of me. For now. I'm waitin' for one of them to jump off.

Same with the wops. Same guys that come around to collect from Saso, same guys that been sending me messages. One thing about the regular mob, they're all the same guys. One crew. And I'm quits with them too. Oo-gotz to all them ghinnies. All the work I did for them people. What did they do for me? They threw me nickles like they was manhole covers. If I had stayed with my own kind, I never would have had so much trouble or done so much time. Later for them too.

Yeah I sound like last legs. Yeah I sound like a retread hoodlum on the overdue list. But I'm mad. I have paid my dues, I have stood up (never was no stool pigeon), and meanwhile, I'm broke. I been hard nose and hard ass all my life and all I get to show for it is hard luck. That's why I can't stand these touch guys walkin' around. Buncha pussy.

All right, I'm at the bar takin' care of business. Got to take the joint serious, it's my rice and beans now. I put a TV screen on top of the bar to spy on the cheaters (wasn't worth a damn). Friday night, place was jammed. I wasn't smilin', or drinkin', or snortin' for nobody. To top it off they kept playin' that "Bad Luck" number. Pachanga's doggin' my heels like I'm steppin' on dollar bills. He's worried I'm gonna get killed before he scores.

"Yeesus, Carlito, I heard about dat chit wiz Guajiro. Yeesus, why joo don tell me, so I can back joo op."

Pachanga's puss been pressed in a waffle griddle, but he had big pearly chicklet teeth.

"Pachanga, that was weeks ago. Some bodyguard you are, you just found out."

"Con-yo, Carlito, joo got me runnin' after that fockin' Kleinberg—"

"Kleinfeld."

"Klein-man. No importa. Gwat a pain in dee ass, Carlito, joo gwon believe it. He got lotta money dat guy, Carlito, lotta money."

I could see his chopper gleaming.

"Pachanga, I owe Kleinfeld my life. Never mind that shit."

"Con-yo, Carlito, mi hermano, Pachanga only foolin' around."

"Well, don't fuck around. Keep your eye on the bar. There's people stealin' money from the bar."

"It's so fockin' dark in here."

Pachanga was right. The joint was almost pitch black. We had these disco strobe lights flashing on and off, but with the pink smoke and all you couldn't read no newspaper in there. But that's the way they like it. Three deep at the bar, can't dance, can't hear, can't talk. That's the way they like it. Main thing is to have a lot of broads, which we had. Saso had all kinds of gimmicks for them. Mailing lists, gifts, contests. Once you scoop up the chicks, the chumps will break their legs to get in. The joint was a gold mine.

So I'm making the rounds of the club. Weekends we had a seven-piece Latin band as well as the disco. Wasn't the Fania All-Stars, but they wailed. People dancin' and carryin' on. Noise drive you crazy. Chinese waiter come over to me.

"Misser Calito, guy say he don't pay."

Oh yeah! Table in the corner, three guys, three broads. Would-be hard ass. Long roll collars, Cuban gold bracelets, etc.

"Somethin' wrong?" I said.

Long nose in the middle talkin'.

"Nah, Saso owes me money. I'm Benny Blanco, from the Bronx. I'm with Walberto."

"You know me?"

"Yeah, I know you."

"Okay. Saso owes you, but I don't owe you. This is my joint. New rule. Everybody pays his tab."

It was dark but they saw me clear. Pachanga was on my left. Long nose raised his open hands.

"No problem. Have a drink with us, Carlito."

"Some other time, kid. Take care of the waiter."

Fuck Walberto Yeampierre. Ex-pimp. Moved a couple of ounces, suppose to be a big shot. Come down hard on all these swado-thugs. Every night. A while later I'm sayin' somethin' to Steffie about gettin' her into show business through my "downtown" connections. (I'll say anything to get alongside a broad, but I don't pull that gorilla "or else" business.) I'm tryin' to bore a hole in her head when I hear the telltale sound of scrapin' chairs, breakin' glasses, crashin' tables, and screamin' women. A bad beef.

The guys were on opposite sides of a middle table. Single-breasted suit came up with a pistol, while double-breasted's hand seemed to get stuck getting through his jacket. Never did like that cut on a suit. He didn't make it. Pow! Pow! He caught at least two close up, but he was sinkin' slow motion, like a junkie dancin' around a streetlight. The shooter ran around the table as Butterfingers hit the floor, still tryin' to get his cannon out. He finished him off with the rest of the clip, shell casings bouncin' off the deck. The shooter pulled the clip out, but before he could throw another one in, Pachanga jumped him from behind, pinning his arms. I hit the guy in the face with my gun. The crowd, of course, stampeded for the door. Blew a dynamite night. This got me mad, so I hit him again. Pachanga let him go and he fell on his face. We waited awhile but nobody called the cops, so we dragged both guys downstairs and propped them on a stool. Everybody took off. We closed the joint for a while. Air it out, in case of heat or fallin' rocks.

Dave came to me with an overseas project that week. He was gonna be out of the office for a few days and he wanted me to track down a witness for him in the meantime.

"Mr. Keene, tracer of missin' persons," I said.

"Who's that?"

"That's me. Nah, he was a radio private eye, Dave, before your time. You're a teevee kid."

"C'mon, this is serious."

"Where I gotta go?"

"Portugal."

"You must be kiddin'. Tico-tico Land?"

"Portugal, not Brazil. You're not on parole. It's only six hours from here. Couple of days. Be like a vacation, at my expense."

"What happens when I find the guy?"

"Call me at home. Just say you found your cousin. I'll tell you what to do."

"This ain't no, eh, gorilla job?"

"I must know this man's whereabouts. It's essential to a case. Here's his photograph."

He handed me an old police BCI picture, complete with license plate around the neck. Young ghinny face, favored Tony Curtis in the Piper Laurie days.

"Wal-yo?"

"Yeah. Old man Nick Petrone's son, Nicky Junior. Or Nicky Peters. Nicola Petrone, Junior, is his legal name. I used to represent him. You know him?"

"I know of him. Knockaround, but a bad kid. I know his old man's a boss. But I don't know him."

"You fly to Lisbon, then take a taxi to Estoril, that's a resort nearby. There's a casino there, by the beach. He may be working there as a croupier."

"What am I suppose to do?"

"You're a lousy private investigator, Mr. Keene. I told you, call me up, say you found your cousin."

"If he ain't there?"

"Just come home. I'll advance you a thousand dollars."

"A thousand dollars? Suppose I get lost? Suppose I gotta roll at the tables to make it look good? That ain't no money."

"All right, two thousand, but keep track of expenses."

"I'm on the case."

5

THE FLIGHT STARTED OFF DYNAMITE. I'M IN AN AISLE
seat and this bandit with long black hair whiffs her tight-
assed jeans right by my face and lands in the seat next
to me. Thank you, Lord. I can see that hair draped all
over me. We'll be married before they serve the coffee.
Meanwhile I'm studyin' the crash-landin' manual. Show
the broad I'm a serious cat. None of that "Hi, I'm Ken"
jazz. Shoo, I got six hours. Then, like fate, the Brigante jinx
on public transportation went into play (have always struck
out with chicks on all movin' vehicles, like the Mummy's
curse or somethin'—includin' gettin' my face slapped in
the subway when I was a kid and I was innocent). This
two-ton lady carryin' shoppin' bags rolls up and starts
talkin' in Portuguese to the fox next to me. Pretty soon
they're yellin'. The stewardess comes over and they move
my broad out and sit Baby Hooey down. I even had to carry
one of her shoppin' bags outa the plane. No doubt the fox is
sittin' in the back with some hippie's dirty toenails in her
lap. Where was justice in this case? These are the things
that shake up a man's faith.

Landed in Lisbon, checked into a hotel, then jumped a
cab to Estoril. It was early afternoon, so I took a locker
and stretched out in the sun on a beach chair. A concrete
boardwalk curled in and out along the shoreline all the way
in both directions. All the houses were white walls with a
red roof. Like usual, the Atlantic was cold but the sand and
sky were clear. It ain't no Luquillo, but wasn't bad for a

193

European beach. Lotta girls around, but I was pissed off
from the plane ride and the bathing suit I rented. Woulda fit
Sydney Greenstreet. Real cool, cigarette in one hand, drink
in the other, and holdin' up my trunks with my elbows. I
hate to pack clothes.

I made the casino in the evenin'. Did a few blackjack
hands and some roulette. Never dug games. Mostly I hung
around the bar. No Junior. Nobody came close. And my
Spanish wasn't workin' too good on the Portuguese bartender
till I showed him a hundred-dollar bill. Now comprendo. He
looked at the photo. No Americano, no Italiano, no dice.
Okay. *Obrigado.*

There was noise around the roulette table, so I mosied
over. Two six-foot blond broads were shakin' up the wheel
and the crowd. Wavin' their big titties and big bucks all
over. Crowd couldn't make up its mind between the li'l
ball and the big boobs. You could see they were sisters
of the North. All they needed were the helmets with the
horns, and the spears. Was ist loose, mein Fräulein? I'm
gettin' ready in case I gotta rap. They ain't payin' me no
mind, just laughin' and flingin' chips. Must be somebody
else's gelt.

"Hola, Carlito."

I turned around. Betancourt. Don Jorge Betancourt. The
ol' silver fox from Madrid. Big heroin connection for Pete
Amadeo, Joe Cass, etc. He used to export it in sardine
cans, wine bottles, caskets, cars, name it. Skag was his
game, but with class. The game's over now, but he ain't
on unemployment, that's for damn sure.

"Como está, Don Jorge?"

Hollywood tan, wavy white hair, looked like Cesar
Romero for Petrocelli. It was plain he hadn't done no
time of late. He wouldn't look half so good if I had ratted
at the trial five years ago.

"Bien, Carlito, bien. You look well. Let's have a drink
at the bar."

The two broads were fish-eyein' me. Where am I goin'
with their sugar-pops? Relax, Schatzie, he'll be back.
Betancourt handed one of them a roll of escudo notes.
Wunderbar. I followed him to the bar.

"Hansel and Gretel?"

"Close. Heidi and Gretchen. I met them at Pamplona, the San Fermín festival. Stewardesses, from Munich. I can't get rid of them. My age. They are killing me, Carlito."

"Then you will die like Mojíca, with a smile on your face."

He got a charge outa this and the bartender, João, served us a couple of hefty belts. I could see I was double okay with João.

"For whom are you looking, my friend?" Betancourt said.

No sense foolin' around. Not on his turf. I told him and showed him the picture. He looked at João, who shook his head.

"This man has never worked here, I can assure you of that," Betancourt said. "I know of his father and that group. They do not range this far."

"You oughta know."

"Amadeo's dead, no?"

"If you see him, make a quick turn."

"I do not blame you, Carlito, he was a very difficult man. The new one, Castaldi, is more reasonable, no?"

"Joe Cass. I ain't crazy about him either. He throws the rocks too, he just hides the hand better."

"The same spoon stirs the soup, eh. I do not blame you for being bitter. They have treated all the Hispanos like dogs. I, too, paid for their broken windows."

"Yeah, but I paid for the inside, Don Jorge."

"Over there, what choice did you have? Better letters to the jail than flowers to the grave."

"The Italianos gave me a bad time. I didn't deserve that, I stood up."

"Since when are we rewarded for doing what we are supposed to do? That was your Calvary. We are all subjected. In 1937 the Republicans put me to the wall twice. I stood my ground. Five years ago, in Madrid, I saw that quality in you. You do not bend under pressure. And as important, you are resourceful. I commented on this to your associate, the unfortunate Fabrizi."

"Yeah. Poor Rocco. Descanse en paz."

"Que Díos lo tenga en la gloria."

"You were the only lucky one."

"Not so lucky, Carlito. My blood did not run to the river, but it rained in Madrid too. Your government tried to extradite me. Conspiracy. I, who have never set foot in the United States. Your laws are insane."

"I've had a lot of trouble with them."

"Fortunately, the Caudillo would never allow one of our race to be deported."

"Would that have included me?"

"Of course, to General Franco, la raza, all Hispanos were sacred, no matter where they were from. Not so the king, but I am retired, so it matters not. I now watch the bulls from behind the barrier. Just close enough to observe my countrymen lacerate themselves, all over again, as in '37. With the Caudillo gone, there is no one to stay the dogs of war. In the meantime, I tour the countryside."

"With Anita Ekberg. Times two. Not bad work."

"You like my bookends? Come with us, we're goin' south to Sevilla and the Costa del Sol."

"I won't be in the way?"

"Nonsense. Where are you staying?"

"The Penta Hotel, in Lisbon."

"We will be in the lobby at nine in the morning. These Germans are early risers."

I ain't hard to convince.

"Just a day or two, I gotta report back."

We pulled out in the mornin' via white Jaguar. The Minnesota Vikings, up front, did the drivin', me and Betancourt in the backseat. Unbelievable, them broads. Two bodies by Fisher. I mean built. In tank tops and hot pants cut up to their schnappes. No-bra nipples. Even my eyeballs had a hard-on. Ménàge a twar was on my mind but my rap with Betancourt was about the Communists in Spain and people goin' to the dogs, etc. Respect for the host, wait for the okay. Had to, the girls only spoke German. He did all the translatin'. When we got past the Spanish border we blew a hose. Betancourt wouldn't let me out of the car.

"Too hot, Carlito. These are remarkable people. Watch."

Sure enough. The wimmen changed the hose, tightened the clamps, poured the coolant in the radiator. We were off again.

Betancourt said, "I was with the Spanish Blue Division in Russia. I still can't understand how Germany lost the war."

We stopped at a small town outside of Seville. Place called Alcala de somethin'. There was a bullfight scheduled. Seems Betancourt was interested in a matador on the card. Campesino (the peasant). The guy was a novillero or prelim fighter. In other words, not in the ratings yet. The bullring was tank town. Circular concrete bleachers, no grandstand, and no shade. The sun grilled the field like a thousand hotplates, bakin' the dirt orange. Dust all over. Hotter'n a stalled subway.

Heidi and Gretchen got a big hand from the crowd when we came into the arena. "Guapa," "maja," etc., they were yellin'. These Nordic "blondas" still raise hell in the Mediterranean, believe that. The Fräuleins sandal-scuffed their way up the steps, wigglin' their asses and diggin' all the fuss. Some broads are born to incite riots. Guys walk into lampposts, cars crash into fire hydrants, they couldn't care less. I say, horray for them.

Betancourt had cushions for their tooshies. I had to cook my ass on them stone bleachers, with a Spike Jones band playin' rinky-dink behind me. This was a new scene for me, so Betancourt was explainin' the finer points. This was not a sport, this was "fiesta brava," sun and shade, life and death, blood and sand, etc. Very complicated.

Came the bull. Out of the chute like a trailer truck curvin' on Route 80. Half a ton, packed at the neck, like a natural heavy-weight. He ran all over the field. You would too (they just jammed a spike into his shoulder before they let him out, Betancourt told me).

Now comes this fat guy on a horse wearin' a mattress and blinders. He's got a long pike. He rams it into the bull's neck, pulls it out, then sticks him again, forcin' the pike deeper with all his shoulder weight behind it. Gotta hurt. The bull's bleedin' buckets now, down his side and leg. Can't see the blood on the sand, too much dust bein' kicked up. Not enough, they bring out another guy who jams six short lances, two at a time, into the bull. Betancourt said the pike was to bring his head down, and the banderillas to bring it back up. Jesus.

Enter the bull killer, tight pants and all. The girls love 'im.

"I figure the bull's been stabbed nine times so far already. Hell of a way to go into a fight," I said to Betancourt.

"You do not understand. That is a diesel train. He weighs over a thousand pounds. He must be bled, or there would be no contest. His head must be controlled or there can be no art with the cape, no ritual with the sword."

Art? Chopped beef. This first stiff used four swords. I was waitin' for him to pull out a pistol. El Campesino (the star of the card) came on second. He had more stuff. He worked close, got decked from a headbutt, not a horn (no fool, he lay flat coverin' his face), and did for the bull with one swordthrust. In up to the handle. The bull went down on one knee, like he was takin' an eight-count. The blood was gushin' out of his nose and mouth. Second knee buckled and he went over. Campesino's banderillero, Bacurri, squatted down and slit the bull's throat. Teamwork. The crowd loved it. The Fräuleins popped their drawers. Campesino! I felt bad for the bull. He kept comin', he was game. Now they rope him to three horses wearin' bells and drag him out through the dust to go for sausage rings. They didn't do that to Jake LaMotta. I didn't go for the brave feast. El Campesino came struttin' around the arena like he was Tyrone Power (if Tyrone was a gnome, 'cause Campesino wasn't much over five feet tall). The crowd went apeshit and the band went oompa-oomp. I could see he had eyes for the Fräuleins. Olé, yo' mammy.

Betancourt had creamed.

"He has it, Carlito! The calm, the serenity in the face of death. The rabble, cowards all, sense this. The matador opens his fly, 'aquí están mis cojónes.' That is what they pay to see. It is a show, a 'sexy.' El Campesino passed this crowd through his balls. He will be a 'matador de toros,' not a novillero, next year. The bulls, the crowds will not pass so easily. If there is a hollow ring it will be heard clearly. . . ."

I was more worried about El Shrimpo passin' Hansel and
Gretel under the balls this year. Sure enough, he showed
up that night. Flamenco Sevilla or some such joint. Rock
cave with a lot of pictures of Carmen Amaya, Manolete,
Lola Flores, etc. Olé tu madre. Tiri, tiri, tiri . . . the singer
wailed, like an Arab at Ramadan or a Jew at Passover. They
all came through Andalucia.

We had a big table against the wall by a fake fireplace.
Me and Betancourt sat facin' the girls. From close up you
could see they weren't sisters. Heidi was friskier, action.
Gretchen was more re-action. Dolls. They sported matched
white peasant blouses, red faces, and blue-icicle eyes. I
was talkin' English with my version of a German accent.
Madon. What they heard I'm not sure, but they seemed
up and we drank wine by the jug. The strain was gettin'
to me, tryin' to make two broads in sign language (with
one eye on Betancourt), but we shall overcome. Ha.

El Campesino made a showbiz entrance, backed by two
of the flunkies from his "quadrilla." Junior lightweight, he
favored Elisha Cook, Jr., 'cept he was Gypsy-colored and
had a knot of hair behind his head. Dressed in black. Everybody gave him a big play. The singers and dancers went,
"Olé, bravo niño!" He struck a few poses around the room
while he was lookin' for the girls. Ah. Big piano smile.
Betancourt sat him down between Heidi and Gretchen. My
buddy.

"Matador, este es mi amigo, Carlito Brigante."

For a jockey shorts, Campesino had a helluva grip, but
he never looked at me. The girls climbed all over him.
Pourin' him wine, purrin' and strokin', with Betancourt as
interpreter. Campesino could hardly talk Spanish, let alone
German. Didn't bother the girls none. Now Campesino's
poker-pussed, just noddin', he's used to this groupie jive.
I'm out in left field, worse, on the 161st Street subway platform. S'okay. Meanwhile I'm guzzlin' vino by the kilo. I'm
gettin' mad at Betancourt too. He's pimpin' for Campesino.
Me he don't give a break. He can't be servicin' both these
broads, he's over sixty. And I showed respect, waitin' on
him. So he puts Campesino in my bed! Li'l red rats I was
seein'. Fuckin' illiterate Andaluz, this Campesino, speaks

worse Spanish than me. Musta been raised, eatin' grass, in one of them pastures they got around here. Betancourt and the chicks are fussin' and he's lookin' off into space, gettin' more arrogant by the minute (lotta dumb guys do this to cover up).

I'm the fifth leg on the table, so I ain't sayin' nothin'. I'm mean as Joe Greene, but I'm cool. "Allá ellos que son blancos y se entienden." I can see Betancourt is tryin' to rope the kid into some kinda deal, but he can't get no traction. He shifts to me, with all his Castilian *s*'s and *th*'s.

"Carlito, tell El Campesino of the glory we saw in the arena this afternoon."

You ask a question. Usually I'm a diplomat. Blame it on the broads, blame it on the booze. I said, "What I saw was an animal cut to pieces before the matador steps out. They don't give the bull a fair shot."

Campesino's face got darker. They blow up very quick down here. Now he looked at me.

"Tauromagia is a science, señor," he said, "and you are ignorant." Then he lit up a cigarette.

Uh-oh. I let it slide. Campesino turned his chair toward the stage. Some guy was standin' on a small table bangin' with his feet. The Fräuleins were clappin' like crazy. Wadda they know. Betancourt, said, "Matador, what happens is that Carlito is from New York. Americano. He is not experienced in these matters. Let us join in a drink to—"

Campesino spun around. Still hot.

"Americano? His name, his language, where are they from?"

"Puerto Rico," Betancourt said. "A sister country. He is of our blood, Matador."

"No, Don Jorge. He is not of our blood. There are no banana stains here. They have a different breed over there."

The more you try to avoid.

"What breed is that, speak your mind . . . Shorty," I told him. Didn't raise my voice. Betancourt put his arms out.

"Gentlemen! Gentlemen, on this peninsula we are Christians, Moors, Gypsies, and whatever else came by. At this table, the most 'castizo' am I, for I am Castilian by over five centuries. And I say, who gives a shit? What difference from where? It is all one Hispanic brotherhood. I will not allow a quarrel over such nonsense. . . . The Fräuleins would not like it, Matador." Betancourt winked.

"If you have no objection, Don Jorge, I will take the girls with me," Campesino said and he got up.

"Right now? Both of them?" Betancourt said, turnin' to me. I wasn't really jealous. I never hassle over stray snatch that don't really mean nothin' to me. So all I said was, "Had the bull, now he wants the cows."

Campesino's nose flaps started twitchin' as the Gypsy came out.

"Tell the women he called them cows, Don Jorge," he said. "Tell them!"

I could see Heidi was tuned in. She knew there was a beef.

"Take it easy, brother," I said to Campesino.

"Brother? Look for your brother in a whorehouse."

Now we gonna play the dozens.

"He's there with your mother," I said.

He splashed a wine glass in my face. I quick-clipped him in the mouth, like a reflex. But I half-pulled the punch. He was just a punk kid. Betancourt grabbed me. It was over very quick. Nobody noticed,'cept Campesino's boys. They came over. His mouth was busted, but he raised a hand to quiet his two guys. Heidi put a napkin on his lip. Nobody gave me a napkin. I'm the bad guy in the movie. Betancourt said, "Matador, he has committed an error. But he—"

"This is not with you, Don Jorge," Campesino said.

The older guy with knots on his face kept starin' at me, noddin' his head. I had seen him slit the bull's throat.

"Bacurri," Betancourt said to this guy, "let us not have a problem here."

"El mata'or told you, this is not with you."

Campesino pointed to the door. The girls filed out behind him with Bacurri and the other flunky bringin' up the rear. Me and Betancourt sat down again. He poured the wine.

"Bonito espectáculo, Carlito. All your shots have come out the ass end of the rifle. In the first place, das Fräuleins are lesbians. At sixty-two and with a prostate condition, I make allowances. You were blinded by the outside packaging. I took you to be more astute. Jail has dulled you."

"In the second place?"

"They did not even like you. I made suggestions. They said your eyes are greedy, too anxious. They have experience, from the airplanes."

"What did they expect? Bouncin' them lung-warts all over my face—where they think I been for five years. Fuckin' boldykes. They didn't fool me."

"No doubt. But you have indisposed me with El Campesino and I am interested in his career."

"Sorry about that. He asked for it. I didn't bust him up out of respect for you. This bad wine didn't help."

"Do not overindulge. The problem continues after the place is closed. It is close to four."

"Oh?"

"You have nothing?"

"Naked." I was soberin' up fast.

"If you can get to the car, I have a pistol. The streets are too narrow to bring the car here."

"Bring the pistol on foot, Don Jorge."

"Bacurri will be waiting."

"Lump-lump?"

"Yes, the old one. You will deal with him. In Sevilla they call them 'facas.' That is the weapon here."

"Facas?"

"Knives. Bacurri is very quick."

"I saw him in the bullring."

"I will walk with you."

"No good. You'll only be in the way. Go to the car, start it up, and wait at the end of the alley. I'll think of somethin'."

"Está bien."

Betancourt paid the bill and split. The singer was up there complainin' again to his guitar. He thinks he got troubles. Always when you least expect it. . . . I'm lookin' around for somethin'. No kitchen, no knives. Besides, close up, Bacurri will take my liver out. A bat, need a bat, always liked a bat against a knife. No bat. The fireplace. There you go. An iron poker. I slid the poker out and backed into the bathroom. It was a long one. I shoved it down my pants leg and one-legged my way out of the joint. Came out to a cobblestoned patio with a narrow street through a small park. Then the main drag and the car. Not far. Unless Betancourt has bugged out on me.

I pulled the poker out and wrapped my jacket around it. Vamos a ver. Didn't take long. Bacurri was by a streetlight, cigarette in mouth, Cordobés hat pulled low (he musta seen *Blood and Sand*).

"Prepare," he said.

"I have no defense," I said.

"Vamos a ver," he said.

He pulled out two daggers, more like short swords with hilts on them. He threw one at my feet. But I ain't bendin' down for nobody to kick in the face.

"Prepare—to trip over your guts," he said.

Jumpin' Jesus! This cat is gonna dis-gut me and he ain't even gonna take the cigarette outa his mouth? The milk of his mother first! I dropped the jacket and took the poker out, two-handed grip. He went into his squat and we started circlin'. He's feintin' and I'm swingin' the poker. Now I'm backin' toward my exit. I'm trippin' on the stones but I'm movin'. Bacurri gets mad.

"Stand still and fight like a man, maricón!"

Fuck you, I'm movin', Jack. He switched hands, comin' in fast and low on my right side. Clang! The knife scraped along the poker. I got in a short kick to the balls. He fell back and I woulda taken his head off but he was bobbin' n' weavin' on me. Then I saw daylight and took off down the alleyway. Betancourt had the car door open. I could hear Bacurri behind me yellin', "Maricón! Cabrón! Hijo de la mala leche!"

I jumped in the car and we rolled. By now I'm laughin' hysterical.

"You sure them broads are lesbians?" I said.

"You are crazy, Carlito, completely crazy," Betancourt said, but he was laughin' too. Probably got his glands up for the first time in years. After we drove awhile, I started feelin' stupid.

"Made an ass of myself, eh?"

"You are in your autumn, Carlito. The fires should not rage so fiercely. Es ridiculo."

"I can't get used to gettin' old, Don Jorge. It's gone by so quick. When you're in prison, you expect time to stand still. It don't. You never catch up."

"Then you adjust, according to the times. How do you think I arrived at age sixty-two in this crazy country? You must curb your recklessness. I have heard stories from Fabrizi and that other unfortunate, Sixto—"

"Meanwhile I'm still here and they're both under grass."

"All the more reason to start using your head. Get killed over a big money deal, not over a bottle of wine and a skirt."

"I'm tryin', Don Jorge, I'm tryin' to make it into the hangar, like everybody else. But somethin' keeps holdin' me back."

"A pity. . . . I'm curious, how did you get away from Bacurri?"

"Wasn't easy. He came at me with this long fuckin' sword, two of them, as a matter of fact. I took my jacket off and passed him through my balls, à la toro, then I . . ."

We went back to the Macarena Hotel where we'd checked in after the bullfight. We picked up our gear and hit the road again. Betancourt checked out on the broads too. Said he was tired of them. He sure likes to keep movin'. We drove south toward the Costa del Sol. Sun is dry but the air is parched, don't move. Just hangs. Mile after mile.

"Sometimes I get bored with retirement, Carlito. I must admit this to you. Some people from Florida have contacted me. What do you think?"

"You'd have to be crazy. With the money you got? Don't let nobody talk a hole in your head. Them are Cubans, and coke, and you as an importer, right?"

"Along that style."

"That's never been your stick, Don Jorge. You'd have to be crazy. Enjoy life. Nothin's more borin' than jail, believe me."

"No doubt. . . . Come, I will show you a Mediterranean coast of gold unlike anything you have ever seen."

We went to his place outside of Marbella. A big white house with a red-tiled roof set on the beach end of a rock and concrete breakwater. Betancourt was livin' better than the Aga Khan with a loaf of bread under each arm. And he's cryin'.

Bounced around Marbella and Torremolinos another couple days. Beaches and discos. Was gettin' bugged up here too. The broads I liked didn't like me, the broads I didn't like, I didn't bother with, so it don't count. Felt very American, one hundred proof. In the U.S.A. I feel like I'm on the outside lookin' in. In Europe I wanna sing "God Bless America." Weird.

Betancourt laid five big ones on me before I left. "You shouldn't do that," I said as I seized the bundle. Me and him promised to keep in touch. I took off for home.

Told Dave I sat in the casino at Estoril for four days hawkin' this croupier and had to blow the whole two thou, plus some of my own. Turned out to be a false alarm. Guy looked just like Nicky Junior. Name was João. Coulda fooled me. Nah, you don't owe me anythin', Dave.

That weekend me and Saso had a gala, grand reopenin' of the club with complimentary booze and chow. Them Po'Ricans ate and drank for days. We were back in showbiz.

6

Supreme Court, New York County, Part E. Brigante slumped low into the rear bench of the courtroom, at once inconspicuous and near the door. Instinctively geared for a hasty exit despite his presence only as a spectator.

David Kleinfeld was addressing the court.

" . . . and it is axiomatic common sense that in a possessory crime there must be exclusivity of possession. There are a host of reasonable hypotheses all nearly conformable to the factual framework of the instant case, only one of which is consistent with guilt. Mr. Mendoza's presence in the apartment in question, absent attendant circumstances of an inculpatory nature, cannot suffice. The prosecutor must clothe the mannequin, your honor. An examination of either the hearing minutes, the Grand Jury minutes, or the Huntley hearing minutes will not reveal—"

"Mr. Kleinfeld, this court has waded through all that, in addition to your fifty-two-page memorandum. Is there anything else you wish to add?"

"No, your honor. Forgive me if I have been unduly verbose. I tend to be carried away whenever I am confronted with that abomination, the Rockefeller drug law, that Procrustean strait-jacket of a statute where a first offender must serve fifteen years before he is eligible for parole—"

"Mr. Mendoza is not, I believe, a first offender. Be that as it may, I have made up my mind. The Jefferson case, cited in your memo, Counselor, is controlling here. I am granting your motion to dismiss the indictment and the defendant is discharged. An opinion will be filed. Call the next case."

Brigante stepped quickly out of the courtroom and into the corridor. Kleinfeld, arms interlocked with his client, Mendoza, and a stocky mocha-colored woman, followed through the door.

"Mr. Kleinfeld," Mendoza said, his eyes brimming with tears, "I swear to my mother I ain't ever gonna forget what you did for me. . . ."

Overwhelmed with emotion, the robust Mendoza threw both arms around Kleinfeld's neck. Spotting Brigante leaning against the wall, Mendoza shouted, "Carlito, mi hermano. . . ."

And with arms extended he advanced on Brigante, who promptly assumed a crouched fighting stance with both fists clenched.

"Get away, you faggot," Brigante said, laughing. The two men exchanged mock jabs and hooks, then embraced.

"I told you Dave was the man to see you go, Papo, but you didn't wanna believe me," Brigante said.

Papo Mendoza motioned to the woman.

"Altagracia, Carlito's the dude put me on to Mr. Kleinfeld. You remember my ol' lady, don'tcha, Carlito?"

Altagracia Mendoza, of the sharply structured features and long Indian tresses, nodded, her luminous black eyes set on Brigante as he bowed from the waist.

"Encantado, señora," Brigante said.

"I gotta get uptown, man. There's a few dudes thought I was goin' away for life, gotta settle up now. Know what I mean? Mr. Kleinfeld, I'll be around your office later on in the week. I got a present for you. Vamos, Altagracia."

The Mendozas departed hurriedly.

"I hope he doesn't get killed this week," Kleinfeld muttered.

"I'll be a rat's ass, Dave, you did it again. I'd give my left ball to be able to bullshit like you. I mean it."

"How about five kilos?" Kleinfeld questioned, a smile playing on his lips.

"Thought they only popped him with two in the apartment."

"They didn't look hard enough. How do you think I got my fee?"

Kleinfeld put his hand out and Carlito slapped it.

"You dawg," Brigante said.

They took the elevator to the lobby and crossed Lafayette Street to the corner restaurant, Doyle's, where they sat at a sidewalk table.

"Why didn't we go to Luna's?" Brigante asked.

"Tired of pasta," Kleinfeld said.

"Know what you mean, Mr. Clean."

They ordered prime ribs and Heineken.

"I recognized her right away, Carlito."

"Who?"

"Mendoza's wife."

"Oh, Papo's ol' lady? Where you know her from?"

"The night of the dance at the Central Ballroom on 125th Street, when you had the fight with her."

"Jesus, you got some memory."

"Especially the part about my not getting paid. That was supposed to be a benefit dance to pay my first big fee. I was in partnership with Woody Cohen on 112th Street at that time."

"That was Walberto Yeampierre's promotion to collect money for Freddie Flaco's murder case. The joint was jammed. They had Machito playin'."

"I didn't get a nickel. I swear."

"Of course not, Walberto glommed all the money. Probably whacked it up with your partner, Woody Cohen. What the hell, you were just a kid learnin' the ropes. Although, what you were doin' in Harlem was beyond me. If I went to Yale, you wouldn't catch me on 112th Street in a storefront. I'd have been on Wall Street with the real hustlers."

"I tried it for a year. They gave me a railroad case, sixteen folders. Locked me in a closet. It would have taken me five years to get into a courtroom. Ten years to get my name on the door. I quit, went uptown to get into the action."

"Beats the hell outa me, but everybody into his own bag, right?"

"You beat the hell out of her."

"Who?"

"Altagracia. Mendoza's wife."

"You got it wrong. I don't beat up on women."

"I saw you myself."

"She hit me with a bottle. She was mad cause I had knocked up her sister, India. I was at the bar mindin' my own business. She started runnin' a game on me. 'Punk, faggot.' I tried to back off. I got heavy hands. She came at me with a bottle. Cracked my head. I had to lay her out."

"You missed with the left, connected with the right."

"Wrong. I feinted with left, dipped to my right, then banged her with a right cross."

"She went against the partition, I saw her eyes cross."

"I don't go for that. Not my shtick, I don't beat on women. I'm a lover. Both them sisters were fine, by the way."

"A lot of women need that, Carlito, a lot of women. . . . I liked the way you handled the bouncers."

"Yeah?"

"You picked up your drink from the bar, turned to me, and said, 'Like I was telling you, Counselor.' The woman was out cold, the bouncers were yelling, and you said, 'Who? I'm having a drink with my lawyer.' With the blood flowing down the back of your head. Cool, man, cool."

"You got some memory."

"So Woody was in on the scam with Walberto, you figure?"

"But of course, fuckin' thieves, lemme tell you."

BENNY BLANCO FROM THE BRONX MUSTA COMPLAINED TO Walberto. Right away I got the word from Pachanga that Walberto was mad at me because he ain't had a chance to chip into my comin'-home kitty. Said he had a gift for me. This egg want salt.

Walberto Yeampierre went back to my time in the Barrio. Never did go for the cat. Pretty boy, right away the whores set him up on 111th and Fifth, rice-and-beans pimp. Thought he was bad. Couldn't use his hands. Way back when, I had a winner out of 113th Street name of India. She was a chocolate mousse with black hair down to here. Would cover me like a tent with that hair. Lord have mercy. Now you know next to that you couldn't move me with a crane. This fool, Walberto, had his own ideas. She was gonna be *his* ol' lady. Over his dead body. So there I was on 106th Street and Madison, hangin' out with some of the boys in front of Raymond's Pool Room, when he pulls up in a black Buick (big deal in them days). He had on a black stingy-brim, black shirt, black pants (thought it was the Cisco Kid or Hopalong Cassidy). He gave his gold watch to Monchín, his cousin, to hold. Then he pointed to me.

"Take to the street, mother fucker!"

Just like that. We went to the lot in front of the Flower Hospital. I caught him a straight right hand in the breastbone—thunk—and let the air out. All she wrote for Walberto. Then I had to go 'round with Monchín. He could duke. Boys called it a draw. Me and Monchín shook hands. Walberto said he was goin' home to get a pistol. I'm still waitin'. Jive-ass. Miss Brown hung aroun'.

That was about the time the Italians gave me a break and headed me up in the rackets. Walberto was steady nickel-and-dime decks and street pimpin'. One of the wops (Bobby Blanch from Pleasant Avenue) said to me once, "He's always cryin' we don't give him a break, we told him, 'You're too pretty, won't stand up in the back of the precinct, they'll have to hit you to stop you from talkin'.' We don't want him."

Irregardless of personal feelings, a man got to go to money. The meet was at the Café de la Paix on 59th Street, near his pad on Central Park South. I wasn't impressed, coulda been a front. I hadn't seen Walberto for five or six years, not since Puerto Rico. He was sittin', sidewalk café style, under an umbrella, with a big bottle of wine. Had like a Julius Caesar hairdo and the pimp scar on his face was gone (musta cost a bundle). Very casual in light blue Madras slacks and shirt, Gucci loafers, and no socks. Looked like money was around. He threw his arms around me (had a black-faced Piaget on his wrist had to go for ten large). Now I was impressed. When you broke and busted out, the shine of joolery is blindin'. We crossed our legs, drank wine, and eyeballed the fine chicks walkin' by. We waltzed a few circles first. To hear him tell it he had missed me somethin' awful. I asked about his cousin, Monchín.

"Monchín is dead, Carlito. Killed last year. Colombia. Medelín."

"The hell was he doin' down there?"

He looked around, then he said, "Rolando. We are friends with Rolando."

"What Rolando?"

"Rivas. Rolando Rivas-Barcelo."

"El cubano?"

"Ese mismo."

"Grande?"

"Grandísimo."

"I'll be damn. I didn't know you was tight with Rolando. Figured he was down in Miami with the CIA. He was raidin' Cuba, in small boats for a while there, you know."

"I know. He's come to his senses. Out of all that political shit. Strictly business. And I mean hea-vy. Got a mansion on the water, private airfield. He's my father, man."

"Baptized you, huh?"

"I got a big pad across the street, I'm in the stock market, couple of stores. I'm okay, bro. Thank God, after all these years."

"Rolando always liked the candy. But for partyin', not for business."

"There ain't no other business. Skag is dead. There's only candy. Rolando said it five years ago. He's a genius. He went down to Bogotá and set a route up. Now he services Baltimore, Detroit, Washington, Philly—"

"And you?"

"Vaya!"

We slapped skin about here.

"He spoke to me about you, Carlito. Crazy about you. Said you knew how to party, but when it came to a beef, you were a man of *armas tomadas*. We all know the bad weight you took when you got jammed."

"Is he still chasin' them young kitties? He used to have a gang of baby-dykes he used to closet himself with at the Americana. For days."

We had a big laugh here.

"Yeah, the old cubiche is a stoned degenerate. But he set up a big thing down there, Carlito, believe me, a big thing."

Guy had me droolin'. We went for a bite, some penthouse Hindu joint nearby. On the elevator goin' up, Walberto slipped me a gee. I took it. "Buy yourself a suit, babe," he said. To me. What a man gotta come to when he loses five years. There were rugs all over the restaurant (no elephants). You could see clear across the park to 110th Street, from up there. With all the lights it looked like a chunk of night sky they laid down across Manhattan. New York, New York—you can't beat it.

When the food came, Walberto got down to the main grits he brought for me.

"Rolando wants to see you, Carlito."

"Monchín got whacked out down there, eh?"

"Wadda ya mean?"

"It's gonna get real hot down there in the Coca-Cola business, right? Meanwhile, the Corsicans have got flags planted all over South America plus the regular ghinnies to back them. They're goombahs. I'm suppose to get into that. The spics are gonna have to lay down, like usual. Lo siento."

"Not in South America, we ain't. We're Latinos. We speak the language. Rolando's got generals and colonels in his corner, he's got newspapers. They can't gorilla us."

"Rolando wants me to go down there as a shooter, right?"

"He wants to talk to you, bro. That's the message. You ain't gonna get a better offer nowhere, Carlito. Times have changed. There's no money on the street. Try it. Lissen, talk to the man."

"Can't hurt. Okay, Walberto. Cuando?"

"Soon. We'll fly down together. I'll call you. In the meantime, I'm around the Hippopotamus and Cachaça a lot."

"What's with this Benny kid?"

"Benny Blanco? Oh, yeah. Young kid, was in Vietnam. He's with me, he's all right. You know how fly these kids are today. They don't wanna pay their dues. But Benny's okay. Tough kid, but he listens. Rolando likes him."

"I gotta get used to the new faces, that's what Dave Kleinfeld tells me. Nobody we knew is left out there, Walberto. Hard times."

"Three times. State-time, fed-time, and—"

"Dead-time."

"Mostly the last one, Carlito. Death Valley out there. You know me, used to take to the street with any mother fucker, but these new kids have no respect for human life. Will shotgun you just to see you go up in the air. It's been hell, the last few years. Better off in jail. I don't go to Harlem. They're crazy. But we got these greasy Dominicans, too. You was lucky with Guajiro, you always been lucky. Don't press it."

"No big ting."

"You got nobody left. Tato's doin' twenty years, I hear he's in the crazy house. Victor got shotgunned right on 105th Street by the school. Colorado, they left him in the trunk of his car in a Burger King. Musta been there a week. Slaughterhouse, bro."

"Lalín?"

"You don't know about Lalín?"

"I know he's in a wheelchair."

"You know I don't like to say nothin' bad about nobody, but keep the 'ojo clinico' on him."

"He's wrong, eh?"

"I ain't sayin' he is, and I ain't sayin' he ain't. Just be cool when he's around."

"Lalín. Coño."

"Them guys are all past tense. You got a place with us, bro. Main thing is you're out and lookin' good. That fuckin' Kleinfeld's a miracle worker. Nobody ever expected to see you again, this side of the wall."

"It took five years, but he busted the government's case."

"Coulda fooled me. I never liked him as a lawyer. I remember when he showed up in Harlem to work for Woody Cohen. Cohen sent him down to represent some of my girls in the old Women's Court. He wasn't no hell."

"He's become a hell of a lawyer, Walberto. You oughta see him in a courtroom now. He was just a kid when he was in Cohen's office. Besides, that fuckin' Woody Cohen was a thief and a half."

"Yeah, but what a personality. Sharp. He looked like the president of the bank. Those pinch glasses without the frames."

"Edward Arnold."

"Yeah, not like Kleinfeld, a shrimp. Looks like a pushcart peddler. I'm amazed how he's come on. Got big wise guys in his stable. Puttin' Steinhardt and them guys outa business."

"Dave is the new wave. Lawyers that do their homework. They can't wing it anymore. Gotta do the paperwork. A big front don't mean nothin' these days. Days of the bullshit artists like Steinhardt and Cohen are over. Dave is the head of the class."

"Dave ain't got no class, Carlito, I been out with him."

"You went out with Dave?"

"Sure, the night he was playin' big shot buyin' me and Woody drinks at the Arcoiris. Showin' off for the whores. Woody took off with Carmen 'Tongolele.' Knob-job. Kleinfeld got drunk as a skunk. I stayed, doin' him a favor, you know the criminal element used to go there. He gets a bug up his ass about me! 'Wadda you think you can sponge drinks off me all night?' I was hardly drinkin'. Then he starts, 'You ain't shit, I can get girls too,' that kind of garbage. I didn't give him a beatin' out of respect for Woody. He's a nasty little fuck. I told Woody about it."

"Woody was no bargain, Walberto."

"They killed Woody, y'know."

"You still believe that crap? Cohen committed suicide, the whores got him in trouble. He was gonna go to jail."

"Suicide? Woody? Bullshit. A man over six feet tall can't break his neck off a five-foot staircase. I been to the house."

"Bullshit. The hang-ups in the joint do it all the time, even without a rope. I see a guy do it with his shirt. They bend their knees when they jump."

"They put the rope around his neck—afterward."

"Who?"

"The Kleinfelds. Dave and his father, who was a DA at the time. I know, Carlito, don't forget I was tight with Woody. Internal Affairs set Woody up with that runaway kid. He was panicked. He wanted to buy his way out. Dave said he had the connection through his father. Woody gave Dave a big bundle. Then there was a meet at Woody's house in King's Point. Woody, Dave, and this police captain. Woody said Dave's old man showed up out of nowhere. The old man started throwin' punches like a wild man, even hit Dave. Deal fell through. Woody was still on the hook, but he couldn't get his money back from Dave. Kept gettin' excuses. Woody was pissed, said if he went to jail, Dave and his father were goin' with him."

"So what?"

"So they dumped him."

"What about all the pimps, includin' you, and cops that Cohen would have ratted out before goin' to jail? Any one of them could have whacked him out."

"Bullshit. Who discovered Woody's body? Who kept the money? Who got the house from the widow? Dave Kleinfeld. Rest my case, Carlito."

"Never hold up."

"We ain't in court, Carlito. I don't give a fuck. I got my own troubles. But nobody can tell me different."

"You should be in the homicide squad, Walberto."

"What, and have to deal with the likes of you?"

El ladrón juzga por sus condíciones. The thief judges by his own conditions.

"Vaya!" We slapped skin again.

We split early. Walberto had to get duded up for a big party at Regine's for some South American diplomat guys he was hostin'. Jive fuckin' Walberto. Never did no serious time. Last guy, from the heap, I woulda picked to score. No class. Everytin' he ever did on the street, el zilch-o. And now, at the last turn, when it counts, he's at the head of the pack. Where is justice? I walked north along Central Park West. There was people around, but I was lonely as the night train whistle. Lotta fags out. "Hi there." In the Barrio, "malas lenguas" said that Walberto and Monchín was swappin' out. Of Walberto, I believe anythin', he's a natural-born pimp, which means he ain't got no mother. But not Monchín, he was "mucho macho." Rolando's a steady degenerate from the old bust-out Havana days with the Superman, the donkeys, the Great Danes, etc. Maybe that's what him and Walberto got goin'? Medellín, city of beautiful women. Best in the west. Rolando musta thrown some dynamite parties down there for the local "colmillu'o." Snort 'n snatch by the kilo. Nobody sets up like Rolando. Yeah, but how'm I gonna hack it by myself? I'll be made soon as I get off the plane. Colombia's wild west, by the time I get it checked out, them Injuns have me blown away. No me gusta, Rolando, no me gusta.

7

By day (regular Clark Kent) I was "gainfully employed" at Kleinfeld's office. And I don't just mean as house torpedo. I mean I would come in wearin' clean threads. Conservative. After all, Kleinfeld ran a class act. Raunchy office won't get the big fees out of the thugs. Gotta give them atmosphere. Even if it's a Mickey Mouse bust, show 'em their case got a big folder (even though the papers belong to somebody else's case). Dave had it all down pat. Unfortunately, he had two flyweight associates, paper lawyers. He probably wanted it that way, only one lion in the cage. For me, "más vale cabeza de ratón, que culo de león." Better the head of a rat, than the ass of a lion. Anyway, these two assistants, if you loaded up what they didn't know, you could fill a warehouse. Wouldn't get past a weekend on the street. Kind of guys that gobble up libraries, meanwhile not only they don't see nothin', they don't even look around. Couldn't find a hooker or a teevee knobber on 44th and Eighth. Could be two pairs of sneakers, size thirteen, carryin' tire irons waitin' on their stoop, three o'clock in the mornin'—they wouldn't see them. Wap! Wap! "They went that-away, officer, two Third World types, however, under the Wade-Gilbert-Stovall cases. . . ." Would not take a piss without the case law on it. What and when, I used to call them, as in Milton Wadleigh and Harry Cox, they were closer than two fags in a broom closet. Cox, specially, didn't have no sense of humor. Kleinfeld loved the story about the time

217

Cox was the Legal Aid and he was interviewin' whores in the pens in the back of the courthouse and the guard stuck his head through the door and said, "Is Cox in here?" and one of the whores said, "Ain't no cocks in here, but a whole lot o' cunts." Cox said Kleinfeld made it up. If they didn't have a spieler with balls like Kleinfeld around, they would starve to death. So with hooples like that, quite naturally, Kleinfeld came to rely more and more on my judgment on tricky matters. It's a goddamn shame a man gotta have a diploma. When are they gonna wise up? There is a brain drain in this country. I read all about it in *Newsweek*. And it's all because a lot of qualified guys are ruled out of bounds in the rain by the diploma crew. "We're aboard, fuck you," they sing as they pull up the gangplank. I ain't worried about it, let the country get fucked up. But you don't need no Phi Beta cap on your head to know what's goin' on. That's my point.

Fact is I was not givin' Kleinfeld my best. Fact is my mind was not on Kleinfeld's cases. It was on Diane Vargas. Diane Vargasesasseses. Once again it was the lower part of the anatomy that got me. Not her face, that wasn't gonna launch no thousand ships. Don't get me wrong, she wasn't no Beulah Bondi, not by a long shot, but it wasn't her best part. It was her body that had me crazy. Diós la bendiga. A body like that turns you to religion automatically. And she used to dress it up nice, every day. She would sit it behind the typewriter. With her tiny waist and them fine chibs spread out all over the chair. From behind she looked like Iris Chacon. Lord. One time she got up and I got down and kissed the seat of her chair. Pachanga saw me and I had to make a joke out of it, but I was lovin' it, Jack. What and when said she had a vulgar ass. See what I mean? Them lames wouldn't know a fine fox if she sat on their face. Which they don't deserve. That hump of a husband of hers was crimpin' on my time. He was in some halfway house or work release program, so the mother fucker suppose to be doin' time was around more than me. That's what's wrong with this country, damn hoodlums suppose to be doin' time and they out in the street, breakin' balls. Shit.

Meanwhile, I was all tripped up behind her (behind). Nose clogged, windows fogged, brain blisters, all the symptoms of an advanced case. Only one cure known to man. Luckily, it comes in a handy-sized box. So drastic measures had to be taken to get my hands on her box. In other words, reverse psychology. I tightened up and held back. None of that fallin' on the floor, "I-can't-stand-it" jive. On the contrary, Mr. Cool. Clean shave every day and a splash of Houbigant cologne all over me. "Good morning, Ms. Vargas" (they go for that mizz bizz now). "Good evening, Ms. Vargas" (I used Saso's voice and posture). Har dee har har. "You are a very good typist, Ms. Vargas. You are a very intelligent person, Ms. Vargas, I mean, Diane, which is why I enjoy conversatin' with you and not these stupid people I have to meet at night who can't even hold a conversation with the drinkin' and jumpin' up and down" (she was interested in the club). I assigned Pachanga to make points for me when I wasn't around.

"Meester Carlito got plenty money, Diane."

"I don't care about things like that, Pachanga. Silvio made money at one time, look where he is now."

"Joo hosban, Silvio, was a 'ratero' burglar. I knew heem on Prospect Avenue and I knew heem een Green Haben. Silvio neber made ten dollar to rub togedda. He gwas, he ees, a lowlife."

"He's still my husband."

"Wassa matta fo' joo, Diane? I got dee guy for joo right here in dees office. Carlito. He crazy for joo. He got lotta money."

"Carlito just came out of prison. I would be crazy to get mixed up again with that life. I've heard stories about Carlito."

"Fockin' lies. Das dee people gwanna get in joo pants, Diane. Don't believe it. They tell joo lies about Carlito. Ebry night I gwork wiz Carlito in the club. Gwat a place. He the boss, I'm dee secon boss. You gonna luv it ober dere, Diane."

"He told you he was crazy about me?"

"Choor!"

Diane was a freak. She was tough, stone face, wouldn't look at me. But I knew she was a freak. That body couldn't tell me lies. So, one rainy evening, Pachanga took Kleinfeld home. Silvio was in for some violation. That leaves me and Diane. Peck, peck, peck, li'l typewriter. I'm goin' around, where is that confounded file? Ha. I squat down alongside her. She's sitting at her desk. Now or never. I made my grab.

Diane! Diane! I can't stand it! I snatched her around the waist and she fell off the chair on top of me, so we're rollin' on the rug, and neckin' and kissin'. But when I tried to get my head under her dress, she said I was rapin' her. So we had to start neckin' and kissin' again. This goes on about a half hour and I'm exhausted. I got to pull all the plugs out. I start moanin' and groanin' that I'm cramped up in horrible pain 'cause she's denyin' me her body. She came around. Kept comin' too, one of them multiple engine jobs. All the time I was bangin', she was bangin' on the floor with her hand, like it was a beavertail. And yellin' "ah-oo, oo-ah," loud, too. I thought it was gonna bring the janitor up. Like to kill me. Even my knees were bleedin' (on account of Kleinfeld's cheap rug).

Copped regular after that. Her desk, Kleinfeld's desk, broom closet, even on the washbasin. But she wouldn't come to my pad. She was a married woman. She were a devil! But during the day, business as usual. If the blue-and-dirty-collar world knew what was goin' on in the white-collar world, the Communists would take over right away.

Later on I got a bad report on Silvio from Pachanga. Seems Diane met this old Italian guy in the office. I think he was giving her money. He was in her apartment when Silvio called up on the phone. Silvio told Diane he knew she had a guy up there and he was comin' over to do her in. She got hysterical, so the old guy got on the phone and told Silvio to get lost. Silvio told the guy to wait thirty minutes while he drove there. He was goin' to do them both under. The old man said, you got a half hour. Silvio made it in twenty minutes, but the old man's people got there in fifteen. Seems the old man was a retired button guy. They took Silvio with them. I figure he is now in the great halfway house in the sky. I figure they did Diane a favor. She never said beans.

THE MERCEDES-BENZ DROVE SLOWLY ACROSS THE BRIDGE to Riker's Island. The expanse of murky water beneath flowed tranquilly, concealing the treacherous currents that lurked under the surface calm.

Kleinfeld had placed the visitors' pass on the windshield. The guards at the two checkpoints waved Kleinfeld and Brigante on. They parked at the open lot and walked to the waiting room in the bus depot, where they mounted the Number 2 bus to the Men's House of Detention, 1414 Hazen Street. They rode in silence. The bus carried several correction officers who were joking and bantering with the driver. An open truck carrying prisoners on a work detail sped by in the opposite direction. A loud exchange of profanities and jeers took place between the officers and the prisoners.

"Men's House," the driver announced. Kleinfeld and Brigante stepped down and crossed the roadway toward a squat, gray building.

"How'd you get me in here?" Brigante asked.

"You're my associate, remember?"

Brigante laughed.

They signed in the register and were led to the counsel room. It was low-ceilinged and partitioned into six glass cubicles along the side walls. There was a uniformed officer behind a desk in the right-hand corner as they entered. No one else was in the room. Kleinfeld handed him a slip. The officer picked up the telephone and exclaimed loudly, "Anthony Tagliaferro, counsel room. . . . Right."

Kleinfeld and Brigante proceeded to the cubicle diagonally opposite the desk and sat down, closing the door.

"Tony Tee, eh," said Brigante. "No wonder you been so quiet."

"I'll tell you about it afterward. You'll sit on the bench outside, but keep your eye on him."

"Tony Tee, eh. Lissen, Dave, I put hands on that guy, we'll be so fuckin' dead so fuckin' fast—"

"You afraid of him?"

"Not a question of bein' afraid. He's a number-one ghee. He's a general. I'm just tellin' you, that's all."

Kleinfeld smiled, displaying a perfect line of capped teeth.

"Don't worry, Carlito. I'll protect you. I'm five feet, six inches of bottled lightning. Long as they don't muss my hair."

Brigante was not appeased.

"Dave, don't fuck around. If something's shakin', you better tell me about it. I been put through too many changes and I done too much time because of these people. Don't be sellin' me no pig in no poke."

"Tagliaferro's had it. He's getting fifteen to life on an A-one state case and he's getting life as the head of a criminal enterprise with the feds. Serves him right for retaining Steinhardt instead of me. He's not going anywhere, he's been declawed."

"Declawed, huh? I got a flash for you, his claws go 'round the world and can reach out from Attica or Atlanta or wherever and scratch the shit outta you, believe that."

"I can't believe it. You're really scared of these people. I'm not impressed by this Mafia bullshit. I've had too many of them begging me on their knees to take their appeals. And the toughest ones you can find will eventually turn informant. They need me. I have the brains. I deal from power with them. They know it and I know it."

"Well, I'm glad somebody knows it. But some of these wops are blow-tops and sometimes even if it ain't good for them—ba-beem! You go!"

"Wait outside. Here he comes."

Brigante walked to a wooden bench by the main desk and sat down. The door was opened by a spindly, black correction officer wearing a uniform hat wedged into his thick Afro. Behind him stood a thickset man, over six feet tall, with heavy, rounded shoulders. His bulk shrunk the small room as he loped past the officer, swinging his long arms. He paused in the center of the floor, turning in all directions until his thick-browed eyes came to rest on Kleinfeld. Coarse hair matted his chest almost up to his chin. He shook his small, balding head in disgust. Captivity made Tagliaferro appear even more simian to Kleinfeld. Now he looks like the Himalayan yeti, he thought, and shuddered.

The black officer announced.

"Himself, Mr. Tee, the main ghee in lower three, to see Mr. Counselor Cleanfield."

Sicilian Asphalt Company—wearing clothes, was Brigante's quick association as he took note of Tagliaferro's finely tailored black slacks and V-necked sweater. There was a white bandana around his neck.

Tagliaferro smiled benignly at the black officer.

"Okay, Floyd, you had your fun. Lemme talk to my lawyer."

His voice was a barely discernible rasp. Throat cancer, Brigante concluded.

"See ya' later, Mr. Tagar—Mr. Ferro—see ya' later."

"Beat it, Floyd."

Tagliaferro never glanced at the desk officer or Brigante. He strode to the booth. Kleinfeld got up, his hand extended. Tagliaferro, hovering over him, refused his hand and pointed at Kleinfeld's chair. Kleinfeld sat down, as did Tagliaferro. There was a small wooden table between them.

"My throat's gone, Kleinfeld. Don't make me talk. Just lissen. Saw that little jig brought me down? His name is Floyd Butler and he lives at 765 Amsterdam Avenue, corner of 97th Street, apartment 17H. Got that? Floyd Butler, 765 Amsterdam Avenue."

"Mr. Tagliaferro—"

"Don't make me talk. I can't talk—"

Tagliaferro grimaced, then went into a violent cough spasm. He stood up, gurgling and spitting into his handkerchief. He sat down again, his face livid, eyes watering. Whispering, almost inaudible now, Tagliaferro leaned forward, his chin close to the table.

"Kleinfeld. Never liked you. Not 'cause you're a Jew. I've had Jew lawyers before. You're a phoney. I said that in Atlanta first time you came down there. A few rabbits came out of the hat and all the wops ran to you. Then you got to Nicky. You were gonna save his son. You got a million dollars for that one. For delivery of one stool. I told the bosses you were a phoney. But Nicky conned them that this was the main stool that was givin' us all up—"

"He was, I swear he was."

Tagliaferro lay his hands on the table palms up.

"Jew. Look at my hands. If you make me talk, I'll snap your neck."

They looked like catchers' mitts to Kleinfeld. He slid his chair back.

"I'm sorry, Mr. Tagliaferro."

"Some of that was my money. Then you got Nicky playin' the big don. You got all the cases. You got credit with the bosses on my parole. That was a con between you and Nicky. The same with Pomeriggio and Specchio. You fuckin' phoney. Now three years later I'm in again from the same stool you're supposed to have bought from the DA. I can see Nicky settin' us up, then splittin' the fee with you. He's the one told the bosses, 'Kleinfeld's got the hook in deep. Foley Square, Special Prosecutor, DA, he's got them all.' He coulda been the stool. That fuckin' greaseball! He's in that river now, right over my shoulder. With the crabs and the eels. I know you guys whacked up the swag between you. I shoulda had Nicky taken out thirteen years ago. He was sellin' buttons to garbage collectors then. Sure! Open up the books, let everybody in. *Buttana!* Ten years out of my life. For what? I come out, niggers and spics got it all. We ain't got nothin'. Three years I been workin' to get it back. Yeah, babanya! It's the only game there is. And if *castrati* like Nicky ain't got the balls for the junk no more? Next! Capisce?"

"Yes, Mr. Tagliaferro."

"That was the good part, now comes the bad part."

With this, Tagliaferro laughed, which caused him to gag and brought on a near convulsion of coughing. Kleinfeld rose to his feet in alarm.

"It's okay. Sit down."

"You should be in a hospital, Mr. Tagliaferro."

There was an interval of quiet as Tagliaferro struggled to swallow and restrain his cough. Completely hoarse, he started again.

"I don't care about the money. You can keep it. Only I

don't know how long, because the contract is already down on you. The cars, the guys, the guns, and the lime pit. All ready. Just the name is missin'. From in here, one button I push."

Tagliaferro pressed his right forefinger onto the table. His eyes disappeared into his brows.

"What do I do?" Kleinfeld asked, breathless.

"Thought you'd never ask. You get me out of here."

"Me? Why me?"

"I got a million-dollar credit with you. Whatever it costs you can cover. You got the brains to do it foolproof. These fuckin' gafones I got around me can't think. And you got the connections in here to get me out of the building. Yeah, the nigger. I know all about the other time."

"You have to swim. That's near Hell Gate."

"I learned how to swim in the East River. I know Hell Gate. I know the currents. I was the champ in the Boys Club in East Harlem."

"Nobody has ever made it across."

"I don't expect to. A boat on the East Side can do it easy."

"It can be done, Mr. Tagliaferro. But it has to be done right."

"Yeah?"

"I don't trust your people. You yourself say there's an informant among them. Do you know what this information would be worth? And with me as a co-conspirator? If I'm going to put my life on the line, there must be complete secrecy. No outsiders. *I'll* have the boat there!"

"Deal!"

"Leave it in my hands. You'll be a free man before the month is out."

"You got three weeks, Kleinfeld. In three weeks I go for sentence in Supreme Court. After that I go to the feds."

"Floyd Butler, 765 Amsterdam Avenue, corner of 97th Street, apartment 17H."

"I said you were a phoney, not stupid. I got cancer, Kleinfeld, I don't give a fuck. But I want out, to straighten out some of these guys who couldn't even wait until I got sentenced to step out of line. I just can't see this thing we built with so much blood go down the sewer. And because of guys who ain't even made, guys who had to pay for their buttons? Guys I sent out for coffee and doughnuts? I gotta settle. Then what happens, happens. *E!*"

Tagliaferro leaned back in his chair and shrugged. The intensity drained from his face as he relaxed and lapsed into silence, staring at Kleinfeld.

"I want to get working on this right away," Kleinfeld said.

Smiling, Tagliaferro reached out across the desk and patted Kleinfeld on the cheek.

"Tell me the truth, you and Nicky set Joe Noonch up, right? They squeezed his brains out of his head with a wire, y' know?"

"I swear to you, Nuncio was the confidential informant on all of those cases. I finally nailed him in Junior's case."

"And you and Nicky took the whole bundle home. *Bellisimo.* I always like the part when the Jew with the briefcase walks up to forty wops with the guns in their hands and says, 'Stick 'em up.' *Meraviglioso!*"

"Butler will be contacted."

"*Ebbene,*" Tagliaferro nodded wearily, rising slowly to his feet.

"Do you know where she is, Mr. Tagliaferro?"

"Where who is?" Tagliaferro raised his eyebrows.

"My wife, Mr. Tagliaferro, my wife."

"What am I, a fuckin' stool pigeon? Wadda you askin' me for?" he said, extending his arms outward.

"You knew everything, Mr. Tagliaferro. You're the boss."

"I don't know what kind of minestrone you people cooked up."

"You know she ran away with Nicky's son."

"*Grazioso.* The Jew got the money, and the Jewish princess got the 'saseetch' from Nicky Junior," Tagliaferro said, snickering.

Kleinfeld glared into his eyes. Tagliaferro shifted his gaze. Finally, he relented.

"I never liked that kind of business, Kleinfeld. A man's

family should be respected. But those fuckin' Petrones, father and son, they got no honor. Junior's in hidin'. Yeah, with her. I got my own beef with him. You do the right thing and I'll find them for you. That is straight business from Tony Tee."

"Thank you, Mr. Tagliaferro. But do you have some idea where they might be?"

"Next! I told you already. That comes after."

Tagliaferro opened the door of the booth, then turned back to Kleinfeld.

"Who's that?"

"That's Brigante," Kleinfeld responded.

"Paisan?"

"No, Puerto Rican, from the Amadeo case. I got him out of Lewisburg after five years. The feds had a rock-crusher case against him. I reversed the conviction, unanimous opinion by the Second Circuit. They'll never try him again, I did—"

"Pete's case, eh? I remember. This guy stood up."

"He always stands up."

"Your new lobby boy, eh?"

"You might say that."

"Have a nice day, Counselor."

"Same to you, sir," Kleinfeld said quietly as he stepped past him out of the booth and walked toward Brigante.

Kleinfeld led Brigante out of the counsel room. They walked to the bus and the terminal's parking lot, treading almost noiselessly over the rough gravel of the open field toward Kleinfeld's car. Kleinfeld entered the car, sitting down heavily. Brigante followed. The doors were locked. Kleinfeld turned the radio on.

"They're all the same," said Brigante, "you know one, you know them all. I been in the rackets all my life. You can't do business with these people."

"Who says I want to do business with these people?"

"You ain't one of them, believe me."

"Who says I want to be one of them?"

Brigante threw his hands up in irritation.

"Aw, man, now you gonna play games with me. Forget about it. Start the car. Do what the fuck you want."

Kleinfeld drove the car out of the lot, across the bridge and in the direction of the Triboro Bridge. They went south on the FDR Drive.

"Why are you angry, Carlito?"

"You're a great one for questions."

"Just curious."

"I'm thinkin' of the favor you did me—doing a lot of my case on the arm."

"Yeah?"

"And how I'm gonna pay and pay and pay."

"Have I bugged you about the fee?"

"No. You got bigger plans for me."

Kleinfeld nodded, his eyes on the road. "Tony Tee. I need your help."

"I knew it."

"We're going to spring him. You will be paid. Fifty, and we scratch what you owe me."

"So they got you over the line, Dave?"

"Just doing a special favor."

"No. You're in the bag, you're not a lawyer anymore, you're a wise guy now. Don't get me wrong, I'm not criticizin', who am I to throw rocks? But you oughta know, right? I mean it's a different ball game on this side. You can't learn it in school, and you can't have a late start. It's none of my business, but for a guy in your position, a top lawyer, it's not worth it."

"I'm just doing this one favor."

"Hear me out. Then you do what you want. There's no one favor for Tony Tee and them guys. That's a lifetime mortgage. I'm just yakkin', right? I know you're locked into these guys, I could see it while you were talkin' in the room with him. Gone city, I said. But what's a mother to do?"

"I can't go back, Carlito."

"That bad, eh?"

Kleinfeld sucked his lips in, his dark eyes set on the road ahead.

Brigante brought his fist down on the dashboard. "Pues, pa' lante, como el elefante."

The tension eased. Kleinfeld looked at him and smiled.

"I don't have an elephant."

Brigante laughed. "We could rent one. They stick their trunk through the bars and pull the whole jail down. Sabu used to get Tarzan out of jail like that all the time. We can hide the elephant in the trunk of the car."

"I have a boat."

"I ain't a Regatta man."

"I'm coming with you," Kleinfeld said, turning his head. Their eyes linked.

"Now I know you're crazy."

"I've done it before. It'll be easier this time. Water's warm. They're understaffed. I have a heavy hook in the place. They'll get him into the water."

"You know a boat?"

"I've been on the Sound for years. I have a house in Kings Point. I know those channels like my hand. We cross Little Neck Bay into the river."

"That's rough for a swimmer."

"Not really. We're coming in from the east, picking him up near the north corner. One quick light."

"He'll drown."

"Not Tony Tee. You saw him, he's an animal. He'll swim to Italy."

"And then come back for you, eh?"

"You need a stake. Where are you going to get it? Selling junk again? Those days are over for you, Carlito. You're not going to risk heavy time again. I can tell. Not that you've lost your nerve. You've matured. You realize, 'Hey, I could get thirty years for what I've been doing.' Once you do that, you're through. If you stay in, you'll get busted and—"

"Turn stool pigeon," Brigante said, leaning against the passenger door, his body turned to face Kleinfeld. "And loose lips sink ships." His tone was glacial.

"Come off it, do you think we would be in bed together if I didn't have faith in you? You're my number-one man. We complement one another."

"I don't consider that no compliment. Looking into your trickbag again."

"I mean that we can work together. My brains and your muscle. I'm expanding my office. Do you think I can rely on Cox or Wadleigh? Do I have to make it plainer? Your future is with me, or do you have something better lined up?"

"I didn't check my mail this morning. Say. Ain't this boat ride kind of tricky for two guys suppose to be in the law business? I mean, couldn't we get jammed?"

"Anybody can try a case. But it's ideas of this type that separate the men from the boys. This is the extra, the edge, that will have me retired at Monte Carlo or St. Moritz instead of carrying my lunch down to the courthouse on the subway, *verstehen?*"

"That's what we need, Dave, a fuckin' U-boat. Yeah, like, eh, Helmut Dantine, with the turtleneck, and the periscope. Pull right up to the pier. In ya' go, mate."

Brigante elicited no reaction to his jest.

Kleinfeld steered the car out at the 63rd Street exit and drove west.

"You never laugh, huh?"

"Sure I laugh, but I'm thinking."

"I'm thinkin' too and I gotta laugh. I was once on another escape job," Brigante said.

"Where?"

"Federal Detention. West Street. Some Cubans."

"What's the story? Who were the guys?"

"Some Cubans. You wouldn't know them. They wanted to get their main guy, Rolando, out of West Street. So they consulted the 'santero,' the voodoo guy. He came up with the scam—and got paid big bucks for it too—that to get Rolando out of the joint, they had to get a live goat and release it in front of the jailhouse. That's the only way Rolando was gonna get out. Don't ask me if the roof was gonna cave in, or the cellar gonna cave up. Don't ask me. And you couldn't ask the Cubans, 'cause they would get mad. They were gonna get their man out of the joint. We were all stoned the night we went out. Fuckin' goat didn't hardly fit in the back of the car. Stunk too. We opened the door on 125th Street when we picked up this other guy and the goat ran out. We had to chase him under the viaduct. Five of us, coked up for days, chasin' that goat, all the way up the ramp on the West Side Highway. So finally we get the goat back in the car and down to West Street. It was dark, so we parked under the highway and one of the Cubans, Pepe Chicago they called him, got out with the goat on a leash. And he's walkin' like he's walkin' a regular dog! I tell you, I was pissin' in my pants. So Pepe gets in front of the door and starts to cut the goat loose. Two guards jump out of the jailhouse door and grab Pepe Chicago. Meanwhile the goat takes off down West Street. Guess he didn't want to get locked up. We hoofed too." Brigante laughed. "Still waitin' for them guys to come out. Crazy Cubans."

Kleinfeld chuckled. "I had one of those voodoo cases. Puerto Rican woman. Policy action. Big, fat. She used to come to court wearing a nun's habit and sandals. When we went to trial, she opened up her pocketbook. A dead frog with its mouth sewn with a sort of leather string. 'This is so the DA will be unable to speak.' I was speechless, I mean I went into shock."

"Did you win the case?"

"Of course. I wiped the cop out on cross-examination. She never thanked me. She ran out to the phone to thank the party who gave her the frog. It was disgusting."

"Probably some botanica in Spanish Harlem."

"I can't understand that kind of mentality."

"It's simple. Where do all the Park Avenue people go to get their head straightened out when they got a problem? They go to the shrink, right? Right in them doors on the ground floor there. Well, uptown the shrink ain't got no diploma, but he uses the same mumbo-jumbo-abracadabra-Wizard-of-Oz bullshit. The customers demand it and the public will be served, believe that. I'm thinkin' of openin' one of them botanicas myself, shit."

They entered the office, the rug under their feet thick and springy. Fuckin' rug, thought Brigante, I still got the scabs.

"Hello, Diane. Any messages?" Kleinfeld asked Diane Vargas.

"A Mr. Rutledge called, no message. And Tyrone James called to say he would be in to see you at six o'clock. To wait for him, it was about money."

"Okay."

Kleinfeld walked past her desk and entered his room, closing the door behind him. She pivoted on her chair and returned to the typing their arrival had interrupted. She cakes too much makeup on, trying to hide her pimples, Brigante mused, don't bother me none, not with that rusty-dusty she sits on, if she farts, she sweeps the floor, ooowee. Lips set, indifferent to Brigante's presence, Diane Vargas concentrated on her typing.

Brigante circled behind her. He leaned forward until his nose touched the back of her head. Then he whispered, "Diane, you got me crazy. I'm gonna eat you right here on the rug."

She hunched her shoulders.

"Get away from me. You don't want to take me out, you're not going to touch me. All you want to do is grab me here in the office. You have no respect for me. Dejame quieta."

Brigante strode quickly around the desk to face her. He put his index finger to his chest.

"Me? I? Do not respect you, Diane? If you knew the respect I have for you. Ask Pachanga. Ask the lawyers. Whenever they kid about the terrific shape you have, I say, hey, respect. Lissen, we're both PRs. The same blood, how'm I gonna put you down?"

"So why don't you take me out to dinner? Or take me to your club?"

"Diane, Diane. If you knew what I'm goin' through now. What with my rehabilitation and trying to get back into the mainstream. They want to put me back in the gutter. There are federal agents followin' me everywhere. They're mad because I did less than five out of thirty. When the coast is clear, then I will come to you with a clean record and say—"

" 'Take me, I'm yours.' You're full of shit, Carlito. I know you have a girl in the club."

"Oh, what a fuckin' lie! I swear to my mother drops dead, I ain't got no girl in the club."

"Your mother dropped dead long ago."

Brigante was stung by this remark. He rose to full height.

"Hey, don't fool around with my mother. I don't go for that shit."

Diane's glare wavered. Detecting her slightly chastened mood, Brigante pressed home his advantage. "How would you like it if your mother was dead?"

"I'm sorry," she said contritely.

Brigante assumed the role of the aggrieved. He took a magazine and walked slowly across the reception room to sit on the large sofa, morose and unforgiving. He turned the pages studiously, with great ceremony. Diane Vargas was upset, that was abundantly clear. He would pounce on her as soon as Kleinfeld left. "Making up is so very hard to do, so make it easy on yourself," Brigante crooned to himself.

The front door opened and two tall black men came in. They exchanged hard glances with Brigante as they walked up to the reception desk.

"Tell him Tyrone James is here and don't want no shit."

James turned to glower at Brigante again. He wore a brown wide-brimmed hat (cowhide), flipped up on one side, a light tan suit, open-collared brown shirt, and yellow alligator shoes. His less resplendent companion wore matching jeans and jacket.

"You may go in, Mr. James," Diane said, opening her eyes wide as the two entered Kleinfeld's private office. Brigante rose from the sofa and stepped quickly into the adjacent library room. Wadleigh and Cox were seated at opposite ends of a long conference table. Hundreds of law books and legal periodicals covered the walls. Engrossed, neither lawyer looked up as Brigante entered the room. Brigante knelt down and removed a large volume from a bottom shelf. From behind the book he extracted a .357 Magnum. He slipped the revolver into his waistband, buttoned his jacket and returned to the outer room, resuming his seat on the sofa.

Diane Vargas sat rigidly, staring at Brigante in silence. The buzzer on her desk rang three times.

"Get in there quick, Carlito," she said.

Brigante rushed into Kleinfeld's office. Kleinfeld was seated behind his desk. Tyrone James was on his feet, his large frame shaking as his right hand, which held his hat, swung wildly.

"Ah ain't fuckin' aroun' witchoo, Kleinfeld. I want mah money back. All of it, y' heah? And ah want it now. Don't wanna be hearin' nothin' about no banks bein' closed." James turned his head toward Brigante. "Bunny, keep yo' eyes on this dude. Watchoo bring him in here for, ain't gonna do you no good."

"He is one of my associates, Mr. James. You have that file with you, Carlito?" Kleinfeld inquired, patting his waist. Brigante nodded, his eyes on James and Bunny. Kleinfeld slid open a drawer of his desk and took out a short-barreled .38 Smith and Wesson revolver. He held it in a two-handed grip resting on the desk. He pointed it at James. Brigante shifted his position so that he was now flanking Bunny. Kleinfeld's voice was even.

"Now take this with you uptown, James. I have filed a notice of appearance, I have conferenced your case with the ADA, I have done some investigation, I have at least earned your retainer. I set the value of my work, no one else—"

"You ain't done no work, and ain't gonna do no work. I checked you out uptown with Dukes and Black Bart. You a thief, Kleinfeld, the word is out on you, you are through, y'heah, through. You must be crazy too, throwin' a gun on me."

"Black Bart asked the impossible. If you want to discharge me, that's your prerogative, but I keep my retainer. Now, get out of my office, and don't come back until you're ready to discuss this reasonably."

"Reasonably? Kleinfeld, put that fuckin' toy gun down afore I climb up there and jam it up yo' ass."

Kleinfeld stood up, holding the gun in the same two-handed grip. He thumbed the hammer back. The soft click of the turning cylinder . . . James heard it clearly. He turned his scowl on his partner, Bunny. Bunny shrugged, then stood up. James slapped his hat on his head, adjusted it with an exaggerated flourish, and turned on his heel, walking calmly toward the door. Bunny followed closely behind.

"Settle with this mo'fucker later," James said as they went out.

Kleinfeld resettled in his chair.

"Thought you was gonna wash that nigger. Scared the shit outa me. Jumpin' Jehoshaphat."

"What do I do with this thing now, Carlito? It's cocked. I'm afraid of it. The noise."

Brigante went around the desk and took the revolver.

"Watch," Brigante said as he pointed the gun downward, inserting his thumb between the firing pin and the hammer block. He pulled on the hammer, then gently released it forward as he simultaneously squeezed the trigger, slowly removing his left thumb until the hammer was resting against the block again.

"You'll have to teach me how to use this thing."

"You're goin' whole hog, huh?"

"I have a permit."

"You're tryin' to be what you ain't. You can't make it on this side. Any more than I can on your side. There's a thousand things you'll never learn."

"In other words, I'm not used to guns, therefore I'm not 'macho,' is that it?"

" 'Machismo' is the poor man's strut, it's all he's got. You got talent, you got brains, don't waste your time."

"I can be pushed only so far."

"Dave. I know you're all right. I seen you get out of the car that time they hosed you down. You showed everybody you had them on right."

"My rite of passage on 111th Street."

"You had the right of way—"

Kleinfeld smiled.

"I mean, like a Bar Mitzvah, for my balls."

"You surprised them guys. But I always give a man his lane, you never know how a guy will react under pressure."

"Know something about me, Carlito. When I'm most frightened, I'm most dangerous."

"Killer Kleinfeld, eh? Don't let's get carried away, Dave."

"I mean it. I surprise myself. I got mugged on the subway once, I was in high school at the time, must have been twenty years ago. Two Spanish guys. They went up and down the car. I hid my face in a book. Didn't help. I was elected. 'Lemme see those books, lemme hold a dollar.' They terrorized me. I was petrified, but I remembered a penknife I had in my pocket. I got up and stood by the door as we pulled into the next station. The taller guy grabbed me by the hair from behind. I spun around and slashed his face open. I jumped out on the platform as the doors closed behind me. Dropped all my books. He was screeching louder than the train wheels."

"Fucked 'im up, eh? Good. You're like me, wasn't born to be pushed around."

"I got that from my father. He's not the brightest, but he's got balls."

"It's all relative, like they say. Balls is who's got the jump. I've only known two guys who always stepped forward no matter what. They ain't steppin' no more."

"You will sidestep a situation, Carlito?"

"Sidestep, backstep, any step that will get me over. That's why I'm still here."

"Discretion is the better part of valor."

"Exactly. Well, now that we know how bad we are, would you mind tellin' me what's goin' around here? Your practice will dry up if enough of these guys start badmouthin' you."

"It happens to the best of them. You get a few bad breaks, they all go running to the new hotshot."

"But you ain't made enough money to get shot down yet. You're just startin'."

"I've made plenty, don't worry. I can tell them all to go fuck themselves. Let's get out of here. I'm not going to the apartment. I'm spending the weekend at Kings Point. Check out the boat."

"Know watcha mean. I got the number. I'll walk you to the car. Then I'll come back and help Diane close up."

"Tell me something, are you humping my secretary?"

"That's one thing I don't do. Shit where I eat, fool around on the job, that's out. Let's go."

8

IT WAS A BIG SATURDAY NIGHT AT THE CLUB. SASO HAD one of his gimmicks goin' again—a beauty contest. All the flyers was out and we had a big turnout.

I'd been pissed off all day again, 'cause by my flags I'm broke. I mean big-money broke. I been jugglin' heavy numbers since I'm a kid, now I'm forty-five and I gotta start worryin' about money? What kind of improvement is that? Mostly I'm pissed off 'cause I'm scared. Yeah, I'm scared to stick my hand in again. Don't know how or when this happened. But I'm thinkin' about gettin' shot, or gettin' jammed and goin' to jail. Never bothered me before. One of the guidance guys at Lewisburg, Mr. Seawald, told me, 'You'll run out of steam, you can't sprint all the way, can't buck it forever.' That's it, I guess, they don't reform nobody, they just wait for you to run out of wind. All they gotta do is keep you locked up in the meantime, after a while you quit by yourself. Was a time, had to roll around in a Lincoln, now I'm in a Cougar. Thing is, it don't bother me that much. Shows you the cougar can change his spots.

But ain't no mood can stand up to a fine broad. They came in bunches. Jersey, Bronx, Manhattan, Brooklyn. All kinds. Even had some American chicks. Hell of a party. Place was a crazyhouse. Everybody runnin' after these fine women. There was somethin' for me too. I'm clockin' the scene. Ankle to knee, you can't beat the American leg. But knee to ass, the Latin women take the prize—and that's the

237

part where all the fun is. (If you doubt my word, check out Channel 47 any Wednesday night.) Which brings me to the winner, Rita Rosario, with her thin legs, fine behind, big red mouth, and big head of red (painted) hair. Look like Rita Hayworth or Maria Montez, that Dominican fox from the Turhan Bey days. (Kind that send you home to either slash your wrists or beat up on your ol' lady.) The conga drum went *prack-a-tan, prack-a-tan, prack-a-tan*, and the brass went *tara-tara!* Saso got Rita up on the little stage. She had on this thin red dress, low cut, and high heels. Everybody's goin' "Yay."

"The winner is Rita . . . Romero! Let's hear it," Saso announced. Yay.

"Rosario," she corrected.

"I mean, Rosario! Let's hear it." Yay some more.

Pachanga jumped out and spun her around a few times. The band picked it up and they did a fast guaracha. Rita could move. Titties too. She stayed with Pachanga all the way, and when he took his jacket off, she kicked off her shoes. Joint went wild. A broad like that will pull in twenty customers regular.

I let the excitement die down. After a while, I'm cruisin' around her table. She was sittin' with four or five chicks. They were all from Brooklyn. Bad start. But I didn't know this yet. I was all After-Sixed with my Zorro shirt and patent leather kicks. Sumooth. You'd think I was on ice skates. I snapped my fingers.

"Pachanga, a bottle of Dom Perignon for this table. Tell Louie. Right away already. Ladies, allow me. Carlito, un servidor. My place is your place is our place."

Made that up on the spot. Then I gave them the ol' bow. Times have not changed. The women still go for a guy with class. Rita spun her head, lookin' around the club, à la Rita Hayworth in *Gilda*. I go for all that. She said, "Saso told us the club was doing terrific business—"

This is true. All the wise guys were around spendin' money, tryin' to make brownies with me. I don't pay them no mind.

"—since you started working for him," she said.

Faggot of a Saso.

"Me work for Saso? You got it wrong, Miss Rosario. Saso works for me. You want me to prove it to you?"

"Call me Rita. No, no, Carlito, I just misunderstood."

She leaned over and gave me a li'l cleavage, plus her hand on my hand, plus that red mouth with them big teeth. There's two guys the broads will go for every time. The boss and the musician. I cannot carry a tune, so quite naturally, I got to settle for the party of the first part. That's cool.

"Look here. My car is at your pleasure to go the airport. As a matter of fact, I may be in Puerto Rico myself, this weekend. I'm thinkin' of opening up a 'Latin Reform Club, Part Two' in PR."

"That sounds terrific."

"Do you dance professional?"

She put her head back and laughed. Now she's doing *Down to Earth*. Who was the stiff in that? Oh, yeah, Marc Platt.

"No, Carlito. I work in an office. My and my girlfriends. Sit down, have a drink with us, these are my friends. . . ."

Can't hurt, right? Home free.

Martita, Dorita, Florita, etc. All the ee-tas.

"Why did you ask me if I dance professional?" she says. They love it, they love it!

"Rita! What a question. The way you dance? Ave Maria. You should be on the stage. As a matter of fact, I'm thinkin' of starting a little 'showtime' gig on Fridays and Saturdays. I'd like to talk to you about it—"

"Oh, they're playing 'Amalia Batista.' "

Gotta dance! Could have eight ingrown toenails. Gotta dance! Fuckin' Latin women. Fast mambo, too, must have lasted a half hour and I ain't no Joe Piro. But Rita's lovin' it. Head thrown back, boobies and ass shakin'. Did what I could. And I hardly ever even dance in the club. We came back to the table. Now I'm all sweated and wrinkled up. All out of breath. Hate that shit.

"That was fantastic, Rita."

"You were terrific, baby. You really surprised me."

"No big thing. Just my ol' Palladium routine."

"Palladium? How old are you?"

"Me? Twenty-five. Not countin' winters and summers."

"C'mon, really. How old are you?"

"Thirty-six. But don't tell nobody. Y'know, my image."
She laughed, I laughed. We was lovin' it. When you team
up with a new kitty, it is the greatest. So here's me diggin'
on this stone-killer of a broad when in come the rain like
it was the Puerto Rican Day Parade. Pachanga.

"I mus' to talk to joo, Carlito. 'Scuse me, ladies." So he
takes me in the corner.

"Carlito, Lalín is downstairs. They breeng heem op, he
een the wheelchair still from the time Kiki shoots heem in
the back. Joo gwan to see heem, Carlito?"

"Lalín? He was like my brother, Pachanga. We grew up
together. He's the only one left from my old crowd."

"Joo gwan to see heem, Carlito?"

"Yeah, I'll see him."

"Carlito, joo been away a long time. Kiki says Lalín a
stool pigeon from before. The feds send Lalín to Springfield
on a beeg bust. All een a sudden he's back. How come?"

"I got out in less than five. They could say the same
thing about me, right?"

"Hokay. Joo the boss. Pero ten cuida'o, Carlito, ten
cuida'o."

Lalín. We went through a lot of changes together. Blond,
good-lookin' PR. Great dancer. All the chicks used to go
for him. Lotta heart, stand-up. In the street, everybody is
always callin' everybody else a stool pigeon. I gotta see
for myself about Lalín.

They wheeled him in. Young kid pushin' the wheelchair.
Lalín. What had they done to you? Hardly no hair. Face all
sucked and scrunched up. No teeth hardly. Good suit on,
but his body was all dried up. When the street's really mad
at you, it don't put you in a box, it puts you in a wheelchair.
Lalín . . . bendito.

I went over and threw my arms around him. My man.
Thought he was gonna cry. I brought him over to the table,
introduced him to the girls. His kid wouldn't sit down, he
kept watchin' Lalín's back. We're all drinking champagne.
Lalín's givin' me a big promotion in front of all the girls.
I'm blowin' smoke in Rita's head. Some of the musicians

from Machito's band showed up and did an impromptu set. Rita asked me to ask them and they played the slow bolero she liked. Me and Rita were dancing very slow, veree tight, lights flickin', but low, beautiful. I got my face in Rita's hair as we're turnin' near the table. Lalín was starin' at me. I could see Pachanga over in the corner shakin' his head. Que sea lo que sea.

We came back to the table and sat down. After a while Lalín said, "Carlito, where can we go for a blow?"

I wasn't too much into candy anymore since I came out. I was paranoid enough already. I knew how I'd get once I started again. I don't do anything by halves. But Lalín was an ol' buddy.

We went to the little office me and Saso had next to the bathroom. When we got to the door Lalín told the kid to wait outside. The kid gave me a funny look. I wheeled Lalín over near a desk, then I locked the door behind us and sat down behind the desk. It was good snort.

We were rappin' about ol' times. Who didn't get forty years, who didn't get shot, etcetera. Then Lalín said. "You're fucked up, eh, Carlito?"

Bam. Just like that. Lalín—straight from the man to set me up.

I knew but I had to hear it from him.

"Times is hard, Lalín. Ain't nothin' out there."

"You mean all them people in Lewisburg and you didn't connect."

I figure I'm talkin' into a mike.

"No, Lalín. Did a lot of reading mostly. And I did a lot of joggin'. Worked on my appeal. I did most of the work, Kleinfeld got the credit."

"Jew mother fucker," he said. The two of us laughed.

"Toma otro pase," he said as he reached over with the wrapper. We laughed some more, then he steered back around to old times and stickball and jitterbuggin'. And I'm waitin'.

"I'm in with some people, Carlito."

Here we go.

"Yeah?"

"Yeah. Italianos. Heavy paper."

"No shit?"

"Mira, Carlito. These people got the money. They'll go up to twenty-five for a key if it's good shit."

"Why don't they go to the chinks downtown?"

"They don't like to deal with them people. And they don't want nothin' to do with the Colombians. Can't stand them greasy mother fuckers. They want regular street people. Old school, y'know."

"Stand-up. Like us, Lalín?"

"Yeah, like us, babe."

I pulled the Magnum out of my pants, and pointed it at his face. He opened his mouth. I put my left index finger to my mouth. He got the message. Then with the same hand I pointed to his chest and jerked my hand back. Lalín put his hand in his shirt and came out with the wire. Never was nobody's fool. His hands were shakin' bad. He put the miniphone on the desk. I threw it on the floor, stomped on it, and kicked it into a corner. I sat down again and put the piece away. I was afraid that with the coke in my head I would do something crazy.

He was crying buckets of tears and saliva. I told him a few things anyway.

"Your gums are leakin', you scumbag. I knew you were a stool pigeon from your teeth. You don't give a fuck anymore, Lalín. You're all fucked up, so you wanna fuck everybody else up, right? I oughta blow you right out of that wheelchair, hijo de puta!"

He reached down under the chair. I went for my pistol. He pulled out a box of Pampers.

"Kill me! Go ahead. Kill me! Go ahead. Pull your trigger. Look. Look what I carry around. Pampers! I shit in my pants. I can't hump. I can't dance—*kill me*, you cock sucker."

He threw the box. It hit the wall behind me. I waited awhile for him to settle down. He was hysterical. I think from the movies all the time. I'm thinkin' of Tommy Udo throwin' the old lady in the wheelchair down the stairs. He stopped blubberin'.

"Can't do it, Carlito, you can't do it. You're gonna say I'm fulla shit, but I was gonna show you the wire. I couldn't

rat you out. I was gonna give you a signal or write it out
for you."

"You're fulla shit."

"They made me do it. They wanna send me back to
Springfield. I'm no good in the joint. I'm in a wheelchair.
Do you know what it is? I know one thing, I ain't gonna
die inside. I was born on the street and I'm gonna die on
the street."

"Who made you, the feds?"

"They're all the same now. The feds, the city, the Special
Prosecutors. They all drink out of the same ditch. They're
gonna get you, Carlito. They want you bad."

"You got names?"

"What names? Buncha white guys, detectives, agents, I
don't know. They come to my house, wire me up, and
wheel me out."

"Get paid?"

"Yeah."

"Fuckin' stool pigeon."

"I wasn't gonna hurt you, Carlito. I swear. Por los huesos
de mi madre."

"Yeah, yeah. Get the fuck outa here, okay? Get your
wheel boy. Hey, what's the story with him?"

"He's okay, he's my kid cousin."

"Nice job you got him. When they come for you, he
goes too."

Lalín shrugged his shoulders. I got up from the chair.
I needed some air. So much shit going down. So many
people tryin' to lock me up. I'm walking to the door when
I remembered something.

"People seen you come in here. Everybody knows you're
a stool, they'll say I'm a stool. Or better, I let you go 'cause
I'm scared, I'm a punk. You are good news, Lalín. Know
what I mean? I oughta throw you down the stairs."

"I got some good news for you."

Then he clams up. He knows I always been a nosy-body
"averiguao." I come back from the door.

"What good news?"

"Remember the 'Americana' you were so crazy about
before you went in?"

"Yeah, Gail. What about her?"

"She's here in New York."

"How do you know?"

"I seen her, last year. Just before I got shot. You remember that schoolteacher, Gloria, I used to go out with?"

"No. Where did you see Gail?"

"At the Hilton. Some kind of teachers conference. I went to pick up Gloria and this blond chick, fine as wine, was with her. They taught at the same school, upper Manhattan, around 200-something Street. She speaks perfect Spanish. We were talkin' about PRs and the Barrio, all that bullshit and this chick mentions your name, Charley Brigante. Char-lee."

"That's her."

"I told her you was m'main man, and all like that. This before I got shot, I was lookin' good. Had me a Toronado—"

"Did she ask about me? I mean . . . you know?"

"I told her you was still in the joint, doing thirty years, and never comin' out. Who—"

"Did she say what she'd been doin', things like that?"

"Gloria told me the chick was really hung up on you for a while, but you put her down. I told Gloria, 'What's the guy to do, he's doin' thirty years.' She married some South American guy and went to live down there. Guy was killed, she came back and was in the school with my girl."

"Where's Gloria now?"

"Florida somewhere. I dunno."

"Where was this school?"

"Upper two hundreds, off Broadway, I used to pick Gloria up there."

"How did she look?"

"Gloria's a fox, she—"

"I mean Gail."

"Un pollo, mi hermano, un pollo tremendo."

What could I say? The mother fucker brought me two baskets. One full of butcher knives and one full of flowers.

"Lalín. We been sittin' on buzz saws all our life. We're on the down side now. I don't want to kill you. I don't even want to fight you. You got things to do. Do them someplace else. Okay?"

"Okay, Carlito. Adios."

"Adios."

The kid and Pachanga carried Lalín down the stairs. I didn't say nothin' to Pachanga about Lalín. In the street, if you accuse a guy of bein' a stool pigeon, either he's suppose to kill you or you're suppose to kill him. None of them kind of ideas were makin' sense to me anymore. Fuck it. I went out to party some more with Rita.

It was broad daylight when we walked over to my apartment on 79th near Riverside Drive, for a nightcap. I got on her case right away.

Oh, Carlito, you're in such a hurry. Thought we were only going to have a drink. Play a record. Let me finish my cigarette. Ave Maria, Carlito!

She wasn't red all over, but she sure had fire down below. I was just about fallin' asleep when she announced I had to drive her to Brooklyn. You wanna play, you got to pay.

I was back on the highway from Brooklyn. My head looped back to the time with Gail. Gail. Mickey Mouse name from the heartland. What heart? They ain't got no heart out there. Gail. Gale Storm, Gail Russell, Roy and Gail Rogers—no that's Dale. Brimfield, that was her name—solid one-hundred-percent Wanglo-Saxon from the Buck Jones country. Roll out the barrel. Miss America from Lorain, Ohio, out to save the unwashed Puerto Ricans and ended up with me. What hassles I put her through. Then she married some "cholo" from South America. Probably another dope peddler. Chick must be a glutton. Always in the Latin bag, instead of stayin' in her own world. She must be crazy. Missionary bag too. They're worried about the poor. People like her, that's what they worry about. The poor. When shit turns to gold, the poor will be born without assholes. That's the poor. I had a million dollars in my pocket, I was one of the poor. Fuck the broad . . . school's closed today anyway. Let's get some sleep.

No sooner I fell asleep the fuckin' phone rang.

"Your dime."

"Carlito?"

"Yeah, who—"

"Monchín's cousin."

"Qué pasa?"

"Can you be at Kennedy at twelve? It's ten o'clock now."

"Yeah, guess so."

"Good. Eastern Airlines. You can fly back tonight or tomorrow if you want."

"Okay. Eastern. Twelve o'clock."

THESE FOUR "MACHETE-FACED" CUBANS PICKED ME AND Walberto up at the Miami airport, in an El Dorado. Everybody wearin' shades. Nobody said very much. "El Comandante" was waitin'. That's what Rolando was called in the old days with Batista. Had his own private army in Cuba through a couple of presidents. Rolando swore Batista had castrated Castro when he took him prisoner after the Moncada Barracks raid and that's why he let him out of prison. But "castrao o no, Castro es el mas empinga'o de todos," Rolando used to say. Rolando had been a chief of police, so you know he had a ticket for "paredón," but he survived. Survived in the Belgian Congo and in the Bay of Pigs. Survived in the knockaround streets of New York. And made it down here to live better than King Farouk (who he favored, with his dark glasses and porno hang-up, only not so fat), and with hardly no English. Nobody's fool, was Rolando Rivas-Barcelo. He always liked me.

The sun was still hot when we got to Rolando's place. Looked like the old Al Capone house down in Miami Beach. *Gone With the Wind* mansion edged on the water with a big boat tied up alongside. Weepin' willows, green · lawns you could land a plane on, white wicker chairs under these big beach umbrellas. Money, babe.

Rolando was out on the lawn under this awning with a couple of other "cara de matones." They were around this table with a big spread of black beans, white rice (Moors and Christians, the Cubans call them), pork, and platanos and scoopin' it up.

"Carlito, mi hermano," he said.

He stood up and we embraced and kissed like we was Jules and Jim. Moustache and hair a little grayer, but he looked the same. His boys moved to the other tables, leavin' me, Walberto, and Rolando under the awning. Beans looked good, so I ate too. We rapped about this n' that until finally I said I had to get back that evening for a big party at my club in New York.

"Está bien, Carlito. Walberto has spoke to you about my problem. I need a man of trust down there. Monchín was a good man, but he was, ah, 'trigueño,' dark-skinned, he stood out too much. You, Carlito, fit in better, have the two languages, and can be more 'astuto,' more clever."

Spaniards used to say, "To be white is a career; mulatto, an illusion; black, sack of coal." Pobre de Monchín.

"You got all these guys here, Rolando."

"Pliz, Carlito. I know what I do. I have men down there too. But I need you. You have the 'malícia' that I need. Let me 'splain. Many years ago I see what happen. The hard-stuff trade is dead. Many reason. No importa. But 'coca' I know from Cuba from the forties. From before Prío. I, myself, have attended coke parties at the presidential palace, locked in for days with movie stars. It was big business, even then, in Havana. I saw the time had come for the U.S., and I prepared. Santa Marta, Cali, Cartagena, Medellín, Bogotá—I have the network set up. The amateurs are gone."

"What's the problem?"

"Corsicans. They have Italian names, but they speak French and Spanish. Tough, Carlito, tough. Una Camorra o Mafia, but more united. Never a stool pigeon. They practice torture among themselves. I know Corsica. When I was there, they brought me Miss France or Miss Paris, for three days. *Quelle femme!* The Corsicans thought they could seduce the old fox. I took the cream and left the water. Ha. But I was impressed. They put the president in, they own the country. When Interpol arrives, they do not let them get off the plane. I have seen with my own eyes."

"Coño, Rolando. No me diga."

"Carlito, the other material is dead, France killed it. Only 'coca' remains for the big money. But it is only in this hemisphere, it belongs to us, los hispanos. Not to this plague of 'Corsos'! Maldíta sea su puta madre."

"Not enough for everybody, Rolando?"

"There could be. The 'altiplano' has leaves for everybody. But the Corsican brotherhood is one of assassins. They are too greedy. They will not eat and let eat. Son unas fieras. I am an exile, Carlito. You know how I came to plant my battle standard in this country, in this house. Puro cojón!" He removed his dark glasses. "Look at my eyes and see if I have lied to you, Carlito."

Rolando was a "santero" and believed in all that voodoo jive. I looked at them red eyes and saw nothin' but lies, blood, and rows of crosses. Uh-uh. Not for me, Jack.

"Never, Rolando. For me, where you put your hand, that is sacred."

"Gracias, mi hermano. I have not come this far to be cast aside by these 'atorrante' Corsicans. I can deal with them. What I cannot deal with is a union of Sicilians and Corsicans."

"American wops?"

"Sí. There was a meeting in Marseilles. They are in league. We are to be pushed out. I am concerned. The Italianos in America have too much money. But you know them better than I do, Carlito. You know how they think, how they operate. You know street warfare, you know treachery. Santa Barbara, Changó, and Yoruba were in my thoughts when I heard of your release from prison. Aquí esta el hombre! Carlito, I want you in Colombia to organize my men for this problem."

"That can cost a lot of money, mi hermano."

"We have airfields, planes, boats, and whatever money is necessary. There are millions of dollars involved here. I do not have to tell you, Carlito, that you will emerge from this a rich man."

"If I emerge."

Rolando put his glasses back on and smiled.

"Nobody lives forever."

"This is true."

"Bueno, mi querido Carlito, qué?"

"Sounds good, Rolando, and I'm flattered that you think I'm the man for the job. I don't have to tell you I can use the money."

"How much money do you want right now? Walberto, call Camilo."

"No, no, Rolando. I'm okay for now. I mean big money for the future. I don't need anything right now. Okay, I have to get back to the club. Lemme see what I gotta do about my apartment and some deals I got goin'. Then we can do business, okay?"

"Sí o no, Carlito?"

"Coño, Rolando, dáme un 'break.' I just come outa jail. Lemme take care of business in New York, then I think I can help you out, okay?"

"Two weeks, okay?"

"Okay."

"You got the five thousand from Walberto already, no?"

Walberto's pretty face held up. Mr. Blah-zay. Didn't get white or anythin'. His ass was out the window for four thousand dollars with that question. Still a popcorn pimp, still a game player, and with all the money he's made with Rolando. I figure I'd let Walberto owe me this one. I can call it in later. Besides, "Ladrón que roba ladrón tiene mil años de perdón."

"Yeah, Rolando. I got the five thousand!" I said.

Happy Birthday, Walberto. See ya in New York.

Walberto stayed behind with Rolando. I left on an evening flight back to New York. Coo-razy, these Cubans. They will be diced into li'l Chinese steak cubes. Rolando wants to fight the Mafia and the union Corse with a couple of Miami refugees off the corner of Flagler Street. He must think I'm crazy. Get me in a hatchet fight without a hatchet. You can't get a fight outa me! I don't wanna hear about it. Just gotta unhook myself easy, so Rolando won't get mad. I need Colombia like Lalín needs an attack of St. Vitus's Dance. Later.

9

A TALL, HEAVYSET, UNIFORMED COURT OFFICER OPENED the robing room door into the courtroom, Part AR3, night court. He banged on the door with his open hand.

"Hear ye, hear ye. All persons rise, put all newspapers away, the honorable Joshua Kleinfeld, judge of the Criminal Court," the court officer mumbled hurriedly as he led the judge down the aisle at a quick pace. The large gathering of police officers, witnesses, defendants, and spectators rose. All eyes focused on the short, ruddy-cheeked man in the black robe carrying a large unlit cigar in his hand. As the two men turned the corner at the forwardmost row in the room, the officer tapped a reclining man on the shoulder. He remained seated, glaring at the officer.

"Keep going, Manny," the judge told the officer, Manny Suarez. Suarez paused just long enough to observe that the man was young, white, wore cowboy clothes, and an elaborate entanglement of hair tied into a braid that from a distance resembled a coonskin cap.

Judge Kleinfeld mounted the bench. Two telephone books were already placed in the seat of the large swivel chair. Kleinfeld remained standing, momentarily. He appeared to be adjusting the calendar on the desk. His eyes scrutinized the room. To his right, the Legal Aid attorneys read complaints, conferred with clerks, interviewed people at the thick wooden rail partitioning the well from the audience, and shuttled back and forth from the prison pens. Directly beneath the judge's elevated bench there was a large table, known as the bridge, behind which the arresting officers, the defendant, and the defense attorney were to stand, facing the judge. The assistant district attorney was positioned on the left side of the bridge, behind a mound of papers. The long bench to the judge's far left, within the well, was crowded with women and male transvestites charged with prostitution, some of whom were mouthing messages or blowing kisses to spectators.

The collective agitation of the spectators exuded a tenseness that rose like water vapor to hang stagnant over the room. Thick as oatmeal, Kleinfeld thought. He flared his nostrils. Long years in that seat of despair had sensitized his antennae. A long night, complete with moonlit sky and a Sunday backlog of weekend arrests was in the offing.

The houselights were dim (by municipal edict). Fading, unpainted walls and a peeled ceiling from which plaster chips occasionally descended, like so many snowflakes, heightened the cheerlessness of the setting. Night court.

Judge Kleinfeld finally sat and those assembled followed suit. He scanned the audience row by row. Flower child, Rastafarian, junkie, wino, skell, pimp, distraught parent, anxious wife, irate complainant, gauze-beturbanned victim, and assorted students and observers. "All ye having business before this court . . ."

A baby let out a loud squeal and started crying. The judge motioned to Manny Suarez, the bridgeman, who stood before him. Suarez nodded to the court officer at the gate (the opening in the rail), who in turn signaled the court officer in the back at the exit doors.

"Git yo' fuckin' hands off me," a woman carrying an infant shouted from the back row as a court officer attempted to usher her out. "I wanna see ma husbin'!"

"Let her stay," the judge said. "Tell her she has to keep the baby quiet."

Always extend the carrot first. Nonetheless, several pimps in the back row elected to walk out, alarmed at the woman's outburst and the attention it might divert to them. High heels clacked their temporary exit.

Kleinfeld chuckled as he thought of the macabre Brooklyn judge who was rumored to have remarked under similar circumstances, "Take that baby out and throw it against a wall." He kept a scrapbook of courtroom cartoons. His favorite being the judge who, "I hereby," . . . doubt on his face, glances at a clock behind the prisoner that reads four-thirty . . . "sentence you to four and one-half years." The judge had learned to curb his volatile temper as well as give rein to any humor salvageable in a situation. It was a way of bracing against the waves of human suffering that battered and, at times, engulfed him.

A cockroach scurried across his desk.

"Remand him," the judge said to the startled bridgeman, Suarez.

Recovering quickly, Suarez said, "There's no hold on him, your honor."

"All right, parole continued."

To his immediate left stood the heavy door to the prison pens. Police and correction officers streamed in and out. Sporadic shouts, screams, and curses could be heard as the door opened. Kleinfeld made a quick assessment of his tools. Penal Law chart, calendar, writing pad, water pitcher.

"Hey, this is the same water from last week, Manny."

Suarez knew he had changed the water before Judge Kleinfeld had taken the bench. It was their little ritual.

"No, your honor, that's fresh water."

"Make sure, somebody might want to poison Judge Pearlman and get me instead. Call the first case."

"Brandy Alexander. Represented by the Legal Aid, Mr. Busch," Suarez read from the court papers.

A giant black man in a miniskirt and white high-heeled boots was led off the side bench and brought before Kleinfeld. His heavy lips were painted red, and a yellow wig, with the ends turned up, was poised precariously on his head. Kareem Jabbar in drag, thought Judge Kleinfeld. Loitering for purposes of prostitution. Five warrants outstanding. Fines totaling a thousand dollars or one hundred days in jail.

"Move to dismiss these cases on the grounds that 240.37 of the Penal Law is unconstitutional," Busch said.

"Motion denied."

"Move that all these sentences run concurrent."

"Cannot, Counselor. These are fine or time sentences. Motion denied. Anything else?"

"No, your honor."

"Is there anything else you or the defendant wish to say before I execute sentence?"

The defendant raised his hand.

"Yes, Mr.—er—Miss Alexander."

"Yeah, you can kiss mah ass!"

"That motion is denied. Vacate the warrants, execute sentence. Put him in. I want him recalled later. We'll have a suitable sanction for his contemptuous remark. Put him in."

The police officers laughed.

Judge Kleinfeld stood up, feigning anger with a scowl. Some of the spectators were aghast at the defendant's audacity. But most had not heard. Kleinfeld had no intention of recalling the case. Anything short of a pistol shot went unnoticed in night court. The case load would not brook delay or interruption for less. Pissing against the tide, Judge Kleinfeld thought. Next case. He sat down again.

An endless array of prostitutes paraded before the bench. Some were obviously in the advanced stages of pregnancy. One woman, a dwarf, wearing sneakers and a raincoat down to her ankles, had to be held up. She was in the grip of withdrawal pangs and had to be remanded for medical attention. A man in the back of the audience jumped up, muttered "shit" and stamped out of the courtroom. A tall blonde, incredibly emaciated, came before Judge Kleinfeld next. She was bent at the waist, apparently in pain, and asked leave to address the court directly. Judge Kleinfeld was nettled. Breaches in procedure were the stuff of which writs and appeals were made.

"Madame, you have a capable attorney beside you."

"Lemme talk, Judge."

"If you insist."

"I'm gettin' out, Judge. I've had it. Can't take it no more. I need a back operation. Looka me, I'm all crooked. Goin' back home. I'm quittin', Judge, gimme a break."

She started to sob, loudly. The courtroom grew quiet. Judge Kleinfeld stood up.

"Madame, calm yourself, please."

He looked down at her print sheet. Twenty-eight arrests. Nine aliases.

"Where's home, lady?"

"Lansing."

"Says Duluth here."

"My kid's in Lansing now. I'm gettin' out of the business, Judge. I can't take it out there no more. Please, your honor—"

She moaned as her body began to quiver. At her side, her lawyer, Busch, kept his gaze on Judge Kleinfeld's face. Kleinfeld sighed and sat down heavily. Busch knew his client would walk.

"All right, madame. I'm going to give you this last chance to get out of your sordid business. Go home, go to a hospital. Plead her, Busch, I'll sentence her to a conditional discharge," Kleinfeld said as he slammed the court papers down on the desk. He knew she would be back before another judge the following week. But he chose not to wrangle over this case. A foreboding that weightier, more complex matters were about to descend enveloped him. Already tired, he was subconsciously husbanding his resources against the impending onslaught. Sixty or seventy whores a night do that to you, he thought, they sap up your time and energy, then you have nothing for the real cases.

"Luther Wilkinson, bring him out, officer," the bridgeman called out.

A black man in a soiled white T-shirt, shoeless, entered the well of the courtroom in rapid, deliberate strides, his head jerking left to right as he combed the audience for a familiar face. The defendant was not tall but appeared as wide as he was tall, with triceps that jutted out beyond his shoulders. He stood, legs apart, rocking on the balls of his bare feet, with his head reared back, bunching thick folds of skin at the back of his close-cropped head and neck. Through heavy-lidded eyes he glowered at Kleinfeld. Kleinfeld averted his eyes. This is not a ghetto confrontation, he reminded himself. Suarez rolled his eyes at two of his court officers and they took positions on each side of the prisoner. The police officers sprawled on the benches throughout the courtroom sat up. They immediately recognized Wilkinson as the quintessential "live one."

"They took my mudda-fuckin' shoes," Wilkinson said, his tone matter-of-fact.

Kleinfeld opted for the soft road.

"One second please, Mr. Wilkinson. I'll be right with you. Let me examine these papers. Uumm. Bus terminal. Robbery. Victim badly beaten, hospitalized. All right, I'll hear you, Counselor."

Busch, who stood a few wary feet away from his client, said, "Your honor, I cannot discuss a disposition. Mr. Wilkinson's on parole now—"

"For another robbery case."

"For *a* robbery case, your honor. He is presumed innocent in the instant case, or we have forfeited all rights—"

"All right, Busch, all right. Let me hear the district attorney on bail."

Assistant District Attorney Lobello was conferring with the two arresting officers; he turned to address the court.

"Your honor, we have a positive ID, and the victim's credit cards were found on the defendant. He was caught running from the scene—"

"Runnin'? Who was runnin'?" Wilkinson bristled. He turned to face Lobello. "I was walkin', they jumped on me," Wilkinson shouted, pointing an indignant finger at the police officers, "and they put the cards on me, and how that cat gonna identify me, he was drunk! Ain't got no case. Damn!"

Ignoring the outburst, Kleinfeld nodded sympathetically, trying to placate the man whom he intended to hold in high bail. A harder line would only serve to ignite an already explosive situation.

"The people are asking ten thousand dollars," Lobello said.

"Ten thou—you must be crazy, man," Wilkinson exclaimed, his face wrinkled in disbelief.

"This is preventive detention. That is completely beyond the scope—" Busch added. He was interrupted by the judge.

"What is the condition of the victim, Mr. Lobello?"

"Satisfactory, your honor, twelve stitches."

"Bull-shit," Wilkinson said loudly.

Kleinfeld's face stiffened, but again he chose to overlook in the hope that he might conclude before the situation escalated out of control.

"All right, Mr. Busch, in deference to you, I'm going to fix bail in the sum of five thousand dollars," he said.

"Thank you, your honor," Busch said.

"Watchoo mean, thank you? What the hell kinda lawyer are you? I ain't got no five thousand dollars—"

"A very good lawyer. Put it on for Wednesday. Put him in, officer. Call the next case, Manny."

"Who?" Wilkinson shouted, incredulously.

Judge Kleinfeld looked around and beyond Wilkinson as if searching.

"Who? What do you mean, who? You! Who else am I talking to? Put him in!" Judge Kleinfeld's patience was depleted. Once more unto the breach.

"Not me," Wilkinson stepped back, into the outstretched arms of the court officers. Judge Kleinfeld knew he was going the hard road with Wilkinson the moment he had cast eyes upon him.

The riot promptly ensued as the frenzied Wilkinson kicked and threw punches at the officers trying to subdue him. All the while, he screamed, "Help, they're killin' me—"

There were six court and police officers rolling on the floor with Wilkinson. The melee lasted several minutes. Kleinfeld stood up to better survey the battle, grasping the water jug, the sole weapon at hand to fend off attackers. The courtroom was already in an uproar when a woman relative of the defendant's tried to vault over the rail, adding to the din.

"They're killin' him, they're killin' him—" she shouted.

Suarez champed at the bit, anxious to join the fray. But he stood his ground, at the bridge, between the judge and all comers, true to the original and ultimate raison d'être of his calling. Like the imperial "Old Guard" of Napoleon, battle was only joined in extreme emergency and as the last of the reserves. Wilkinson never came close. Handcuffed and held high in the air as if by pallbearers, he was carried into the detention pen by a flanking crowd of officers. His parting note was, "Ain't suppose to take my mudda-fuckin' shoes!"

Kleinfeld banged on the desk several times.

"Order! If we don't have order, I'll have the courtroom cleared and no one will be arraigned."

The arresting officers in Wilkinson's case came back into the courtroom, dusting and rearranging their clothing. Kleinfeld gestured to one of them to approach.

"Why was he barefoot?"

"He threw them away, your honor."

"What do you mean?"

"I mean when we started chasing him, he kicked them off his feet so he could run faster, they were high heels."

"So if he's a mugger, why does he wear them in the first place?"

"I guess he forgets or he don't plan it. Just jumps on the first guy he can get his hands on. I dunno, your honor."

"Okay. Call the next case, Manny."

Kleinfeld leaned back in his chair. He looked at his hands. They were trembling slightly. I'll have a stroke in here one of these nights, like Ryan had, he thought.

"Beverly Castro," Suarez trumpeted. "Bring him out, officer."

A tall, fair-skinned Puerto Rican with a startling Afro hairdo of various colors, including a green stripe up the middle, walked briskly out of the holding pen. He wore sunglasses, sandals, hot pants, halter, and pancake makeup. To no avail, his dark jowls, doorknob knees, and wire-tight legs belied the female trappings, he was macho. Suarez instructed him to place his pocketbook on the table. There had been several incidents of objects being thrown at the judge.

A burly-shouldered construction laborer type, complete with heavy, mud-caked boondockers and hard hat, arose from the spectator rows and ambled up to stand alongside the police officer, who in turn stood next to the defendant, Castro.

"You Pasquale Farenga, the complainant in this case?"

"Yeah."

"Swear the trooth this affidavit?"

"Yeah." Farenga raised his right hand. His face had several contusions and abrasions. His haircut and dour expression reminded Kleinfeld of Moe from the Three Stooges. Legal Aid attorney Levy requested permission to approach the bench accompanied by the assistant district attorney. Kleinfeld detected an aura of surliness, not in keeping with Levy's usual countenance. He immediately determined that Busch ("anarchist bomb thrower and general pain-in-the-ass") had poisoned Levy (and Bailey, the third lawyer of the complex) against him, as if he were to blame for the Wilkinson donnybrook. Commie bastard.

"This is the worst, Judge, the pits," Levy sighed, shaking his head.

"Judge, this is robbery. This is a workingman. Look at his face, look at it, Levy," Lobello insisted.

"I don't have to look at it," Levy replied with disdain.

Ha, Kleinfeld concluded, Levy's got one up his sleeve.

"Look at this!" Levy said, triumphantly exhibiting a photograph of Castro sitting in Farenga's lap at a table in a cocktail lounge. Lobello took the photograph from Levy. He held it at arm's length, he held it close up, he even held it upside down. Then he handed it to Kleinfeld. Kleinfeld smiled.

"What do you think, Lobello?"

"Bunch of queers, Judge."

Levy bridled.

"Gay people, Mr. DA, and he's not a spic, either!"

"Who said anything about spics, what are you trying to pull, Levy?" Lobello said, pointing his finger at Levy's face.

"All right, all right. Take it easy, take it easy, we've got a long night. Farenga's Italian, Lobello," the judge said.

"Nobody's perfect, Judge."

"Tell you what. The complainant will withdraw the complaint. I will admonish the defendant to stay away from him. Okay, Levy?"

The two lawyers stepped back to their respective parties, conferred briefly, then nodded affirmation to the judge.

"All right. The complainant agrees to withdraw his complaint. You, Castro, are to stay away from Farenga, look what you did to his face, you ought to be ashamed of yourself. All right, case dismissed."

Castro was enraged, he screeched, stamped his feet, and did a little dance of outrage.

"And what about me, look." He removed his sunglasses revealing two black eyes. "Tell him to stay away from me! I don't want to live with him anymore, so he beats me up, look." Castro raised his halter to show bruises on his ribs. "And look." Castro proceeded to lower his shorts to reveal a large black and blue mark on his buttocks. Kleinfeld stood up and shouted, "Enough! Get them out of here. Call the next case."

Castro exited rapidly, Farenga hastened to catch up with him. "Beverly, please," he pleaded.

"Walter Mahoney. Bring 'im out."

A uniformed police officer escorted a middle-aged man wearing a baggy, ill-fitting suit, tie, and house slippers, into the courtroom. Chalk-faced, with a thick, shaggy head of gray hair, he shuffled into place in front of Kleinfeld, swaying on unsteady feet, his eyes focused on some distant star. This cosmic journey would have to include a stop at Bellevue, Kleinfeld quickly concluded, the man was manifestly out to lunch. Accordingly, he addressed Bailey, the Legal Aid lawyer.

"He's out of it, Bailey. I think the defendant should be remanded for psychiatric examination, article 730. You consent?"

"Not at all, Judge, I was able to communicate with Mr. Mahoney in the pens. He understands the charges—"

Bailey had no sooner uttered these words than Mahoney dropped his head back and opened his mouth wide, wide, wider, until it was stretched to an astonishing expanse. Kleinfeld, at first, assumed the prisoner was yawning.

"What, is your client bored with all this, Counselor?" he questioned, then noted with alarm the prisoner's continuing rearward descent.

Bailey turned to his client. By now, Mahoney, feet fixed in place, was curved backward completely. It appeared to

Kleinfeld he had arched a perfect upside-down U. Must be a contortionist, he thought. To the people in the audience, Mahoney had almost sunk from view behind the rail. Some of them stood up to see better. "Damn, look at that," somebody said.

"Article 730, Bailey?"

Bailey capitulated.

"Request an article 730, Judge."

"Let the record reflect that the defendant has executed a perfect—eh—somersault, I guess, eh, for no particular reason. Article 730 ordered. Remand."

The officers lifted the rigid Mahoney, still arched backward, and carried him into the detention pens. Fucking full moon, Kleinfeld thought, I knew it. "Next case."

Suarez leaned over the desk and whispered to Kleinfeld.

"Judge, we gotta clear the courtroom. Clerk just told me. Bomb scare. FALN called up."

"Call another case."

"Judge, the boss says we gotta clear the courtroom. We gotta search."

"I'm the boss around here! Did you look in the garbage can? Ah—shit! I'll be in the robing room. Where's my cigar? All right, clear the courtroom."

Fifteen minutes later, Kleinfeld was back on the bench. "There's a hundred and fifty cases in the system tonight, Judge," Suarez, gravely, informed Kleinfeld.

"With all these goddamned interruptions we'll never finish by one o'clock."

The stenographer, a young woman, stood up to protest.

"I can't stay past one A.M., your honor. I have to drive to Jersey. I have a baby-sitter."

"What can I tell you, miss? I'll do the best I can—"

A group of pimps filed into the courtroom with the returning crowd. Some pushing and shoving took place in the back of the courtroom between the court personnel and one individual wearing a wide-brimmed black velour hat with a white band which he had refused to remove. As he was dragged outside by the officers, he shouted to one of the women on the prisoner's bench, "I'll be outside, Dawn."

Dawn promptly got up and waved cheerily as from a passing boat. She resumed her place in the midst of the crowd of prostitutes, announcing to no one in particular, "That's m'man, Chauncey."

The audience was still focused on Dawn when the exit doors slammed open and two court officers reentered the courtroom pushing a reluctant Chauncey from behind as they held him by the scruff of the neck. Chauncey held himself stiffly, reclining his long, angular body at a forty-five-degree angle, in silent protest against the indelicate handling of the officers. They force-marched him down the aisle toward the detention pen door.

"Took a swing at us," one of the officers said as the small procession approached Kleinfeld. Chauncey now removed his hat, a gesture of respect, as the three men went by the bench. The judge received them on his feet, solemnly, as if they were passing in review.

"Call the next case," Kleinfeld said and sat down.

A seemingly endless host of accused felons and misdemeanants were arraigned before Kleinfeld. Shootings, stabbings, rapes, burglaries, car thefts, assaults with acid, assaults with baseball bats, and one particularly revolting case where a husband had forced a bottle of bleach (Clorox) down his pregnant wife's throat (she insisted on withdrawing the charge).

By 1:15 A.M. Kleinfeld was reeling. He had arraigned 147 defendants that night and was nearing the end of his tether. He was also one year shy of his seventieth birthday and mandatory retirement after twenty-four years on the bench.

The stenographer wailed. "Your honor, it's after one, I have to get home to my child."

The Legal Aid was unyielding. "Judge Kleinfeld, you *must* arraign this defendant. He's been in custody for two days and there's no case! Have we suspended the Constitution? The quality of justice is—"

"All right, all right," Kleinfeld interrupted Busch, "one more case. Close it down after this one."

"Bring out George Devereaux."

Devereaux stepped quickly in front of the bench. A pleasant expression on his pale face, he bowed respectfully. Of medium height, he was neatly dressed in a blue blazer, ascot, and gray slacks. His thin dark hair was plastered down. Bulging watery eyes and tight, dry lips signified an alcoholic to Kleinfeld.

"Thank you for calling my case, your honor," Devereaux said in an amiable tone of gratitude. Only his nicotine-stained hands twitching behind him revealed his apprehension.

Kleinfeld's eyes raced down the arrest sheet. Sexual abuse, impairing morals of a minor, sodomy, rape . . .

"Approach the bench please."

Busch and Lobello stepped up.

"Loitering around a school, eh?" Lobello said.

"The loitering statute is a travesty. What is loitering?" Busch asked.

"Wandering around the schoolyard with a bag of jelly-beans," Lobello said.

"Who said he had jellybeans?" Busch demanded.

"He looks like Peter Lorre in *M*, look at him," Lobello added. Devereaux, out of earshot, smiled and bowed again.

"He's only kidding, Counselor. How about a violation and a fine?" Kleinfeld suggested.

"He's only charged with a violation. The DA and I have already discussed an ACD," Lobello agreed.

"This son of a bitch preys on kids. Look at this sheet. He shouldn't be walking the streets. Agh—what's the use? Step back, case adjourned in contemplation of dismissal, both sides consent."

Devereaux walked up the aisle to the back, where he was joined by the young man in the cowboy clothes who had refused to rise when the judge entered the courtroom. They went through the doors together.

"Lookit Daniel Boone there, Judge. No respect for the court and now he teams up with the short-eyes. I shoulda kicked his ass," Suarez grumbled. Then he announced to the audience, "There being no further business, this court is adjourned to nine-thirty in the morning."

10

LALÍN HAD TURNED WHEELS IN MY HEAD. GAIL. SPIDER
spinnin' cobwebs, round and round she went. Some broads
can do that. Had me jumpy. Couldn't sit around. Not even
teevee and the late movies I go for. I ankled over to the
club early, about one A.M. Had to go over some numbers
with Saso, who is a juggler and a half and who sooner or
later I'm gonna throw down the dumbwaiter. I came east
on 79th Street on the downtown side. I see this gypsy cab
doubleparked in front of the club. Two guys pile out and go
into the club, leavin' a guy behind the wheel. I crossed the
street like I'm goin' past him, on the driver's side. I can see
he's like an Indian guy—little, with the bristly hair. South
American. Hmm. Like the three cholos in the gypsy cab that
been hittin' all the after-hours joints. After the stick-up they
gang-bang the barmaids for bonus. I see this creep slidin'
down in his seat and turnin' his head away. Case closed.

I strolled to the corner and ducked into a hotel. I waited
a few minutes then I came out walkin' fast along the curb,
tryin' to keep to his blind side. He's beamed to the entrance
of the club on his right, so I cut behind the car and got to
his window before he spotted me. I jammed my pistol in
his ear and pulled the car keys out.

I said, "Policia!"

"Qué pasa, qué pasa?" he said. I knew he was a Peruvian
or Ecuadorian. This is the crew, sure as shit. I dragged him
upstairs, all five feet of him, bouncin' him off the walls.
Had him by the hair in front of me, with the Magnum at

his neck, when we stepped on the club floor. The stupid Saso is talkin' to the other two cholos by the bar. When it comes to street smarts Saso's the original guy who carries a fork in case it rains soup. Nobody else around. The thugs are workin' their con on Saso that they want to rent the joint for a night. I'd have had the jump on them but the guy I got gave a yell. They moved quick. They grabbed Saso, put pistols to his head, and got behind him. Ha. Peruvian (or Ecuadorian) stand-off. Saso and the little guy I got are screamin' "Don't shoot!" Me and the two cholos are screamin' curses back and forth.

"We choot heem!" they yelled.

"G'head. But I'll kill li'l brother here."

Li'l brother was already bleedin' bad from a rap I gave him comin' up. Saso's yellin', "No, no." This went on for a while. I think Saso fainted. Anyway, in between callin' each other maricón and cabrón, we worked out a deal. We switch around and they get by the door. Then they leave Saso there and back down the stairs, guns pointed at his back. When they're at the downstairs door, I let li'l brother come down behind them. I knew soon as he was clear they would open up.

"Down, Saso!" I yelled, soon as li'l brother was loose.

Saso hit the deck and all hell broke loose. I emptied my piece. They musta fired twenty rounds. All over Saso's prone ass. He wasn't even nicked. Was over quick. I had the car keys so they hadda hoof. But this is the shit that goes on in after-hours joints. A man is not safe no kinda way. You don't get no police protection, so every night you gotta wait for a couple douche-bags to come in and shoot up the place. It's unbelievable what you gotta put up with.

I couldn't get Saso off the floor. Wouldn't budge. Had like a hysteria freeze. Then he got mad at me!

"You would have let them kill me!"

He went total bananas, cussin' me out instead of thankin' me for savin' his raggedy ass. But that's the element. They're all like that. Lucky for Saso I was outa bullets else I woulda fired him up. Fuckin' low-life.

Gotta get out of this rut. New crowd, new faces.

* * *

THE FEW REMAINING SPECTATORS LEFT THE COURTROOM
as Kleinfeld lumbered to his feet. Suarez reached over and
lit the judge's cigar. Kleinfeld shook his legs, they felt
cramped. His armpits were wet, sticky. Tension. There were
not too many more of these nights left in him. The weary
judge trudged down the steps from the bench. A tiny mouse
scurried around the wastebasket and disappeared into the
woodwork.

"Did you see that, Manny, a rat?"

The court officers and clerks laughed.

"That's our mascot, Judge, he's here all the time."

Kleinfeld turned to Lobello, who was stacking papers at
the table.

"How can we inspire respect for law and order in a
shithouse like this? How can defendants respect such an
environment? It breeds disrespect for the whole system. Go
into the federal courthouse, spotless. The worst hoodlum
would be intimidated—"

"They got the money, Judge," one of the clerks observed.

"Money. Everything is money. People want law and
order but they don't want to pay for it. We're dealing with
amputated limbs and they give us corn plasters. The city is
hemorrhaging. Agh! I'll be glad to retire next year."

Kleinfeld gestured with his hand, then followed Suarez
up the rows of benches to his robing room. Lobello and
Levy walked behind him. It was called the Solniker Room in
honor of Kleinfeld's revered predecessor, Hyman Solniker,
who had inaugurated the blockbuster parts that were gen-
erally credited with recranking a system that had virtually
ground to a halt. The room had three chairs, a table, a leather
couch, a filing cabinet, a water cooler, overhead fluorescent
lights, and the smiling, cherubic face of Judge Solniker on
a photograph.

Kleinfeld removed his robe aided by Suarez. He put on
his suit jacket. The two young lawyers, Lobello and Levy,
were sitting on the sofa, smoking cigarettes.

"Did you read that decision in Friday's *Law Journal*,
Judge?" Lobello asked.

"Which one?"

"The search-and-seizure case, the guy with the ten-inch knife."

"Where they reversed and suppressed?"

"Yeah. Second department."

"Yes, I read it. It's like I was telling Levy here, just the other day, after my own reversal. We are, literally, awash in a sea of technicalities that will soon drown us. Multitiers they want. By compartment. Inquiry but not detention. Detention but not arrest. Arrest but do not search. Search but do not seize. These decisions have spun themselves into a sophistic knot that a Spinoza could not unravel. I certainly can't. I want to know how the cop on the street is supposed to."

"He's not supposed to, we are. After the smoke clears, we're supposed to weigh the balances of society's interest vis-à-vis the individual's rights. We're supposed to examine the so-called articulable reasons. Presumably in the dispassionate environment of this building. Or do we abandon the Fourth Amendment to every trigger-happy cop on the street?" Levy demanded.

Lobello pointed his finger at Levy's face.

"It's people like you, Levy, sitting in the appellate courts, that concoct this gobbledegook. Never held a gun in your hand, never stared at the shitty end of a knife or gun, never saw a sawed-off shotgun come out of a glove compartment while you're writing a ticket. What the hell do you know?"

"And you know?" Levy said, nodding his head.

"Goddamn right. I've been out on the street. I know what it's like."

"Goddamned police state is what you advocate, Lobello," Levy shouted.

"Boys, boys, take it easy. Let the Appellate Division worry about the balances. Let's go home."

"You should have been up there, Judge," Lobello said as he got to his feet, pointing upward with his finger.

"I'd probably be the same as they are. I think when they insulate you, when you're limited to exhibits and documents and you don't see the people, you get like that. It's inevitable."

"And that is the objectivity that our system requires," Levy said.

"Bullshit!" Lobello said, his color rising.

"Go home, you guys, get some sleep," Kleinfeld said as he stepped into the bathroom.

The two lawyers exited the room, carrying their dispute down the hallway.

Judge Joshua Kleinfeld emerged from the bathroom drying his hands and face with a paper towel. The door opened, and his son, David Kleinfeld, entered, followed by Suarez, the bridgeman, already changed to civilian clothes.

"You won't be needing a ride to the Bronx, Judge, will you? Your son says he'll drive you."

Judge Kleinfeld stood motionless. Slowly, his features were drawn into a frown.

"Hello, Dad," David said. His voice was buoyant. The older man sighed. "Okay, Manny. You take off. I'll be all right," the judge said.

Suarez closed the door behind him as he left.

The judge stared at his son. David went to the water cooler, took a sip, then turned to face his father.

"To taste of the sea you need but swallow one gulp," David said, smiling.

The judge's eyes remained cold.

"What is that supposed to mean?"

"Nothing, Dad, I was just thinking of our trip to Russia with Mom."

"Mom, huh? Since when do you have time for your family? When's the last time you came up to see us? Agh, you make me sick, David."

The judge walked around and sat behind the desk, picking up his cigar.

David sat on the sofa facing his father. Carriage erect, legs crossed, immaculate in his dark suit and tie. His smile remained affable despite the rebuke.

"You're right, Dad, you're absolutely right," he said, nodding his head in agreement. Puffing slowly on his cigar, the judge's eyes traveled the length and width of his son.

"You're like the Bionic Man. Changeable parts. New nose, new teeth, new hair. What the hell do you do to your hair? You put brake fluid on it or STP?"

David shook his head.

"That's why I don't come around, you're always criticizing me. I'm thirty-five, you're sixty-nine, can't you allow for any differences? Why are you so inflexible?" He gestured helplessly. "Dad, I want to get back to the family."

The judge paused. "You're in trouble."

"Of course not! What's the matter with you? I'm your only son and all I ever hear is reproach. It's this goddamned lunatic asylum you've been in for ninety years. I saw some of your cast here tonight. Right out of *Marat/Sade*. How can you stand it?"

"Oh. Now you're worried about me? All these years, now you're worried about me?"

"Of course. Let's face it, you're getting old. What have you got to show? The good-conduct medal from the Appellate Division or maybe honorable mention in the *Law Journal*—"

"I got reversed last week."

"Of course. They've never given you a break. You should be in Supreme Court. How many times have they passed you over?"

"I don't like it up there. The real work is down here."

"But what do you have to show for it? You're still in the subway, still on Walton Avenue—"

"Concourse."

"Dad. They've made you a workhorse and given you nothing for it. Nothing. I want to get you and Mom out of the Bronx."

Judge Kleinfeld rocked his chair slowly, his eyes fixed on his son.

"You must really be in trouble."

David uncrossed his legs and leaned forward, looking down. "Can you talk to Haynes, Dad?"

"You cock sucker," the judge said softly through clenched teeth.

David bounded to his feet.

"Talk to him. You broke him in, he respects you. Tell him to take the heat off me. I haven't done anything wrong. But they keep poking around. They start rumors. Scare my clients. They're trying to ruin me."

"Are you crazy, boy? You want me to interfere with an ongoing investigation? Don't you read the papers? With that nut, Norwalk, trying to indict every judge in the city. Are you out of your mind?"

"But Haynes is not like that. He would never hurt you. He knows you've always been clean, he told me so. He idolizes you."

"You've been across the street already?"

"Yeah, but nothing serious. Listen . . . I'm begging you. I can't sleep, can't eat, throw up my food. I'm thinking of what happened to Barney Thurston's son. They hounded him into suicide. And he was innocent. You told me that yourself."

David sat down heavily, laying his head on the back of the couch.

"I remember Denny Thurston as a rookie cop," the judge said, his eyes moistening. "Horrible tragedy for that family."

Judge Kleinfeld rose stiffly to his feet, walked slowly around the desk, and stood in front of David. The judge pointed with his cigar hand.

"You are asking me to put my neck on the chopping block."

David waved his hand in resignation. "Do what you want, do what you want."

"The question is, what do you want? What can slake your thirst? How many steaks can you eat? You have a house, a boat, a Mercedes-Benz, money in your pocket. What the fuck do you want out of life? Tell me. I want to know."

David put his hands to his head and spoke upward, toward the ceiling.

"I come to my father for help and he gives me a ques- tionnaire. We're going to plumb my psychic wellsprings, is that it?"

The judge would not relent. "It's Judy. It's Judy's running away, isn't it? That's what's untracked you."

David vaulted to his feet, shouting. "I've *told* you ten times. Don't mention her name to me. I don't want to hear that shit, I don't want—"

The judge shoved him back down on the couch.

"All right, all right! I'll see what I can do with Haynes. I'm not promising anything. And don't call me on the phone. Last week, that call you made sounded ominous. Don't call me here."

David's body seemed to contract. The muscles on his face constricted and he grew silent. The judge became uneasy.

"David, I said I'd help. All right?"

"Yes . . . Dad."

"What's it about?"

"The Petrone case."

"That's over with."

"They're never over with, you know that."

"That the one where the witness disappeared?"

"Was killed. Nuncio. And Nicky Junior walked. It's that fucking Bill Rutledge. He's after my scalp. He's trying to reopen that old-piece-of-shit case."

"I don't know Rutledge, David."

"He's nothing, Mitchell Haynes is the boss. You can talk to him. You don't know what it's about, but you came to show support for your son. In other words, 'What the hell is this all about and what is this Rutledge trying to pull on my son?' You know. Dad, we . . . we have to do something. I'm going crazy. If Rutledge gives this to Norwalk, he'll splash me all over the headlines. They'll destroy me." He rubbed his face. "I meant to tell you. I made some points with Haynes. I gave an old client of mine, Brigante, a job around the office as a messenger. He begged me, out of work, you know. Anyway, I found out he was still dealing in narcotics. Heavy. Making calls out of my office. I immediately went to see Haynes. They're working on the case. They want him bad. Made a good impression."

"David, David, lay down—"

"With dogs, wake up with fleas. I know, Dad, I know now. But how can you compare my years with yours? Believe me, this nightmare I've gone through, by myself, with no one to turn to, has opened my eyes. You were right, Dad, it's just not worth it. The paths of glory—"

"Lead but to the grave," the old judge said as he made

his way to the water cooler. He drank water, then walked back and sat down behind the desk.

"You know, David, that trip to Russia before your mother got sick was the last time the family did anything together. I remember your reaction when we chanced on Khrushchev's small tombstone in that obscure cemetery in Leningrad—"

"Moscow."

"Moscow. Remember what I told you, David? I told you, 'This man banged his shoe and the earth trembled, armies were mobilized,' and you said, 'Look at him, practically in a potter's field.' "

"Yes, Dad."

"That's why I asked you before, what do you want out of life? For years I've been trying to tell you your values were twisted. I've seen people go up and I've seen them come down. They don't realize that all there is to life is a good wife, health, and a name nobody can point a finger at."

"You're right, Dad."

"I tried to tell you that years ago when you got hooked up with Petrone, the old man. You had a godfather, he got you all the big cases. Big office, big car. They seduce you, exploit your talent, then discard you like a squeezed lemon. I tried to tell you, but no, you know it all."

"He's gone, Dad."

"Who?"

"Petrone. The old man."

"Gone? Gone where?"

"Gone."

"I'll be damned. Petrone, huh? Well, I hope you've learned something from all this."

"I'm changing my whole life-style, Dad."

"I'll talk to Haynes tomorrow."

"C'mon, I'll drive you home. We'll wake Mom up!"

11

I PULLED UP IN FRONT OF THE SCHOOL. 212TH STREET NEAR
Broadway. And I waited. All the kids and the teachers
came out. I can't even wait on money, I'm waiting an hour.
Coulda been in Phoenix by now. What the hell am I doing
here? Gonna mess up her life again, that's all I'm gonna
do. Besides, the big glamor days are over. Carlito Brigante
ain't big-timin' anymore. So what am I sitting here for? Just
to break balls? Ego-trippin'? "I can do it again?" Stupid,
what can ever be done twice? Nothin'. All you do is spoil
the first time you was there.

Safari shirt and pants, tan colored, I'm pressed, but not
like them vines Cye Martin used to drape on me. Ain't no
Patik Philippe on my wrist. Drivin' a Cougar. Me who was
drivin' Lincolns and Caddies since I was a kid. But I mean
who cares? Who's lookin' at you? Only me, from across
the sea, said Barnacle Bill the sailor. Who dat ol' man in
the rearview mirror? Carlito Brigante, also known as United
States of America versus Charles Brigante. You old! Ain't
so pretty anymore, babe. Wadda they call them, laugh lines?
Meanwhile you ain't laughin, but you got crow's wrinkles
all the way 'round your head. Got my hair though, teeth ain't
bad. Body is solid. Was doin' five miles a day at Lewisburg.
What the hell, for a cat that been shanked, shot, jacked,
brass-knuckled, I'm doin' all right. I ain't even suppose to
be here, shit. Let's get outta here, leave this chick alone.
Coulda made Albuquerque by now. Why you always gotta

piss on somebody's parade? Leave off. But I wasn't goin' nowhere.

She came down the steps. Jeans, plaid shirt, carrying a bunch of books. Must have been four o'clock. I put my shades on, got out of the car. I came around and sat on the fender, with my hand around my mouth. She came up the block. Her hair didn't seem as blond as I remembered it. She was fuller, more woman. By my signs, still the best thing that ever came my way. She went by, with her serious city face.

"Dropped somethin', lady?"

She gave me a hard look, which made me smile. She froze.

"Charley!"

"Martha!" I said, trying to horse around. We used to do that "Martha and John" routine. She lit up and smiled big, happy. I had to hold on to the car. She was tanned (from the Hamptons), but her eyes were still the same Caribbean green from the other time. They came down on me like tropical rain, cool and fresh. It had been almost five years. Still felt good.

"Dr. Stanley, I presume," (I knew it was Livingston) I said, and she laughed. She just stood there, saying "Charley," like she was in shock. I took her books and we ended up in a fake-Mexican sidewalk joint in the west seventies. I got off bad. Ah-in' and eh-in'. Even spilled my drink on the red checker squares.

"Qué pasa, Charley, estás nervioso?"

In perfect Spanish, no less.

"Joo peeky pany, lady?" I said, but I had blown my cool, so I stopped fartsin' around.

"Am I out of line, Gail? I mean, poppin' up like this, still crazy, after all these years?"

She green-beamed on me from across the table. Lit me up again.

"You will never be out of line with me. Never."

Well all right.

So now I got her by the hand. The waiter could drop a tray on my head, I ain't lettin' go of that hand. So now we're both leaning over the table and we go into vertigo. Like a wheel within a wheel.

I'm drinking heavy (which I can't do too good anymore) and we're reminiscin' about the islands and the boat and the beauty times we had together, when she was young and I had bread. About the time we anchored near Caneel Bay, not another boat in sight, and I climped the "quenepa" tree (she loved quenepas) and them cows (or bulls) wandered down to the beach, scaring the hell out of me. What did I know about cows? Gail fell down in the water laughing. She was a country girl, what the hell. And the time I climbed a cliff on a deserted island off Tortola, me wearing a snorkel and flippers (cut my feet bad but I wouldn't give up in front of her) and she took a photograph from the boat (I hate photographs). That was the island the current caught us swimming over the reef and I got a little excited and she led me out (you can't beat American chicks in the water).

And on and on. We're hookin' up, I felt it.

Then she told me something I didn't remember.

"Remember the airport at San Juan when you left?"

"Yeah, Gail, you came to see me off."

"There was a little boy with an old man carrying bags. And you gave him a ten-dollar bill and told the old man to look out for him, that he was a good boy. Remember that, Charley?"

"Eh-yeah."

"I was, well, a little frightened of you, until then, Charley. It showed me your insides," she laughed . . . "rotten to the core." We said it at the same time. That's what she liked about me. I didn't take anything serious. She never said so but I figure. Broads go for a fun guy.

"The whore with the heart of gold, eh? Don't you believe it, Gail. Lead plumbing. Give up on it."

She squeezed my hand.

"I never gave up on you, that's why I went to that horrible jail, under the highway, to see you. All the way from Ohio and you threw me out."

"The biggest favor anybody ever did you."

"It was bad inside, Charley?"

"No big ting. Just a lotta push-ups and a lotta waste of time. Everything's changed, nobody left in the street I know.

I got old, I'm broke. Other than that, everythin's okay."

"But you told me you had a nightclub."

"Really an after-hours joint. Bust-out. Somebody will get shot in the place and the cops'll close it down."

"Charley, you sound so bitter. Maybe it's time you got off the street."

"And do what, Gail? Do what?"

That stumped her. This is why I hate gettin' involved heavy with a chick. Everything gets heavy. Somebody played an old Tito Rodriguez record in the jukebox. I wanted to change the subject.

"Remember the singer I took you to see in that hotel lounge in Puerto Rico? Tito Rodriguez. That's him. Rest in peace. Greatest singer PR ever had. A Frank Sinatra. Same breath control, same feel for a lyric. Every time I hear him, I get a lump in my throat." I was stoned by now.

"I remember, Charley, he came over to shake your hand."

"That was him, a gentleman. I knew him from the old Palladium days. The good die young, and I'm still around."

Now I was all fucked up. Don't know if I was feelin' so good, it felt bad. Or feelin' so bad, it felt good.

"Julio Gutierrez wrote that song. 'Inolvidable,' " she said, her pronunciation perfect around that tongue twister.

"You learned Spanish while I was away, Gail."

"Portuguese too."

I just nodded.

"I know Julio too. Cubano. Used to play at the Torero in Washington Heights. Dassa me, Gail, in with all the big stars."

We drank and talked a long while.

"Why did you come for me, Charley?"

"You ask hard questions. I don't know. Lalín said he had seen you. I'll be honest with you, when I was inside I never thought about you."

"Never?"

"Gail. When I want to, I can block something out of my head, good or bad. Cross it out. X marks the spot. That's why I do good time. Don't be moonin' over technicolor movies in my skull. But since Lalín said he saw you—"

"Yes?"

"I had to see you for myself."

"Y qué?"

"No sé."

"That song, 'Inolvidable,' it's in an album I brought from Brazil. A singer called Roberto Carlos. Would you like to hear it, Charley?"

Would I like to hear it? Do it rain in Indianapolis in the summertime? She shared an apartment with another schoolteacher, near West End Avenue, the nineties. The roomie was out. Worse luck. Small pad, full of books, posters, paintings, statues swinging in the air (other broad was an art teacher), and stacks of albums (Gail's the music bug). We had some wine out of a Spanish "bota." I'm on a giant cushion, clockin' Gail. Hair was short now, curly, the cut of her face always reminded me of that chick in *The Graduate*. Right out of Hollywood, and drinking wine with me on the floor. I must have been crazy to ever let her go.

The place was heavy on Brazil. Rio, São Paulo, Brasilia. A big poster of Sugarloaf Mountain with all the lights and skyscrapers around it, Corcovado, Ipanema. The albums were strong on Jobim, Bonfa, Laurindo Almeida. Them guys. Orfeo negro, mucho Brasileiro.

She played an album by this guy, Roberto Carlos. One of the big singers in Latin America. I didn't know him. She brought a guitar down from the wall. Strumming softly, she sang in a low voice (in Portuguese) along with the record. I don't know from the wine or what, but it was beautiful. Then the guy sang Julio's song, "Inolvidable," in Spanish.

"En la vida hay amores que nunca pueden olvidarse . . ."

Her pretty green eyes were tearin'.

"Those were for me the last time I saw you at West Street."

She said nothing. Just plucked lightly on the guitar strings. Good as Byrd, but not in my key. I've caught too many beatin's in my time not to know when I been wasted. And by a fuckin' ghost. I bit.

"What was his name, Gail?"

"Roberto. Roberto Pereida." She could hardly talk.

"What happened?"

"February of last year. Rio de Janeiro. Last day of carnival. We were drinking. One of the other musicians was driving. He died in my arms."

"You were very close?"

She moved her head up and down. She wouldn't look at me. Miss Otis regrets. Okay. I got up as quick as I could (hard to get out of those fuckin' floor cushions), put my drink down, and tippy-toed out, closing the door quietly behind me. Hauled ass out of there. Didn't even look at the number on the brownstone. Let's roll, Carlito. Got no time for this moon-over-Miami bullshit. Go out and get the bread.

CHIEF ASSISTANT WILLIAM RUTLEDGE AND DETECTIVE Frank Rizzo were in a late afternoon conference with the Special Narcotics Prosecutor, Mitchell Haynes, in his office. Rizzo paced back and forth, hands deep in his pockets.

"There was two big dons put up the money, according to Nuncio, also known as Joe Noonch or Nunzie. He said Petrone, the senior, from Pleasant Avenue, and Tony 'Tee' Tagliaferro, from the West Village mob. Nicky Junior, Petrone's son, was the go-between with the cops from the Special Unit. He made the buy. Joe Noonch saw the junk pass, himself. The case blew up when Kleinfeld put up some money and bought Nuncio's name. *Ciao*, Joey Noonch. Then Nicky Junior disappeared, now old man Petrone too. David Kleinfeld runs through the whole thing. Eventually they'll kill him too. The property clerk case is like a jinx, Mr. Haynes. Everybody gets burned."

Haynes looked up.

"How does Brigante fit in all this? I mean, the junk was stolen, switched, and sold while he was in jail."

Rutledge nodded. "Easy. Brigante was hooked up with Pete Amadeo, Tony Tee's goombah. It's all one conspiracy with Dave Kleinfeld at the hub."

"Jesus, how could one man be in so much trouble?" Haynes pondered, almost to himself.

Rutledge leaned across the desk.

"Mitch, has it ever occurred to you that maybe *his* old man, the judge, is behind him, like a boss, like a Meyer

Lansky? In other words, his poverty thing may be all a smokescreen, a scam? How about that, a *judge*?"

Rutledge sat up straight, looked at Rizzo, who shrugged his shoulders, then back to Haynes.

Haynes shook his head.

"Bill, for Christ's sake, I love you, but you can weave the craziest theories. Will you come off it? Jesus—"

Rutledge's face flushed but he said nothing.

Haynes turned to Rizzo.

"Frank, what do we have on Brigante so far?"

"Nothing. Stool pigeons say he's not doing anything. Maybe he's waiting on this big move Kleinfeld's talking about. Kleinfeld hasn't produced anything for us, says Brigante's being cagey. Personally, I think Kleinfeld's giving us a handjob."

"All right, stay on top of it. Bill, did you get those figures for me? I want to look at them before I leave."

"They're almost ready. How long will you be in Washington?"

"Three or four days, I'm not sure."

"We'll watch you on TV, Chief," Rizzo said. His dark jowled face broke into a grin.

The phone rang on Haynes's desk. Rutledge picked it up.

"Mr. Haynes's office. . . . Judge Kleinfeld? Yes, sir, he's right here." Rutledge handed the phone to Haynes. Rutledge dead-panned it, but Haynes caught his eyeshift to Rizzo. Haynes put his hand over the speaker, "Will you come off it, Bill, he's an old friend. You're watching too many movies."

"When I point the finger—" Rutledge said, smiling.

Haynes spoke into the telephone.

"Judge Kleinfeld, how are you? Fine. Fine. She's fine, kids are fine. Yeah, he's at Cornell. Fullback like me. Yeah, yeah. . . . Nedick's? Kind of early, isn't it? . . . Eh, okay. Got it. Take it easy, Josh."

Haynes replaced the phone on its cradle, slowly with deliberation.

"For Christ's sakes, Bill, I told you to have those reports on my desk days ago. How soon will I have them?" he said.

"Mitch, do yourself a favor, put a wire on, okay?"

"Listen, do me a favor, let me run my office, okay? It's late. Get me the reports."

Rutledge rose, and strode quickly out of the room, followed by Rizzo.

12

So comes the time of Diane Vargas's birthday. God forbid the question, but I calculated from the effect of gravity on her body, thirty-five, give and take a year. We was still coppin' a pop once in a while but nothin' regular. She was keepin' company with an old Greek that owned a belly dancer joint near the Statler Hilton. Dave Kleinfeld sprung the office staff to a big feed at Sal Anthony's on Irving Place. Me and Pachanga, Dave, Cox, Wadleigh, and Diane. We put Diane at the head of the table. Did the cake and the happy-birthday number. She was good people. Her trouble was she was waitin' on some guy to solve her problem. May as well wait for the Park Avenue bus on a snowy night. Pachanga was mad because they didn't have no red beans, or "gandules" (pigeon peas).

"Pachanga, this is an Italian restaurant," Dave told him.

"So gwat, they can't make no lousy bean? Wasumata from dem, I ain't gonna eat."

He ate. Ate out the joint. Wanted a bowl of linguini with clam sauce to take home with him. Kleinfeld liked to play with people, used to put him on. Call Pachanga by his real name, Gremildo.

"Gray-mildew, that is an extraordinary outfit you're wearing. A plaid shirt with a plaid suit. Might start a trend." What and When thought this was a scream.

"Meester Kleinberg. I'm de kinda guy like different colors. Joo see dees two guy ober here," pointing at Cox and Wadleigh, "every day dey got de same suit. You got lotta money, why don you give dem more money so they dress pretty. I don go to no lawyer look gworse dan me."

Gimme a street guy anytime. In the give or take of repartee you can't beat them (specially if they done time—the greatest school of all).

Pachanga always remind me of that guy in the sarong, used to play bad guy in all the Hawaii movies—guy was always stirrin' up the natives against the old chief—then the volcano would blow up on Bora-Bora or Manakora and he would go "Aiee" when the lava got to him. Look just like him. But Pachanga could get around people. Right away he scooped up two girls from another table and sat them down with us. They weren't sayin' too much to look at, so Kleinfeld passed, but Cox and Wadleigh got interested, and likewise the broads. Plain to see they was the three-button-suit-and-vest type. Pachanga winked at me. He had "cache."

"Somebody gotta look out for Cox and Watz. Son pendéjos," he said.

About one A.M., Diane insisted on seeing the club. We were all a little high and feelin' good. I called Saso and told him to have a table, that I was bringin' a party of downtown pipples. We drove up to 79th Street. It was early, but the club already had a nice crowd (Saso was rafflin' off a car). We was a party of eight, so we took a long table along the wall. It was a weekday, so we didn't have no band, just the disco, but loud as hell. It was Diane's day, so I had to dance with her. I ain't no rock-n'-roller. Hate that noise. As usual the bar was packed. Kleinfeld had come down from his buzz and was acting glum. Saso (big-ass bird) landed at the table. He sighted on Kleinfeld like crosshairs.

"Counselor, I have heard so much about you from Charles. I wanted a career at the bar, but the fortunes of war—"

"What war was this? Sixty-day war, Ethiopian war?"

Kleinfeld was a ball buster. But you couldn't faze Saso.

"No. The war in the ghetto. The war against poverty. A war that knows no quarter. I'm with a community organization in the Bronx, and sometimes we recruit lawyers who are interested in helping the community—"

"Mr. Saso," Kleinfeld said. Serious-faced.

"Ron. Call me Ron, Counselor."

"Am I a member of the community?"

"Of course. We all are, the human community."

"All right. Then I need help . . . Ron."

"Help? What kind of help, Mr. Kleinfeld?"

"See that little black piece of tail over there on the dance floor . . . ?"

It was Steffie, the barmaid. She was on her relief and she was out on the deck dancin' in a pair of white pants that had been sprayed on her (no drawers either). Kleinfeld was about to pull rank. Lord of the manor.

" . . . I want that, bring it over here . . . Ron."

Kleinfeld's hair was a little unpressed by now and his eyes were gettin' beadier and beadier. Saso looked at me and said, in Spanish, "She belongs to Benny Blanco."

"What happened to Rudy, the waiter? I thought him and her—"

"Benny chased him."

Now I got hot.

"Fuck Benny Blanco. Bring her over here. She got the rest of the night off."

So Steffie come over and lit a fire under Kleinfeld's ass. "You rilly sump'n, Mr. Kleinfeld. You puttin' me on, Dave. Man got hisself a Mercedes, got hisself a yacht. Damn, Carlito, where you been hidin' this man?"

She gave him both barrels. Kleinfeld had his tie off, hair standin' straight up, and he's boogeyin' with Steffie. Lovin' it, too, Jack. She's shakin' and turnin' and doin' her thing and Kleinfeld's beads are glued to her ass. Look like somebody hit him in the forehead with a rubber hammer. He's staggerin', but he ain't out. Then they go into that Pendergrass "Bad Luck" number and Kleinfeld really goes ape. I hadn't had a laugh like that since I come outa jail.

About this time comes Benny Blanco from the Bronx. Along with his two water boys. Three white Puerto Ricans with the short sideburns covering the top of the ear. Roll collars long as the lapels on the suit. Rice and beans mafioso. They was "boys." Very up-tight about findin' out that they was bad. Like, "damn people are scared of me." They took a table facing us on the other side of the dance floor. Steffie still hadn't seen them even after she and Kleinfeld sat down again. Saso turned white (shoulda took his picture).

Pachanga got up and went to the side of the room. Diane's a veteran, so she's already panicked. She can hear a beef comin' up like thunder. Kleinfeld's got his hands all over Steffie and he's wooin' n' cooin'. Benny is sittin' straight up, with both hands on the table. Then he smiles at me, and waves. I can see the flash of his fancy joolery. He points a long finger at Saso, still smilin'. Saso looks at me. I nod. Saso goes over, talks awhile, then comes back.

"He says he wants to send a bucket of champagne over. He says he wants you to send Steffie over." Steffie spun quick, saw Benny, and pitched a fit on the spot.

"Saso! Carlito! What—?" She's gaspin'.

I tried to calm her.

"Take it easy, Steffie. There's no problem here. You're with Mr. Kleinfeld. Benny will understand."

Kleinfeld is total stoned now. He's swingin' his head around.

"What Benny? Fuck Benny. C'mon, Steffie, wassa matter, baby?"

So the pot thickens and I ain't lettin' Steffie go nowhere. And Kleinfeld wants to dance. To improve matters, the air conditioning breaks down and the joint is gettin' hot. Wadleigh is dancin' with one of the girls, jumpin' up and down in the same place, bumpin' and knockin' into people. Cox is passed out on the table with his broad puttin' ice on his neck. Fuckin' squares, can't take them nowhere. By and large, the squares when they get drunk is worse than the hoodlums. Then they go to a wise-guy joint, get outta shape, catch a beatin', then they call the cops, "hoodlums attacked me from behind." Diane knows I'm runnin' a game, so she gets real quiet. She got her pocketbook under her arm. She's lookin' for a foxhole.

Rudy, the waiter, brought over a bottle of Piper-Heidsieck in a bucket of ice.

"You know who this is from," he said.

"Send it back," I told him.

Rudy was grinnin'. He took the bucket back to the service bar. Now we got both feet out the window.

Kleinfeld jumped up.

"Hey, where's he going with that bottle? Tell him to bring it back, Carlito. Champagne for everybody. Atta baby, Steffie."

I pulled him back down.

"Wrong table, Dave."

But he didn't hear me, he's strokin' Steffie. Saso leaned into my ear about this time. Even his moustache was sweatin'.

"Charles, please. Benny spends a lot of money here. Why do we need this? We can't afford another incident?"

"Plus you owe him money, right?"

"I paid him."

"That's your lookout, Saso. He's just another nickel-bagger to me."

"Why do you push the kids so much? They bring in the money."

"I was doin' time. They was out here. That's why."

"Charles, something's happened to you. You used to be a fun guy. Now you're always in a bad mood. We go back a long time, so I'll tell you. People are talking about you, say you're stir crazy. They're afraid of you. You should see how you look at people. You won't have a drink with anybody. Bad for business. I'm serious."

"You're serious? You and your phoney community 'guisó'—"

"What do you know about my work? I'm down at the Welfare or at Landlord-Tenant every day. You're always putting down my work. What have you done, besides racketeer?"

"Bailed you out, didn't I? You put your sticky hands on it real quick-like, didn't you?"

Saso leaned back. Started sliding his upper plate around in his mouth. The clickin' meant he was thinkin' heavy. Ha.

"It doesn't make sense that you should hate these people. They're what you were twenty years ago. . . . And they bring in the money."

"We gonna do 'This Is Your Life' now, right? Look, Saso, you ain't got no diploma, you ain't no shrink, so get off that kick."

Saso got up.

"He won't back down, Charles. You'll have to kill him."

"Do that too."

"What about Walberto?"

"He bleeds."

"Me lavo las manos," Saso said. He turned and walked toward the bar. Diane got up and followed him, so I knew Benny was crossin' the floor.

Except for his white shirt, he was all in gray. Gray suit, gray tie, gray stickpin, no cufflinks. Lad was clean. He was a smiler, had a little Bronx gold in his teeth. Big nose. His two flunkies were behind him. He came up behind Steffie and Kleinfeld, facin' me. I had my back to the wall. He put his hands on Steffie's shoulders and leaned over her head toward me.

"That's the second time you turned down a drink from me, Carlito."

I could see a big stone on his left pinkie. Diamond watch, silver bracelet.

Steffie froze in her chair. Kleinfeld turned to look up at Benny.

"Say whatcha gotta say, Benny," I said.

"I say Steffie's at the wrong table. Right babe?"

And he pulled her up. Pachanga, Rudy, and two of the bouncers jumped from behind, grabbin' Benny and his boys. They couldn't move. We dragged them into the office. Kleinfeld insisted on comin' along. They only had one gun between the three of them. Musta been on parole. Kleinfeld had a snub nose in his hand. And that room was crowded.

"What the hell you doin', Dave?"

"I'm going to shoot this cock sucker. Trying to take my girl away."

He was swacked out of his skull.

"Put that away," I told him, but I had to laugh. Dave, the hit man. I didn't want Benny hurt too bad. Out of respect for Rolando.

There was no back door, so we tried to sneak them out past the bar, but people knew what was going on. We went through the first door and had them on the landing. I told Pachanga and the bouncers to put these guys out and they were barred from the club "for life" (if not sooner). This got Benny hot.

"Carlito, you better fuck me up now,'cause next time we meet I'm gonna kill you. I swear by my mother—"

I kicked him down the stairs. He went ass over teakettle. It was a long flight and he didn't miss a step. He was sprawled out on the street floor. His punks carried him out. Faggot.

Typical of me. Twice I had to rumble over this black broad and I ain't laid a glove on her yet. But I can see Benny's point. Never was a Latin cat could pass up on a fine black kitty. God invented black and God invented white. But it took the Spanish to invent the mulatto. And the mixture was better with the Latins, softer. Put 'em all in the blender and you get women like the "mulatta" chorus girls from the Tropicana in Havana (before Fidel). Never seen women like that. The U.S. of A. is going that way. We're all mixed up here already. When you see so many white guys walkin' around with kinky hair. This is the wave of the future. In other words, the man of the future is here already, and he's a PR.

The party broke up. No air conditionin' and too much excitement. Diane stayed at the bar with Saso, who was gassin' her to death. Cox was on his ass, we put him in a cab with Wadleigh and the two bimbos. Dave was becomin' a pain in the gazool. Wanted to snort coke. Pachanga scored off a reliable guy upstairs gamblin', and me, Steffie, and Kleinfeld took a blow. Didn't do nothin' for me. Kleinfeld, of course, wouldn't stop talking now.

"Leave your car, Carlito. You drive me and Steffie. I'll bring you back in the morning. I want to show you and her my house. Cohen's Coliseum. Taj Mahal of Little Neck and Manhasset Bay. C'mon. We have to talk. Our boat ride's coming up on Sunday."

He was talkin' this shit in front of Steffie. Leave it to the candy. So we split the joint. I'm drivin' the Mercedes-Benz out to Kings Point. Kleinfeld and Steffie in the back, like

I'm the chauffeur. Didn't bother me none. Dave's m'man.

It was the wee hours, so the roads were clear. Little Dave is smokestackin' for Steffie about what a tough guy he was. Booze and coke had him believin' it himself. How he pulled his gun on this big spook in his office and how he was gonna shoot Benny but I stopped him. Everybody wants to be what they ain't. Paloma por gavilán.

"I'm getting tired of these hoods coming to my office and pushing me around. I can be rough too, eh, Carlito?"

"Meanwhile, you don't know enough to close the windows when you're in the car wash." Dave hesitated, then he remembered.

"Tell Steffie how I stood up to that whole gang on 111th Street."

"Yeah, but if I ain't there, you ain't here."

"They would have killed me."

"For sure. That was Bobbie Duke and some of the Viceroys. That pipe wouldn't done you any good."

"It was a crowbar. I've kept it as a memento. I showed that rabble I was a man."

"Nobody ever questioned that. You showed 'em where you was at. You shoulda seen him, Steffie—"

Always puff a man up in front of his ol' lady.

Women get bored when men start macho-trippin' but Steffie was doin' her "wow, don't tell me" routine. I could hear her wheels schemin', "this li'l Jew-boy gonna take care of business, home free." I looked for her face in the rear-view mirror, but all I could see were dollar signs. Guys don't wanna be loved for their money. Wish somebody would love me for my money. She-it. Dave was funny-lookin', so he would get shook up if you told him that. He wants to be "luv-ed." What he don't know is that them's the best kinda broads, lookin' out for themselves. Them other kind, romantic broads, walk around with their own rhythm section in their head, get you in trouble. And he thinks he's a tough guy.

"Truth is there ain't no tough guys, Dave, only actors. The whole street is an act. You oughta hear the tough guys scream and cry in the back of a station house or on New Year's Eve in prison."

"Actors? What do you think lawyers are? That's all law-yers do, act. I can laugh, cry, rant, rave, all on cue. Like an Olivier. I can assume any shape or form. I can adjust to any speed, any psyche. Try pleading for mercy in a courtroom for some miserable pederast who hasn't even paid your fee—"

I figured a foot doctor.

"If you an actor, recite somethin'," Steffie said.

"Okay."

He musta tickled her because she started laughin' loud. They were horsin' around awhile, then things got quiet in the back. I figured he had his face between her legs. Divin' for black pearls, no doubt. Dave, you dawg. Then I saw the lights behind us. Empty highway and this car's blinkin' his brights behind us.

"Don't let him pass us, Carlito. Step on the gas."

I hear Dave. He's sittin' up and scared. I push the car over ninety, but they were gonna pass. The first bullet is always for the driver, so you know I was concerned. Tried to squeeze my head through the steerin' wheel. They were right alongside. Kleinfeld is stretched flat on the floor by now. He squeaks, "Don't let them pass on the outside. Keep them on the right."

He was on the left side, of course. Steffie, dumb broad, is straight up, she doesn't know what the hell is comin' off. They passed. False alarm. Couple of kids in a souped-up car. Me and Dave felt stupid for gettin' excited.

"See what I mean, Dave?" I said.

He kept quiet. As a matter of fact, he kept quiet all the rest of the way to Kings Point.

Taj Mahal all right, ranch style. House had to go for a quarter mill, easy. Had a giant fireplace maybe twenty feet wide in the middle of the living room. Made out of all kinds and colors of stone. The floor seemed to be made of marble. There were sliding glass walls with wooden panels behind them that went up and down. The place could be sealed up like a shoe box. Coulda had a stickball game easy inside that house. Dave apologized that the new fur-niture and decorations were not in yet. Steffie came out of the bathroom saying there was a red marble tub she could

fit her apartment into. She was dazzled. Doin' all right,
Kleinfeld.

"This used to be Woody, my former partner's house. I
fixed it up."

"Too bad about Cohen, huh?"

"Tragedy. He was a beautiful guy. Taught me a lot."

We're sprawled out around the fireplace. Steffie fell out.
Dave wanted to talk. His nose was stoked, but he still made
a lot of sense. There's no subject he's not into. We got to
talkin' about Russia, which I was into heavy because of a
buddy I had in Lewisburg, Antinov. He was a Ukrainian,
from Canada, in for check forgery. Antinov had been with
the Red Army in '41, was captured by the Germans, and
switched to the German army under Vlasov. Then he was
turned over to the Russians again. He told me his buddies
were jumpin' offa rooftops and eating glass so they wouldn't
send them back. Stalin sent him to the Gulag. Lost all his
teeth (he had iron teeth in his mouth). Guy had wrists like
ham hocks. Could do a Pennsylvania winter in an undershirt. Gave me the scoop on the whole war. Talk about a
survivor. He's the one turned me on to Solzhenitsyn, the
greatest convict in history. Man did eleven years (same as
me, altogether), did cancer, and still out there raisin' hell.
It was readin' Solzhenitsyn and his troubles that got me to
thinkin' about me. In other words, unless you been inside,
you ain't ever looked inside yourself. . . .

"And examined the infinity of the inner space, which
cannot be contemplated without the indispensably purifying,
spiritual experience of confinement," Kleinfeld said.

Exactly. It is a pleasure to talk to an intelligent man.
Unfortunately, I mostly only meet these guys inside, because
the street these days ain't got nothin' but clowns and stool
pigeons.

Then he said, "Bullshit," and laughed. Dave was a cynical
sombitch.

I had read all of Antinov's books on the war. So me
and Kleinfeld got into Stalingrad, Sevastapol, Kursk and
the Carel, Werth, and Guy Sajer books. Dave told me he
had been to Russia (his mother was from Odessa) and had
stood at the spot where they stopped the Panzers, sixteen

kilometers from the Kremlin. Could see the onion domes. Stood in front of the Winter Palace, where Lenin kicked off the revolution. Dave had been everywhere. Meanwhile, I had spent my life on a barstool.

It was dawn and I wanted to conk out. He walked me to a bedroom. Bed was mounted on a platform; you fall off, you'd be killed.

"We go this Sunday, Carlito."

Damn. Thought we passed on Tony Tee. I need to bust into Riker's Island like I need another felony. I musta had some puss,'cause he added, "Think of it as a commando operation, like St.-Nazaire."

"You know what you're doin'? I mean I got two felony convictions already."

"It's been done before."

"I don't go for this."

"Wait a minute. Not too long ago your issue was very much in doubt. Remember that long trip I made to Lewisburg to see you? Remember what you said to me?"

"Said a lot of things."

"You said, 'Today for me, tomorrow for you,' that's what you said."

"Yeah, 'Hoy por mí, mañana por tí.' "

"I want you to come with me. You're lucky, Carlito. You don't think so, but you're lucky."

"How about lights? Dogs?"

"No lights. No dogs."

"What about patrol boats?"

"A joke. There's no security, the cutbacks. Sunday night. The boat will be ready. Be here about eight P.M."

"Fifty large?"

"Plus a bonus."

"He'll never make it. Tony Tee is too old, he's sick."

"What do you care? You still get paid. You can buy out Saso or do whatever you want. Beats selling dope."

"You got the balls of a flat burglar, Dave."

"I know. Go to sleep. I have to wake Steffie up now."

"For a little man you stretch a long way."

"I'll be up by nine A.M., making phone calls to Geneva."

"That's where your stash is, eh?"

"Fuck you, Brigante, go to sleep."

"Oh, before I forget, do me a favor."

"What?"

"Leave the piece home. You're gonna get hurt or you're gonna get me hurt."

"Bullshit."

"Dave, you're gonna wave it at the wrong guy. He's gonna take it from you, and then what?"

"You don't think I'll use it?"

"Something like that, yeah."

"You may be right, but then again, you may be wrong. Irrespective of which, the gun remains. Good night, Alexandre."

"Good night, Nikita."

Slept good. Once my mind is made up, I don't sweat for nobody.

13

JUDGE JOSHUA KLEINFELD, WEARING A FADED BLUE SUIT, stepped off a stool at Nedick's on Foley Square. It was nine-thirty A.M. The District Attorney, Special Narcotics Court, Mitchell Haynes, was crossing Duane Street diagonally, his bulky frame filling a seersucker suit. The sun was burning through the haze of the hot August morning. They met at the curb.

"Hello, Josh."

"You're late, Mitch, I was just leaving. Not like you to miss an appointment."

"Traffic was bad."

The judge nodded. "I know my call disturbed you, but I have a problem. Let me walk you back to your office."

Haynes shrugged and turned on his heel. They proceeded together across the street toward Foley Square Park. They passed a bench facing west in the shade of the park's overhanging trees.

"Let's sit for a second," Kleinfeld suggested. "I get tired right away these days."

Haynes felt his insides clench. They sat. Kleinfeld looked up at the leaves.

"Shit. He's my only son. His mother almost died at childbirth. He was small and sickly. He had a hard time with the Irish kids in the Bronx. I've never made any money, but we managed to put him through Yale. He waited on tables, hustled odd jobs. Was left out of a lot of the social life. I'm not making excuses for him, especially to you, coming out of Harlem—"

"Go ahead, Josh."

"But you were a football player, and just plain, basically sterner stuff. My boy, David, had all kinds of complexes. First his height, then his acne, then the girls didn't like him, all the specters of adolescence. All in his mind, not real. But brilliant as he is, he was *Law Review* and second in his class, he never seemed to outgrow them. Then his wife left him for another man—"

"Josh—"

There were tears streaming down the old man's face.

"Mitch, please, just another second. He's in trouble. I know he's in trouble with your office. I'm not asking you to do anything wrong. But he's my only son and I know him. He is highly emotional. I'm afraid he'll hurt himself. I am haunted by what happened to Barney Thurston's son, Dennis, from that Knapp Commission smear. I believe he was innocent. He blew his brains out, anyway. Everybody turned their backs on him. He was a pariah."

"I knew Dennis when I was in Hogan's office."

"I was with Barney for four days while his boy was in a coma. That's not going to happen to my boy. And if my boy is innocent, and I believe he is, I don't give a fuck about you or that crazy Norwalk or anybody else, you hear?"

"Take it easy, you're getting yourself all excited," Haynes pleaded as the judge dabbed at his face with a handkerchief. "I don't like to see you like this. But what can I do, Josh? Really, what can I do? Do you want me to quash a case because he's your son? Get us both indicted?"

The judge reddened. He got up slowly from the bench and faced the still-seated Haynes.

"No, goddamnit, I'm not asking you to quash a case because he's my son. I'm asking you to keep in mind that David Kleinfeld might be innocent, and that the pressure your office is creating might kill him, and failing that, the publicity alone, even though he be found innocent, can destroy him professionally. I'm asking you to bear up to a special responsibility in this case, yes, because he is my son."

Haynes stood up, dwarfing the defiant Kleinfeld.

"You're overstepping your bounds, Judge."

The two men stared at one another. The judge removed a cigar from his pocket, then fumbled for a match. Haynes lit the cigar for him.

"Still smoking old wrestling trunks, Judge?"

Kleinfeld smiled.

"What I did for you when you first came downtown, I did because you deserved it. I'm not calling in any markers on you. But if you can, spare my boy. I know this conversation could have fatal consequences for me. You might even be wired up right now. I understand your position. But please understand mine, he's my boy."

"I'm not wired, Josh. And this conversation never took place. Good-bye, Judge."

"Good-bye, Mitch."

The judge walked north toward Leonard Street as Mitchell Haynes crossed Centre Street toward the State Building.

IT WAS R DAY, AS IN RIKER'S ISLAND. IT WAS ALSO THE third Sunday of August. Old-timers day in the Barrio. Pachanga called me early and I drove up to 111th Street and Fifth Avenue. Every August the old stickball (and fighting) clubs from the forties and fifties get together for a block party and stickball game. Pachanga said they started having them while I was away and it had become a big thing with guys coming from all over the country. The Devils, the Falcons, the Zeniths, the Turbens, the Rockies, the Viceroys, the Madison Flashes, the Home Reliefers, and other distinguished alumni from Coxsackie, Elmira, Dannemora, Mattewan, Green Haven, not to mention Atlanta, Lewisburg, Danbury, and others too numerous for lack of space. Ha. It was a real boola-boola reunion. Sun was shinin', all the guys with handkerchiefs wrapped around their heads, Apache style, and their pants rolled up. The game was on full blast. Pink rubber ball (Spaldeen) comes in on one bounce, batter gets one swing with a broomstick handle (foul tip is out). Don't need no glove but some guys use them. Goddamn ball is always goin' up on the roof. In the old days, the bulls used to come around and break the bats, now they stand and watch the game. The sidewalks were crowded with people, guys I hadn't seen in years and years. A while back, in the "jitterbug" days, these guys would have shot each other on sight. Most had been through the prison system, but most had quit the street. Drivin' a hack or a truck, workin' in a factory, like that. A few were still stumblin' around on junk or wine. Or methadone cocktails (kill ya faster'n junk). And a few were still out there jugglin' like me, tryin' to get a break. Ha.

There was garbage cans full of ice and beer along the sidewalk. Most of the tenements were abandoned, but the few that were up had people on the fire escapes and windows. There was a couple guys tryin' to peddle smoke or a deck, or run a three-card monte but on the sneak, 'cause the old-timers would chase them. There was guys sellin' "cuchifritos," "pasteles," "alcapurrias." It was a regular party and everybody felt good. Year before they had a shootin' but everything was cool. A few arguments, but no fights (a miracle 'cause some of these guys were dukers for days). Pachanga hit a double and tore his pants slidin' on a sewer. After the game they had a salsa band playin' on the sidewalk and people were singin' and dancin' in the street. The rains came and they danced holdin' umbrellas. Like in the movie, 'cept Gene and Debbie couldn't make it. Prior commitments.

Me and Pachanga took a walk around, for "Auld Lang Syne." The Barrio is shot. All the landmarks (bars and poolrooms) are gone. No more neighborhood. Nothin' but the lousy projects with a piss-in self-service elevator (that don't work) and some teenager with a switchblade waitin' on you. Ain't the same faces either. I mean, we wasn't no Derby winners in my day, not by no long shot, but people didn't walk around with that "they-owe-me-but-ain't-paid-me" look. I know, I'm gettin' old. Still.

Felt "raro" walkin' around the old turf. The old buildings still standin', boarded up with planks and sheet metal. People gone. Like them old cowboy movies, only instead of tumbleweed and cow dung, we got stripped car wrecks and dog shit. I stood on 110th Street and Fifth Avenue, and like happens in the old musicals, I was waitin' for the people to come pilin' out of the old Park Palace with the bands and the excitement of the old days. No haps, just a bus stop now. I remembered the night Filete shot Chulito (Li'l Pimp) right there by the pump. He was breathin' through the hole in his back. "Turn me over, don't let me die on my face," he said. Couldn't see the difference, but we turned him over anyway. He wasn't about to make it on either side. I couldn't walk ten feet without remembering somethin' that went down for somebody. We got to 106th and Madison. How many guys turned this corner (including me), maybe holdin' their guts in, tryin' to make it to the Flower Hospital Emergency? Only to have that ugly nurse say, "What, you here again?" Or maybe she wanted your Blue Cross, Social Security, and license plate numbers, meanwhile your shoes are fillin' with blood. Was a bitch in them days. Where did they go, all them hyperenergy guys? All them balls and hearts, where'd they go? Shoulda climbed mountains, crossed deserts, invented things, wrote songs, sang poems, done somethin'! They just all pissed and bled their way down sewers. With the sanitation guy washing out the stains with a broom so nothin's left. Can't even hear an echo.

If this was a flick, I'd do a soft-shoe Ted Lewis bit about now, "li'l ol' trip down memory lane." Right there on 106th and Madison Avenue. For the boys. Ha.

So the wind blew, and the shit flew, and everybody went down. And I'm still standin'.

I told Pachanga, "Nothin' here for me."

And we took off. Mi barrio ya no existe.

I went home to change and rest up. No tellin' where I'm gonna sleep Monday night. About seven P.M. I started out for Kings Point.

Right away I didn't like it. He was coked, to the gunwales. The flaps of his nose were red and swollen. I don't care what anybody says, you ain't as good. Bad start, Jack. Blue indigo blazer, white ducks, like we was goin' to a yachtin' party, he was spiffed out. Right away he's givin' orders like he's Captain Bligh and I'm a deck ape. He had all these charts and maps and diagrams, kept checking the time.

"We're coming in on the La Guardia side, through the Sound. I've timed the run. We pull out at one A.M. When we get there, he won't be in the water ten minutes. The water's not bad there."

"How are you gonna spot this guy in the water in the dark, Dave?"

"We get a light. We line up with that, come straight in. Will you stop worrying. You're supposed to be the tough guy, not me. I'm paying you a fortune for this. Stop talking negative. I'm getting sick and tired of it."

"Okay, Warden. Where's Steffie?"

"I sent her into the city."

"She'd make a good alibi witness."

"Are you crazy? Trust a woman?"

Dave had a funny nose. Long from the front, short from the side. Like somebody planed it down, leavin' the tip stickin' out. It was twitchin'. Guy was becomin' a regular candy man.

"You know, Dave, two romances come out of that party. You and Steffie, Saso and Diane. I now pronounce you ham and eggs."

"Bullshit. Bitch is just here because of what I can do for her. You think they care?"

"Damn straight they care. They care about what you can do for them. Nothin' wrong with that. That's the healthiest relationship in the world. Guaranteed longevity, as long as the gold-ivity holds out."

"Who wants a fucking gold digger around?"

"Babe, I'm older than you. You have to understand that you go with what you got. If you ain't Clark Gable, you show 'em your wallet. They will break their legs to get in your bed."

He got very beady on me, here.

"What? Something wrong with the way I look? What? Because I'm *short*? What do you think *you* look like? Just another *fucking* Puerto Rican, that's all you look like."

The coke will do it every time. I let it slide. Around twelve-thirty A.M. Kleinfeld got the call.

The boat was a beauty. It was a thirty-seven-footer with a flying bridge. He'd had it painted a darker color. We left Kings Point at one. Kleinfeld at the wheel. I was on the forward deck with a grapplin' pole. The water was calm, but the moon was clouded, and soft spray of rain was fallin'. I was wearin' sneakers, slacks, and a windbreaker, but I felt a bad chill. Specially in the balls. Two pistachio nuts in a freezer. Captain Video didn't feel nothin', he was stoned.

We crossed Little Neck Bay, movin' west, under the Throgs Neck and Whitestone bridges into the East River. Kleinfeld cut to the left a little, southward toward La Guardia. I could see the lights of the airport, but Riker's Island was pitch black. Visibility was zilch. This is one "Don Cheech" that's gonna have to swim to Italy. Then I saw the light. Kleinfeld gunned the boat forward, making a helluva lot of noise. We came in awful close. No Tony Tee. Madonna! Dave started zigzaggin' the boat. If the guy's in the water, the screws could chop him up. Dave is crazy. Then I spotted Tagliaferro's bald head. He was practically drowned, but his eyes stuck out like hard-boiled eggs. I reached out with the pole and he grabbed it. Kleinfeld cut the engine. I was workin' my way back with the pole to the lower rear deck, pullin' Tagliaferro along. Kleinfeld jumped down the ladder from the flyin' bridge.

"Give me that fucking pole," he said.

Dave had a crowbar in his right hand. What the fuck is he doin'? He grabbed the pole with his left hand, straddlin' the rail with his body, so he's half in, half out the boat. He's pulling the pole in, but slowly, he's only using one hand. I reached over to snatch the pole. There must be twenty boats out there coming our way, or at least, a squadron of planes, and this nut's fuckin'—

"Get your hands off the pole, Carlito—This is between Tagliaferro and me. Get back!"

The man is definitely bananas. Things got very quiet. Could hear a flea pee. And maybe the water bloop-bloopin' along the sides of the boat, which was rockin' badly. I saw Tagliaferro reach out with a hand.

"Kleinfeld, please . . ." he said, garglin' slime water, his head bobbin' in and out of the river.

"Where is Judy, Tony Tee, where's my wife?"

Kleinfeld's askin' about his old lady, like we were rowin' in Central Park Lake. Then Tony Tee pulled hard on the pole and jumped up out of the water, grabbing the rail of the boat with his left hand. Crunk! Kleinfeld smashed Tagliaferro's hand with the crowbar and he fell back into the water. Splash. He was gone. Then his head came up again! Like the guy in *Diabolique*. Jesus. Kleinfeld jabbed him with the pole and Tagliaferro grabbed hold again. His eyes were closed tight, all you could see were his teeth, clamped, I don't know from anger or fear or pain. His left hand was bleeding bad. Kleinfeld hauled him in again. I'm dancin' around the fishing chairs, in a panic, I figure, the Coast Guard, somebody's comin'.

"Tony, for the last time. Where's Judy? With Nicky? Where? Rome? Palermo? Just tell me and I'll pull you aboard. You want to drown like a rat? Tell me!"

Tagliaferro gasped something about London, I couldn't make it out, but Kleinfeld did, he nodded.

"Okay, Tony. Come aboard," he said, as he pulled on the pole. Then he swung overhand, hard, with the crowbar. It caught Tagliaferro on the forehead. Musta split him like an eggshell. He went back with both arms sticking out, Christ on the cross. Stayed under that time. Arrivederci, Roma.

"Drown, you ghinny bastard," Kleinfeld said. He threw the crowbar into the water and ran up the ladder. I just stood there. Cosa más grande! He turned the boat around and we made for the Sound. I sat in the fishing chair all the way. It was rainin' and I got all wet. Didn't bother me none. My mind was blown. Crazy Jew. I was thinkin' of a movie title from somewhere, "Who is David Kleinfeld, and why is he breakin' my hump this way?" Somethin' like that.

I got paid, plus an additional ten thousand. I kept my mouth shut. I didn't contract for no hit, but I figured the less I know, the better. He walked me to my car. It was rainin' hard now. He leaned over and said, "Call it anticipatory self-defense. He would never let me live. He's even had some of the cops killed."

"Why didn't you just let him drown?"

"He would have made it back. He's an animal. He would have made it back. I'm not worried about an autopsy if they find him. All kinds of barges and scows around there to account for a broken head."

"You know what you're doin', Dave." I started the car

up. He stepped back and said, "I'm getting wet. I'll see you at the office in the afternoon."

I came over the Triboro Bridge on the outside lane lookin' down on the East River. He's slidin' along the mud bottom now. Tough Tony Tee. With the fish. Con-yo!

14

THE SPECIAL STATE PROSECUTOR, LAWRENCE NORWALK, stood behind his desk on the fifty-seventh floor at number-two World Trade Center. He faced west, toward the Hudson River traffic beneath his spacious window. It was eight-thirty A.M. Norwalk had run five miles at the Central Park Reservoir, showered and breakfasted (on oranges, lemons, and Hoffman's Super-Protein). The freshness and rosy color of his face exuded health and temperance. His tall, regal frame was clothed in a custom-made tan suit and yellow tie. Solid brown brogues shod his large feet. He favored a white sidewall cut to his black, gray-flecked hair, consistent with the functional, no-nonsense image he cultivated. His small, even features were drawn in a slightly pinched expression that detracted from their symmetry. That and his lightly tinted metal-framed glasses evoked a mildly sinister air. The *Times* had earlier that week editorialized on the need to prosecute errant judicial officers and the inefficiency of Norwalk's office in obtaining convictions in this area. Norwalk pondered the indescribable injustice of the situation.

A massive cover-up. Of Watergate proportions. The whole judicial system is shot through with corruption. From the club-house, all the way to Albany. It's deals, contracts, nepotism, favoritism, from the starting gun to the finish line. And to date I've only nailed two of the cigar-smoking bastards, both reversed on appeal. These newspapers don't realize that a judge's career will, of necessity, wind in and through the system. And no matter where you confront him, there's always someone to bail him out, exert pressure, feed him information. They all run from my name, like a scourge. Of course, the bastards are corrupt. But you can't fool the public, the public knows that I alone can weed them out. I have no favorites and owe no favors. And yet, I have to justify my existence to the legislature on a yearly basis, like a goddamned retainer. The district attorneys are all out to destroy my office. They want to hide the corruption in their own houses and grab my budget. I'm alone in this fight. Under siege from all sides. My only hope is the man in the street. You can't fool him. He knows the whole judiciary is putrid. That you have to get down on your knees and pull it out by the roots. Clean the bastards out.

Shaughnessy. Supreme Court justice. Thief. A common thief is all he is. Goddamned jury must have been crazy. Rock-cruncher facts I presented. Pulverizing case. I missed nothing. Stupid, blind bastards.

Maybe it's these dark glasses. Maybe I should have let Duncan try it. Nonsense. Who knew the case better than I? Nonsense.

There was a prudent knock on Norwalk's door.

"Come in."

Jeffrey Duncan, Norwalk's chief assistant, entered the room followed by William Rutledge and Frank Rizzo. The three men padded in on the thick, wall-to-wall rug. The two visitors took in the luxurious ambience of the setting and its magnificent view. The desk, like the person, was ordered and clean, most antiseptic.

"Please sit down, gentlemen," Norwalk said.

He remained standing, his arms at rest on the back of his chair. Norwalk elected to erect a glacial facade on this occasion. This was detected by Duncan, who quickly parried the awkward absence of the extension of hands by plunging into a recitation regarding some commonplace office business of no consequence to either Rutledge or Rizzo. Duncan's tenure turned on his ability to adjust the various office scenarios to conform to Norwalk's unpredictable stances. Norwalk likened himself to a virtuoso actor capable of rendering impromptu variations on a stale script, ever expanding to new dimensions with each performance. "I get these flashes of intuition, Jeff. I never know how I am going to react when you march them in." He had known Norwalk to almost vault over the desk and embrace someone in an effusive display of camaraderie. At times Norwalk would sink into his chair, hands in pockets, buried in an abyss of gloom and despair that the "guest" (as in target) should have come to such a pass. He had also been known to shout at Duncan (the "guest" being a Supreme Court justice charged with accepting a plane ticket to Miami), "What is this man doing here, Duncan, why is this man not in jail, that's all I want to know, why is this man not in jail?"

Norwalk had a trunkful of ploys and guises from which he would select a pair as soon as he and the "guest" made eye contact. It was up to Duncan, as stage manager, to scurry about arranging the sets. He was nimble, and in tandem he and Norwalk had shattered the defenses of many a recalcitrant visitor. Their modus operandi was merely a refinement of the old police "high and low" technique. The rarefied air of the fifty-seventh floor with its sumptuous rugs and the exalted title of Special State Prosecutor, however, invigorated the formula. As the "guests" were invariably lawyers, judges, and persons of substance and standing in the community, it was not necessary to pounce in the night upon them. This factor was vital to Norwalk's apparatus, in that, as he put it, "the call is made on Friday, late in the afternoon, the appointment is for early Monday morning. The fool will run amok on Friday, make two hundred phone calls on Saturday, and stare in the mirror all day Sunday, envisioning his ruin. By Monday, he marches in through that door, wrists extended, happy at the prospect of handcuffs."

The lower echelons of the staff, properly manipulated, were purveyors of rumors of "unimpeachable source." One incident that reduced both Norwalk and Duncan to paroxysms of laughter was the volunteered confession of an attorney regarding some chicanery in a bookmaking case.

Inexplicably, rumors began to waft through the Criminal Court Building that he (the lawyer) was in the talons of Norwalk. The anticipated second shoe so weighed on the lawyer's fragile shoulders that he hied himself up to the World Trade Center and purged his soul. The astonished Norwalk and Duncan knew nothing of the transaction and had never heard of the lawyer.

But rumors alone had served to create social and professional lepers from whom colleagues would flee. Like so many plague carriers, even their wives were not spared the ostracism. Newspaper leaks numbered in Norwalk's battery of weapons. Carefully nurtured, tailored, and wielded, the press could prove a valuable, even indispensable ally in the battle against corruption. "The infinity of arrows in the prosecutorial quiver," he would say. Norwalk's sharpest arrows were disgruntled employees and subordinates of public officials.

Nevertheless, the investigations had, of late, suffered a series of what he regarded as untoward coincidences that bedeviled their successful termination. This only hardened his conviction that the district attorneys and the state legislature were bent on the abolition of his office. Norwalk's misgivings were not visible to his terrified peers of the legal establishment, who saw him as a fusion of Vishinsky, Roland Freisler, and other demonic forces too horrible to contemplate.

The time and place, then, found Norwalk bestride his narrow world like a Colossus, and petty men condemned to walk under his huge legs and peep about to find themselves dishonorable graves.

Duncan cleared his throat.

"This is Bill Rutledge, chief assistant to Michael Haynes, and Detective Frank Rizzo, Mr. Norwalk."

"Have Rizzo wait outside."

Duncan, his manner apologetic, walked Rizzo to the door, then came back.

"I want the two of them, Rutledge. Father and son," Norwalk said.

"The father's an acting judge, Mr. Norwalk. You can have him right now. The son is still a little ways off."

"It was I, in this very office—Duncan here is my witness—who broke Nuncio. He was *my* informant. Do you know what that meant?"

"Yes, Mr. Norwalk. The police property clerk case. The four hundred pounds of narcotics that were switched."

"Rutledge. I had that case here." Norwalk extended his curled hand, palm upward. "*Here!* And that bastard David Kleinfeld whisked him out from under my nose and had him killed. Joseph Nuncio, the best kept secret in this office, and Kleinfeld found it out. I will see him imprisoned and disbarred—"

Norwalk strode swiftly around his desk and began pacing back and forth in front of the two seated men.

"Go ahead, go ahead, I'm listening," he said.

"Bill figures we get the old man first. Use that as leverage to flush out the son," Duncan said.

Norwalk scoffed.

"Nonsense. David Kleinfeld will give up his father and his mother if it would spare him one day. The man is completely amoral. And from my school, of all places . . . never made Skull and Bones, though!"

Rutledge said, "Josh Kleinfeld's a sitting judge. He has one year to go for retirement. I figure he's calling the shots behind his son. I don't see that little jerk in the elevator shoes as no mastermind. But the old man's been around a long time, a cagey fox."

Norwalk stopped in his tracks, turned, and said to Duncan, pointing to Rutledge, "Man has imagination. I like that. Let's hear the rest of it."

Rutledge continued, "We've got him on obstruction of justice or governmental administration. Interfering with an ongoing investigation, conspiracy, using undue influence—"

"You're talking misdemeanors, Rutledge," Norwalk interrupted.

Rutledge colored. "It's more than enough to throw him off the bench. Judge Kleinfeld is a legend in the court. He goes back to Dewey. Think of the coverage, Mr. Norwalk."

"We can ensnare the son too, Boss," said Duncan. "You

watch. You know how these things are: You kick in the door, the whole house falls down."

Norwalk walked back and stood in front of Rutledge, his arms folded.

"What do we have against the judge?"

"Okay. You got the call from the judge to Mitch Haynes right after the son has been in to see us and is under the hammer. Then you have the meeting between Mitch and the judge at Nedick's. Rizzo saw them in a deep powwow on a bench in Foley Square Park. Mitch came back upstairs, all shook up. I got him to say the old man had put pressure on him. Not in so many words, but clear enough."

"Were you wired, Rutledge?"

"How could I be wired, Mr. Norwalk? He's my boss."

"You're here now, aren't you?"

"This is different. I'm not about to get myself in trouble over old school ties."

Norwalk turned to Duncan.

"I never liked Haynes. He used to make a big hoop-la about knowing the street, the jargon, when we were in Hogan's office. You can learn all there is to know about street people in two weeks. Like shooting fish in a barrel. Special Narcotics District Attorney! House nigger, that's all he is. They don't give him any money. Couldn't find an addict on 117th Street. And he tried to pirate the Nuncio case from me. Those were his cops that stole the junk to begin with. And he's in cahoots with the rest of the DAs to eradicate my office. . . . I think we can nail him on official misconduct. Yeah, 195 of the Penal Law."

Duncan nodded assent.

"Suppose Haynes denies his conversation with the judge?" he asked.

"We'll throw the whole thing in the Grand Jury. The meeting, the admission to Rutledge here, the prior relationship, the tape," Norwalk said.

"What tape?" Rutledge questioned.

"We had a wire in the judge's robing room when the son came down. We knew Judge Kleinfeld would get to Haynes sooner or later. That's why we got to you. Lucky for you that you're not covering up under any misguided sense of loyalty. Don't worry about Haynes. We can use an experienced investigator like you in our office."

"Thank you, Mr. Norwalk."

Norwalk extended his hand to Rutledge and they shook hands. He walked around his desk and sat down for the first time.

"You will, of course, say nothing to Mitchell Haynes about this matter. I will handle him personally, from my level. He's tough, but I can swoop down on him, surprise him, break him. Then I pull the plug on Judge Joshua Kleinfeld. Maybe even a felony perjury, if we can get him before the Grand Jury. All right, remain in contact with Duncan. Say nothing to Rizzo. We'll take it from here. You've done good work."

"Thank you, Mr. Norwalk."

Rutledge was led out by Duncan.

"We going to hire him, Larry?" Duncan asked as he returned to Norwalk's desk.

"Are you crazy, a goddamned stool pigeon? We'll just nurse him along for now. Jeff, I have a feeling, just a feeling, that this is going to lead us to the property clerk case. Listen carefully now. I want surveillance on both Haynes and the judge. Make it obvious. Start the rumor mill. They'll start circling around, dying to meet, but afraid. Then the distrust. 'What's he doing, what's he saying behind my back, he's giving me up,' and so on. We'll drive a wedge between them. Divide and conquer."

"Maybe they'll show up at the same time. Like those two lawyers who came over here the same day to inform on one another."

"Oh, yeah, the partners."

They enjoyed a hearty laugh.

"Move on this right away, Jeff. Call the judge on Friday. This is a big weekend. Nobody in town. He can simmer all weekend. Have him in here nine A.M., Tuesday morning."

Duncan affected a Cockney accent.

"'e shall 'ang from the 'ighest yardarm in the Royal Nigh-vy."

Norwalk, in high spirits, elaborated.

"'e shall be drawn and quartered at the Tower and 'is 'ead impaled on the gate, wot?"

Peals of laughter echoed down the corridors. The staff knew by the volume that somebody's ass was up for grabs.

JUDGE JOSHUA KLEINFELD TOOK A STOOL NEAR THE SHORT-order cook. The lunchroom at the Criminal Court Building was almost empty.

"What'll it be, Judge?"

"Just a cup of coffee, Henry," the judge said as he put his cigar down at the end of the counter. A tall, husky blond man approached and sat on the adjacent stool. He was Leo Donnelly, a detective attached to Mitchell Haynes's office.

"Cup of coffee, please," he said.

The judge turned his head to the left, mildly curious. He saw a gold shield cupped in the man's left hand, resting on his lap.

"I'm Leo Donnelly, Judge, from Mitch Haynes's office. You and Mitch are in trouble—"

The judge's temples tightened. The coffee arrived. Both men poured sugar and stirred their cups silently. They remained at profile to one another, sipping slowly.

"Go on," the judge said.

"My partner, Rizzo, a stool pigeon, ran and told Bill Rutledge, the chief assistant, that Mitch and you had a meet in the park. Mitch talked to Rutledge about it. Mistake. Norwalk was on Rutledge's ass already. Rutledge ran down to Norwalk, he brought Rizzo along. Rizzo is scared to death, he survived the police property dope switch case, and he's trying to be more Catholic than the Pope. I got it from him and I told Mitch. Mitch said to tell you all you talked about was old times."

"Thank him for me." The judge felt a pain shoot through his chest into his left shoulder.

"I'll be around here every day for lunch, for a while anyway," Donnelly said, and motioned to the counterman. "Separate checks, please. See ya', Judge."

Judge Kleinfeld lit his cigar.

So it's finally happened. . . . Pebble in a stream. But the ripples will drown me. One year to go to retirement. My wife, what will I tell my wife?

15

I͟T͟ ͟W͟A͟S͟ ͟A͟ ͟J͟U͟M͟P͟I͟N͟'͟ ͟F͟R͟I͟D͟A͟Y͟ ͟N͟I͟G͟H͟T͟. ͟T͟H͟A͟N͟K͟ ͟G͟O͟D͟ ͟T͟H͟E͟ ͟A͟I͟R͟ conditioning was workin'. I'd spent some time in the Hamptons, just drivin' around. Didn't see anybody I knew, but got a lot of sun. I was decked out in my off-white suit, open black shirt (no faggot medallion) and black Guccis. I had a thousand dollars in my pocket, people was lined up to get in the club, and I'm pissed off. Didn't wanna know from nothin'.

I was hangin' around the bar checkin' out this new barmaid, Elena, that Pachanga brought down from the Barrio. Steffie was stayin' with Dave now, and I think she was startin' to dig on him. Camera on top of the bar to catch the help cheatin'? Suppose to relay into office? Bullshit. Never worked. They're gonna steal? They're gonna steal. Even the customers. Like right away I see this well-dressed guy glommin' customers' change bills off the bar. Pachanga! Get this guy outa here. Pick on the wrong guy and he be blown away on the spot. Trouble, always trouble. Wherever you got booze, babonya, and broads, you got trouble.

Babonya, the wops called it at Lewisburg. That's what really been buggin' me since I come out. Dope. And now that I got fifty thou in my kick, I can make a real move. But I'm scared. Face it, Carlito, you've lost your confidence, that's all, your confidence. Don't think I can get away with it anymore. I see the jailhouse in front of me all the time now. Like a spaghetti stain on a silk tie. And I can't get next to people on the street anymore. Can't stand these new punk faces. With a head like that, how'm I gonna make a move?

Pachanga looked very swelegant. I brought him down to Leighton's and got him a couple of outfits. Had him in blazer and ascot and put two large in his pocket. If I got it, you got it. He was worried about Benny from the Bronx, suppose to be walkin' around with a pistol and a hand grenade, lookin' for me. "I'm here, ain't I? He knows where I'm at. Why don't he come up here? Don't pay these punks no mind."

After a while these Chinese kids came up. Two of them, sharp, well dressed. They didn't come out of no laundry. Couple of those Hong Kong boys from Chinatown. They got all the fan-tan bosses gorillaed down there, now they wanna be dope peddlers. Right away I put on my street face. "Watchoo mean, so-and-so said you could talk to me? Don't know so-and-so. I am a A-one legitimate businessman. You must be crazy. Come in here to talk to me in riddles. I don't know what you're talkin' about."

First rule of junk, never deal with strangers. Meanwhile, the jails is full of guys that only deal with friends. Don't leave much room, do it? The best one I heard was the two buddies in Lewisburg who was goin' back in the dope business when they got out. Whoever got busted first could rat the other one out! That's what it's come to.

I know them chinks thought I was nuts. Maybe I was. Coulda been a dynamite score. Coulda been a big dope hookup for me in Asia. Never know now. Can't seem to hold the dice in my hand no more.

Rita showed up from Brooklyn with a whole gang of broads. I made a fuss and got them a big table. She was mad at me, but I told her I lost her number, plus my car broke down, plus I been sick. She didn't go for it too strong, but she was good people about it. Right away I sent them over a magnum of champagne. We had the band wailin' and everybody was partyin'. Pachanga came over and right away him and Rita did up the joint with a fast mambo.

I was back at the far end of the bar and beginnin' to loosen up behind the action. I saw this American chick come in the door. Long, low-cut white dress, with a kind of little white cap coverin' her hair, long earrings, and one of them blond American tans. Tremenda gringa! Then I recognized the cheekbones. Gail.

She stood by the door, lookin' around the room. Meanwhile, the room was lookin' at her. I motioned to Rudy. "Traela pa'ca." He wheeled her around to me. I'm feelin' very up-tight. I sat her on a stool, against the wall. A 747 coulda landed in the room, I wouldn't have heard it. She crossed her legs and got her knee against my leg. Oo. Lovin' it, but I'm not lookin' at her. Stone-face (don't wanna be seen droolin'). I signaled Elena to come over. I pointed at Gail. Gail ordered somethin' that sounded Brazilian to me. This got me sore. We gonna do the Carioca or what?

"Enough already, Gail. Carmen Miranda is dead. Elena, bring her some of the wine I'm drinkin'."

Not a peep. The wine was set down and I turned to tink glasses with her. Now I focused. Trouble, Carlito. She was set, confident, like she'd turned the corner on somethin', somebody. Me. Funny, they make you chase 'em till they catch you. She kept starin', smilin' with wet lips. The crazy lights played with her skin, eyes, and teeth. She knew it, women know about these things, I knew it, but she had me a little groggy, anyway. She held my hand as I lit her cigarette. Steady, babe.

"What is this with the helmet?"

"I was out to the Hamptons, didn't get a chance to wash my hair. You don't like it, Charley? What about my false eyelashes, you don't like them either? I did my best. For you, Charley." She leaned forward on me. Green fire eyes.

What could I do? I put my arms around her. I don't know how long we were clinched. In an after-hours joint, no less, and me suppose to be halfa boss. Very uncool. Like Dave says, ludicrous. But I'm through worryin' about people. You do what you gotta do.

I heard Pachanga say, "Sunsin wrong, Carlito?"

He probably figured she was drunk. I rolled my eyes at him. Pachanga caught the scene and split. I sat on a stool and took her by the hand. I'm a sentimental cat, I admit it.

"I thought it was Gloria Vanderbilt comin' through the door."

"You're dating yourself, Charley."

"You really know how to hurt a guy."

We always laughed easy together.

"You never called, you never came by," she said. "Blocked me out again, right? Never a second thought, eh?"

I snapped my fingers.

"Like that, babe. Now I see you, now I don't."

"Liar, liar, Charley. You should see your eyes."

"You should see yours."

We went into another clinch. It be's that way, sometimes, what can I tell you? They played a slow piece and I took her out on the dance floor. Me who hates to dance. I told the singer to do "Inolvidable" next. He ain't no Tito Rodriguez, but in the mood and in the dark, holding my girl after all these years, and all the guff I been through, he was the next best thing. As we walked back to the bar, I caught sight of Rita. She was noddin' at me. Like "lost my number, eh, you mother!"

Gail went home with me. It had been five years. No phoney prelims. As soon as we came in the door, she went into the bathroom and came out naked. I was fixin' a drink. She caught me by surprise. I stood in the middle of the living room as she unbuttoned my shirt and started kissing my chest. Ave Maria! She stepped on my feet (we used to do this in Puerto Rico) with both of hers, I held her against me and marched her backwards into the bedroom. I gobbled her up inch by inch. And it didn't seem enough. Not nearly.

There's a famous saying: "Upside down they're all sisters." Hadda be a faggot to say it. Not true. Some got it for you and some don't. Just a question of findin' the right one. But it's like hittin' the number. Most guys never luck up. The same people say sex don't get better with age. What they don't tell you is it don't get worse either. In other words, in the bed, you can hit a home run same as before. Just don't get up to the plate as often, that's all.

The apartment looked down on the Hudson. You could see the lights on the highway, the Palisades and the GW Bridge from the bedroom window. String of pearls, I used to call the bridge at night. A pretty sight.

She lit a cigarette for me, then she spotted the Roberto Carlos album on the stereo. I could make out her eyes, in and out of the shadows, searchin'. They were as hungry as mine. She was on top of me, her hair wet and curled, and I could see specks of light running down her back, even in the darkness. She ran her fingers up and down my face, whispering the lyrics of "Inolvidable." In Spanish, no less. Heavy-duty chick.

"That record's been drivin' me crazy," I finally admitted. What the hell.

I kissed her eyes and felt their wetness.

"Why did you come for me, Gail?" I wanna be stroked.

"When I asked you that question, you said you didn't know."

"Yeah, but you're smarter than me."

We clung very tight. When it's goin' right between two people, the after part is almost as good.

"You're my man, Charley, you always have been. I respond to you, I feel more alive . . . I don't know. Call it chemistry. The green and the brown chromosomes."

"Chemistry? How about an erection set? Got one of them too."

"Charley, you—"

We laughed and rolled around the bed a while. Then I got up and brought back a bottle of wine and two glasses. I sat on the edge of the bed and poured drinks. In the dark.

"Tell me about him, Gail. I want to know."

I'm a glutton too. She was quiet for a while, then she said, "Roberto was a beautiful, sensitive boy. And I loved him. He looked a little like you. Younger."

"You ask a question. You get an answer. Rots-a-ruck!"

"Do you want me to say that every shadow on every wall for five years reminded me of you?"

"Yeah. Lie to me." She wrapped her arms around me.

"I never forgot you, Charley. God knows we went separate ways. But I never forgot the time we had together. And now you're back inside me and I'll never let you out. And I want to have a baby, your baby. How do you like that?"

I stood up. "Whoa—Gail! Old as I am, if we have a baby, it'll be born with wrinkles."

"All babies are wrinkled. I'm thirty-one years old. I have wrinkles too, touch."

She took my hand and put it between her legs. I got back in bed. Like I said, I knew I was in trouble this trip.

16

NORWALK STOOD AT HIS OFFICE WINDOW, ENGROSSED in the sight of a small tugboat towing an immensely long barge. He immediately perceived a parallel with his own strained efforts to haul the ponderous criminal justice system upstream, up to the standard he saw so clearly. As befit the occasion (the anticipated "guest" was a judge), Norwalk wore a somber gray suit and a dark tie. His morning had begun badly with a six A.M. argument at the Reservoir with two black prizefighters who took up the whole track instead of running in single file. He had been told, "You better get yo' ass outa here," and had chosen not to protract the issue or assert himself, but it grated. His reverie was interrupted by a gentle knock on the door. He looked at his watch. Nine A.M.

"Come in."

Judge Joshua Kleinfeld's short, slightly rotund figure stood in the doorway, as Duncan held open the door.

"Come in, gentlemen. Sit down."

Norwalk remained by the window, facing the two men as they sat, his hands clasped behind his back. He smiled at Kleinfeld.

"You come to joust with the dragon minus lance and armor, Judge Kleinfeld? I should expect a battery of lawyers to precede you."

"Mr. Norwalk, if after forty-five years, I need a lawyer—"

"He who hath himself for a lawyer—"

"Hath a fool for a client. I recite that daily to hardheaded defendants."

"Time, advice, and clichés are a lawyer's stock in trade, wouldn't you say, Judge Kleinfeld?"

Duncan nodded approvingly at his boss's newly minted aphorism, but Norwalk's gaze remained fixed on the judge. Duncan remained alert for some telltale sign of the tack to be pursued.

"I've been known to spout a few. Do you mind if I smoke? I know you're a health advocate," the judge said.

"Not at all. Go right ahead."

There was a pause as Norwalk and Duncan observed Judge Kleinfeld light a cigar with dexterity and a steady pulse. Norwalk continued.

"This office would not have it said that there was any attempt to intimidate you in the absence of counsel. Personally, I feel that if a man is innocent of any wrongdoing, he has no need of barriers or procedural shields. Those are the safeguards of the habitual offender. For an innocent man, the truth is the only weapon. Surely, Judge Kleinfeld, your vast experience has made this clear to you."

"The truth shall make ye free, Amen," Judge Kleinfeld said, without expression, but the intonation was sardonic.

Norwalk, discomfited, looked toward Duncan, who again nodded approvingly. The Special State Prosecutor moved away from the window and took up a position behind his chair. The judge, hands in his lap, puffed away as a few bits of ash settled on his dark suit.

"I know, Judge Kleinfeld, that there are those who depict me as an ogre. Self-serving as it may sound, there are no horns and tail on me. I'm merely part of a team trying to do a difficult job. My ideals are the same today as they were fifteen years ago when I was in the DA's office."

"I remember you."

"Of course. So be assured that what I am about to say to you is not a tactical ploy or some devious stratagem calculated to lull or deceive you."

"I'm listening."

"You are merely ancillary to this investigation. The prime target is Mitchell Haynes. It is he who has violated the public trust with official misconduct, a serious misdemeanor in one so highly and delicately perched. Think of it, the District Attorney of the Special Narcotics Court remaining silent when it was his sworn duty to speak. How can such a man occupy a position of trust in the most important area of law enforcement, narcotics? The public is convinced that collusion, cronyism, and clubhouse 'old boyism' permeate our system. How could they think otherwise with a political hack like Haynes flouting the law and subverting the efforts of decent law enforcement people?"

"Mitch Haynes is one of the most decent and effective law enforcement officers I know, Mr. Norwalk."

"Judge Kleinfeld. Yours was a mere fatherly indiscretion. A distraught father going to the aid of a beleaguered son. This office understands that. This team never loses sight of the ball, and the ball is Haynes. Your conversation with Haynes is a minute portion of the mosaic. But we need it to complete the composite, to frame the picture, as it were, of the kind of official Haynes is. For this bears on his handling of a matter of colossal significance, the police property clerk narcotics theft."

Norwalk paused here for effect and to canvass his prey for signs of fatigue or capitulation.

"You didn't tell me about that, Larry," Duncan whispered, feigned anxiety for the judge clouding his face. Norwalk stared at Duncan, then he said, "Jeff, this is a delicate matter, as you can well appreciate."

Duncan shook his head at the magnitude of it all.

Norwalk turned to the judge again.

"Judge Kleinfeld, Haynes is in murky waters. Do not immerse yourself. You have much to lose, your pension, your reputation. Do not compromise yourself for Haynes's sake. You cannot save him, all you will do is destroy yourself and further jeopardize your son."

"My son again."

"Yes, your son. David is at the core. His hysterical pleas would have moved any father."

"You had a bug, Norwalk. You had a bug in the judge's robing room!" Kleinfeld said loudly, as he rose to his feet. "You were a slimy son of a bitch when you were in the

DA's office, and you've gotten worse. You couldn't shine Mitch Haynes's shoes the best day you ever saw. All Mitch and I ever discussed was the weather and old times. Got it, the weather. Convene your Grand Jury. Any time and place. I'll be there. And you and your flunky here can go fuck yourselves."

The choleric Kleinfeld reimplanted his cigar in his mouth, clamping it between his teeth. He turned and stomped out of the office, leaving the door ajar.

"Now we'll get him for perjury," Duncan said, closing the door.

"Call up Haynes. Tell him I'll be up there at two-thirty. Get this in front of a Grand Jury immediately, Jeff. Subpoena everybody, before they start comparing notes. Is the word out on Kleinfeld?"

"The word is out."

"Move, Jeff, move. We're going to bag ourselves a sitting judge."

DETECTIVE LEO DONNELLY escorted NORWALK AND Duncan down the long corridor to Haynes's office at 80 Centre Street. Pausing at the open door, Norwalk observed Haynes sitting at his desk in shirtsleeves. Haynes looked up, then leaned back, putting his hands behind his head.

"Jeff, why don't you and the detective go have some coffee?" Norwalk suggested.

Duncan nodded, turned and doubled back with Donnelly. Norwalk entered the room, closing the door behind him. He strode across the room, smiling brightly, arms outstretched. He vigorously shook hands as he took a chair by the side of Haynes's desk.

"Mitch, baby, what the hell have you been doing with yourself? Haven't seen you at the Association meetings or even Forlini's. Let's get together for lunch soon. All I ever see of you is on television." Norwalk leaned across the desk.

"Yeah, Larry, crying for money. Trying to keep this office afloat. I just got another report about the revival of the Turkey-Marseilles route. People are dying and all we can bag are the nickel and dime pushers. You don't know what it's like. They allow me one finger for forty leaks in the dike. Like shoveling shit against a propeller."

Norwalk slapped his thigh and laughed raucously.

"That's what I miss from the old days. That uptown mother wit of yours. Never lose it. . . . But seriously, Mitch, I'm going through hell. Our office is under siege too. I'm even more frustrated than you are. At least no one seriously proposes abolishing your office. And all because we are trying to remove the few rotten apples that are discrediting our judiciary. We keep getting reversed by the Appellate Division. Even attacked personally in gratuitous dicta opinions. These judges are powerful. I tell you. They've banded together to destroy the Special Prosecutor's office. Superfluous, they say. Are they going to police themselves? Nonsense. These corrupt judges have to be flushed out before they infest other agencies. And there has to be an independent investigatory body. Not necessarily with me at the helm. I'll be a soldier in the ranks. I don't care. But if they're not purged, they'll devastate the entire law enforcement apparatus," Norwalk said, jabbing down with his index finger on Haynes's desk for emphasis.

Haynes was mildly amused. Norwalk was known for his ninety-degree turns from fervor to rejection, then the reshunting to a new course with renascent zeal. This inability to hang in sapped Norwalk's effectiveness as a prosecutor, Haynes decided.

"You never were one to do things by halves," said Haynes.

"How do you mean?"

"I mean you didn't show up at the district attorney's office 'til the sixties. Yet you've passed us all like a shot. Larry Norwachefsky grabbed the baton and ran the whole relay by himself. More power to you. I wish I had your drive and singlemindedness of purpose. I've got too many kids and distractions."

"I hear the older one's a good fullback."

"Yeah. Cornell. He's going to be another Marion Motley. You remarried, Larry?"

"No. You know how it is."

"Are you kidding? Stay that way, have some fun."

The colloquy ground down by degrees until an uneasy quiet settled between them. Norwalk sat back in his chair. Finally, Haynes said, "What's on your mind?"

"I know you've written Rutledge off."

"That's between me and Bill, the treacherous son of a bitch. But go ahead, speak your mind, just like you always do. And don't give me that prosecutors alumni bullshit because you know and I know that it doesn't mean a fucking thing when someone's in trouble. Speak your piece."

"Mitch. You've only seen the tip of the iceberg. You don't know what's involved. I'm not at liberty to divulge particulars, but it appears Judge Kleinfeld is tied up with his son, David, on the police property drug switch. Do you know what that means? The biggest case in New York's history! I tell you, they're starting to fall. It's like a row of matchsticks, a house of cards. Nuncio, David Kleinfeld, the judge—doesn't that ring a bell?" Norwalk said, half rising from his chair.

"What is this, guilt by association, by consanguinity?"

"Is there any other kind?"

"I'm serious."

"So am I. Mitch, please. Don't stand in the way. This is bigger than you, bigger than me."

Norwalk held his arms outward as if to encompass the width and girth of the project before them.

"What the hell does all this have to do with me?"

"You're going to nail Judge Joshua Kleinfeld for me."

"How am I, pray tell, to do that?"

"The undue influence, the intimidation he brought to bear upon you, a public official, to obstruct you in the performance of your duty. All in dereliction of his sworn duty as a judicial officer."

"What the hell are you talking about?"

"Your conversation with the judge in Foley Square Park following a taped conversation he had with his son, David. Witnesses observed your meeting in a setting visible from this very window. Also your statement to Rutledge as to the nature of the conversation. And last but not least, Judge Kleinfeld, who was in my office this very morning, sans defense counsel. He may have a thing or two to say about that little parley you had. Shall I continue?"

"Bullshit! Josh and I just reminisced about the old days and—"

"The weather?"

Haynes rose from his chair. His large frame towered over the seated Norwalk.

"Larry," Haynes said, his nostrils widening. "I'm beginning to get annoyed."

"Don't you understand? You can be charged with official misconduct. Tried, convicted, and disbarred. Don't you realize the position the judge has put you in? Gratuitously he has put you on the spot to save his son, who is up to his ears in murder and narcotics. Sit down a minute. Mitch. Sit down, goddamnit, and reflect. If not for yourself, then think of your wife and your children. Think of them!"

Haynes, momentarily benumbed by Norwalk's outburst, sat down hard. Norwalk renewed his tirade:

"And how long do you think old man Kleinfeld is going to stick to that weather story? How much heat can he take? And you know it can be applied. By the tablespoonful. How long? By then, you will have been before the Grand Jury. Oh, yes, the subpoenas are out now. By then, you will have laid the predicate for a perjury indictment against yourself. A felony! Automatic disbarment. Reflect, Mitch, reflect. That's all I'm asking you to do. You can't have it both ways. Josh Kleinfeld created this situation. He sought you out. He literally set you up. Are you going to sit on a wooden stake, all out of some twisted sense of loyalty? Between you two, one will be the witness and one the defendant. Believe me. I would prefer you as the witness. You are less culpable and more worthy."

Norwalk rose slowly, dramatically. The effect was lost on the bewildered Haynes.

"I am done, Mitch. Think over what I've said. You know where to reach me."

With rapid strides, Norwalk made for the door. As he prepared to exit the room, he heard Haynes's voice behind him.

"What is it Hogan used to say? . . . Let the chips fall where they may."

"You'll be buried in chips," Norwalk said and he closed the door behind him.

17

Eᴀʀʟʏ ɪɴ ᴛʜᴇ ᴡᴇᴇᴋ ᴀɴᴅ ꜰᴏʀ ɴᴏ ɢᴏᴏᴅ ʀᴇᴀꜱᴏɴ ᴛʜᴇ club was crowded by three ᴀ.ᴍ. Saso brought up this wacky Cuban singer from Miami and she jammed the place. Suppose to have been a big deal in the good old Havana days of Montmartre and Tropicana and Cubita la Bella. I didn't go for her. Couldn't sing to save her ass (nothin' could save them oppressed masses, big as they were). She'd scream, sweat, tear her clothes and scratch herself. Sometimes she'd drop her jugs (big too) on the head of the conga player, or if the fever (Ñañigo) really got to her, she'd crawl on all fours around the stage, shakin' her head like a wet dog. She'd knock the band and herself out, though. After a set, Pachanga and Rudy would have to carry her off the stage. Caña, she was called, like in sugar cane, as in candy, which she'd snort by the kilo. A stone butch, she had a cute li'l chick, Sarita, she used to abuse for days. But lissen, nobody's perfect, and she was pullin' the customers in. People who'd never been in the joint before.

Pachanga said, "Walberto called. He commeen wiz a beeg party of beeg chots. I gotta set op a good table, eh, Carlito?"

"You're impressed, eh?"

"Summata wis joo, Carlito? Choor. Dees de guy gotta gib joo the break. Wan break and joo be the main connection right away again. Es verdad o no es verdad?"

Pachanga—another nut-job.

Walberto showed up with about seven or eight people.

Downtown disco crowd—models, dancers, fags, designers. He was all tanned and dressed in a white Pierre Cardin suit, maroon patent-leather loafers, and a big red kerchief around his neck. No socks and no shirt at all. This sucker must be swappin' out. Wasn't any wise guys in his party, so he ain't worried about his back.

Pachanga almost had a beef with some guys he had to move out to make room for Walberto and his crowd (no small thing, twice I have seen men killed over a chair). Set 'em up right in front of the small stage. Walberto insisted I sit with him. Right away I said no tab for Walberto. His American women were very tall, blond and skinny—kind that right away wanna take their shoes off and do the mahm-bo! "It's so chic to go native, my dear, let it all out, be yourself, Clarissa." That was this little guy with like a pirate outfit on and espadrilles (coulda been one of them Aragon "jota" costumes), Whatever, he was the centerpiece of this crew.

"Gastón is from Chile, but he's really French, Carlito. He says my name, Yeampierre, is not Puerto Rican, that it's really French. Very talented man. Makin' me over, my wardrobe, my pad—"

"I really want to get Walberto into acting," Gastón said, "those dark features, those eyes. I think you're going to see a return to the Latin leading man, à la Gilbert Roland type, again. . . ."

Yak yak. Walberto protested with his hands, but his puss said, "Mirror, mirror on the wall." Luv-in it. The women kicked their shoes off and got up to dance with some of the fags from the table, while Walberto and Gastón worked on Walberto's future in Hollywood. Never fails. A hustler is slick on one side, but a chump on the reverse. So he gets away over here, but they take him off over there. Walberto, Saso, they're all the same. They don't see the big picture, like me. Meanwhile, I'm broke, and Walberto's flush. "Melissa, you're all perspired, why don't you and the girls go freshen up before the show starts and all the lights come on—" Gastón, the majordomo, told the girls when they returned, then back to his spiel for Walberto, yesterday's Puerto Rican, tomorrow's superstar. Enough to make ya sick.

Showtime. Caña came out with a different dress, a long one this time. She wanted all the lights out except one, on her, and she sat next to the piano player to sing a soft ballad you could hardly hear. Then she jumped on top of the piano stool and started screamin' a hopped-up "guaracha." Next she jumped down and took the sticks from the timbalero and started bangin' on top of the piano, the musicians, even the wall, singin' and shakin' like the "santera" she was. Finally, she laid down on the floor with the mike. She spotted Walberto. "Walberto, mi hermano!" She dragged him out to, the stage, took his jacket off, and they did an old style "guagnanco" that was a mother. Dance good too, Walberto, got back huffin' and puffin'. Gastón was in shock. "Walberto! But you never told me you could dance like that. Did you see him? I mean, did you see him?" Etcetera, etcetera. Make ya sick.

Seems that Caña was an old girlfriend of Rolando's from Cuba. She started out in one of his de-luxe AC-DC cathouses in the suburbs of Havana. In those days, she was a switch-hitter, now she was straight dyke. Walberto, total degenerate, was the next best thing to Rolando, specially with twenty decks of coke available.

Me and Walberto got into a corner by the bar.

"I haven't heard from you, Carlito."

"You were supposed to call me."

"And?"

"Can't make it, Walberto."

"You're gonna hurt Rolando's feelings."

"Can't get away. Too many hassles here. And I'm lookin' to retire. Basta ya."

"He was countin' on you."

"Sorry about that."

"I have your four thou. I thought Rolando meant a thousand in front, not the whole five. But don't worry about that. One of my girls has the money in her pocketbook."

"Keep it. Send it back to Rolando. You throw in the other thousand. That'll give him back his five. We're even."

"Beautiful. No sweat, Carlito. You had to hurt the kid, eh? Benny Blanco. I heard he got outta line."

"Yeah, he got a little frisky."

"Benny don't mean no harm, bro. He's young, gets his head bad."

"He's a punk."

"He's a tough kid."

"I know—Vietnam and all that. Still a punk."

"Well, I had to calm him down."

"He made a threat. I was suppose to finish him right there. I didn't, out of respect for you, Walberto."

"I see. Okay. It's all straightened out. Don't worry about it."

"I ain't."

"Lemme get back to my party, man. Hey, keep in touch. Us old-timers gotta stick together."

Yeah.

Saso, for once, lookin' pressed and clean, brought me over to a table with some Italian kids from the West Village. Vito country. Fancy dress but rowdy, beep-a-reebeep. I didn't go for them. Sal, Scoonge, Dom, Yumpy, Mezzomafioso.

You was with Rocco, right? Right. Beautiful guy. Yeah. Ya got some joint over here. Thanks. This Canna broad is a riot, we'd like to bring her downtown, but without them jigaboos behind her. Okay, talk to Saso, my partner. Beautiful broads,'ey, madon, lookit that one over there with the nigger. When-a the moon hit-a you eye.

I cut it short. That's all we need now, crazy wops in the joint along with crazy spics and spooks. Caña was Saso's party and I didn't want to be around Walberto when he got paranoid behind his coke. "Wadda ya mean ya can't—?" I could hear him from here. Some cats can blow themselves up to lions behind a couple of snow-decks. Who needs it. These nights were killin' me. I had a bad headache from all the noise and carryin' on. The afterhours man got battle fatigue, after all these years. I cut out early. Didn't say good-bye to nobody.

CAÑA SAT NAKED IN THE CLUB'S MAKESHIFT DRESSING room, staring at her large, pendulous breasts in the mirror. Her thick, tawny-colored body reeked perspiration. The mascará from her heavily made-up eyes dripped in black streaks down the round cheeks of her smooth face.

"When we get back to Miami, I go to the clinic. Only surgery can save my 'tetas.' Qué opinas, Sarita?"

Sarita stood behind Caña, holding a large white towel.

"You still drive the men wild, querida," Sarita suggested cautiously.

"Fuck the men. I am only here because I owe Saso a favor. Hijos de puta—"

There was a knocking on the door.

"Soy yo, Caña. Walberto."

Sarita let Walberto into the tiny room.

"Sarita," Caña said, "go outside. But if I catch you with any mens, I kill you, okay?"

"Caña, por favor," Sarita said, handing Caña the towel as she stepped out, closing the door behind her. Caña rubbed her arms and shoulders with the towel slowly. Walberto stood silently behind the chair, his eyes on her image in the mirror.

"Estáte quieto, Walberto, I don't fool around."

Walberto diverted his stare, then he said, "You saw them out there tonight?"

"Los italianos? Of course. They are the same group that came to Miami to see Rolando. They belong to a man named 'Cheek.' Cheek Mason. Rolando acted like the president come to his house. I do not remember the other three so much, but the blond one, Dom, Dominick, I remember. He's the 'descarao' who took his pants off when I took him out to dance during my show at 'Los Violines.' Imagínate que escandalo!"

"Ghinnies, wadda you expect? Cerullo, Dom the waiter. The light-haired one in the dark suit against the wall, right?"

"Sí."

"He seems quiet tonight, Caña."

"Of course. With his music inside. This is Carlito's club, Walberto. The place is full of killers. Los mafiosos no son estupidos. They were smart enough to make a fool of Rolando, who is supposed to wear such long spurs. In Miami, they told Rolando they needed him in South America. Partners. Ha. The setup, the 'parapeto' was a

French 'puta' they had for Rolando. You know how he is. He was so grateful to the Italians for their friendship, he told César in Puerto Rico unlimited credit at the casino for this one outside, Dominick. They gave it to Rolando without Vaseline."

"I heard. Two hundred thousand Dom the waiter dropped at the tables."

"Their boss, 'Cheek,' said he would pay. 'Mielda' he pay. Rolando had to pay the casino. This 'Cheek' make a fool of Rolando."

"That's Mazzone, Chick Mason. He's the big boss. The underboss, Castaldi, Joe Cass, promised the same thing. He's the one came out of jail with Carlito Brigante. They are all in bed together."

"The bed is being made for Rolando."

"He says he didn't pay the two hundred. Ha!"

"Rolando will not admit it, but he paid. They have made a 'pendejo' of Rolando. I am with him since I was a child in the chorus at Tropicana. He does not change. Twenty years ago he left his wife, a white society woman, for me. I know him. His head is good till they put a 'papaya' in front of him, then with one cunt hair they can pull him from here to France. He does not change, Walberto."

"Then they will kill him. I know these people. Not talk, not money, they want Rolando's liver."

"And Carlito?"

"Carlito's hooked up with them. Are you blind? Why do you think the Italians are here? To see you?"

Caña rose to full height, then cupped her breasts together.

"Y mis tetas, ya no valen?" she said, smiling.

Walberto laughed loudly. Reaching into his jacket pocket, he removed a tinfoil packet.

"La coca vale más, Caña," he said.

18

For Steffie's birthday Dave wanted to run a little affair for her. I come up with the Copacabana for Wednesday. They were givin' a big testimonial for Machito and figured we'd have a ball. I knew Steffie would go for it, she loved Latin music. There were six of us, Dave and Steffie, Pachanga and Elena, and me and Gail (Gail was practically living with me by then).

We ate at the Sacred Cow (not too far from my house), then we jumped down to the Copa in Dave's Mercedes. One of the boys from the old neighborhood was parkin' the cars on 60th Street (used to be a good pug, had decisioned Bethea in the Garden). Here comes me lookin' dap out of the backseat of a new Mercedes with a dynamite blonde under my wing. My man fell back, he say, "Damn, Carlito, you still out there lookin' whippy. Thought you was long gone."

Always did have a surprise for them people uptown. They love it when you on yo' ass. They in the basement, they wanna see you in the sub-basement. Your own kind too— "Who he, think he can fart higher 'n his asshole, fuck him, jive Po' Rican." Like an indigested dog, don't wanna eat, don't want nobody else to eat. Whole gang of them people out there. Like them hotel clerks that wanna see luggage. Here you been workin' on a kitty for three months and the sombitch behind the desk wants to see luggage. "Ain't got no goddamn luggage." "No luggage, no room, this ain't no sportin' house, what kinda place you think we got here,

329

for shame (yuk, yuk)." He ain't gettin' none, why should you? Mother humpers. Yeah, they hate it when you got a fine bandit witchoo. Fools ain't got no sense. You take this shrimpie Filipino or Guamguy back in the 1950s in Harlem. He looked like Mr. Moto. So what? Still had a big-ass redhead livin' with him on top of the poolroom on 108th Street and Madison. Everybody (includin' stupid me) was sayin "What does she see in that fuckin' midget submarine?" (Cat was a merchant marine.) Ignorance of the man on the street (specially 108th Street) was unbelievable. Could be the lady come off some "prettyboy" trip where she couldn't get in front of the mirror from her ex-dude's primpin'. Who knows but she come off a bumpy ride and li'l brown brother was steady lookin' out for her? Maybe he just had a heavy pork-leg. Coulda been any one of these or any combination therefore. But them fools in the poolroom could never figure that out. These (I admit) are some of the things used to puzzle me before I did heavy time and got my act together. Thank God.

I had bought Gail one of them tuxedo outfits for women and black suede pumps with little fake diamond buckles. My idea. She was fabulous. Dave had Steffie wearin' tailored clothes, kinda conservative (soon as a guy get hold of a fox he wants to hide her from everybody else, right?). Which brings us to Elena, Pachanga's main squeeze now, who was all right 'cept she was a little heavy on the bulges, the makeup, and the charm bracelets. Didn't bother me none, long as she was holdin' Pachanga up. Never question or mess with a man's old lady, one of the golden rules of longevity. "Para el gusto se hicieron los colores."

Dave knew some of the new lawyer owners, so we rode in smooth. Checked out the lounge upstairs. There was a trio playin' Irving Fields music (mostly 'cause it was the Irving Fields Trio). There was some old-time swingers wearin' French cuffs on their wrists and doormats on their heads, standin' at the bar waitin' for lightnin' to strike. At the other end was some beehive Lolas leftover from the fifties waitin' for Troy Donahue, Sonny Tufts, or Guy Madison. Take your pick. The wanderin' eye that sees all, only got eyes for the door. They're all waitin'. Next stop, Roseland.

Musta been ten years since I been in the Copa. I caught a nostalgia fit right away. Talk about landmarks. If these walls could talk (better they don't talk). Golden memories of Joey the Blond, and Sonny, and Frank C., and Junior, and all the stars of yesteryear. And the star of stars, Podell, who could orchestrate two hundred "Italiano brava gente" with Chinese food. ('ey, Jools,'ow come you got that hump, Angelo, down in the lower tier, wadda you out of yer fuckin' mind or sumpn'?) And do it regular. And die in bed. That little Jew had more balls than all the wise guys in the joint. Knew his showbiz too. Spotted talent early. All the heavyweight performers, Sinatra, Nat Cole, Davis, Tony Bennett, Rickles, they always came back to pay their respects to the man and the place that got them off. Was a magic room, fit them people like a shoehorn. Nat Cole was the class, even the ghinny waiters would admit that. New Year's Eve we used to reserve tables (hundred a head, big money in them days) for Sammy Davis, who'd sit on top of the piano the joint was so jammed. As Barbra would say, memrees. . . .

Downstairs it was frantic. Like most Latin affairs. Everything confused and everybody jumpin' around. Joint was packed, so we had to buy a fuckin' table on an upper tier, but we could see the stage pretty good. Who's who, who think they're who and who ain't, was there in the Latin world. A regular "asopao" from the TV, magazines, and newspapers. I shook hands with José Torres (Chegui), who was there with Pete Hamill. Last time I'd seen Chegui was when he knocked out Charley (Devil) Green at the Garden in the second round, then climbed up on the top strand of the ropes and jumped into a fight at ringside his brother and Norman Mailer was having with some guys. Turned out to be the best fight on the card.

You had people from the unions, poverty programs, doctors, lawyers. Hell of a wingding. Every Latin musician, Puente, Celia Cruz, Pacheco, Vicentico, Patato, and so on, came out that night. Even Federico Pagani, who prompted the first Latin dances at the old Palladium in the forties.

(No easy trick to talk to the "Don Cheech's" who ran the joint to give the okay in them days.) Payin' their respects to Machito. Greatest musician the PRs ever had. And he's a Cuban. I knew him over thirty years from the ol' Park Palace days on 110th Street and Fifth Avenue. Seems like all my life he's been up on a bandstand singin' and shakin' maracas and I been circlin' around him dancin' with one broad or another. Looked the same as he did in '45. Spotless clean, big smile on his brown face. He was like a father to all the Barrio kids (he lived there all his life on East 110th Street). How many nights in how many joints I heard him. "Take advantage, you are American citizens, stop the fighting and the dope, you don't get nowhere." He was always tryin'. But you can't do nothin' with fuck-ups (includin' me) who can't get up on a Monday mornin' 'cause it's rainin', or Tuesday 'cause it's sunny. By Thursday they'll jack somebody up to get money for the weekend. I tried to explain that to the "therapy" crew in the can. They don't understand that a hustler can't find no fun in a regular job 'cause he ain't gettin' over on nobody. And he only moves in spurts, at night, or on the weekend. He can't watch no clock. Just ain't his stick.

Macho never gave up on me. Him and a whole gang of people tried to help me. Couldn't talk to me. I was slicker than wet cobblestones. I thought.

And Macho caught hell too in them bust-out dances we used to have. How many times him and his band had to check out a side door while the chairs and bottles been flyin', or have a guy dance by one minute and see him stretched out on the sidewalk the next, dead. Ahead of his time, always, it was way back in the forties when Stan Kenton cut a record in his honor, "Machito." We knew Macho was great by then in Harlem, but to have Kenton know it was a big thing for us in them days. As a matter of fact, it was guys like Machito and Tito Puente that gave a whole lot of Latins their only "descarga" in a whole week of bumps and lumps behind some salad bar or steam press. Hats off to all them band guys.

After the speeches, Macho, Puente, Celia, all of them got together and worked a jam session. Blast-off! Thought the joint was gonna fall down. I been to a lotta gigs but this was somethin' else again.

Me and Gail was still holdin' hands. Couldn't let go of this broad. Follow her right into the shower (had fun in that shower). Seem like every day I found somethin' new I liked about her. She was workin' her points, cool, about us goin' to live in Puerto Rico (she loved PR). I wasn't sayin' too much, but the idea was growin' on me. Who'm I kiddin'? If she said, "Let's rent in the Gobi Desert," I'd have said, "We get gas and electric included?" Sold American.

The six of us were dancin' and drinkin' Dom Perignon. Everything paid by Dave. Couldn't put your hand in your pocket. I ain't ever been no zipper pockets, always been down with the bread, ask anybody, so I didn't go for this; but the cat would sneak out and pay the bill before you knew what was happenin'. Didn't bother Pachanga none.

You could see Pachanga's act was in for a few changes with this new broad, Elena, around. She wouldn't push him, but she'd lead. Thought he had God by the tail. Dave, meanwhile, was gettin' heavier by the minute. He wanted to trade stories where I look like a chump and he comes out the hero. In front of my old lady. Fuck him.

Macho came over with some of the musicians and made a big fuss about me ("I know him since he was a kit") and told Gail what a big deal I was and all like that (never knew the man to say anythin' bad about anybody). So Pachanga and Gail (and me) are agreein' with him and life is beautiful. Macho gets up and we're huggin' and kissin' good-bye.

Now I look at Dave. I know he's gettin' stoned 'cause his hair is startin' to stand up. And he starin' at me with his bad-drinker puss. He hadda say it.

"You know, Carlito, since you're such an attraction around here, I ought to let you pay for everything, right?"

He laughs and looks around the table for his chorus. This flies like a lead-ass bird, so now he gets all outa shape.

"I mean I just greased you for sixty big ones and I've been carrying you since you came out, right? What the hell, you could show a little appreciation."

He's sittin' up straight now, like, "Hey, I'm the main event around here." Nobody's agreein'. I wanted to slap him in the mouth, but I'm really mad at myself. When you take favors, this is what happens, you got to gargle Tabasco sauce. I choked, but I didn't blow up.

"Dave, I think you're a little high, so we'll let it slide. I haven't asked you for a mother-fuckin' nickel, but I'll spring for this or any other fuckin' tab you want—"

Now I'm thinkin' I'm goin' to throw the table on top of him, when Steffie butts in.

"The man's only playin' witchoo, Carlito. He's only funnin' witchoo. Ain'tcha, Dave?"

Elena said, "*Sixty* thousand dollars."

Pachanga stood up.

"Sharrap, Elena, pliz! He only playin' wiz joo, Carlito. C'mon, let's dance, dis is a fun party. Everybody dance dis guaracha. Qué pelicula! Vamos, Elena."

Kleinfeld musta seen my face because he started pedallin' backwards.

"Goddamnit, Carlito, you can't take a joke? For Pete's sake, I was only tryin' to get a rise out of you. You're moonin' over Gail all the time now. Forget about it, c'mon, tell them the story about the goat. . . ."

It blew over. But I'm still anglin' in my head. Maybe he's got a hoodlum complex, thinks I'm a tough guy or somethin'. Lotta buffs like that. Wops (and even cops) scoop them up. They gotta pay for everythin'. Just so they can hang around the tough guys. But the gangster gets the short end 'cause the buff will turn stool pigeon soon as anythin' happens. Then I'm thinkin' maybe Dave is a fag. He baits me, like a broad would. But I hear from Steffie he whips it on her steady. Maybe he's one of them bifocal fags.

He took Gail out to dance, so I took Steffie. Pachanga was already out there goin' crazy with Elena. And the music went round n' round. We jumped up and down awhile, but I was still annoyed about Dave. Then Pachanga came around from the other side of the room and said, these guys, Dynamo and Sapo (Frog) had said that Lalín had gotten whacked out on the Lower East Side. Was on the radio that Eladio Flores—Lalín—had been blown out of his wheelchair with a shotgun in a social club. I felt lousy about it. I don't know why. Don't make me no never mind. Pa'pichon bastante voló. He was a stool and he was in a wheelchair. That's what he wanted, to be put out of his misery, like them skells you see in the middle of East Side Highway on a foggy night. Maybe I felt bad for myself. Like the numbers are dwindlin' down to me. They have washed gobs of people in front of me, alongside me, behind me, and I'm still standin'. They stomped Mayagüez to death right in front of me at St. Nick's Arena dance one night. They blew Mikie "Blue Eyes" away at the Shelton Hotel right alongside me (Lee Marvin was almost a dead hero when he tried to grab the shooter). And I'm steppin' out of Korman's Drugstore on 111th Street when another Mikie (Li'l Mikie) ran behind me just as Romulo (whose face he had cut) blew him up. He skidded all over them tiles.

But I'm still standin'.

I figure I'm smarter. I know if you had a beef in the bar and you come out late and your car don't start on the street, don't stick your head under the hood. They've pulled the wires out and the car on the corner is waitin' on you. I know if the guy says, "Wait here, mother fucker, I'll be right back," finish him right there. That don't mean you can't get killed, but you get a better point spread. It's them little things that make the difference.

I'm feelin' so bad I need air. So I went outside and walked toward Fifth Avenue. Gail caught up with me on the run. We sat on a bench and I told her about Lalín and growin' up and hangin' out. Stickball player, dancer—he was terrific guy, cover your back in a minute. Now he's laid out on the fuckin' Bellevue butcher block. Nobody to say, "Hey, Lalín was a helluva guy, used to bat clean-up in all the money games, always the prettiest cat at the Easter dance at the Manhattan Center." Yeah, he hit a couple of clinkers at the end, but that's because he was hurt and down on his luck. "Buena gente was Lalín, buena gente." I saw she was cryin'.

"Why you cryin', Gail?"

"Because you're crying. Because the tears are running down your face."

She held me tight. I hadn't meant to get goopy in front of her, but if a woman don't hold a man up, who's gonna do it? She was always in my corner.

We went back to the table and I paid the bill. I told Dave I'd break his hole if he didn't let me. When we got home, Gail said to me, "He's sick, Charley. Dave is sick. When he took me out to dance he started rambling."

"He was tanked up."

"The real Kleinfeld came out of that bottle, Charley. Not a pretty sight. He said he'd had a beautiful wife. Like me. A cunt to be exact. That she'd run away with a—an Italian."

"I heard about that. He don't talk about it."

"We're all whores. All women are whores, leeches, bloodsuckers, and worse."

"He told you that? Little cock sucker. Wait till I see him."

"He won't even remember. He's been very badly burned. Listen, I don't care about him. I only care about you. I don't think it's healthy to be around a man like that."

"What about Steffie?"

"He said she's the only kind of woman he would have around him because she can hustle a dollar for a man, that sort of thing. He's fucked up. I don't want to be in his company."

"Don't use that language, Gail. Look, I'm backin' off from him. Had some business to set up. It's done. Me and you'll be makin' our move soon."

"When are we leaving?"

"Where we goin'?"

"Anywhere outside of New York."

"Two for the road, eh?"

She snuggled up close and I did my "Two for the Road" hummin' number, in her ear.

"Ol' brown eyes," she said.

So I sang (lousy) "The Music Stopped" like in Frank's first big flick in the 1940's, complete with the gestures and a big finish. Right in the bed. She clapped her hands. Then I put my hands on her.

* * *

THE TELEPHONE RANG IN THE BACK OF GASTÓN'S PARI-sienne Boutique on East 57th Street.

"It's for you, mon cher, long distance. Rolando," Gastón said as he handed the receiver to Walberto Yeampierre. Rolando Rivas-Barcelo was on the line from Miami. "Hola viejo," Walberto spoke into the phone. . . . "I'm positive. . . . Cerullo, the one they call Dom the waiter. . . . Yeah, I'm telling you, the blond one that come down with Chick Mason that time and you okayed in Puerto Rico. . . . They were all in the club, very cozy with Carlito, the big host. . . . No, Joe Cass wasn't there, but this Dom is the tip of his dagger. . . . Why are you hesitatin', Rolando? Carlito will never throw in with us. He is with the Italians. I saw it with my own eyes. He always has been. He must be attended to. . . . You are comin' to New York? . . . . Okay, if you insist. . . . I'll set up a meet. . . . Public place. Hasta luego, mi hermano."

Walberto put the phone down.

"Rolando's coming here?" Gastón inquired.

Walberto nodded and said, "I'm goin' uptown. If Benny Blanco calls, tell him I said, hold everythin', y'hear. Hold everythin'!"

"Esta bien, Walberto. Don't get yourself upset."

"Fuckin' Rolando. Can't make up his mind."

19

THE FIFTH AVENUE HOTEL ON 12TH STREET WAS THE scene of the District Attorneys Alumni Association dinner. Appellate Division and Supreme Court justices, Criminal Court judges, district attorneys and assistant district attorneys, past and present, were in attendance. As were members of the private bar and assorted clerks and officers from a multitude of law enforcement agencies. They numbered over two hundred.

The cocktail reception was in full swing by seven P.M., with many of the invitees gathered at a long bar. There was a table in the middle of the reception room covered with hors d'oeuvres. A crowd had coverged around the table as the guests dipped into the steam plates.

Mitchell Haynes filled a small plate with sausages and handed the large spoon to Detective Leo Donnelly at his side.

"Take a piss at seven-thirty," a voice whispered behind him. It was Judge Kleinfeld.

"Leo?" Haynes said.

"No. You, Mitch. You. Downstairs. Half an hour." Haynes nodded. The judge extended his hand, exclaiming in a loud voice.

"Mitch Haynes, how are you? How's Cathy and the kids?"

"Fine, Josh, just fine. How have you been?"

"Never better! Oh, there's Judge Howell, let me go curry favor for a minute. See ya, my boy."

* * *

SPECIAL STATE PROSECUTOR LAWRENCE NORWALK STOOD at the end of the bar, surrounded by a small coterie of his assistants, including Jeffrey Duncan. These younger assistants regarded themselves an elite band, uniquely equipped (under Norwalk's aegis, of course) to ferret out the pernicious corruption rampant in the body politic. This belief bore them up under the subtle ostracism to which they were subjected by the colleagues. The DAs Alumni dinner was no exception.

Norwalk reveled in it, nonetheless. His entry into the reception room, flanked by his entourage, had caused a lot of heads to turn.

"No wonder I feel a slight tremor in the building," remarked an attorney. "Larry just walked in."

After assuring a commanding position at the bar for Norwalk, Duncan, as chief honcho and spear carrier, would sally forth and spear a passing judge or district attorney. "Come over and say hello to Larry, he won't bite you, ha." Norwalk's scrubbed, almost collegiate look and engaging smile rendered him quite personable under these circumstances. But most chose to skirt his perimeter warily, and likewise he was avoided, if not shunned, by the private practitioners. All of which only served to buttress Norwalk's conviction that they were all tainted and guilt-ridden.

He had long forsworn alcohol and took note of Duncan's third drink with interest. Might bear watching, this Irishman who was privy to all his secrets.

It was Duncan who spotted her first.

"Larry, it's Allison, she's here."

Allison Norwalk, the former wife of the Special State Prosecutor, entered the room in the company of two attorneys from her law firm. The daughter of an admiral from New London, Connecticut, she carried herself with all the assurance of her patrician upbringing. A successful attorney in her own right, she had borne Norwalk two children and an acrimonious divorce suit, recently finalized. Slightly drunk, despite the attempted diversions of her male companions, Allison Fenton Norwalk made straight for the bar.

Lawrence Norwalk found himself cornered. Her wounds were still fresh.

"Double scotch on the rocks," she said. Her sharply defined features set as she followed the movements of the bartender. Wisps of her fine, chestnut-colored hair came down over her eyes. She blew them away. Forty years old that fall, she thought, and feeling every year of it. Whereas this bastard of Larry Norwachefsky was looking younger and fitter than he did eighteen years before, when they met at the Penn Relays. A gangling Jewish boy from the Bronx wearing thick horn-rims. It was his very vulnerability that had drawn her to him in the face of the vehement protests of her family. With the years, his skin had cleared up, he wore contact lenses under tinted glasses, and the idling motor within had accelerated and raced him beyond her, the children, and the life they had shared together. Norwachefsky became Norwalk, the scourge, if not of God, then of Rockefeller.

"Allison," one of the partners said, "I was just telling Walter that the transfer tax—"

"Paul, I didn't come here to talk shop. Let me have my drink, please," she said, her voice loud.

Neither Paul nor Walter was as disquieted as Norwalk, who hastened to put his ginger ale down on the bar. Too late.

"Norwachefsky. Hey. I said, Norwachefsky!"

Norwalk took a deep breath, then leaned toward her across the bar.

"Allison. There are people present. No scenes, please," he pleaded.

Norwalk's assistants were mortified. Duncan put his hand on her arm.

"*Allison*," Duncan sang out. "I understand you've been made a full partner of Fenwick, Heath and—"

"Get your hands off me, you lousy son of a bitch. Tell your boss here to take care of his family first. Dragged me through the courts for over a year. Son of a bitch of a Larry!" she said and flung her drink at Norwalk.

The glass was empty save for the ice cubes, which fell to

the floor at his feet. He made for the door in long swift strides as his companions hastened to regroup and catch up.

JUDGE KLEINFELD CONCENTRATED ON THE CUBES IN THE urinal against which he stood. Haynes was at the adjacent urinal. They were alone.

"I hear the mountain went to Mahomet," the judge said.

"I'm a Catholic myself. Yeah, he came up."

"I went before the Grand Jury. I bearded the lion in his den."

"I heard, Josh. Big mistake."

"I got angry, Mitch. I got boxed in. It's not in me to be ducking and hiding. I've always been an up-front man, all my life. Never cheated a dollar. And now on this piece of shit, I break my neck."

Haynes stared silently at the older man.

"I'm through, Mitch. There was a bug in my chambers, on top of the fluorescent light rack. Can you believe the malevolence of this bastard? The tape is loud and clear."

"I don't know what to say, Judge."

"Don't say anything. Just listen. I'm releasing you from any obligation to me. Just tell them the truth."

"I already told him we only talked about the weather."

"You weren't under oath, Mitch. He's going to subpoena you before the Grand Jury. If you lie there, he'll back you into a perjury count. Then he'll throw in conspiracy, official misconduct. Even loitering on a park bench. You know his indictments. You're the Special Narcotics Prosecutor. You have to be like Caesar's wife. He'll bury you. I put all this in motion trying to bail out that miserable son-of-a-bitch son of mine. I leaned on you. I had no right. You're off the hook. Just tell the truth in front of the Grand Jury."

Kleinfeld stepped down from the urinal. He relit his cigar. Haynes turned and walked to the washbasin.

"They'll indict you for perjury, Josh."

"I'm sixty-nine. My career is over. I should have known better. Keep Leo away from me. I'm cancerous. I have to go it alone now."

Haynes put his hand out. They shook hands and the judge walked out of the bathroom.

Haynes spoke aloud to himself.

"God bless you, Josh."

20

THE WEATHER WAS GETTIN' COLDER AND MY TIME WITH Dave was windin' down. All I gotta see is a guy's pointy teeth one time. It ain't ever the same after that. So after the beef at the Copa we kind of leveled off. I still enjoyed talkin' with the guy about the world and politics. The guy was sharp. But it wasn't the same between us. He was too wild for me.

Like he called me up to ride shotgun with him to some used-car joint near Pleasant Avenue in what was left of ghinny Harlem. Hard to believe that in the middle of that garbage can you still got a few wal-yo left. Kind of rear guard the bosses left behind in case they gotta double back.

It was still daytime. They had the same three used cars in the window that were there when I was in Harlem, ten years before. Every so often some dumb PR would wander in. "How much for that car, man?" "Get the fuck outa here." "What the hell kind of business you got, man, treat the customer like that?" They would throw the PR out the door.

We went into a small office. There was three of them standin', one of them, a fat guy, sat in a chair the wrong way. Toothpicks, turned up brims on the hats. Bad eyes. These guys was no Mickey Mouse. Fatso tilted his head toward me. Dave said, "He's an associate of mine, Renzo. From my office. Carlito Brigante."

Renzo looked at the goombahs, then he reached into a drawer in a small desk and pulled out a thick stack of court minutes. Soundin' like a cement mixer goin' uphill, he said,

"Read 'em and give us a figure, Kleinfeld."

"I already know the case. I told your people I want fifty thousand in front. I came here to pick up some money, not to quibble with you. I'm the best, I'm doing your boss a favor. I'll tell him you guys aren't ready to do business yet."

The San-Gennaro-feast boys didn't go for this nohow. Fatso Renzo, specially, got worked up.

"*Aba-fangool!* Did I say that? Don't talk like a *cafone*, awright? We're gonna do business here. We're gonna do business. But you gotta clean up yer routine a little there. I hear you ain't pullin' the rabbits out so good no more. We want a guarantee, Kleinfeld, that's all."

"You got it!" Kleinfeld pointed at Renzo.

Renzo pointed to a big spitter leanin' against the door. They all look like Tami Mauriello to me.

"That's Minghee. When you see him, you got your score."

Minghee? Pleasant Avenue . . . Joe Cass.

"When is that, Renzo?"

Renzo looked at me, puckerin' his chops.

"Think I'm gonna say in front of him? We know he's your, eh, *pezzonovante*. Ha. You get your money. One thing, Kleinfeld. You gave the okay. You don't do the right thing . . . pizza oven. You'll fit."

The boys thought this was a scream. Before we left, Minghee pulled my coattail, too.

"Joe wants to know when you comin' around," he said.

"Soon, Minghee, soon."

Hold your breath.

We took the transcript. When we got into the car on 116th Street near Patsy's, I said, "It's a wonder you can walk, Dave, your balls must weigh a ton apiece."

"Fucking wops. I can run circles around them on one leg."

"Suppose you can't deliver?"

"Carlito, it's too involved for you."

"Try me."

"I've never given a nickel back yet. I can always smokescreen the money. Had to be used for this, for that.

Pay the cop, pay the DA, pay the judge. Then these people are always getting killed or going to jail. But sometimes I do deliver. One way or another I keep the money. I just make up as I go along. Something always comes up and you get by. I don't worry about these people. The only one I couldn't talk to was you-know-who. He was an animal."

"Oh, yeah. I read in the paper he disappeared off the Rock."

"I sleep like a baby. Me? I'm going to lose retainers because some jerk lawyer will give a guarantee and I won't? Bullshit."

"You're a worse bandit than me."

We were drivin' south on Second Avenue. He turned left to the East Side Highway on 96th Street and laughed.

"You don't even have a learner's permit, Carlito."

"If I had your license, I'd be a millionaire."

"What makes you think I'm not?"

"So wadda you hangin' around for?"

"The action is the best part when you're the best. I know I am. Look what I did for you."

"That brief was a masterpiece, Dave." (I had to admit it.)

"Of course. You have to understand that I try cases geared to the appeal. In the higher courts they don't see the junk in front of them. It's just a different atmosphere. Abstract, cerebral. They fancy themselves innovators, intellectuals. But they can't break new ground upholding old decisions. The fun, the exercise is in the new twist, the new approach. In other words, give them something new to hang their hat on, and you have a reversal."

"That's easy?"

"Of course not. I don't want to toot my own horn, but the appellate courts have used some of my briefs verbatim. No one has won more conspiracy cases than I. . . . But you can't win them all. And with these ingrate bastards you're only as good as your last case. So I had troubles with the Saunders case—Black Bart. I'll straighten it out. I'm more worried about my father."

"Yeah, I read somethin' about it in the papers. Your name came up. He's indicted, eh?"

"That lunatic, Norwalk, trying to smear us."

"You can't talk to him?"

"Norwalk? Are you crazy? He sits up there in the World Trade Center like he was Genghis Khan. Nobody can talk to him. I used to watch him at Yale. His class was a few years ahead of mine. Trackman. Ran around in his BVDs. Jew-boy like me. Unpronounceable name. Changed it. Married into society. Became a regular whirling dervish after the governor appointed him. I wouldn't get near him with a ten-foot pole."

"Your father's in trouble, eh?"

"I have a few aces up my sleeve, yet."

"Goin' in the ol' trickbag again, eh?"

"I'll deal with Norwalk when the time comes. Fucking JASP."

"Ey, I forgot. Can you drop me off at 79th Street? I want to pick up Gail."

"What is it with you and this new girl?"

"Not a new girl, we go back quite a ways."

"I don't believe you."

"What?"

"I mean a guy like you. Married? Tied down? You're an action guy."

"Not really. It's not all party, babe. Been a few rainy nights when I've been lonely. I don't deny it. All I know is the best time of the day is when I see her. What can I tell you? Maybe I'm getting old."

Dave got a little riled up here.

"That's ridiculous. They're all the same. You go out of your way for them and they take advantage. All they want is a meal ticket. Give me, take me, bring me, and what have you done for me lately. Period. I'm surprised at you, Carlito. Really surprised."

"We'll see. I'll be takin' off soon . . . for good."

He looked at me, then he got real quiet till we got to 79th and West End.

"Drop me off here."

"Steffie wants to give a dinner on Saturday at my house in Kings Point. Small, just a small gathering. We'll make it a kind of farewell thing for you."

"You're goin' pretty strong with this chick yourself."

He shrugged. "Just a steady piece of ass to me. Listen, if something works out, I may have a going-away present for you."

I got out of the car. He leaned over the seat and said to me, "What is it Renzo said you were?"

"A *pezzonovante*. Like a heavy hitter, ninety-centimeter. That's Sicilian. I only met about five hundred of them down in Lewisburg. They know a class act when they see one. Shalom, Hymie."

And I gave him the Sidge "salute." He got a kick out of it. He cracked up.

"Get the fuck out of here," he said.

SMALL? THERE MUST HAVE BEEN FIFTY PEOPLE AT DAVE'S house. Steffie didn't do no cookin', she was in a long hostess gown, playin' lady of the manor over a couple of cooks, two waiters, and a bartender. Buffet spread all around the big fireplace. Of the guests me and Gail only knew Cox and Wadleigh. There was a whole gang of lawyers, doctors, and look-alike money guys. Some fine foxes too. Why I gotta look at salami, when I got prosciutto under my arm? Still.

Had these big vats with all kinds of food. They had "ordefiva" (as a friend of mine used to say) for days. They had roast beef, turkey, lasagna, a giant salad bowl with chunks of avocado, fruit. Even had ham and pork sausages (them Jews were scoffin' them up). Was a loaf of Italian bread, musta been ten feet long. Big bowls of Sangría. Scotch and champagne by the case. Regular Charles Laughton orgy. I didn't really stuff my face. I can't enjoy a good scoff with a whole lot of fancy people around. A man can't talk intelligent with the tomato sauce all over his chin. Plus you stain your shirt. Then what?

So me and my old lady is drinkin' wine and hawkin' the action. The people were sprawled all over the place. I was waitin' for some broad with her hair tied in a bun to come over, stick her nose in my eye, and say, "And what do you do?" Pretty soon a broad with her hair tied in a bun . . . "I am an interior decorator" (I have decorated a whole lot of interiors in my time). I play everythin' off Gail, like to crack her up. She's my best audience.

Steffie was hoppin' and hostessin' around. Thought it was Elinor Ames of the *Daily News*. Dave was takin' care of business too, but his nose looked a li'l puffy. Like he'd been sniffin' in the cookie jar again. His man, Cox, drunk (and disorderly again), was arguin' with Wadleigh about People versus Ossobucco or somethin'. If them two guys saw the UFO come out of a toilet bowl, What would say to When, "What's the case law on this?"

They played some slow music and me and Gail danced. Mostly we were sitting on this ledge around the fireplace. Along comes this chubs, wearin' a beard, dandruff, pipe, and Hush-Puppies. Wants to dance with my ol' lady. Chump should go dance with his ol' lady, gotta come over and bother mine. More than one clown has been wasted in the Latin dances for this shit. You could be in a clinch with your chick, some guy'll reach over and pry you apart, "Can I dance witchoo?" Deserve to get smacked. But I was on my good behavior in Dave's house, so I let her go. Gave me a good view of her though. She put all them broads away.

They got a thing goin' telling jokes. Right away I stopped the show with my joke about the guy on Lenox Avenue talkin' to God. Cracked everybody up. Chubs makes an announcement he don't go for no ethnic jokes. I'm the house ethnic and I gotta stand still for that guff from a Lung-Island liberal. Tryin' to make me look bad in front of my ol' lady, who he was puffin' smoke rings at. Like he was sendin' signals. Mickey Mouse intellectual. Still showin' off, he got off on Dave and the two of them went into a heavy literature gas-bag. They went shot for shot. The crowd went—wow. I went—yawn.

" . . . the rogue and the scamp have ever fascinated, witness the unflagging popularity of Candide or Lazarillo de Tormes—" Now Chubs sights on me. "You're Hispanic, Mr. Brigante, what do you think of the Lazarillo as opposed to Candide?"

Naza-who? I could see the shit-eatin' grin on Dave's face. There was a lotta people there.

"I go for the two of them," says me, slippin' and slidin'. Fuck you, dandruff-flakes. Gail moved up quick.

"Yes, Charley, but the Lazarillo precedes Candide by centuries. You usually lean toward the Lazarillo."

"You're right, Gail, Nazarillo's really my favorite."

Nine ball in the corner pocket.

Chubs leaned toward her, where he'd been aimin' all along.

"Spanish literature, my dear?"

She nodded.

"Where?"

Fuckin' intellectuals will examine all your drawers, whether you're wearin' them or not. No respect.

"Ohio State. I was an exchange student at Granada for a year," Gail said. Now we gotta hear Chubs's life story.

"Granada? The Alhambra. Of course. I was at Salamanca for a spell . . ." (yakkity yak yak for a longer spell). "You're fortunate, Mr. Brigante, to have met such a beautiful Hispanophile."

"I was thinkin' the same thing," I told him.

"Carlito's strong suit," Dave said, "is Russian literature, isn't that right, Carlito?"

Cock sucker.

"Only Solzhenitsyn. Mainly 'cause he done time. I ain't no expert."

"Politically, he's lost his sense of proportion. His literary style, I don't care for . . ." (fuckin' commie, I knew it). "Have you read Dostoevsky? Or Gorky's *Mother?*"

"Never heard of him or his mother."

"My dear man, you have not plumbed the Russian soul. . . ."

More yakkity yak. Him and Dave were plumbin' over my head when I got attacked from the side by some Brillo-hair in sneakers wanted my opinion of a French guy I thought was a hairdresser. I got all tangled up. I'm talkin' hair and he's talkin' philosophy. Gente loca. And he was buggin' me all night (think he was a faggot).

The music went round 'n round. Went to the wee and the pee hours. Time for the Sinatra sides. All the guests were gone. Gail was in the kitchen with Steffie drinkin' coffee. Me and Dave were laid out on this big sofa. He was zonked, total. Quite a few of them people had brought their own stash. They went home singin' "Come Fly With Me" (wasn't on no gossamer wings either). They're doin' coke in the boondocks. It be's an outrage. For shame.

Dave said, "You're right. Get out of all the shit. I've been thinking about it. You've got a good woman in Gail. I'm going to help you. I made a few calls. Remember Lloyd, black guy from uptown?"

"Lloyd Simpkins?"

"That's him. I spoke to him about my problem with Black Bart. He's a beautiful guy."

"Yeah, I hear Lloyd did all right while I was away."

"Your name came up. Seems your mutual buddy, Earl, was asking about you."

"Yeah, Earl Bassey."

"He's got a big car-rental agency in St. Thomas. Might have a place for you. Interested?"

"Yeah, I'm interested. That's only twenty-five minutes from San Juan."

"I can set it up for you."

"Okay, give me the bad part now."

He sat up, annoyed.

"You see the way you are, Carlito. Try to help you out to retire in one piece—"

I had to laugh.

"Kleinfeld, I been around people all my life. I know human psychology. C'mon, quit fuckin' around."

He lay back on the couch again, rollin' his head around.

"It's part of your going-away present. A little trip to London, with me. You get paid."

"That thing worked out for you?"

"What thing?"

"What you told me before."

"Yeah. Whatever. I need your help. Last time out."

"Pig in a poke again?"

"Less you know the better, right?"

"Wrong, Dave. Last time out with you, you did a nasty. I got two felonies, remember?"

"This is personal." He looked away. Nervous.

"The facts, ma'am.'"

"I'm getting tired of fucking around too. I want my wife back. I want Judy."

"How am I supposed to do that? I ain't no Mr. Keene."

"All right. Here's the whole story. You know the police property clerk case?"

"Sure. That's while I was in. Where they switched the junk—four hundred pounds. Unbelievable. Suppose to be old man Petrone. Balls like a pawnshop, buyin' that shit back from the cops. Whew!"

Kleinfeld's eyes were half lidded, with his muzzle all puffed up.

"Way more than four hundred. Brains, Carlito, brains. I had to coach him all the way. Dumb ghinny."

A swindle like that scares anybody, but I had to hear the rest. I took a blow with him, wheezing a little bit.

"Crime of the century," I said. "But you shouldn't talk about it." My eyes watered. Out of shape.

"Bullshit. Statute of limitations had almost run. Old man Petrone only put up the money. Not even, he got it from Tony Tee and some other bosses. I had the connection, I set it up. The old man used his son, Nicky Junior. Also Joe Noonch and two other guys. They made the actual moves. Millions were made, mostly by Petrone Senior. I know he gave me a bad count. So did the bosses. I couldn't complain. I needed him as a buffer from the crazier guys. The mob went berserk, Carlito, you can't believe the money."

"Ave Maria!"

My hair stood straight up. Money is a bitch.

"It was too big. A lot of jealousy. All kinds of trouble. Norwalk turned Joe Noonch around, something to do with Nuncio's wife. Everybody was going down: Junior, the old man, a couple of bosses."

"Not you?"

"Nuncio didn't know me. Only the Petrones."

"You would have gone too."

"Maybe. Anyway, the old man got word that there was a stool. All their money and connections and they came up with zilch. It took ol' reliable Dave to bail their balls out of the fire. I got to a clerk-typist. Simple as that. Fifty large for one word, Noonch. Joe Nuncio."

"John's Bargain Store for a name like that? I *know* you raised the ante, Dave."

I stuck my right hand out and high where he could see it. He slapped skin and laughed. His nose started to run and I gave him my handkerchief.

"Damned right. I made up for all the money old man Petrone stole from me. The ghinnies paid through their Roman noses. I scored a bundle. While all this was going on, I had to wet-nurse Nicky Junior. Fucking crybaby, supposed to be a tough guy like his father. Had him over to my apartment, treated him like he was my own family. All the time he was scheming after my wife. But I didn't know about it. I blame old man Petrone, he knew about it. I was supposed to be his protégé. Cock sucker. I hope he's down there holding hands with Tony Tee. After Joe Noonch, the other two guys disappeared too. Tony Tee was having everybody in the deal wiped out. Junior panicked and ran away, and Judy, stupid cunt, took off with him."

"Now you've tracked her."

"I want her back."

"None of my business, but one: Why do you want a woman that put the horns on you? And two: what makes you think she'll come back to you?"

"Well put, Counselor Brigante. In converse order, let me worry about whether she'll want to come back with me, and two, that's only you macho Latins that stay up nights, worrying about horns. She was my girl on Walton Avenue, she will always be my girl. I gave her a hard time, but that's while I was hustling to make a buck. You've never had to work for a living, Carlito, you don't know what it's like. It's worse than the street."

"Where do I come in?"

"That's what the trick said to the he-she."

"You mean the shim."

He slapped skin again. I wasn't feelin' no pain either.

"Junior's a gunman," he said. "The old man told me he made his bones when he was nineteen."

"Yeah, but you got a pistol now. Still don't like the noise, right? Lotta guys like that."

"Cut the shit, Carlito. I just want you there to keep the peace while I talk to my wife."

"Won't be easy. I been checkin' on Petrone's kid."

"What do you hear?"

"Suppose to be another Johnny Stompanato. All the chicks crazy about him. Meanwhile, he drove the father crazy. Booze, dope, loved black women, degenerate gambler, into all the bookmakers and shylocks."

"That's Junior."

"Also heard he stuck up games, shook down connected people, and even put a lighter to some boss's face at the ol' Pussycat. Bad kid. No respect."

"His father had to call a sit-down for that one."

"Yeah, the bosses wanted him hit. I know all about your boy. In the joint we know everything. It's only out here that we get into trouble."

"Old man Petrone packed a lot of weight. He said they'd have to kill him too. He knew he'd made a lot of money for them. But the old man's gone and I hear Junior has changed. He's broke, working as a croupier in London. Definite information this time. He won't be too much trouble."

"All right, Dave, last time out. I'll do you this one last favor. When we get back, I split."

"You get five thousand when we go. Five thousand when we get back. With Judy."

"I'll go for nothing. Just pay my expenses."

"That's a bad precedent. I don't want any favors. You get paid."

"You're learnin', m'man."

"Now that's a laugh. . . . Hey, tell me that story about you and that broad in the Hotel St. George. . . ."

Dave was fallin' out. I went to the john in the back. When I came out, I noticed this old guy in one of them Prohibition-style tuxedoes sittin' by himself in the study, watchin' teevee. The big room was dark, but I could make out racks full of books, rugs, fancy leather, and sea paintings. The old man had a bottle next to him. He wiggled his finger at me from the leather armchair he was in. I walked over to him. A short red-faced guy with white hair and a cigar stickin' out of his mouth, I hadn't noticed him at the party. He was tanked up good.

"I know you," he said. "You're Brigante. You're the guy my son got out of the can. You pay him back by using his office as a screen for your monkeyshines. Boy, do I know you."

Like Pigmeat used to say at the Apollo, "Here come de judge!" Didn't look like Dave, looked Irish. I tried to talk nice.

"No monkeys, no shines, Judge. I was just helpin' Dave out for a few days."

"What law school did you attend, Brigante?"

There's somethin' about me, soon as a judge lays eyes, *wham*, "Yo' ass is out the window." I kept quiet. He got up from the chair, about up to my chin, and poked the long finger of the law into my face.

"David thinks everybody's his friend. He takes the likes of you into his confidence, into his home. Criminals he wines and dines. He's got a hoodlum fixation, that's what he has. Ever since he teamed up with that whore lawyer, Cohen, fifteen years ago. I rue the day I ever let him get involved with that shyster. Almost got David disbarred. But the trusting fool still prefers the company of felons to that of decent professionals who can do him some good. These bore him. He can't grasp the fact that it is the likes of you that are going to betray him."

Now I'm a stool pigeon. But I kept cool.

"Can I leave now, Judge?"

He turned around and went back to his chair and drink. I left the room. Dave was out cold on the sofa. All the Kleinfelds are crazy. Lemme get my old lady and blow this joint.

ON THE WAY HOME I TOLD GAIL ABOUT GOIN' DOWN TO St. Thomas to see my man, Earl. Maybe expand the car rental business to Puerto Rico with him. Very emotional chick, Gail. Right away her eyes got shiny, and she curled up next to me in the seat. All she wanted was to be with me. I understood that,'cause I didn't need anybody else around either. Not like before when I used to walk around

with the entourage like I was Frank Sinatra. Just to get
haircut would cost me fifty balloons what with five or six
"arrimao" hangin' on. I was thinkin' about an apartment
down there, near the beach. I'm like a crab, gotta be near
the sea. Gail was the same way, she'd been raised on Lake
Erie around boats and water. Sometimes you look at two
people. They ain't got nothin' in common. He's this, she's
that. Meanwhile, there's a whole gang of little quirks they
got goin' for them under the covers. Like they don't bunch
up the toothpaste in the tube, or they go for old movies,
or maybe they both come to life in the evenin' but wanna
be left alone in the mornin'. And what about the boudoir?
They could be two freaks and nobody know it. Little things
that the people lookin' through the window can't see. Guy
could be wearin' dreadlocks and a bone through his nose,
some sociology broad or teeny-bopper will dig on him. It's
a mystery can baffle an Einstein or a Paul Muni.

When we got in the sack, I told her, "Hispanophile, huh?
No wonder you got the hots for me. It's a disease."

She laughed.

"Bailed you out, didn't I?"

"That fat guy had eyes for you. My dear. I would've
straightened him out except I had this guy looked like Irwin
Corey followin' me around with the extensionist bullshit.
Had me up to here."

"Existential."

I gave her a dirty look.

"You said you wanted me to correct you. Remember,
Charley?"

She was gigglin' up a storm.

"It's easy for you, smarty-drawers, you went to Ohio
State, where did I go?"

"Upstate."

"Oh, wise-ass, eh?"

She ducked under the sheet and we started wrestlin'
around the bed.

"I'm only quoting you, Charley."

"Don't repeat what I say, I make up as I go along."

"What about Operation Bootstrap, your program to
improve your mind?"

"Gail, how many times have I gotta repeat? It's not my mind. I'm faster with figures than you are. And who can break down off-the-wall ideas faster'n me? Includin' you with your crazy commie yin-yang. Don't need no Third World, this one's good enough. Just give me the money."

"Now I'm a communist. Politically and philosophically incompatible, that's what we are."

"That's what I'm talkin' about. The words. It's the words that are holdin' me back. People hear a guy say, 'undubitably,' in a crowd, right away he's ahead on points. Big words. That's where I, meanin' well, fart n' fell."

"In—"

"In what?"

"Indubitably."

"Stupid fuckin' language. I give up."

"Charley, words are just props. Don't be taken in by fancy parlor talk. It doesn't mean anything."

"If I'm so smart, why don't I sound like it? Like Dave, say?"

"Read the books I gave you. You'll dazzle everybody with your verbal footwork."

"Cannot read that Marcel Prowse. Not enough goin' on. I like the war books or the one about the Gulag, where the cons wiped out the stool pigeons. Somethin' that really went down."

"Haven't you gone that route long enough? I mean, the violence? Where's the poetry in you? I'm going to bring you a book by Luis Borges. You'll thank me for it."

"I will. Ave Maria!"

"You want to dazzle people at parties?"

"True."

"So?"

"Okay, heavy check-out on the books. But 'ey, I ain't gonna read about daffodils and trippin' through the tulips. Gotta be somethin' goin' on."

"Behold. The liberal arts, Charley Brigante."

"Never too late for a man to get rounded out. M'man Walter, from upstate, used to say, 'A dude gotta be, the three gees, like the suit label. Good lookin', good ball,

and good rap.' I got the first two out of three. My rap I
gotta work on."

"Oh yeah? Let's see about the second gee. I'm not so
sure."

"No, I'm too stupid. I don't deserve it. Too much second
gee, that's what's holdin' me back on the third gee. Don't
wanna be loved for my body alone. Suspended sentence
for you. Seventy-two hours. Next case."

She shoved me and I fell off the bed. I chased her
around the apartment till I cornered her in the kitchen.
We second-gee-ed by the refrigerator. Only place left we
ain't balled is the hall closet (don't fit). In that area (I mean
bedtime activities) we were very compatible. For the rest of
it, who knows? But I used to make her laugh a lot.

In the morning I told her I had to go to Europe with
Dave. She pitched a fit. She wouldn't stay in the house.

"I'm going home to 90th Street. I don't want to hear
anymore," she said. I'd never seen her like this. Even her
eyebrows turned red. I took her home and double-parked
in front of her building near West End Avenue.

"Charley. He's going to get you killed or worse—sent
back to prison for the rest of your life."

"It's just for a couple of days, Gail. To see his wife."

"He needs you for that?"

"Well, there's a problem, no big thing."

"Like her lover?"

"Well, yeah. But I'm just goin' to, ah, keep the peace."

"You're a policeman."

"Gail, don't be that way. No need to get excited—"

"Why shouldn't I? It's my life too. Are you blind? Can't
you see Dave is sick? You're always talking about the street
and what it taught you about people. Can't you see how
Dave manipulates you? He plays you like a banjo. Flattering
you, consulting your opinion, steering conversation in your
direction. He condescends, that's the word, he condescends
to you. He's more clever, more subtle. When he talks to
you, four fifths of his mind is programmed elsewhere.
You should hear yourself parroting his big words. Since
you heard it from him, your every other word is, 'this is
ludicrous, that is ludicrous.' I'm not saying this to hurt or

belittle you, Charley, It's because I love you and want us to be together that I'm saying this. And because I know he will take your decent qualities and twist and entangle them. Friendship and loyalty are what you live by, Charley. Kleinfeld—"

"Can run circles around me on one leg."

"Exactly. He has no feelings, no morals. And he bares his fangs regularly, like at the Copa. He's fascinated by you. But basically he resents you, and if you let him, he'll destroy you. And me."

"I hate to say it, Gail. But you're a little jealous of Dave's friendship with me. And as a matter of fact, I have given him some ideas on cases that he has used—"

"What's the use."

She got out of the car and walked around to the curb. I reached her on the stoop.

"Don't walk me upstairs. I don't know what I'm going to do, Charley. I don't want to see you for a while."

I was in shock. I didn't say anything. What she didn't know was that I had made money with Dave. He wasn't playin' me for no banjo. I was hip to his jive.

"He's going to kill those people, Charley. Remember that I told you."

And she ran up the steps.

21

I FOUND OUT WE WERE BOTH HARDHEADED. I WOULDN'T call her, she wouldn't call me. Like to kill me. Before I left, I sent her flowers and a little card I wrote somethin' on. Me and Dave flew to London. On the jumbo jet. Love that plane. Didn't cost hardly nothin'. Dave got us on a gambling junket. This is why the rich get richer, unlike the other kind. He was in a big hurry. Was comin' back to do his father's trial in Supreme Court. Cox and Wadleigh had done all the motion work, but Dave had to be there for the trial or the old man would go in charged with perjury and come out convicted of sodomy and promoting prostitution. That's what Dave said.

Of course, first class. We stayed at a fancy hotel on Strand Street. We had time to kill to Sunday, so we wandered around. It was the first time for the two of us. I had been in Madrid and the wide avenues of London reminded me of it. Beautiful clothes on Regent Street. The women got rosy cheeks. The cabs were unbelievable, clean, polite. The pizza was lousy, like eatin' a radial with ketchup. Whole bunch of Arabs ridin' around in bathrobes in their Bentleys and Rollses. We were standin' around Trafalgar Square, almost got our picture taken. You shoulda' seen Dave hoof. Like a regular wise guy. We went to a play that night. Theater was right downstairs. Another first for me. Guy named George Barnard Shaw wrote it (think they named a girls' school up near 120th Street after him). It's about a lot of people standin' around yakkin'. *Man and Superman,* but no Superman showed up (the one in Havana, I hear, Fidel put in the army). Me and Dave ended up eatin' on a boat docked on the Thames. Spanish food no less. Mezzo, mezzo. He talked all night about what he was goin' to do to Norwalk at the trial. Somethin' sensational that was gonna knock the whole courthouse on its ass.

"What are we going to do about this guy tomorrow, Dave?"

"Let me worry about it. One thing is sure. He's not going to keep my wife. We're still legally married. They're living in a state of adultery, you know."

"God-zooks."

"I'd be justified in killing him, you know."

"Just hold it right there. You're not going to kill him with me around. Do that on your own time. I'll bug out right now."

"I didn't say I was going to kill him. I was just pointing out to you the unwritten law. Like in Texas or in Sicily."

"You mean like the mind goes blank. Temporarily crazy."

"Precisely."

We went into the finer points of insanity. I have wide experience in this area. In the old days, anybody charged with homicide would be taken out of the Tombs and sent to the Bellevue Psychiatric Ward for thirty days. They'd give you a robe and a pair of toilet-paper slippers and throw you in this big cage with about thirty or forty other guys. Homicide crazies. Who didn't throw somebody off the roof, who didn't stuff somebody in the furnace, who didn't sleep with the corpse for a week. Try sleepin' in that ward. No sooner you'd close one eye (that's all you're allowed), some guy with electric hair would peer over at you in the dark. I mean eyeball to eyeball. I mean scare the shit out of ya. The doctors said I was a malingerer. I said I only liked regular sex. Then I found out they meant I was goofin' off. Okay. The real whack-jobs would get mad if you said they was crazy. You had to agree they were malingerin'. Crazy house.

Dave (early bird) got me up early Sunday mornin'. He'd been up for hours, been out, come back. We took a cab

along the river. Passed a lot of bridges (no London bridge).
Saw Big Ben. After a while we got out of the cab and he
made me walk for about ten minutes. Then we got to this
big project. Dolphin Square. Nice, not too fancy. Junior was
not livin' like no Lucky Luciano in exile. Self-service elevator. We had it rehearsed. Knock, ask for Mr. Peters, that
there had been some problem at the casino this morning.
I was suppose to fake an English accent. Madon! I heard
a woman's voice and went through the routine real fast.
She opened the door. Kleinfeld's Marjorie Morningstar.
Small, dark-haired, a beauty, Judy was. Scared to death
too. Kleinfeld went right past her into the apartment. Thin
chick, wearin' a housecoat, she was in a daze. Kleinfeld sat
her down on a couch. She didn't say a word. Junior was in
the shower, we waited for him.

He came out in a short robe, barefoot, hair wet. Nicky
Petrone, Junior, former contender for the Rossano Brazzi
award. A little down on his luck, but with all the curls
in place, still a pretty boy. He was, irregardless, a known
shooter and I was nervous. Junior looked at me and Dave
like we was the meter guy, then he walked into the living
room, where Judy was on the couch, all bunched up. She
had big, dark eyes and thick, black hair. I could see why she
had both these guys' balls in an uproar. Judy, Judy, Judy, as
Cary Grant would say. He stood in the middle of the room,
in his terry cloth, hands on hips. Didn't look scared. It was
a small apartment with hardly any furniture.

"If he makes a move, kill him. And her," Dave said.

I nodded. Just meant to keep Junior honest ('cause any
guy used to stick up connected crap games don't give
a shit).

"Leave her out of this, Dave. I'll go anywhere you want,"
Junior said.

"Don't worry, you're not going anywhere."

Junior eyeballed me.

"This is your killer, Kleinfeld?"

"They killed your father, Junior. Tony Tee gave the okay.
You're on your own" was Dave's answer.

Didn't budge him.

"He's in hiding," Junior said, weak.

"Tony Tee had him plucked right out of his house in Fort Lee. Lucky they didn't take your mother too."

"Pop . . ."

Junior started to fade. He got a little rubbery. Then he had to sit down. Had to plop next to Judy, and she grabbed his hands in both of hers. You're in trouble, Dave, if you think you're gonna take this broad away from this guy.

"Nicky, I'm sorry—" she said. Now she wants to stroke his hair. I mean, enough is enough, already. Dave went bananas.

"Shut up, you whore! I came to take you home, but now I'm not sure I want you. Look at you. You used to be a beautiful girl. You look like shit. Look at this dump. Look at the mess you've made of your life. I'd have had you living like—like somebody. Not in this shithouse."

"David, I don't care about those things. I've tried to tell you—"

"How could you get mixed up with this greasy bastard? They're going to come for him. This is Mafia. They always get even. And I'm glad. But they'll kill you too, Judy. They'll kill you too!"

I got my eyes on Junior. I figure he can't have nothin' under the robe. He went to get up. I pointed him down again.

"Dave," he said, "I told her twenty times to go home. I'm not going to make it. My father's friends in Italy let me down. I don't speak the language. They took all my money. I never got a break. Tony Tee thinks I have the other money. I don't have that money. And I'll never rat. I was born Mafioso. They can squeeze my brains out too. I'll never rat. But they won't believe me." He put his hands over his face. "Go with them, Judy, just go with them."

Judy wasn't having any of this. She grabbed Junior and held him against her chest. Nice chest too. She was not about to let go. She started to cry, loud.

"Leave us alone! Go away, David. Don't you understand? I love him!"

Dave moved too fast for me. He grabbed a lamp and smashed it against the back of Junior's head. Judy screamed as Junior slid to the floor, his head bleeding bad. Dave

pulled a revolver from his waist. I finally got off here.
I jumped from the side (I was on his right) and grabbed
his gun hand, which was already pointed down at Junior's
head. I jammed the cylinder, it wouldn't turn, so he couldn't
squeeze off a shot.

"*Dave*! Dave! Think what you're doin'," I'm yellin.
Lucky for me Dave ain't too strong. I wrestled him down
and he fell on his knees. I got the gun. He was cryin' now,
like a baby. I knew he would have killed them both. I had to
sit in a chair. I'm getting too old for this shit. I put the bullets
in my pocket. I'm watchin' these three people in all their
mess and misery. I felt like a burglar, or a peepin' Tom.

"Get him a towel," I told Judy, who was helping Junior
up on the couch. She came back with a wet towel. Junior
just had a gash on his head, looked worse than it was.
She was cradlin' him. Poor Dave, had to get up by himself. I gave him my handkerchief. They all quieted down.
Too quiet.

"Let's go home, Dave," I said, and he nodded. I got up.
Junior couldn't figure me out. Thought I came to bury him,
instead I saved his ass. But I came to keep the peace, right?
Gonna cost me five thousand bananas to be a fuckin' hero.
Dave was a sore loser. Had somethin' for everybody.

"I hope the wops come soon for you, Junior. You look
like shit, Judy."

With me, he would settle later. All these early risers are
like that. Their day is too long, they get nasty.

Later on I'm thinkin'. We all have our "adorado tor-
mento." Don't have to be Natalie Wood. Could be anybody.
Of course it's in the head. But that don't help the loser.

Wouldn't talk at the hotel, wouldn't talk at the airport
(there was a fuckin' strike), wouldn't sit next to me on
the plane. I figured we were through. Gail was right. Fuck
Dave Kleinfeld.

22

$\mathbf{C}$ARTHAGINIANS ANTICIPATING THE RETURN OF SCIPIO could not have made preparations more elaborate than David Kleinfeld's mobilization for the battle with Norwalk. He marshaled food, beverages, medical supplies, clothes, cots, and linen. The statutes on perjury and obstruction of governmental administration complete with all the decisional authority, both state and federal, lay in one stack in the middle of the floor; another stack of books and papers contained pertinent out-of-state case law; a third pile of papers contained summaries on cases with references and dicta bearing secondarily on these issues; there were thick transcripts of the legislative session minutes that had passed the statutes; memoranda of law on every evidentiary question they could foresee and a contingency memorandum in the event of an adverse ruling. Texts, treatises, and *Law Review* articles were scattered about the office. A special private agency in Boston was contacted to investigate the prospective jurors. A psychiatrist was retained to help in the selection of the jury. Norwalk's public and private life were already under scrutiny by a New York private detective agency, with heavy emphasis (at David's insistence) on the remote possibility of homosexual liaisons in Norwalk's past. Even a hypnotist was considered.

This drastic war footing so engaged the energies of the firm that all other matters were at a standstill. No matter. Kleinfeld called a conference. In attendance, Cox,

Wadleigh, and Diane Vargas, the latter taking copious notes of Kleinfeld's proclamations.

"We suspend all other activity. We adjourn all pending cases. I will accept no new retainers until my father's trial and acquittal are accomplished. I have a fifty-thousand-dollar war chest to pay for this all-out legal effort. Twenty thousand for Cox, twenty thousand for Wadleigh, and ten thousand for you, Diane. Half paid in front, the other half at the successful conclusion of my father's trial." Kleinfeld paused to note the impact of this portion of his manifesto upon the proposed beneficiaries. Then he continued, "But you will earn it. You will not go home for the duration of the trial. Except for some extraordinary reason. This will be a twenty-four-hour-a-day commitment. Forget you have a home or life away from this office. If you don't think you can cut it, there's the door, and no hard feelings." Kleinfeld halted and pointed to the door. His dark eyes, ignited as from some inner core of energy, probed their faces. All three vowed their unceasing efforts and appeared, to Kleinfeld, to be imbued with requisite enthusiasm.

"Okay. We're going to the mat. I want every single case Shepardized, from the advance sheets to the founding fathers. Strike that. Back to Runnymede. I want every single opinion and decision that Judge Schrader has written. Let the psychiatrist read them also. Can't hurt. Stupid bastard Schrader ruled against us on the bug. That's a firm grapple hook for appeal. There's no way they're going to sit upstairs for an indiscriminate monitoring of a judge's chambers! That would be ludicrous. Reinvestigate those sealing dates also. The bug is the appeal. No question about it. But this case has to be won on trial. Any other result will kill my father. You understand? Kill him. His heart is already bad. My mother doesn't even know he's been indicted. Saving a life, that's what this is about. Day and night we will eat, drink, and sleep perjury. That is the target, the perjury count, the rest will fall with it. And the linchpin of our attack will be intent. The lack of criminal intent in my father's mind. Where will the jury find the necessary *mens rea* if his state of mind was one of total anxiety and bewilderment? A profligate son panicked and put inhuman pressure on his father. 'Father, save me, I'm being framed.' 'What would you do, ladies and gentlemen of the jury, you have children too?' Get the idea? Make sure you get that down, Diane."

Cox, rising to the occasion, submitted, "Is the father to be stretched on the rack for the sins of a dissolute son?"

"Good, Cox, good, I am the villain. That's a good phrase for summation. Put it down."

Diane nodded and continued writing. Not to be outdone, Wadleigh volunteered, " 'Danger invites rescue.' Cardozo."

Kleinfeld and Cox exchanged pained glances.

"Wadleigh, please stay on the citations, leave the court-room oratory to me. You can start drafts on requests to charge now and ideas for summation. It's never too early. Know one thing, I mean to wipe out Norwalk in that courtroom. If it means my license."

Wadleigh lowered his head to stare at Kleinfeld over the frames of his eyeglasses. His eyes rotated slowly toward Cox, his mentor in all mundane matters. Cox nodded. Reassured, Wadleigh nodded.

Cox put a question.

"Are you putting your father on?"

"I honestly don't know, Harry," Kleinfeld said, his tone slackening.

"What?" Wadleigh said. "How can we formulate tactical plans without knowing whether the defendant is going to take the stand in a criminal case? That's absolutely pivotal. What good is a mountain of research if we don't know that? We have to have a basic strategy."

"He is not a defendant. He is Judge Kleinfeld. Don't ever let the jury hear different. And we prepare for either eventuality. We will have alternate plans set up. Think of a river crossing. Several feints, find the weak spot, concen-trate our forces, and pour through. . . . Like the Russians across the Oder, with two thousand searchlights," Kleinfeld said.

"Or the Germans across the Meuse," observed Cox, wryly.

"Yeah, you fucking Nazi," Kleinfeld said. All laughed except Diane, who heard only the sounds as she wrote.

"Let's kick it around," Kleinfeld suggested, "the old man was born in Russia, but was brought over as a baby around 1908, 1909. Raised around Delancey. That would be good on summation, 'ghetto kid clawing his way out of the gutter.' We've got to get a lot of old Jewish guys on that jury."

"But they may not like judges. You know, coddling criminals," Cox said.

"He's right," Wadleigh said, "nobody likes judges. That's where the right and the left meet, their mutual dislike for judges."

"It's not going to be a lead-pipe cinch. . . . The more I think of it, the less I like him on the stand. My father is long-winded and bad-tempered. Norwalk will bait him, draw him out, then choke him on his own rhetoric. Dad's liable to have a stroke right on the stand. My problem will be to keep him off even if it's best for the case."

"You're the lawyer, Dave, he has to defer to you," Cox said.

"He's a regular Kulak, once he makes up his mind, he's like a mule."

"The jury will hear the tape. Somebody's got to explain it our way or Norwalk will make them draw all the wrong inferences," Wadleigh said.

"The fucking tape is loud and clear. They had the bug right on top of the fluorescent lights. But it could be a twin-edged knife, because I sounded like a man near the breaking point from the pressure, eh, of trying to make a living and support my office. In other words, you can argue from the tape that the father cracked up in order to save the son from cracking up."

"In other words, he acted instinctually. The preservation of the young. A phenomenon characteristic of all species," Cox elaborated.

"Get it down, Diane," Kleinfeld said.

"What about you?" Cox asked Kleinfeld.

"What about me?"

"How will you play it?"

"Believe it or not, I have a strange feeling about this case. I'm going to play a lot of it by ear, the way Norwalk does. I see myself starting the case as the trial advocate, low key. He couldn't indict me, so he doesn't have any real hidden ammo I'm going to worry about. He can't call me as a witness, but by the same token he doesn't expect me to take the stand and expose myself to all the petty shit he's going to throw at me. He figures I won't have the balls to risk getting disbarred. I know how he reads me—that I'll never take the stand."

"Would you?"

"Like I said, I'm playing it by ear. But as we're talking, I can visualize a little scenario. Stop writing, Diane. I'll tell you when to start again. I start off, but my nerves break because my dad's life is on the line. You, Harry, take over until I compose myself. Then you call me to the stand. Maybe I'll break down again under cross-examination. Then at the end, you get one of your asthma attacks and I have to sum up. We'll drive Norwalk up the wall."

"I haven't had one in a while."

"Harry, every time you try a case, you know you end up with an asthma attack. You have a hospital record. This won't be any different."

Wadleigh stood up, adjusted his glasses, and said, "I don't like that. I don't like that at all. That's obstruction, that's collusive—"

"Sit the fuck down, Milton. You made fifty thousand dollars last year. Try making it on your own sometime. You will starve to death contemplating the lint in your navel. You know it and I know it. Now cut the bullshit and sit down," Kleinfeld said, sweeping his hand down.

Milton Wadleigh looked at Cox, who pointed to Wadleigh's chair. He resumed his seat.

Cox tapped the yellow pad balanced on his knee. "With your father on the stand we could bring out some of the highlights of his career with people like Seabury and Dewey and Hogan. That sort of thing. That would go over big with a jury. Besides, a judge not taking the stand? What's he hiding? There's a different standard. I think he has to go on, whether we like it or not," Cox said.

Kleinfeld tilted back in his chair. "Nine out of ten defendants sink themselves on the stand. They're too immersed.

They drown. Ever see the look on the face of a prosecutor when a defendant takes the stand? The lousiest DA's case in the world comes to life. I've seen it a hundred times. Of course, when the defendant doesn't take the stand, it leaves a vacuum, but it's the lesser of two evils. And if I take the stand, I can fill the gap. At least, divert attention. I can take the weight, I'm not on trial," Kleinfeld said.

"The Brigante portion of the tape, is to be redacted or not?" Cox asked.

"Stupid Schrader can't make up his mind. Latest I heard is he's going to let the jury hear the whole tape."

"But won't that jeopardize an ongoing investigation?" Wadleigh said.

Kleinfeld made a sour face. "You think Norwalk cares about a Haynes investigation? He's going to bag a sitting judge no matter what. Besides, Norwalk's got Judge Schrader convinced that I made the whole Brigante thing up. As if a person would gratuitously fabricate something like that."

"Ridiculous," Wadleigh said.

"Norwalk is totally irresponsible," Cox added.

There was a pause as the three lawyers pondered the repercussions that might follow the divulgence of the Brigante segment of the tape.

"Why didn't you tell us Carlito was using the office as a blind? We could have all been embarrassed," Cox said mildly.

"Harry, I don't like to accuse a man unless I'm sure. Especially a friend. You don't know the torment and soul searching I went through. I'm the guy that's down there in the trenches digging up clients. You just have to sit here and theorize. I guess I didn't want to alarm you guys."

"That's what we're here for," Cox said.

"Goes without saying, Dave," Wadleigh added.

"That's why I didn't say it, Milton. All right, let's make believe I'm Norwalk. Diane, please. Now in my opening, I would . . ."

I DROVE UP TO THE SCHOOL IN INWOOD. SHE WAS ON THE top floor. I stood at the open door of the classroom. Tiny wooden tables and chairs. Like a dollhouse. Must have been twenty kids around Gail as she read from a book, in Spanish, no less. She had her back to me. Goldilocks. I'd have played less hookey if they'd had teachers like her around.

I remembered old Mrs. Connaughy throwin' rulers and erasers at us in Patrick Henry Junior High. She was right, we just hung around to break balls. The Comanches used to stand around on the street and make the squares jump up and down to hear if they had money on them. Used to keep the zip guns right in the desk. Mrs. Connaughy said, "I'm going to the office. You're the monitor, Carlos. I don't want to hear a sound, especially from André Pettiford." He was the local looney tunes. Better you put pantyhose on a grizzly. Had to hit André with a metal washpan (musta been six-two and still in junior high) and they took *me* to the principal's office. Police brutality. Never did like a cop's job. Times sure have changed.

One of the kids said "mira" and she spotted me.

"I'm the new kid, ma'am. Remedial reading." She stood up. She was wearin' a sweater. Had them good, long-term boobs. Pretty girl. No way I'm gonna let this go. We went out to the hall. She only gave me a little smile, so I had to keep my hands to myself. But I was happy just to look at her.

"Brought you a Harris Tweed jacket. Got it in the car."

"Match the one you have on, Charley?"

"Yeah, his and hers. Elbow patches and all. From your homeland."

"I am an American."

"You don't look like no Indian to me."

Her eyes twinkled. She was loosening up. Beware of PRs bearing gifts.

"Am I still bein' punished, Gail?"

"Forever and ever."

I took her in my arms and spoke into her ear.

"You were right about Dave. Me and Dave are finito. He tried to hurt those people just like you said."

"And?"

"I stopped him. We haven't spoken since."

She squeezed me, then she pulled back. I could see the wetness in the corners of her eyes. She smiled and one drop slid down her face. I figure I still got a shot.

"Charley, the kids. I have to get back inside—"

"One second. I made contact with an old friend of mine. He's in St. Thomas, doing great in a car rental business. This guy was like my brother. He wants me to come down and talk about me teamin' up with him. Maybe open up a branch in Puerto Rico. You and me, babe?"

She threw her arms around my neck.

"When are you going down?"

"When are *we* going down. I got two tickets for Friday night. Figure five days. Tell your people here it's an emergency. It is, Gail. Behind this move we could turn a corner and leave the whole pack behind, right?"

"Charley, Charley—"

Always had a few surprises for her. Right out of the ol' trickbag. On top of bein' crazy about her as a woman, she was my kind of people,'cause she was always down for the action, for whatever had to be. And that's just as important and lasts a whole lot longer.

I DROVE DOWN TO THE CLUB EARLY IN THE EVENING. SASO wanted to see me before Pachanga showed up. We locked ourselves in the office.

"I think you're going to have to get rid of Pachanga, Carlito."

"That bad, Saso?"

"You're hardly around anymore, Carlito. The man is impossible. And his woman, Elena, is worse. I haven't caught her yet, but she's playing the piano behind the bar. But I won't accuse her. I'll let you do that. He's your buddy."

"The broad, huh?"

"Elena is all Harlem. Her whole family is in dope. They come around here to see Pachanga. It doesn't bother me, but I don't want him making any serious moves while we're around. You certainly can't afford another conspiracy and the agency I'm with is coming up for refunding. Now how will I look?"

"I'll talk to him, Saso, he listens to me."

"I'll tell you something else. You might as well know. I heard from Rudy that Pachanga has been complaining that you're not into anything, that you're afraid to make a move, and that he's wasted a lot of time without making any money. Don't quote me."

"That's that skank Elena talkin'. I'll come around later and talk to Pachanga. I'm goin to St. Thomas over the weekend so I'll have to talk to him tonight."

"He thinks he's the boss. Get him out of my hair. Please!"

This beef between Saso and Pachanga had me bugged. I had to sell my piece of the club with the minimum static. Otherwise I'd never get my money out. I called his house and his old lady, Elena, said he was in the barbershop around 107th Street and Lexington Avenue. I went over. He was in a chair getting his hair cut. I saw him through the window. Couldn't find a meter so I double-parked and waited for him to come out. He was waving his arms around, so I figure he was explainin' to the guys what was what. Around here, Pachanga's opinion counted for something. After all, he spoke English.

That was a big corner in the old days. Guys used to talk about Vincent Coll having a shootout right down the block. Italian mob had a movie house, a big diner, and a bar on the corner. Plenty of the "*guapi*" (pretty ones), Neapolitan and Sicilian, around in them days. But they wasn't all pretty, least not to the Irish, who tagged them "wops."

The "Don Cheecheros" would pull up in the big cars. The button guys would be lined up along the window of the bar on the street in front of the diner. Big hats, shiny shoes. The bulls were no problem, everybody got paid. The tires, the nylons, the ration stamps during the war. Then later, the hot cars, the shylockin', the numbers, until the hostess with the mostes' arrived—the white lady. Heroin was better than Prohibition. The mob invented a whole new industry, wasn't in *Mechanix Illustrated* either. The Sicilian express, Istanbul, Marseilles, last stop to Harlem. They made millions. But like they themselves say, "Dope money is cursed." After a while, the "babonya" destroyed the neighborhood and they got chased. But they had their

time on the sunny (west) side of the street. The stoops will
tell you, "Ya seen Botch? Botcha who? Botch-a-galoop!"
"Ey, wal-yo, wadda ya know?" . . . And where'd ya go?

No more mob. Any ghinny bartender or truckdriver in
Greenpoint puts up a couple thousand dollars, right away
some wise guy sells him a button. He sticks a cigar in his
mouth and thinks he's Mafia. Wants everybody to know it,
puts an ad in the paper. In the real mob, in the old days, you
could be connected twenty years and never hear the words
cosa nostra. Nowadays it ain't secret, it ain't a society. Just
bust-out, like everybody else. *Ciao*, Rudy.

Pachanga came out of the barbershop. I think his old lady
was pickin' his clothes. He was lookin' more like a person,
he had on a nice black leather jacket. I pulled up alongside
his Pontiac.

"Sube, Pachanga."

He jumped into my car.

"Carlito, mi hermano, qué pasa? Elena said joo was
lookin' for me."

"Pachanga, me and Gail are leavin' New York, maybe for
PR. I'm not sure. But I gotta sell my piece of the club. I'm
gonna need money to retire from the street, right? I mean
we ain't got no pension system, right?"

"Right."

"I want you to stop breakin' balls with Saso. He don't
go for you nohow."

"Dat ees a moder focka, dat Saso. He go behind my
back to joo, Carlito. I lookin' out for joo. Not for no
fockin' Saso. He's a fockin' seef, robbin' all the money. Das why he don won me around. So he can clean
joo ass out. I think he's a 'cheeba,' a stool pigeon. I
think he gonna set joo up. Das what I think. Dat way he
keep all the money. What you gonna say? You in jail for
life, eh?"

"Be careful, Pachanga, be careful. Don't call a man a
'cheeba' unless you can back it up."

"Saso's a stool pigeon. I tell heem to the face. Fockin'
stool pigeon. Why he go around tryin' to find out my
business, your business, all the time? He gonna set us op,
baby, he gonna set us op."

"All right, all right. Let it be. Le'me check it out. You just be cool around the club. Don't say nothin' to Saso. I'm goin' away for the weekend, and when I get back, we'll settle up with him."

He grabbed me in a bear hug, laughin'.

"Joo sonabambiche! Joo gonna get married with the gringa. Das what you gonna do. I gonna be the padrino for the firstborn."

Crazy guy.

23

ME AND M'MAIN SQUEEZE FLEW TO ST. THOMAS FIRST
class. Honeymoon special. Here I go again. Nothin' like
sneakin' away to the islands with a fine fox. What are you
gonna do better than that? We was all cuddled up in the
front of the plane and I'm feastin' on those pretty greens
of hers with the thick curly lashes. Plus doin' a little sly
neckin' when the stewardess (fine broad) ain't lookin'. I
don't care if the goddamn plane don't ever land. Gail was
lookin' spiffy. I had her all dolled up in a new wardrobe.

"Want to hear something, Charley?" she said.

"Ain't got no money."

"No, serious."

"Flyin' up high with some gal in the sky . . ."

"C'mon, Charley."

"I'm up here in the clouds and you want me to get
serious."

"I'm late."

"That's serious. How many?"

"I figure my friend has missed attendance about three
weeks."

"Eh—you ain't been to the truant officer or nothin' like
that?"

She got mad: "I can see you're crazy about the idea."

"Of course I am. It's just that it scares me a little."

She was getting red. I grabbed hold and held her tight.
With women, you can't just accept something, you gotta
love it.

"Anything you got for me is beautiful. But it's gotta look like you. Comprende?"

"Comprendo. We'll call him Carlos, like you."

"Never. You crazy? I want one of them 'good-guy' names like Wayne or Lance. I ain't gonna raise no Puerto Rican."

We was laughin' and carryin' on. Then the stewardess brought us two drinks, compliments of some old guy across the aisle. He lifted his glass.

"Here's to love. Salud."

I guess it showed.

We landed after midnight. Scared the shit out of me when I got off. A mountain right in front of the plane's nose. I saw Earl's shiny, black face as soon as we got into the terminal. His hair was short, almost white now. He looked fit, terrific. He picked me up in the air. We was always aces, as far back as Elmira, we was tight. Still had them yellow eyes that did most of the talkin' for him.

We drove up a mountain to a place called Ma Folie. It looked down on the bay and lights of Charlotte Amalie. String of pearls. Earl had a million questions.

"Is you or is you ain't, brother Brigante?"

"I'm ready, Earl. I swear on the head of my old lady right here."

"Never mind my head, Charley, swear on your own," Gail laughed.

"Look at this, Earl. Women's lib. Nothin' but lip. How's Millie and the kids?"

"The kids are all grown up. They're in school in the States. Millie had to go to St. Croix. Moms is sick. Y'know, gettin' old."

Millie was never too crazy about me. She figured I'm down here on some dope scheme or maybe even a set-up for the feds. Like a guy named Skokie showed up from the fed joint in Marion with five kilos of federal junk for a pal of Earl's, Randy. Randy was retired, but Skokie bugged him for weeks: "You m'man, got to help me, my last break. I can quit, like you, behind this move." Etcetera. He moved Randy into twenty years. Almost buried Earl too. Bad part was Randy's wife, she was in the car. She got ten years. She's still on the lam. Skokie got fired up later on, so what, he buried Randy. I don't blame Millie. West Indian gal, I wouldn't mind Gail lookin' out for me the way Millie looked after Earl. Was her got him off the street when the big sentences started to come down. But he always had sense than me anyway.

"In the morning, I'll take you to the office. We're big here on St. Thomas. But I can get bigger in PR. I got this guy, Molina, in San Juan, near the airport. But he's robbin' me. You could expand that operation for me, Carlito, no sweat."

"What do I know about car rentals, Earl?"

"You learn. I learned. Wadda you think, they got a school? Who could ever beat you out of a nickel? You'll be great. This ain't no charity bit. You can do this job. . . . Long as you got religion."

"This lady right here is my religion. But I wanna buy a piece of the action if I'm comin' in. Like you say, no charity."

"Money never hurt nobody. How you sound, turkey?"

"Sixty, maybe seventy."

"Mmm. Got yourself a lil' stash, eh? Okay, come on down. We're goin' into business. You're stayin' at my house. I only work in the mornin', afternoons I'm on my boat. Forty-seven-footer, Hatteras, secondhand, but wait till you see the way I got her fixed up."

"I ain't goin' on no boat with you, Earl. You could hardly drive a car when I met you."

"Been down here six years. I go to St. Croix, Anegada, you name it. You'll see. I'll take you to the office in the morning, then we'll go on the boat."

Sunday was the best day. Hummin'birds, summer skies, and us cruisin' lazy-like, in and out of island coves splashed blue and green and white. The Virgins, God bless them all. Earl was up to the bridge, under a big awning, doin' his thing. Me and Gail stretched out on the deck on a big towel, catchin' sun and the spray the boat's kickin' up. I was rubbin' oil on her. Lovin' it too, Jack.

"Pretty soon I won't be able to wear a bikini, Charley."

I kissed her belly button.

"This where he's coming through?"

"A little lower."

I looked up and sure enough Earl is lookin' down, laughin'.

"Don't be doin' that on my boat, Carlito," he said.

We were high on the air. Day like that could put a smile on a parole commissioner's face.

Gulls and pelicans were loopin' and divin' all over the water. You could see fifty feet down, it was so clear. Bunches of fish swam and jumped across the bow as we cut through. So many colors! Like skimmin' on rainbows over a sea of emeralds with a white-blue sky roof. Mar Caribe. It must have haunted Columbus to his dyin' day. No wonder the PRs always come back.

I framed the set in my head. For the rainy day waitin' on me. Hoard the good times up. They can bury you in solitary, but they can't part you from your mind. Them windmills can turn in a dead calm.

I rested my ear on her stomach. Listening. Stupid, I know. She put her hands around my head.

"I still have the card you sent with the flowers," she said.

"I was a little stoned. You know how it is."

"Maybe we can divide our sadness, maybe no more Aprils without flowers. You got that from the album. Beautiful, Charley."

"No big ting."

"I know you love me."

"Who told you that lie, lady?"

"The way you look at me, I can tell. I knew you'd come back for me."

"Suppose something happened to me and I couldn't."

"I don't know, Charley."

"You'd go back to Brazil. I know you get mail from Roberto's family. I hate them, don't ask me why. I hate them."

"They're a wonderful family. But I don't think I could ever go back."

"What about this little crumb-catcher you got in the oven here?"

"That's mine. He goes where I go. And I'm not going anywhere without you. You can't live without me."

"Baloney."

She pulled me on top of her.

"Uh-oh!" Earl said.

"He's attacking me, Earl. Call a cop," she said.

"Don't do that, brother," I said.

We anchored off a white beach with a long row of palm trees almost down to the water line. I climbed up on the flyin' bridge and dove off head first. Looka me, Gail. Lousy dive too, but Gail applauded.

"Damn Puerto Rican can't dive for shit," Earl said, from up there, didn't see him jump off though. We were drinkin' chilled wine from the bottle. Me in the water and Gail leanin' over the rail and pourin' it into my mouth. She stood on top of the icebox and dove in like Esther Williams.

"She-it, she swim better than you do, Carlito. You can't do doodley-squat," but he wouldn't get in the water. "You kids play, I'm here every day," Earl said, sitting in the fishing chair, drinking cold Brillante and smokin' a ciga- rette. In the bright sun, in chinos and blue yachting cap, he looked like retired money.

I never could swim with Gail. She beat me by ten lengths to the beach. I thought of coppin' a quickie behind the palm trees. I mean we were in the middle of nowhere. One million B.C. But she wouldn't go for it. Then I tried to shimmy up a tree to get a coconut and I fell on my ass.

"I thought all Puerto Ricans could climb for coconuts," she said.

"When's the last time you saw a palm tree in Harlem?" And we chased around the beach like two kids. What the hell, you gotta let loose sometime. We knocked around in the boat some more till we got to a reef near Drake's Anchorage. Me and Gail went snorkeling. I had the speargun. A long one with three slings on it. Thought I was Buster Crabbe. She saw the fish first. No more than ten or fifteen feet deep. Came right up out of the ground. A big, black stingray with a white belly. Like a space ship with slow flappin' wings. I'm gonna harpoon this sucker. I dove quick, but Gail pulled me back. He was gone. She was shakin' her head, let him go.

We swam the length of a long fire coral reef. All kinds o
life down there. You could almost hear the organ music
There's just nothin' like it on land.

I had to adjust my mask, so I came down on a rock ledge
Ugh! Right on a sea urchin. Quills went right through th
heel of my fin into my foot. Son of a bitch. I climbed bac
in the boat in agony and Earl is hysterical laughin'.

"You is accident-prone. I don't believe you, Carlito. O
all places, you had to land on top of a sea urchin," he said
and he brought out a long huntin' knife.

"You ain't gonna use that on my foot!"

"Not, just the flat of the blade, needles dissolve quicker
No way you can cut them out."

And he started bangin' on my heel with the flat of th
blade. Earl and Gail were laughin', but I was worried. Ma
could lose a foot, I thought. What the hell did I know,
ain't no country boy.

Later we caught some of the night action on St. Thomas
Some cruise ships were in and the clubs were packed. I
ain't no calypso now, it's reggae, mon, like in Rasta-mon
I got stoned and tried to compete with this steel-drum guy
goin' under the limbo bar but I fell on my butt, again
Earl steered us around the spots, knew everybody. If
had the dude's personality, I woulda been in showbiz
believe that.

Gail was havin' a hell of a party. She was high and al
lit up from bein' under the sun, showerin' sparks all ove
them joints. Everybody was clockin' her. What's that fine
broad doin' with that Puerto Rican? They don't know, do
they? Best part came later, at Earl's house, up on a hill
with a breeze blowin', didn't need no air conditionin'.
knew the pores on her body like I know the hairs on my
thumbs, but it just got better. She wanted to know if I loved
her. She was the whole damn life support system for Carlito
Brigante, bar none. And if she wanted to have a kid, tha
was okay too.

Before I left, me and Earl got down to nuts and bolts.

"This is a business you gotta learn by doing, Carlito
Don't have to be no Einstein. Just gotta stay on top of th
heap. They will try to rob us on the gas, on the repairs

Even rentin' their own cars, instead of yours. That's why you're a natural. Been a thief all your life, ain'tcha? What are they gonna pull on you that's new?"

"I'll get my bread together and call you from New York, Earl. We'll meet in Puerto Rico, say about a month."

"I know you're scared, Carlito. Don't be. You'll adjust. It's the second half of your life. You been reborn, like the Watergaters. . . ." I got a laugh outa that.

Watergate. Best thing ever happened to the prison system. Best recreation we ever had. Better than Kojak or the FBI show (the robbers love cops'n'robbers shows). Five years in the joint, that's all I heard, Watergate. They'd all lived it. Everybody was in the joint on a conspiracy rap. So they was all hypnotized watchin' the presidential "pezzonovanta" get jammed one by one, on TV, no less.

Oh, there's Dean, looka that puss, gotta be the stool pigeon. He ain't gonna stand up. Oops, there goes Colson, attaway Chuckie baby. Not Mitchell, not Honest John that signed all the wiretap orders that put us all in here. Yep. They can't get Herlickman and Alderman. Nah, too close. I'll be damned. Watch out, Dick, easy baby. They're throwin' banana peels all over. Don't believe it. They got the Man. The main man. And with all that money? Can't be. Somethin' wrong in this country when a man cannot buy his way out of a jackpot. Can't be G. Gordon's the only standup guy in the whole crew. Stonewall. "I'll stand on any corner and you can whack me out." Beautiful. But the boys was terribly disappointed when the Watergaters got shot down. That's what ruined the American dollar. If you can't get off the hook with all those millions, what good is it?

"And lissen up, chump, stay out of them after-hours joints. Lloyd told me you runnin' a bucket of blood. You will be killed next time. Believe that. Get yo'ass in the wind or be left behind."

At the airport he told Gail.

"Do him a favor, Gail, bring him back. He listens to you. He don't listen to nobody else. Later, Charlito."

He split, lookin' kind of sad. Like he didn't believe it. On the plane, Gail wanted to know about me and Earl. I told her we went back twenty-five years. Done time together. Didn't have to see one another regular. If he needed me or I needed him. That was it. No questions asked.

"He told me you saved his life."

"I wouldn't let anybody hurt Earl Bessey. Have to go through me first. He stepped out for me more than once."

"He is a good friend, Charley. What kind of person is his wife?"

"Good woman. She's been in a lot of hassles because of him. But they made it. I think she's got a bad idea on why I'm down here. Can't blame her."

"We'll work it out. If not here, anywhere you say, Charley."

"I know you love me."

"Who told you that lie?"

She was laughin' and I grabbed hold of her. Somebody said, "Can I get you something?"

The stewardess (mezzo-mezzo).

"Yeah," I said, "I want to report this lady for makin' improper advances."

She musta thought we were crazy.

We got back to my apartment late and went straight to bed. Around seven in the mornin' I hear bangin' on the door. I went to the door. Three bulls. From the Special State Prosecutor's office. I was worried about my pistols. They were very polite. Still I got my rights.

"You guys got a warrant?"

The short, blond guy in the middle did the talkin'.

"Mr. Brigante, we didn't come here to make an arrest or conduct a search. We're here to escort you to Mr. Norwalk, the Special Prosecutor's office at the World Trade Center. I've been authorized to tell you that Mr. Norwalk wants to play a tape for you."

"Never happen. If I'm not under arrest, I'm not goin' nowhere, period. Especially without my lawyer."

"It is your lawyer, David Kleinfeld, that this is all about. He tried to set you up with the Special Narcotics Prosecutor. Believe me, it behooves you to hear this tape."

I had to hold onto the door frame and take a nine-count. Pal' ante, mi hermano.

"Wait in the lobby for me while I get dressed," I said.

"Mr. Norwalk insists that Miss Brimfield accompany you!"

"Is he crazy?"

"He wants me to make certain there will be no allegations of coercion later. He wants a neutral witness present."

"Bullshit."

"All right. We feel Miss Brimfield should hear the tape in order to help you make up you mind about helping us in Kleinfeld's case."

"I'm going with you, Charley, I'm getting dressed," Gail called out. They had me all shook up. They always jump off early in the mornin' when your head's not wrapped too tight.

"I'm not gonna be no rat. I'm tellin' you in front," I said.

"Suppose you reserve judgment until you hear the tape. My name is Duncan, these are Detectives Speller and Valentín."

Valentin, a PR with a big bush on his lip, looked familiar, but I wasn't sure from where. He and Speller weren't sayin' nothin. I insisted on drivin' me and Gail down on in my own car. If they ain't gonna keep me, why not? I followed them down to the World Trade Center.

24

MADON, WHAT A JOINT. AIN'T NO PHARAOH BUILT A pyramid bigger than Rocky's. High in the sky was Mr. Lawrence Norwalk. Early riser, wasn't even eight A.M. Tall, clean, pinstriper with light shades. Came across the rug, loose, twinkle-toed, athletic cat.

"Good morning, Mr. Brigante, Miss Brimfield, please sit down. We tried to reach you before, but you were on holiday. So please forgive the early morning intrusion, but we're on a hectic schedule. Would you like some coffee?"

No, no, none of that.

"I'll be as brief as possible, I know you have to get to work, Miss Brimfield. Okay, the situation is as follows. We obtained, via a lawful tap order, a tape of David Kleinfeld in conversation with his father, Judge Kleinfeld. We know that before that he had been to the office of the Special Narcotics Prosecutor, Mitchell Haynes, with a horrendous story about you, Mr. Brigante, being involved in narcotics trafficking, and that you were using his office as a cover-up."

"Vicious bastard—" Gail said.

"That is an understatement, Miss Brimfield."

"Let's hear the rest, Mr. Norwalk," I said, giving Gail a dirty look. She was red all over.

"He depicted you to Haynes as groveling for a handout or a menial job. And that you rewarded his generosity by using his office to shield your criminal enterprises. Accordingly, he had no choice but to go to Haynes and tell all in order to protect himself. But our own inquiries as well as input from other agencies persuades us that your hand has shied from the fire since you came out of prison. The word on the street is that you are gun-shy. Insofar as narcotics are concerned, of course. You follow me so far, Mr. Brigante?"

"Go ahead."

"David Kleinfeld, as Miss Brimfield put it, is a vicious bastard. We have concluded that this is all a fabrication on his part. A poisonous concoction to cloud and divert attention away from himself. He knows he is a prime target in the police property clerk case. He set you up as ballast or leverage against my investigation. A multikilo case could strengthen his bargaining position. I wouldn't put it past him to plant something on you. Your apartment, your car, your club. Even implicate Miss Brimfield. He is a special breed."

He stopped talkin' and went to his window to look out, then he sat down behind his desk. There was a tape recorder on it. He stared at us. He'd thrown all the knives, now he wanted to see the blood ooze. Gail was sick.

"Lemme hear the tape," I said.

"Play his portion, Speller."

"It's all set up, Mr. Norwalk," Speller said, and he pressed a button. I heard Dave loud and clear:

" '*He's nothing. Mitchell Haynes is the boss. You can talk to him. You don't know what it's about, but you come to show support for your son. In other words, 'What the hell is all this about and what is Rutledge trying to pull on my son?' You know, Dad, we have to do something. I'm going crazy. If Rutledge gives this to Norwalk, he'll splash me all over the headlines. They'll destroy me. Oh, I meant to tell you, Dad, I made some points with Haynes. I gave an old client of mine, Brigante, a job around the office as a messenger. He begged me, out of work, you know. Anyway, I found out he was still dealing in narcotics. Heavy. Making calls out of my office. I immediately went to see Haynes. They're working on the case. They want him bad. Made a good impression.*'"

" '*David, David—*' "

"Cut it there, Speller," Norwalk said. "Play it over."

"That's enough. What's all this to me?"

"We want you to get David Kleinfeld for us, Brigante."

"You know my record, Mr. Norwalk. You know it from jump street. You got to know I ain't no stool pigeon."

Norwalk got up and came around the desk.

"Not even to protect yourself from a frame-up artist like Kleinfeld?"

"Nobody's perfect and two wrongs don't make a right."

I'm dazzlin' him with footwork. His lips got very white. He looked at busy-mouth, Detective Valentín.

"You don't remember me, Carlito?"

"No, I don't."

"Johnny Valentín from the Renegades. 106th Street?"

"Sounds familiar," I said. I don't want nobody to get mad at me.

"The poolroom? Stickball? I used to play the drums at the Settlement House dances."

All these PRs look alike.

"Sounds familiar."

"Sure. I was one of the boys. Mi hermano, they got you from the short and curlies. They got Butler."

"Who's Butler?"

What the hell is he talkin' about?

Valentín looked at Norwalk. He got the nod.

"Butler is the correction officer at Riker's Island. Skinny black guy, Afro. Was caught dealin' some stuff up there. We knew he set up the Tony Tagliaferro break. He's talkin'."

"Never heard of either one," I said.

"Allow me, Valentín," Norwalk said. "Brigante, we knew you and Kleinfeld were up to see Tagliaferro before the escape. We know Kleinfeld made the arrangements. I'll level with you, Brigante, we don't have enough from Butler yet. Of course, it's only a matter of time. But we don't have time. Judge Kleinfeld's trial starts in two weeks and I need this information about David Kleinfeld now. Do you understand?"

"No, I don't."

"Brigante, we need corroboration of Butler's testimony. With your help we can break Butler down more. Get his cooperation *now*. You'll be accorded complete transaction-al immunity. Then we'll have Kleinfeld, father and son. You see?"

"No, I don't see. I don't know these people. I'd love to help you, Mr. Norwalk. But I don't know what you're talkin' about. Besides, even if I were a rat, there's the attorney-client privilege between me and Dave, right?"

He started hoppin' around, look like he was goin' to hop on the desk or out the window.

"What privilege? Are you insane? Since when are you a lawyer?" Now I get the finger in the face. "Let me tell you something, Mr. Convicted Dope Peddler, we know all about your club. All the gambling, dope, and guns that are run up there. It will get hot on 79th Street for you, Brigante. Smoke will pour from the chimney. Comprenday?"

Fuck him.

"No peeky pany," I said. He rolled his eyeballs at Valentín.

Valentín was real worried about me. Now I got me a buddy. Shee-it.

"Carlito, the dude pulled the rope-a-dope on you. You don't owe him nothin'. Cat tried to set you up. Bury you, Jack. You gonna stand still for that? Watchoo gonna do, shoot him? Not you. I know you lookin' to cut out with your old lady here. Get off the street. Beautiful. But when Butler opens up, and he will, all the way, you best be on the right side of Mr. Norwalk here. That's the way to settle up with Kleinfeld."

"I'm very confused, gentlemen. I need time to think."

"*Bullshit*," Norwalk was screaming now. "You are a jailhouse lawyer, Brigante, and have been from year one. You know *exactly* what's going on here and you've chosen to cross me! *Me*, Lawrence Norwalk. Remember that name, Brigante. You're supposed to be doing thirty years now. Through some cockamamie appeal you're back in the street. You think you're going to sail into the sunset with this lady here? Well, think again. For starters, forget about your club. Then get ready to go in again. You're not doing so hot now. Picture yourself in another twenty years. You'll be hearing from us. Get them *out* of here."

He was still hoppin' around. Regular mother-hopper on roller-skates was Mr. Norwalk in his sky-high pad in the "2001" tower. Thought I was gonna pee in my drawers. But I bowed out with style:

"Good morning, gentlemen. No hard feelings. Shall we, Gail?"

Stuck my elbow out for her and went truckin' on out.

Superjuggler Dave can pull forty-eight rabbits out of a yarmulka. Lemme see him wriggle off this hook.

We drove up the East Side Drive toward the Dyckman Street exit to Gail's school. She hadn't said a word since we left Norwalk's office.

"That's why they brought you down. To bug me into turnin' stool. That ain't ever been my stick."

"That miserable, lousy bastard Dave . . . why don't we just take off? We can go to Rio or São Paulo. I have friends there. I have a little money saved."

"What the hell am I gonna do down there? I don't speak Portuguese."

"Everybody can speak Spanish down there. You'll learn Portuguese in a month."

"What about my business deal with Earl?"

"I'm afraid. Let's just get the hell out of New York, Charley."

"Norwalk's smokestackin'. I haven't done anything. I don't have to go on the lam. Besides, I have to sell my interest in the club. At least get my money out. Just a couple of weeks, babe. That's all it'll take, I promise you."

I was scared worse than she was, but I ain't goin' nowhere without my money.

And you always have to say good-bye to a stool.

25

DAVID KLEINFELD PICKED UP THE PHONE IN HIS OFFICE.
He heard a husky voice.

"Mr. Kleinfeld?"

"Yes."

"This is Patrolman Williams. We're down here at your
garage. Your license plate is DK777, right?"

"Yes, yes. What's the matter?"

"Somebody tried to steal your car. There was an accident."

"My car? Was it badly damaged?"

"Well, you better look at it, Mr. Kleinfeld."

"I'll be right down. Jesus."

Kleinfeld stepped rapidly into the hallway, pressing impa-
tiently at the elevator button. He did not notice a tall black
man leaning against the back wall. Smartly dressed in a
three-piece suit and short-brimmed white Panama, he held a
New York Times under his left arm. The man strode forward
quickly.

"Mr. Kleinfeld," he said.

Kleinfeld turned to face him. The stranger plunged a
short army bayonet into Kleinfeld's left side, below the
heart. The impact stood Kleinfeld's hair on end as he reeled
backward, grasping the protruding handle with both hands.

"Black Bart said you should hold that for him," said the
stranger as the elevator door opened and he stepped
in.

*　　*　　*

RIGHT AWAY, THE COPS STARTED TO DRIVE US CRAZY AT the club. They even put a uniform guy near the door downstairs. Saso was in a panic. And I'm trying to find a buyer! Pachanga said he had a line on some wise guys from the Bronx who wanted to buy my piece. Saso didn't go for the idea, but I knew when they put the food in front of him, he would eat. He was always up-tight for money. I just wanted out, didn't care a shit who it was. I was stayin' away from the club till the heat wore off. Askin' for fifty, but I'd take twenty-five and love it.

Then I read in the paper that Dave Kleinfeld was in Roosevelt Hospital recuperatin' from a stab wound. Big articles. He was givin' press conferences: "Why, on the eve of my father's trial, did they try to kill me?" "Who wants to keep me from defending my father?" "What are they afraid of, what are they hiding?"

Norwalk is lucky Dave didn't get *him* indicted. Papers said Dave would try the case if they had to wheel him in front of the jury on a stretcher. Fuckin' Dave. Horse could break three legs, he still come in the money. I wasn't sure what I was goin' to do, but I went to see Dave. I knew Roosevelt Hospital from the old Palladium days. Anybody got shot or stabbed there or in the old Starlight Bar downstairs would end up in Roosevelt Hospital. Stayed busy.

He was in a private room with the door open. Propped up in bed, with his concrete hairdo, reading a stack of legal papers. He wasn't in no "extremis."

He like to shit. He threw the papers up and tried to get his hand under the pillow, but he was all bandaged up and stiff.

"Freeze, faggot," I told him. He froze all right.

"If I was here to waste you, Dave, you wouldn't even know it. When you had to use the piece, you didn't use it. Why don't you wise up."

"What do you want, Brigante?"

I sat in the chair by the bed and stared at him awhile. He was layin' down but the little fuck still gave off sparks. Reminded me of the other supercharger, Norwalk. Same size hairshirt.

"I heard the tape, Counselor."

His eyes popped like Peter Lorre, but his voice could fool you. Like who, me?

"Fucking Norwalk. Bunch of bullshit, Carlito. I'm surprised at you. They doctor those tapes, play them out of context. What's the matter with you? Falling for that shit."

Just like me. Never admit nothin'.

"A lo hecho, pecho, eh?"

"Yeah, whatever that means. What does Norwalk want from you?"

"Bury you. Offered me transit immunity. Complete."

Kleinfeld laughed. He was enjoying himself. Cock sucker.

"Immunity from what?"

"Tony Tee. Butler's talkin'."

"Bullshit. I don't know any Butler."

"But you know me. See, Norwalk figures between me and Butler we can jam you on the Tony Tee caper. Too bad he don't know about you, your old man, and Woody Cohen. Walberto told me about that."

He took about a six-count.

"Listen, Carlito. I won't even comment on Woody. He was a suicide, plain and simple. That's your old Harlem crowd mentality. They even tried to blackmail me. I told them to go fuck themselves. They're all a bunch of Jewbaiters anyway, anti-Semites."

"Bullshit. That's your cop-out. You know the clients hate the lawyers, period! Natural enemies. If the lawyer's a Jew, 'damn Jew sold me out.' If the lawyer's black, 'dumb nigger don't know nothin'.' Like that. Ain't political. You expect a thug to give you money and love you too? You'll get your lovin' from Tony Tee's crowd and Norwalk. Either way you pay."

"Only if you turn rat. Are you going to get on a stand and be an informant? C'mon. Norwalk's running around like a chicken without a head. He hasn't convinced a judge yet. He's trying my father's case himself. I'll wipe him and his office out. They're hanging by their fingernails now. He's a Jew-boy. Norwachefsky. A Yalie like me. I'll wipe the floor with him. I'm not worried about Norwalk."

"You better start worryin' about the wops. When them

lungs explode, that stiff will come up. The mob will come for you, sure as potholes on the West Side Highway."

"Maybe yes. Maybe no."

"They find out everything. What the FBI, CIA will never know, they know. Believe me, you will be notified."

"Fuck them."

"That message from the spooks was light stuff compared."

"What are you talking about?"

"I know they got a beef with you uptown. Black Bart, Tyrone, and them guys. Everybody's mad at you. You're unbelievable."

"Fuck them too. Listen, it's all a racket, isn't it? You on the street, me in the office. The idea is to make a buck and beat the other guy. Always been that way, always will. What, you got religion all of a sudden? What are you going to do? Open a car wash in Siberia? I know you're trying to sell the club and live happily ever after with your girl. Forget it. You'll never make it. That's not your destiny."

I got up.

"You're a real buddy, Dave, a real buddy. Okay. You got a beautiful future. I'll see you around."

"I got an anonymous call that you were dealing out of my office. I got scared, Carlito."

"Good to the last drop, eh? Fuckin' liar. You would have thrown me out. You wanted me as a backstop. If you got jammed, you would have planted some shit on me. Used it for leverage with the narcos. 'Look who I got for you.' You're an natural stool pigeon. I know you got old man Petrone killed that way. The trouble with me is that I came up at a time when a man could have friends. That don't exist no more. What am I wastin' time for? You don't know what I'm talkin' about."

"All right, I owe you. I'm quitting after the trial. Going to Europe. Come with me. I've got money. We'll have a ball."

"What happened to Steffie?"

"Black bitch. We had a fight. I threw her out. She's going around with some landsmen of yours. What do you say? We'll go to Tel Aviv, it's right on the water. Then jump around to Switzerland. We can go into business."

"Dave, you're headin' for London like you were shot out of a cannon. I don't even think it's Judy. You just can't take a loss. Why don't you wise up. She's gone. You'll never get her back."

"We're quits, Carlito?"

"Not really. You were never my friend. But that's my look-out. I won't hurt ya. See ya."

"Stick with me anyway. I'll make it up to you."

He stuck out his little hand, with the stubby manicured fingernails. I just turned on my heel and walked out. I guess I just went up there to hear for myself. Like say it ain't so. Like a chump.

26

" . . . **N**OT ONLY DID THE DEFENDANT, JOSHUA KLEIN-feld obstruct, impair, and pervert an investigation into corruption in the criminal justice system, but he appeared before the Extraordinary Special Grand Jury and lied about it. I, the Special State Prosecutor, will prove this beyond a reasonable doubt, nay, beyond a scintilla of doubt, I promise you." Norwalk paused here. He stood directly in front of the foreman of the jury. The jury sat erect, attentive, as the tall, rectilinear Norwalk paced in front of them. Supreme Court, Part 40, was in session.

Harry Cox rose to his feet.

"Justice Schrader, I don't mean to interrupt the prosecutor's opening, but I must object to his constant allusions to special this and special that. It is prejudicial to my client, Judge Kleinfeld."

"Objection overruled, Mr. Cox. Agencies have titles. I see no undue prejudice in referring to one by its proper name. Continue, Mr. Norwalk."

Norwalk slid his thumbs under the lapels of his charcoal-gray suit.

"Thank you, your honor. I repeat, this is going to be an extremely short trial. The issues are simple and clearcut. And simplicity and clarity will keynote our presentation of the evidence. Without recourse to hyperbole or subterfuge.

"Perjury is what this case is about, ladies and gentlemen of the jury. Simply put, did Joshua Kleinfeld, the defendant seated before you in the dark suit, one, lie to the Grand Jury? and two, did that lie or deliberate misstatement pertain to a material fact?

"The proof will flow, as follows:

"First, the Grand Jury stenographer who took the minutes of the defendant's sworn testimony before the Grand Jury. You will hear that testimony.

"Second, the testimony of Mr. Mitchell Haynes, the District Attorney for the Special Narcotics Court, who will testify to a conversation he had with the defendant prior to the defendant's Grand Jury appearance. And which totally contradicts the defendant's sworn testimony.

"The testimony of Mr. Haynes will, in substance, describe the defendant's attempts to obstruct, impair, and pervert an investigation of the defendant's son, one David Kleinfeld, by exerting undue pressure and influence upon one of the highest law enforcement officers in the city, Special Narcotics Prosecutor Mitchell Haynes.

"These acts constitute the separate misdemeanor count of obstruction of governmental administration.

"Finally, we will play a recording of the defendant engaging in a conversation with his son, David Kleinfeld, in which the son solicits the unlawful intervention of the defendant in his behalf. You will hear, and the recording will clearly establish, that the petition of the son to the father dovetails exactly with the testimony of Mitchell Haynes, insofar as what was asked of him by the defendant. As you will see, this recorded conversation immediately preceded the defendant's unlawful demands upon Mitchell Haynes.

"If you keep your eye on the ball, ladies and gentlemen of the jury, the following questions will emerge:

"Did the son ask the defendant to interfere?

"Did the defendant interfere?

"Did the defendant lie to the Grand Jury about his interference?

"Simply framed, those are the issues. I will not engage in any prediction as to the outcome of the case or venture any tiresome comments as to its merits. I would never insult the intelligence of this jury. I ask only that you listen to the witnesses and render a fair and impartial verdict, devoid of passion or sentiment. Thank you."

Norwalk bowed, then turned and walked back to the prosecutor's table, where he was greeted by nods of approval from his assistant, Duncan.

"Beautiful, Larry, beautiful. Bare bones. That's what you gave them," Duncan whispered.

Through set lips, Norwalk asked, "Was I lovable, Jeff?"

"Lovable. Surgical, but lovable."

Harry Cox, wearing a new suit and vest, sat at the defense table, Joshua Kleinfeld at his side. The older man's face was lined with strain as he sat, holding the stub of an unlit cigar in his hand. Cox was rearranging a sheaf of papers that were in front of him.

The batwing doors in the back of the courtroom were flung open and two white-smocked ambulance attendants wheeled in a man wrapped in a blanket, his right arm in a sling. David Kleinfeld, in a wheelchair, was rolled up to the gate of the courtroom well.

Cox rose, pointing dramatically to David.

"With the court's permission, my associate, David Kleinfeld, begs leave of this court to be allowed to participate in his father's defense."

Supreme Court Justice Matthew Schrader came to his feet, riled by the unexpected flourish of activity. The jurors' heads were swiveling back and forth. Norwalk and Duncan sat unruffled. They would not dignify such a crass sympathy play with so much as an expression.

"All right, wheel him in."

The attendants pushed the wheelchair up to the counsel table. They sat three abreast, Joshua Kleinfeld in the middle, David to his right, Cox to his left.

"Thank you, your honor," David said, his voice hoarse and low. The attendants took seats in the front row. David reached over his wheelchair and embraced his father with his left arm. This gesture taxed Norwalk beyond endurance. He jumped to his feet.

"Can we proceed with this trial, your honor. I mean, after all—"

"Yes, yes. Proceed with your opening, Mr. Cox."

"The defense waives its opening," Cox said and sat down.

Norwalk commenced his case.

"I call my first witness, Steven Hollander, stenographer for the . . ."

The stenographer read from a transcript of his stenographic notes of Joshua Kleinfeld's testimony before the Grand Jury.

" . . . *and you sat under a tree in the company of Mitchell Haynes, did you not, Judge Kleinfeld?*"

"*Yes, I did, Mr. Norwalk.*"

"*And did you not initiate a conversation regarding your son?*"

"*No, I did not.*"

"*Did you not go into a long discourse about how cruel life had been to your son, David Kleinfeld?*"

"*No, I did not.*"

"*Did you not compare his plight to that of one Dennis Thurston, a police officer who committed suicide while under investigation?*"

"*No, I did not.*"

"*Did you not make reference to 'markers' outstanding between you and Mitchell Haynes?*"

"*No, I did not.*"

"*Did you not say, or use, the expression special responsibility, special treatment, with regards to the investigation of your son?*"

"*No, I did not.*"

"*You neither sought nor asked for special treatment for your son from Mitchell Haynes?*"

"*No, I did not.*"

"*Did you know your son, David Kleinfeld, was having difficulty with various law enforcement agencies, including Mr. Haynes's?*"

"*All criminal lawyers have these difficulties.*"

"*Specifically, your son?*"

"*I don't recall.*"

"*Specifically about the Nicholas Petrone case?*"

"*I don't recall.*"

"*Did your son ask you to intervene in his behalf with Mitchell Haynes?*"

"*No, he did not.*"

Norwalk maintained his gaze steady on the jury as the testimony was read. He found them properly alert. David Kleinfeld started to emit gasps of air, lightly but audibly.

"Are you in distress, Counselor?" Justice Schrader inquired.

"No, your honor," David said. He turned to look at his two attendants seated at rigid attention. They raised their eyebrows solicitously, but David shook his head. He did not fail to spot the equally solicitous expression of number-six juror, a heavyset lady with gray hair. He rolled his eyes upward just a trifle.

"Continue reading, Mr. Hollander, please," Schrader said.

By the noon recess the testimony of Joshua Kleinfeld before the Extraordinary Special Grand Jury had been read in its entirety.

"Mr. Cox," Schrader said.

Cox rose.

"We have no questions of Mr. Hollander. And further, we have no objection to the admission of the transcript, *in toto*, into evidence as People's Exhibit one," he said.

"I believe that more properly lies in my province, your honor, I am presenting the People's Case," Norwalk said as he rose.

"And?" Schrader said.

"And I move the transcript be marked and received as People's Exhibit one in evidence, your honor."

"Marked and received. I believe this an appropriate time for our lunch break."

After being admonished by Justice Schrader as to their obligation not to discuss the case, the jury was filed out of the courtroom. The jurors focused on the small, huddled figure in the wheelchair as they walked past. David kept his eyes down.

"Is your honor ready to rule on our new memoranda regarding materiality?" Cox said as the last juror cleared the courtroom.

"A complex and convoluted area, materiality, Mr. Cox.

I am now roaming in the thickets of the brief your office submitted. I hope to be properly steeped in the subject matter by the end of the People's case. You shall have my ruling then, be assured."

"That time is fast drawing near, your honor, this is going to be a very short trial," Cox observed.

Norwalk added, "It would so appear. I expected a much longer session with the previous witness. I'm not sure we can produce Mr. Haynes this afternoon."

"You will proceed, forthwith, with your case this afternoon. I have the McLain case hanging fire now. I have twenty motions pending. You will proceed immediately following the noon recess. You were in such an all-fired hurry before. No excuses." Justice Schrader's admonition was met with silence by Norwalk.

Joshua Kleinfeld, careworn, fatigued, rose to his feet. He stood, legs spread, shoulders back, and adjusted his suit jacket. In a loud voice, he said, "Matt, I'm going to save you and a lot of people a lot of trouble. I want to change my plea. Let the chips fall where they may."

Cox reared his head back, stunned. As were the court personnel and the remaining spectators. Norwalk and Duncan stood passive, watchful.

David Kleinfeld seized his father around the waist and pulled himself upright from the wheelchair. The blanket fell from his shoulders.

"Justice Schrader," he said, "please disregard that statement of my father's. He is not himself. My mother, a semi-invalid, knows nothing of his indictment. He dies every morning in the fear she has discovered his disgrace. He will do anything to end this ordeal, even destroy his chances of vindication. You cannot accept a plea of guilty under these circumstances, your honor, you cannot—"

"It seems to me," Norwalk interjected, "the defendant is a judicial officer of long standing. If he wishes to plead guilty—"

David pounded on the counsel table with his left hand.

"Have you no decency? You cut off the head, now you want to hack the limbs and trample the entrails, you miserable son of a bitch!"

This brought Schrader to his feet, shouting.

"Counselor! Remember where you are. I realize you're under stress, but that is no excuse. Another outburst and I will hold you in contempt."

Apparently chastened, David slumped down into the wheelchair. The attendants rushed to his side, but he waved them off. There was an uneasy lull during which all eyes were on the gray-as-ash face of David Kleinfeld.

Cox rallied.

"Your honor, we respectfully request a recess until tomorrow morning. My associate has taken ill, and this unfortunate incident has—"

Norwalk interrupted.

"Your honor, we would accede to that request."

"All right. Court is recessed. Ten o'clock tomorrow morning."

ROLANDO WAS IN NEW YORK AND WALBERTO WAS GIVIN' him a party at Cachaça, an East Side club. He said Rolando was goin' to Madrid and wanted to talk to me about a friend of mine there. Gotta be Jorge Betancourt. What the hell, I'd give Rolando a line on the guy.

I brought Gail along. Had her all in white, off the shoulder, just enough on her ears and neck to match the gold of her color. I didn't want nothin' on her hands or arms, she's got these velvet smooth arms and shoulders. Like Bergman in *Casablanca*. Drop the horny Latinos through their assholes. Had to show Rolando who I was sailin' into the sunset (like Norwalk said) with. Was a clear night, I was sportin' my Zorro getup, tux, and a white ruffled shirt opened at the neck (with a tiny medal Gail had given me). Mala hora, buena cara.

The club was on top of the Hippo on 62nd Street. Me and Gail took the elevator up. A knocked-out joint this was. Rugs up to here. Mirrors up to there. Regular botanical garden and the lights were right, I mean you could see the people sprawled out on these long couches around glass tables. No funny lookin' people around. Altogether a very together operation. Kinda joint I always wanted (not no roach-coach like Saso got me into). There was a band in the middle of the room playin' a samba. Brazilian, I could tell by the instruments, and loud.

"Brasileiro, Gail, you're gonna love this joint."

"It's beautiful. I love it already."

We were standin' by the bar when Gastón from the Three Musketeers came around.

"Carlito—et la belle dame sans merci. Bonjour mam'selle, bonjour, Carlito," he said.

"How'ya doin', Gastón? Gail, this is Gastón, from the Waldorf."

"But I am not a chef, Carlito. I am an artist of haute couture, mam'selle at your service. I have a shop on 57th Street, come by sometime, I will have something for you."

"Thank you," Gail said. "I think I've seen your place. Very smart."

"We try. Come, Walberto and Rolando are over there."

Walberto, Rolando, and two killers were seated against the wall facing the band. Three or four American chicks sat facin' them. Young, very young, like teenagers. Buckets of booze around the table.

Rolando got up and threw his arms around me. Walberto was starin' at my old lady.

"Gail, this is Rolando, my friend of many years. This is Walberto Yeampierre."

Rolando kissed Gail's hand and bowed almost to the floor.

"Señorita, you are so beautiful it is painful. Carlito, te felicito. These are friends of mine from Miami, Camilo and Pepe," he said.

The boys nodded and gave me that shoot-you-in-the-back-of-your-ear smile. I recognized Camilo from the time I went to Rolando's house in Miami. The kiddie-chicks were just gigglin', nobody paid them any mind. Their party would start later at the Americana Hotel with Rolando and a soupbowl full of coke.

"Pliz, everybody sit down and enjoy yourself. Walberto, call the waiter."

Walberto glanced at Gastón, who got up to get the waiter. Everybody was keyed on Rolando, so when he loosened up, everybody went along. The band played nonstop samba music with whistles and giant maracas. The booze oozed. I had a borrowed, miniature .45 Colt in my crotch with a round in the chamber, so I was comfortable. Let's make whoopee, what the hell.

The band finally slowed down to "Feelings," and me and Gail went out to dance. When we came back to the table, I said, "This Cachaka place is all right."

"Cacha-sa, it's pronounced. Brazilian, not Spanish," Walberto corrected.

Stupid Puerto Rican, correctin' me in front of people. I gave him a look. Gastón looked at Gail and said, "You are, by far, the most stunning woman in the room. But I can see you with longer hair, pulled up on this side—"

And he starts spinnin' his arms around like a fuckin' helicopter. Walberto, in a sky-blue suit and shirt, with white tie, sat starin' with his arms crossed. Then he sat up.

"Roberto Pereida," Walberto said to Gail, "that's who I saw you with. You used to come here with him. I never forget a face."

"Walberto, you're amazing," Gastón said. "Of course, Gail, you used to have your hair longer, right? Poor Roberto, we heard about his accident. What a shame, such a talented boy. . . ."

They musta looked at my mug because things got very quiet. Rolando stepped in.

"Qué cosa! What nonsense is this, talking about past history. I propose a toast. To the liberation of Cuba—"

"And the restoration of private property," Gail said (sly like).

"And the restoration of the Tropicana." Rolando raised his glass.

"And United Fruit and the American Tobacco Company," she added. I banged her knee. Enough needle. Damn liberals don't know when to quit. Gastón stood up, "I propose a toast to the Superman of Havana, wherever he is."

This got a laugh and a clinkin' of glasses. The party went into gear again. Walberto and Gastón danced with the giggle sisters, but the Cubans wouldn't budge.

After a while, Rolando motioned me to the bar. He got on a stool. I stood.

"Don Jorge sends you a warm embrace, Carlito. He looks with favor on my enterprises."

They all slurp outa the same bowl.

"Me too, you know that."

"So far I am very disappointed in you."

"We gonna go through that again?"

"We still have our problem in Colombia."

"Your problem, Rolando. I am retired."

"You will not reconsider?"

"Case closed. I'm retired."

"You had a better offer?"

I stared at him. But, as usual, I couldn't read him behind the dark glasses. He backed off. He put his hand on my shoulder.

"Mi hermano, I should be more understanding. I have seen the girl of your choice. If I could but find someone like that. . . . ay, Carlito, my destiny is to wander around the world, an exile, like a golondrina, never to come to a place of rest. . . . Ay, mi Cuba, cuando te volvere a ver."

He sighed himself into a heavy slump. I knew his exile routine. I countered.

"Rolando, you will live to see Cuba again under a free flag. And you will have the last laugh over all your enemies, everywhere. The 'santos' are with you, you cannot fail."

Meanwhile, I kept my hand near my waist band. We walked back to the table, arm in arm. Ha.

"Camilo, give me the ring," Rolando said. The ring was for real, didn't come off no plaid stamps. Couple of carats at least. He held it out to Gail.

"Señorita Gail," he said, "allow me this small token. A wedding present to you from your 'padrino.' "

Gail turned pale. She knew things wasn't kosher between me and this crew. I did a quick buck-'n'-wing.

"Mil gracias, Rolando, but Gail has made a secret vow to the saints not to wear joolery on her hands until her mother recovers from her illness. Una promesa."

Gail nodded.

"That's true, Rolando. I have vowed. But the gesture is what counts and I appreciate it from the bottom of my heart. Con todo mi corazón, Rolando."

Vaya! Love a broad with a good rap.

Rolando looked around a li'l bit, then he said, "I can sympathize, Gail. I have not seen my sainted mother since 1959, when Fidel—"

He hadda take his handkerchief out and blow his nose hard. Very emotional, this Cuban. Everybody said, it's okay, Rolando, poor Rolando.

Quittin' time. Time we got to the parkin' lot me and Gail were hysterical laughin' about Mrs. Brimfield bein' sick (her moms was longtime gone) and Gail's "promesa." I was so proud of her I forget to get mad about the fuckin' Roberto Pereida. I got mad the next day though. Brazilian faggot, sneakin' around with my old lady.

27

" . . . And who initiated the subject regarding the defendant's son, David Kleinfeld?" Norwalk questioned.

"Judge Kleinfeld," was Mitchell Haynes's reply.

"And did he not go into a long harangue about the cruelties that life had visited upon his son?"

"Well, yes, Judge Kleinfeld made reference to his son having problems in his adolescence. Problems of adjustment and growing up."

"You, of course, immediately detected that he was, to use the vernacular, copping a plea for his son?"

"Objection," Cox said, rising to his feet.

"Sustained. Please refrain from the use of such terminology. Most unfortunate."

"Inexcusably bad taste," Cox persisted. He looked at David, who spread his left hand on the table. "And I move for a mistrial on the grounds that Mr. Norwalk's gratuitous remark is unduly prejudicial to my client, Judge Kleinfeld."

"That motion is denied. Continue with your examination, Mr. Norwalk. You have been cautioned."

Norwalk bowed. "I apologize to the court and the defendant. I merely intended to capsulize for the purposes of brevity and simplification."

"Continue."

"Mr. Haynes, did the defendant make reference, in the context of his son's difficulties with the law, to one Dennis Thurston, a police officer who committed suicide while under investigation?"

"He did."

"What did the defendant say?"

"That Dennis Thurston was innocent and that he didn't want to see his son similarly victimized. I'm paraphrasing, of course, Mr. Norwalk. I tend to agree with Judge Kleinfeld's evaluation of the Thurston case."

"We're not interested in your opinion of that or any other case, Mr. Haynes. This jury is only interested in the exact words used by the defendant at the time of your meeting in Foley Square Park."

"Encounter would be more exact."

"Was not your meeting prearranged by telephone, Mr. Haynes?"

"Loosely, informally. Judge Kleinfeld and I go back many years. I have a great respect and love for him."

Norwalk recoiled from the witness box as if a bushmaster had risen from it. He retreated to the rail in front of the number-six juror and pointed to the jury.

"This jury is only interested in what the defendant said to you and you said to the defendant at the time and place cited. Not in your personal predilections, likes, or dislikes. We don't give a tinker's damn for any of that, Mr. Haynes. Judge Schrader, the witness is being deliberately circuitous and evasive in his answers to the questions propounded."

"And?"

"I want you to caution the witness."

"Mr. Haynes, you are hereby cautioned that if, in fact, you have been circuitous and evasive in your answers to the questions put to you by Mr. Norwalk, you are to cease and desist from so doing."

"Your honor, I have answered Mr. Norwalk's questions as truthfully and forthrightly as I am capable of. Mr. Norwalk demands total recall and that is beyond my capacity."

"All right, Mr. Norwalk, continue your examination."

Norwalk stepped rapidly toward the witness box, placing himself before it, hands on hips.

"You are the district attorney in charge of all narcotics cases, are you not, Mr. Haynes?"

"I am, Mr. Norwalk."

"A most delicate and important position?"

"I think so."

"Yet you did not think of coming forward and reporting to my office this blatant example of judicial corruption?"

"I do not leap to hasty accusations concerning someone of Judge Kleinfeld's caliber and integrity. I ascribed it more to an emotional outburst from an anguished father."

Norwalk stiffened. The serpent had stung.

Duncan whispered from across the prosecutor's table, "Larry, Larry . . ."

Justice Schrader interceded.

"Mr. Norwalk, you are baiting your own witness, you cannot impeach—"

"Judge Schrader, I demand Mitchell Haynes be declared a hostile witness!"

"You demand? Application denied. Continue your direct examination."

"Larry . . ." Duncan whispered again. But oblivious to all, the irate Norwalk commenced pacing in front of the witness stand. Haynes sat, solid as a stone quarry. His large, brown face placid, almost amused.

"Mr. Haynes," Norwalk resumed, "is it not a fact that it was only after you yourself were prodded and threatened that you came forward and related the nature of your meeting with the defendant? And this despite the fact that you are a highly placed law enforcement officer?"

"Objection," Cox said.

"Sustained. Mr. Norwalk, I suggest that you are treading on uncertain terrain. I have already cautioned you."

Duncan, unable to restrain himself, got up and walked to the side of the discomfited Norwalk. They spoke briefly and Duncan returned to his seat.

"Mr. Haynes, what was said with respect to 'markers' in the conversation between you and the defendant?" Norwalk said.

"Judge Kleinfeld, near as I can recall, stated that he was not calling in any 'markers' on me. But if I could, to spare his boy."

"Very good. And what was said about special treatment?"

"Nothing. He asked me to own up to a special responsibility with regard to his son. Words to that effect."

"From your conversation with the defendant would you say he was aware, profoundly aware, that his son, David Kleinfeld, was in serious difficulties with your office, as well as other agencies, regarding the police property clerk case?"

"He knew his son was in difficulty, but there was no mention of a specific case."

Cox came to his feet.

"Motion for a mistrial, your honor. The question has injected into this case a collateral matter of no probative value to these proceedings, but fraught with such sensational and prejudicial overtones as to deprive Judge Kleinfeld of a fair trial. And I request the removal of a juror and the declaration of a mistrial."

"Denied and you have an exception. Once again, I must caution the prosecutor against straying into collateral matters. Next question."

"Would it be fair to say, in sum, Mr. Haynes, that the defendant set up a meeting with you for the express purpose of requesting your intervention on behalf of his son, and, in fact, at that meeting made such a request?"

Haynes's composure wilted slightly here. He dared not look in the direction of Joshua Kleinfeld.

"The question calls for a mere yes or no answer, Mr. Haynes," Norwalk said.

Haynes shifted forward in the witness chair. He clasped his hands, cleared his throat, and finally looked toward Justice Schrader. A stillness descended upon the spectators.

"I request that your honor instruct the witness to answer the question," Norwalk said.

The stenotypist sat poised in anticipation.

"Tell the truth, Mitch." The strong voice of Joshua Kleinfeld splintered the silence that had settled over the courtroom.

"Yes," Haynes said, leaning back in the chair, his moustache clamped in his lower teeth.

Norwalk turned to stare at Joshua Kleinfeld, who sat with lowered head. He returned to his seat.

"You may cross-examine, Mr. Cox," Norwalk said as he sat down.

"May we have a recess to examine the Rosario and Jencks material, your honor?" Cox said.

"Of course. There will be a half-hour recess. I have an attorney on another matter."

COX AND THE TWO KLEINFELDS HAD AN EMERGENCY parley in a courthouse corridor. The elder Kleinfeld sat on the radiator panel by the elevator banks and lit his cigar. Cox stood alongside while David sat in the wheelchair facing them.

"The only ritual left," said David, "is your prostrating yourself on a rug in front of Schrader and committing hara-kiri."

"This inquest is your idea, David, I wanted to pack it in from the beginning. Get the hell out." Joshua spat his words out through his cigar.

"We have to work together, let's not waste time with recriminations," Cox entreated.

"You want to be drummed out like some Captain Dreyfus, epaulets and all, so you can blame me," David said, ignoring Cox.

"I don't blame you, David. I blame myself for being stupid enough to listen to you. And for having sucked Mitch Haynes into this mess. All because of your hanky-panky and monkeyshines. Agh—what's the use. I'll plead guilty and get it over with," Joshua said.

"After all these years you're going to give them the satisfaction of riding you out of town on a rail? After all those night courts and all the contracts you walked away from you're going to let this fucking Galitziana, Norwalk, destroy your career, your reputation, your name? And what about Mom? What will you say to her? That you didn't do anything wrong but you pleaded guilty anyway? What happened to your balls, Dad?"

"All right, you little son of a bitch. Do whatever you want. But I'm telling you now, no character witness. They all ran, the sons of bitches. I don't want any part of them. They're all scared shitless of Norwalk. Agh—I don't blame them. I brought it on myself."

"Okay, okay. Harry, wheel me to the toilet. Dad, I'll see you in the courtroom."

Cox pushed David down the hallway to the public bathroom. Once inside, David instructed Cox to examine all the stalls. Satisfied that all was clear, David said, "Waive cross-examination of Haynes."

"Waive cross? Dave, the jury doesn't even know what I sound like yet."

"We're rattling Norwalk. We're slicing everything down to the bone. His timing is haywire now. Leave Haynes alone. He set the stage for me. All you will do is make a character witness of him."

"A character witness?"

"Yeah."

The jury was impaneled and the trial was resumed after a forty-five-minute recess.

"Your witness, Mr. Cox," Schrader said.

"Thank you, your honor. Mr. Haynes, we know how busy you are as District Attorney of the Special Narcotics Court, so I will be as brief as possible."

"Thank you, Mr. Cox," Haynes said.

"Now, then, you have known Judge Kleinfeld for how long?"

"Over fifteen years."

"And, in the course of that time, you have met and known other people who know Judge Kleinfeld?"

"Dozens."

"Who might they be?"

"Members of the legal and law enforcement community. Lawyers, judges, prosecutors, police personnel, clerks."

"Have you had occasion in the past to discuss, within this community you speak of, the reputation of the defendant for honesty, decency, and truthfulness?"

"Yes, I have."

"And what is that reputation?"

"That he is one of the finest men to ever grace the bench."

"I object." Norwalk sprang to his feet. "The answer is not responsive to the question."

Haynes continued his testimony before Schrader could

rule. "Judge Kleinfeld's reputation for honesty, decency, and truthfulness among his peers is the highest a man could aspire to."

"Thank you, Mr. Haynes. We have no further questions to this witness, your honor," Cox said and returned to the counsel table.

"Your honor, I demand that this court admonish the witness not to volunteer statements," Norwalk said.

"You demand, Mr. Norwalk?" Schrader said.

"I request, your honor."

"Mr. Haynes, you are to limit yourself to answering questions."

"Yes, your honor," Haynes replied.

"May I cross-examine the witness?" Norwalk said.

"You mean redirect, Mr. Norwalk. He's your witness," Schrader said.

"His hostility is apparent."

"Now who is volunteering statements?"

"May I continue, your honor?"

"Go ahead, Mr. Norwalk."

Norwalk remained behind the prosecution table. "Mr. Haynes, was there some question as to the defendant's reputation for all those commendable traits that engendered a discussion?"

"We lawyers, as you well know, Mr. Norwalk, are a garrulous lot, particularly in prosecutorial circles. People's reputations are often bandied about."

"Tell this jury about the last specific occasion when the defendant's reputation arose as a subject of conversation," Norwalk said, turning his back to Haynes, crossing his arms, and facing the jury.

"I specifically recall the occasion, because of an unusual occurrence, Mr. Norwalk."

"What was that?"

"Your former wife threw a drink in your face and stormed out of the Fifth Avenue Hotel. It was a District Attorneys Alumni dinner and shortly after your, eh, precipitous departure I sat at a table with a group of present and former prosecutors and we all spoke quite highly of Judge Kleinfeld, who was at a nearby table."

"I move for a mistrial," Norwalk gasped. He gripped the table for support.

"*You?* You move for a mistrial, Mr. Norwalk?"

Norwalk was frozen.

Jeffrey Duncan quickly stood and said, "Your honor, could we recess until tomorrow? We assumed that the cross-examination of Mr. Haynes would continue for at least the rest of the day. The rest of our case requires the setting up of technical equipment and so forth. This is totally unexpected."

"Be prepared to proceed at ten o'clock in the morning. I will tolerate no excuses. Ladies and gentlemen of the jury, please forgive this curtailment of the day's proceedings. But that is the unpredictable nature of a trial. Ten o'clock. I repeat my admonition. . . ."

Norwalk sank slowly into his chair. Chin tucked into chest, Norwalk pondered his public humiliation. The jurors, filing out, were reminded of that other picture of dejection, the defendant, Joshua Kleinfeld.

The massive Haynes bounded down lightly from the witness stand, buttoned his jacket, and strode past the prosecutor's table.

"Up your ass," he muttered as he walked past Duncan and the still-seated Norwalk.

28

NORWALK ARRIVED AT THE COURTROOM, FRESHLY shaved, cologned, and wearing a blue pinstriped worsted with a light shirt and tie. What was he getting excited about? He was shooting fish in a barrel. It was the unexpected speed of the trial that had disconcerted him. That malicious aside of Haynes was of no consequence. The jury was too sophisticated to be taken in by a vicious and slanderous irrelevancy. Today he would play his trump. The electronic equipment. He had implicit faith in the layman's infatuation with gadgetry. Machines had no biases, no hostilities, no axes to grind. They were irrefutable, immutable, and incapable of recantation.

Joshua Kleinfeld will choke on this tape, he thought. It will twirl around his neck and hoist him by his own petard to the roof of the courthouse. Turning and creaking slowly in the wind, Kleinfeld's tanned hide would make believers of all the other corrupt bastards. Larry Norwalk means business!

The speakers were set up at both ends of the jury box, and each juror was handed a transcript of the recorded conversation. Whatever garbling or lapses existed in the tape were promptly rectified by the written transcript the jurors had before them. David and Joshua Kleinfeld's voices sounded clear and audible. The robing room had been a perfect echo chamber, even the water running in the cooler could be made out. The jurors nodded their heads in unison as they followed every word uttered on their written copies. The tape had survived a barrage of motions from David Kleinfeld's office including illegality of origin, improper seal, and indiscriminate supervision, to arrive intact. Norwalk was elated. For "clarity's" sake, he insisted that the middle portion be replayed.

"All right, all right I'll see what I can do with Haynes. I'm not promising anything. And don't call me on the phone. Last week, that call you made sounded ominous. . . . David, I said I'd help. All right?"

"Yes . . . Dad"

"What's it about?"

"The Petrone case."

"That's over with."

"They're never over with, you know that."

"That's the one where the witness disappeared?"

"Was killed. Nuncio. And Nicky Junior walked. It's that fucking Bill Rutledge. He's after my scalp. He's trying to reopen that old-piece-of-shit case."

"I don't know Rutledge, David."

"He's nothing. Mitchell Haynes is the boss. You can talk to him. . . . "

OBSTRUCTION, CORRUPTION, MURDER, NARCOTICS—IT WAS all there. Good-bye, Messrs. Joshua and David Kleinfeld. The defendant, out of his own mouth, provided all the materiality and corroboration the statute required. Norwalk had completed his presentation. He could sum up from the top of his head, he felt. He would not even require the minutes.

The conclusion of the People's case signaled the commencement of definitive legal argument by the defense. The jury was excused and Cox delivered a long dissertation on the origins and evils of wiretapping, "big-brother," Orwell's *1984*, the four freedoms, fundamental sense of fair play, and numerous case citations. No avail. The tape held up. The case held up. Duncan and Norwalk shook hands with their eyes.

Cox sat down, gloomily. David reached over with a reassuring hand, nodding his approval of Cox's effort.

Cox, drawing heavy breaths, was visibly distressed.

"Your honor," he said, "could we recess now? I'm not feeling very well. I'm going to have to go to my doctor. Asthma. I feel it coming on."

Schrader, concerned, rose to his feet.

"I will recess now, Mr. Cox, but the defense must put in its defense tomorrow."

David Kleinfeld said, "The defense will be ready to proceed tomorrow, your honor."

"Very well. Recess till ten o'clock in the morning."

Norwalk and Duncan remained seated after Cox and the Kleinfelds had left the courtroom.

"Jeff," Norwalk said, "this is a put-up job. They're going to pull an end run on us."

"What defense are they going to put up, Larry? They can't put the old man on the stand. He's already thrown the towel in, the jury sees that."

"Not the old man, Jeff, I mean David, the son. He's going to play a *mea culpa* role on the stand. I can see the whole scenario from here. The son of a bitch will get up from the wheelchair, like a phoenix, like one of the Holy Rollers at a Revivalist meeting."

"Elmer Gantry."

"Exactly. The wayward son rising to the defense of the father. 'It's all my fault, I inveigled my father, I exploited his love for me, blame me, condemn me but spare him.' He's come back from the grave to save his father. That sort of trashy, two-bit scene. He'll take the stand, Jeff, David Kleinfeld's going to take the stand, sure as can be!"

"You'll tear him to shreds, Larry."

"Not that easy. He'll evoke a lot of sympathy with his wheelchair routine. And I don't want to overdo the Nick Petrone tie-in. Might be reversible error later on even if Schrader lets it in."

"You're right. The jury's liable to focus on him and lose sight of the ball, the old man."

"Sure, he'll embrace all the spears, and there will be none left for the old man. He's got nothing to lose."

"But his license."

"Maybe he doesn't care anymore. Maybe he doesn't give a shit. That could make him dangerous. We need more ammo, Jeff."

"Such as?"

"Such as tonight you get hold of Brigante. Take Valentín and Speller with you. Track him down. Read him the riot act. Tell him I'm working with the Southern District to reopen his old case. Talk about Internal Revenue. His girlfriend. Tell him we're going to close the club down entirely. If he won't come down as a rebuttal witness, at least to give us the information on David Kleinfeld. On Tagliaferro, on anything. Tell him I'll give him written blanket immunity. Get on his ass, Jeff. Tonight. It won't make any difference tomorrow."

"Okay, Larry."

JEFFREY DUNCAN, ACCOMPANIED BY DETECTIVES JOHN Valentín and Howard Speller, arrived at the Latin Reform and Progress Social Club on 79th Street shortly after midnight. A uniformed police officer stood in front of the entrance to the brownstone building. Speller, who knew him, engaged the officer in a short conversation before joining Duncan and Valentin as they went up the stairs.

There were only a few people in the club, mostly around the bar. The stereo was playing a slow Latin ballad. Pachanga, wearing a sports jacket and an open-neck shirt, stepped off a barstool and walked over to them.

"Pachanga," Valentín said, "I'm Johnny from 106th Street. The Renegades. Remember me?"

"Ah-si! Timbalero. Joo use to play timbales with Papi y sus diablos?"

"Right. Last time I saw you was in Queens, open class, they robbed you of the decision. I remember."

"How joo like that? Joo got some memory, boy. They rob me that night. Que pasa wiz these pipple, Johnny? I know joo wiz the bulls."

"This is Jeff Duncan and Howie Speller, Pachanga. Can we sit down somewhere and talk? Pachanga is the boss here, guys."

"Choor, why not?" Pachanga said.

He called out to the bar.

"Elena, send Rudy over. I gonna sit down wiz these guys."

Pachanga led them to a corner. The four of them sat down and ordered a round of drinks from the waiter. Valentín proposed a toast to the health of the club.

"We need it, we don' doin' so hot," Pachanga said, cheerlessly.

"They're breakin' your balls, huh, Pachanga?" Valentín said.

"Fockin' bulls,'scuse me, but fockin' bulls don't give us a break. Scare the pipple away. Before this place was worse than the subway. Plenty womens. Now I gotta dance wiz the fockin' waiter."

Valentín turned to Duncan.

"How about it, Mr. Duncan?"

"How about what?"

"The cop downstairs?"

"Oh sure. Howie, go downstairs. Tell him to take off until further notice. Orders of the Special Prosecutor," Duncan said.

Speller got up and left the room.

Valentín leaned over the table closer to Pachanga.

"You see, Pachanga, the power of positive thinkin'?"

All three laughed.

"So what joo got for me, Johnny?" Pachanga said as he sipped his drink.

"We want to help you and Carlito Brigante."

"Why you wanna luv us so much, all in a sudden?"

"We're after David Kleinfeld, bad."

"He don't talk to me, he only talk to Carlito, Johnny."

"But you talk to Carlito. He's your boy. This Kleinfeld tried to set Carlito up for a dope pinch. A frame-up. We have the proof, a tape recording. We played it for Carlito. He heard with his own ears that Kleinfeld tryin' to set him up."

"So?"

"So we want him to get even. We want him to tell us about some of Kleinfeld's swindles. He can even do it on the QT, nobody gotta know about it."

"So what joo got for me?"

"He's givin' us a hard time. You can talk to him. You guys are partners, he owes it to you. What's gonna happen to the club? With all this heat, you're gonna fold up. Then what, Pachanga?"

"We ain't doin' so hot, Johnny."

"You ain't seen nothin'. They'll close this place up tighter n' a flea's twat."

"I don't suppose to tell him his business."

"You can if it's your business too. Believe me, te convience, mi hermano, te convience."

"Está bien."

"Call him up, Pachanga. Tell him to get over here. We know he lives down the block. Tell him if he don't come over here, we're goin' over there. Tell him we're waitin'. If it takes all night. Okay?"

"Okay, Johnny. I call Carlito."

ME AND EARL HAD TIGHTENED EVERYTHIN' UP WITH THIS guy, Molina, in Puerto Rico, and me and Gail were flyin' down to stay. In about a week. I had sublet my apartment. Earl had set up a beach-front condominium for us in San Juan. I had sixty big ones in a safety deposit box in Gail's name. For once, I was doin' things right, plannin' ahead. Only hassle was sellin' my piece of the club. I figured Saso could send me money, little by little (ha). I could fly back if he found me a buyer. Pachanga could cover my back on any deal (ha). Wanna friend, look in your pocket. No further. But I was leavin' anyway.

I took Gail to a party at the Lincoln Towers. Record company guy, Beto, used to throw dances. Good hustler. In the money now. He had a gang of music people there. Kind of people, me as a no-talent cat, been chasin' after all my life tryin' to get close to their fire. Always been a music bug, except I carry a tune like the banana in the ear. Tito Puente was there, playin' the piano, no less. Graciela, Machito's sister, was singin' some of the oldies. We were all crowded around the piano. Gail loved it. I got to Beto and he made Gail sing. She sang "Amanheceu," and a couple of Jobim songs in Portuguese. She knocked them

Cubaricans on their ass. Crazy about that chick. She really had me crazy. Kept lookin' for bulges. Wasn't even seven weeks gone.

Julio Gutierrez sat down and played and sang some of his own songs. Including. You can't beat that. Even if a guy can't sing, you can't beat 'em when they do their own stuff. Because then they don't sing so much with the throat, as they do with the head. And whose head is better into a song than the guy who created it? That's true of people like Manzanero of Mexico, Julie Styne, Aznavour. The soul inside is so big it comes out on top of the voice, which they ain't got. Only one guy got the head and the throat, that's Frank. But now you're talkin' about the head "pezzonovante." Who I have bird-dogged for over thirty years. Bill Miller's Riviera on the Palisades, D'Amato's 500 Club, Forest Hills, the Sands, Caesar's Palace, the Fontainbleau, name it, I been there. I say he always holds back ten points for himself. That's his bank, that's what he builds on and that's why the walls of the Paramount came tumblin' down, but Sinatra is still standin'. He says, "'Scuse me while I disappear," but then the lights go on and he's still there. Now a Judy Garland, she makes a human sacrifice to the crowd. You could be in the top balcony, she had somethin' for you, even if she had to pull her insides out. I seen her, toward the end, in Atlantic City. Ten thousand people stood up on wooden foldin' chairs (includin' me and a few gangsters) and the faggots were hysterical throwin' flowers on the stage. "We love you, Judy, we love you," people were screamin', with their arms thrown up in the air. Nobody can pay them kinda dues for long. She sure tried that night. San Francisco. . . . She bled for that crowd. Like a Manolete. I guess they need to. They burn up quick.

Julio got a big kick when Gail asked him about "Cuban Jam Session." Knocked me out that she should even know about that record of his. Was cut in the fifties in Havana with the greatest musicians from all over Cuba. Had to be one of the all-time classic sides of Latin music. Nobody (includin' Fania All-Stars) has made a better one since. That's another beef I got with Fidel.

Gail wasn't no groupie. She knew, she felt. I got a kick out of watchin' her in this kind of crowd. She was into her own kind of high. And me with a wooden ear. Well, can't have everythin'.

Pachanga tracked me and got me on the phone. Mother fuckers. Wanna panic me right up to the plane. I told Gail I'd be right back for her and drove up to the club. Pachanga was waitin' downstairs.

"Johnny Valentín and two bulls, Carlito. They be here all night."

"Where's Saso?"

"He go out with Diane. He don't gib a chit about the club. They waitin' upstairs."

Joint was draggin' ass. Wasn't ten people in the place. Never get my money outa here.

"Carlito, over here."

My asshole buddy, Johnny Valentín.

"Carlito, you've met Jeff Duncan and Howie Speller. Sit down. Pachanga, get him a drink. Get a round for everybody."

We was all comfy and cozy.

"I can't stay. I have to pick up my wife," I said.

"She's a beautiful woman, Mr. Brigante. What is she, Irish?" Duncan wanted to know.

"Not sure, Mr. Duncan, they all look alike to us. Right, Johnny?"

It was a riot, to hear Valentín laugh.

"You're sumpin' else, Carlito."

Ho, ho, ho. He had to hold his sides.

"Who goes first?" I said.

Duncan leaned over to gimme the ol' raccoon coat, saddleshoe, American sincerity, gas.

"Mr. Brigante, it pains me to see your place like this— empty. I understand you were doing quite well until recently."

"Seasonal, Mr. Duncan."

"Look, cards on the table, Brigante. We think David Kleinfeld is going on the stand. We need your cooperation. You owe us. We played that tape for you. He could have set you up for another thirty years."

"Mr. Duncan, I want to be of all the help I can. But Mr. Kleinfeld never told me his private business. I was like a messenger, that's all."

"He must have discussed the Nuncio, the Petrone case, with you."

"Doesn't ring."

"Tony Tee. Tagliaferro. We know you know about that, Brigante. Don't play games."

"Love to help you. But Dave is very cagey. Keeps his business to himself. What can I tell you?"

"Anything. Anything that would help us show the jury what a scheming, conniving shyster he is. We'll give you blanket immunity."

"Let me sleep on it. Maybe I can think of something later on."

"Won't do us or yourself any good then."

"Gentlemen, what can I do?"

Duncan leaned back, looked at Valentín, then at Speller. He stood up. Sure enough, there come the ol' index finger.

"Get ready. Get ready for Norwalk. Get ready for the Southern District. Get ready for the IRS. Get ready to close this club down. Get ready to say good-bye to your girlfriend."

"In other words, get ready. I get it."

"Fucking wise-ass! Let's get out of here. C'mon, Howie, Johnny."

Valentín lagged behind.

"Carlito, watchoo doin' to yourself? You pass gas, they'll be on yo' ass. You actin' like a Rican just off the boat. You don't owe Kleinfeld nothin'. What are you tryin' to prove? That you're a stand-up guy? That shit went out long ago. Everybody gives everybody up. Trouble with you is you're runnin' a 1950 model. You're past your time, babe. Agúsate."

I'm noddin'. Long as they don't hit me, I agree with everybody.

I drove back to pick Gail up. And I had rainbows planned for tomorrow. Ha.

29

A**T TEN A.M. THE JURORS TOOK THEIR SEAT IN THE BOX.**
They noted the absence of David Kleinfeld. The old man,
Joshua, wore the same dark suit and dour expression. Cox
appeared equally downcast, his pallor and the puffed sacs
under his eyes denoted a sleepless night to the watchful
jurors. He sat with his arms folded.

"How do you feel this morning, Mr. Cox?" Schrader
asked.

"I will do my best, your honor," Cox wheezed.

"Call your first witness, Mr. Cox."

"Mr. David Kleinfeld," Cox said, as he stood up.

The back doors opened and the small slender figure of
David Kleinfeld entered the courtroom. He leaned heavily
on a cane and the arm of an attendant, who accompanied
him as far as the rail. The attendant veered off and took a
seat in the front row. A uniformed court officer removed
the rope from the gate and David Kleinfeld, alone, entered
the well of the court. He paused, bowed to the jury and then
with painful, hobbled steps walked to the witness box where
he ceremoniously surrendered his cane to the court officer
and took the oath. The truth was to be his only weapon.

Cox made his way past Norwalk and Duncan, who sat
expressionless, to stand by the jury box. Walking wounded,
thought Schrader, let's see them pull this one off.

"May I commence my examination of the witness, your
honor?"

"Proceed, Mr. Cox."

"Thank you. Mr. Kleinfeld, you are an accredited member of the bar, are you not?"

"Yes, I am, Mr. Cox."

"You were an honor student at Yale, having made *Law Review* and summa cum laude."

Yes, sir.

Norwalk rose.

"Objection. That is not a question and we are not interested in the witness's academic credentials. He is not here in the capacity of an expert."

"I'll allow it. Proceed, Mr. Cox."

"Thank you. You are, Mr. Kleinfeld, the son of the defendant, Judge Kleinfeld?"

David sat rigidly. He wore a dark blue suit and tie. His right arm was in a black sling. Laboriously, he turned his head away from the jury, toward which he had fixed his gaze, and looked in the direction of his father.

"Yes, he's my dad."

"Here we go, Andy Hardy," Norwalk murmured to Duncan.

Cox whirled.

"Would your honor instruct Mr. Norwalk to refrain from making remarks? I can hardly speak. Do I have to put up with his comments as well?"

"Mr. Norwalk, please. Proceed, Mr. Cox."

"Straight to the issue. Mr. Kleinfeld, you heard the tape?"

"Yes."

"Was it accurate?"

"Insofar as it went, yes."

"What do you mean."

"I mean it is a fragment, a piece of the mosaic, taken out of context."

Norwalk rose.

"Objection. The witness is attempting to qualify the evidence."

"Overruled. Proceed, Mr. Cox."

"Can you elaborate, can you fill in the missing portions, Mr. Kleinfeld?"

"I will try." Here David flinched and closed his eyes.

"Is the witness in pain?" Schrader said, standing up, staring at the contorted face before him.

"It's my stab wound, your honor. Can I have some water?"

He was served water by the bailiff. He handed the glass back after gulping half the contents.

"All right, I'll try to project the whole picture. I had been under investigation by numerous law enforcement agencies, as a result of having obtained favorable results in various organized-crime prosecutions."

"Objection. Self-serving," Norwalk exclaimed.

"Overruled. Continue, Mr. Kleinfeld."

"Thank you. I became paranoid. Obsessional. I have a fragile nervous system to begin with. I saw myself disbarred, convicted, imprisoned. Constant nightmares. The disgrace. My father, a distinguished judge, how could he live it down? He, who was a symbol of integrity to the entire bar. How could I do this to him?"

Norwalk rose again.

"Objection. Need we probe every nook and cranny of this witness's state of mind? Where is the probative value?"

"I'll allow it. Overruled."

"Thank you, your honor. In this state of hysteria, that's the word for it, I even contemplated suicide, I went to see my father in his chambers. It was about two in the morning and he had just processed over a hundred and forty cases. He was literally reeling from the impact. I went there, at that ungodly hour, to seek advice, only. Who else could I turn to? I am his only child. We have always been very close. Instead, I turned into a sniveling, cringing coward and tore at his heartstrings with my cries for help. When I heard the tape, I realized what a reprehensible and loathsome act I had perpetrated against my father. How I had, through my own near-insane fears, infected my father, so that he, almost in a craze to save my life—I had threatened suicide—went out and spoke to Mr. Haynes in my behalf—"

David's voice broke here, and a sob racked his throat. He took a handkerchief from inside the sling and blew his nose.

"Forgive me, your honor, I don't want to play on any-one's sympathy. I just want the jury to hear the whole story."

"Do you want to take a recess? To compose yourself?"

"No, your honor. I want to finish what I have to say."

Norwalk's eyes were riveted on the jury. They were alert, gaping at David. Norwalk was disgusted. How could this jury listen to such Stella Dallas claptrap? He snickered, shaking his head.

"Mr. Norwalk, please!" Cox said. "Continue, Mr. Kleinfeld."

"Thank you. The tape leaves out the after portion, when I drove my father home and threatened to stop the car and throw myself off a bridge. The tape leaves out the part where I threatened to tell my mother, an invalid, and his wife of forty years, that he refused to help me. The tape leaves out the unnatural terror I instilled in his heart for the life of his only son. I took that great love he has for me, I took that unimpeachable reputation of his of almost seventy years standing, and threw them off the bridge. Instead of myself—"

Kleinfeld broke into uncontrolled sobs, with tears running down his face.

"Mr. Kleinfeld, you must control yourself. Call a recess—" Schrader said.

"No, no, your honor. I have to return to the hospital. I have to get this over with. Let me finish here today. I will control myself. I'm sorry, ladies and gentlemen of the jury."

"Will the court instruct the witness not to address the jury that way?" Norwalk demanded. He and Duncan were thoroughly panicked now.

"Eh, yes. Mr. Kleinfeld, please refrain. Continue, Mr. Cox."

"What else transpired between you and your father in relation to the matters referred to on the People's tape?"

"I cried and whined and pleaded and literally forced him to speak to Mr. Haynes. I am the culprit, I am to blame—"

"*Objection*. The witness is summing up. I have been

patient long enough, your honor. That the witness cajoled the defendant is of no relevance. Nobody put a gun to the defendant's head. This is travesty, this is Restoration farce. The witness is an experienced and cunning criminal lawyer, he can't—"

"Former lawyer, Mr. Norwalk," David said. "Former lawyer. My resignation from the Bar was delivered by messenger to the Bar Association this very morning, effective immediately. It will not expiate my sins against my father, but it will serve to assuage my conscience."

Norwalk was numbed into silence. Joshua Kleinfeld stood up from his chair at the counsel table.

"David, *what* did you do? You have a whole career in front of you. It's not worth it—"

The uproar was instantaneous as David, Joshua, Cox, Norwalk, and even Duncan started talking and yelling at once.

"Order, order—" Schrader shouted as he banged on his desk. The tumult subsided by degrees as all the parties resumed their seats.

"Your honor," Cox said, "in the interest of brevity and adhering to the limited issues we have raised, to wit, Judge Kleinfeld's state of mind and lack of criminal intent, we respectfully request that your honor circumscribe Mr. Norwalk's cross-examination to these very same issues. In other words, tailor the cross to the dimensions of the direct examination. Else Mr. Norwalk will drag in every extraneous and collateral matter extant, and protract and cloud the true issue, I repeat, Judge Kleinfeld's state of mind."

Norwalk smiled broadly.

"Mr. Cox is now endowed with the gift of prophecy. He professes not only to read my mind but proposes to limit my cross-examination to the issues he would frame. He would presume to delineate the parameters of this trial and usurp the functions of this court. If it did not smack of arrogance, I would call it arrant nonsense," Norwalk said, pacing up and down before the bench.

"We all acknowledge yours as a kinetic and dynamic

personality, Mr. Norwalk," Schrader said. "But would you mind standing in one place so I can rule?"

"Of course, I'm sorry, your honor."

"The formulation of the legal issues," said Schrader, "is my exclusive domain and will be in my charge on the law. The permissible extent of cross-examination is also my province. You will register your objections *seriatim*, Mr. Cox, as they appear. Not in anticipation. Proceed, Mr. Norwalk."

"Thank you, your honor," Norwalk said and bowed slightly to the bench. He walked rapidly to his table and was handed a folder by Duncan, two inches thick. David Kleinfeld's dossier.

"Mr. Kleinfeld. Mr. David Kleinfeld," Norwalk began, turning the folder to the first page as he advanced toward the witness chair.

"Yes, Mr. Norwachefsky. I mean, Mr. Norwach, Mr. Norwalk," David said.

Norwalk put the folder down.

"Are you trying to be funny, Kleinfeld? You know his name," Schrader said.

"Your honor, I knew him as a famous runner at Yale, Norwachefsky, from the Bronx. I'm sorry. Norwalk, Norwalk. Okay."

Some of the jurors tittered, drawing a glare from Norwalk. He lifted his glasses, adjusted them, and attempted to smile, but the muscles on his face were almost knotted. Norwalk reopened the folder.

"Is it not a fact that you were walking around the hospital before you appeared here in a wheelchair?"

"That's a lie. The nurses helped me around the floor, but I am still confined to a wheelchair. I insisted on coming here on my own feet against doctor's orders. I still bleed inside. I have to go back to the hospital. But I'm here. Somebody didn't want me on this stand. I don't know why, I don't know who. Maybe you know, Mr. Norwalk."

Norwalk stepped away from the witness stand.

"What kind of nonsense are you spouting now, Kleinfeld? With all the crooked deals you've engineered, your list of enemies would stretch from here to Battery Park."

"Objection. Argumentative, and move for a mistrial," Cox said.

"Objection sustained, motion denied. Put a question, Mr. Norwalk."

"Yes, your honor. The Petrones, let's talk about the Petrones, also father-and-son team. Big racketeers, no? Clients of yours, yes?"

"Objection."

"They're on the tape. I'll allow it."

"Yes, Mr. Norwalk, clients of mine."

"Tell us, Mr. Kleinfeld, on the tape you said Petrone, the father, was gone. It's clear you mean dead. How do you know this? His body has never been found."

"By gone, I meant disappeared. I don't know where he is, or if he's dead or not."

"This relationship of yours with the elder Petrone alluded to in the tape, what was its nature?"

"Attorney-client, Mr. Norwalk."

"You went on a European tour with Petrone, did you not? Palermo, Geneva?"

"Yes, Mr. Norwalk."

"You know, of course, that he was in the top hierarchy of organized crime in this city?"

David Kleinfeld began to shake. Sweat particles glistened on his forehead as all color drained from his face. He rose slowly from the witness chair on unsteady feet and stood upright, his body swaying back and forth, eyes opened wide. He slid his right arm out of its sling and with both hands seized hold of his neck.

"You want my head, Norwalk. Here it is, take it. I'll wrench it off my shoulders for you. But leave my father alone, you fucking—"

Blood appeared at the corners of his mouth and he gagged, still holding his throat. He fell back into the witness chair, unconscious. The courtroom was turned into a shambles as court officers, ambulance attendants, emergency unit personnel, and even members of the jury all commingled in a confused mess scurrying back and forth.

Justice Schrader's shouts could not be distinguished above anyone else's, including Judge Kleinfeld's.

Miraculously, David Kleinfeld was not totally drained of blood by the time they got him to the hospital.

30

THE FOLLOWING MORNING JUSTICE SCHRADER ORDERED summations to commence, irrespective of the incomplete cross-examination of David Kleinfeld.

"The witness has undergone emergency surgery. There is no telling when he will be available again, Mr. Norwalk."

"You could grant a continuance, your honor. Or convene the courtroom at the witness's bedside."

"With all the jurors?"

"Yes, your honor."

"And you cross-examining the witness through a maze of bandages and glucose bottles?"

"There's a precedent for it, your honor."

"I can't believe you are serious, Norwalk. Application denied. Bring in the jury. Mr. Cox, you will deliver your summation first, followed by Mr. Norwalk. I will charge this afternoon."

Cox rose and advanced toward the jury box, empty-handed, not a sheet of paper in sight. Joshua Kleinfeld shifted to Cox's seat to bring himself closer to the action. Harry Cox leaned on the railing of the jury box in front of juror number three, a florid-faced Con Edison employee.

"Justice Schrader, Judge Kleinfeld, Mr. Norwalk, Mr. Duncan, ladies and gentlemen of the jury. This is not my cracker-barrel, just-plain-folks routine. I'm leaning here because I can hardly stand up. You can imagine what Judge Kleinfeld and I have been through at the hospital with his son. Fortunately, at least for me, we've reached the

end of the line. I can go no further. Mr. Norwalk told you at
the outset that this would be a short trial. He was right. And
I am going to make the shortest summation on record. If I'm
supposed to dazzle you now with oratory, forget it. I'll leave
that to Mr. Norwalk. As must be painfully clear to all, I am
not a trial lawyer. That was Dave's forte. By the way, he's
still hanging on.

"Also by the way, I'd like to say something before I
forget. See that old man there, Judge Kleinfeld? Well, with
all the faltering and stumbling that I've done around here,
he has yet to complain one iota. I would like to express my
appreciation, if I may. I'll tell you something else about
this man that you'll never hear again in a courtroom but
was evident throughout this trial. And that is that Judge
Kleinfeld himself doubted his innocence. We had a hard
time convincing him. That's the kind of man he is. That's
the kind of standards he has always lived by. But even he
is human, and a parent, and subject to all the frailties that
parenthood exacts from us when dealing with our children.
Particularly an only child. Even he didn't realize how deep
the instinct to protect one's young runs. It is a primeval
force within us all and I challenge any parent worthy of
the name to deny it. And it was in a state of blindness
and emotional turmoil from the cries and exhortations of
an almost deranged son that he went to see Mr. Haynes and
then the Grand Jury. Mr. Norwalk will tell you he went to
the one to obstruct, to the other to perjure himself. I ask
you, ladies and gentlemen of the jury, a man of his stature,
in such a total state of anxiety and bewilderment, subjected
to the panic and the inhuman pressure of a profligate son,
could such a man have formulated the necessary criminal
intent, the *mens rea* if you will, to commit perjury and
obstruct justice? You have seen the state and condition of
David Kleinfeld. It does not require the vaunted clinical eye
to visualize what Judge Kleinfeld was subjected to. Dwell
on that for a moment when you retire to deliberate.

"The underpinning of any criminal activity must, by
definition, be criminal intent. Lust, greed, self-enrichment.
Here, the mind of the actor was not on any of these.
It was on salvation—rescue. Perhaps of one not worthy,

not deserving. But who can say that to an anguished parent? Look into your own hearts before you answer that question.

"You have, no doubt, noticed that I have not been enumerating fact one, fact two, and so on. But it is not because I fear to confront them or seek to skirt them, or sweep them under the rug. No. It's because we concede them. We never quarreled with the facts adduced by Mr. Norwalk. We, however, vary with him on their interpretations and significance. And if we have erred, it is on the side of humanity and compassion and understanding. Not on some inflexible slide-rule computation of guilt or innocence. Not when the human heart is involved.

"Nor have I embarked on a lecture on the law. That is his honor's sovereign province. But you will, no doubt, hear the word materiality bruited about. It is a troublesome concept that has intrigued legal minds all the way back to Lord Coke, who may have been its original conjuror. In that regard, let me say merely this. And I repeat, I do not intend this to be a legal definition of materiality. But wherein was the material profit to Judge Kleinfeld in this case? Or conversely, wherein was the body politic diminished or made poorer by Judge Kleinfeld's acts? Did anybody line his pocket because this old man faltered before the Grand Jury to save his son? These people of the state of New York that Norwalk keeps talking about, how were they hurt? Was anybody so aggrieved that we must now destroy Judge Kleinfeld? Use your God-given common sense in determining these questions.

"I will conclude now. I have, as I promised, made this a short summation. Mr. Norwalk will speak last. In the final analysis, he is just a lawyer, as am I. He is not the people, you are the people. I won't embarrass you, or myself, by waving the flag. But you know what's at stake for this man. I know you will uphold your oaths and do what you think is right. Please don't make a mistake. Thank you."

"THERE WILL BE A HALF-HOUR RECESS," JUSTICE SCHRADER announced. The courtroom emptied out, except for Norwalk and Duncan, who remained seated at their table.

"What did you think of it, Jeff?" Norwalk asked Duncan.

"This is a hard-as-nails jury, there are only two women on it. They're not going to be taken in by this sappy routine they worked up. I mean, maybe they scored a dinky base hit when Dave Kleinfeld threw his fit, but not—"

"Not wide as a church door, nor deep as a well. But . . . I'm worried. I'm worried. All right, let's go over the notes again."

31

HARRY COX CRANKED THE HANDLE UNDER THE BED IN
David's private room at Roosevelt Hospital.

"Everybody got their check?" David said, sitting up under
the sheets.

"Yes, thanks. Milton and Diane sent their love."

"You all did a hell of a job. Especially you, Harry. A
jury acquittal in less than five hours. Norwalk must have
shit. I'd have given anything to have been there."

"No, you wouldn't, Dave. He's coming after you, like
gangbusters. Special task force. You'd think you were Jim-
my Hoffa or somebody."

"Fuck him. I don't want to talk about Norwalk. Harry,
you were great. There was something likable, decent, about
you up there. You really looked good. You'll be okay.
You'll make it without me fine."

"Without you to pull in the cases, I'm worried about
Milton and me making that rent. It's a big nut."

"I'm glad you said that. A lot of shit is going to come
out about me when I'm gone. Before you sit in judgment on
me, think of your monthly nut. Then think of what I had to
do, to carry it all this time."

"You're really going, eh?"

"Before the end of the week."

"But where will you go?"

"Better you don't know."

"None of my business anyway. What about your father?"

"He's been in to see me. He's still pissed off. I figure

we're even. I got him in, I got him out. He doesn't see it that way. He's putting in his papers. He told the administrative judge to go fuck himself. Maybe he can join up with you guys."

"Why not? We can use him. Keep the name on the door. That's a hell of a good idea."

"Have you seen the *Law Journal*?" Kleinfeld asked almost proudly.

Cox nodded. "Had your resignation right on the front page."

"Well, I went out with a bang. And I played for all the marbles. Tell you the truth, I'm not complaining. To coin Carlito, 'For a sparrow, I flew pretty high.'"

"What happened to him?"

"I think he went to Puerto Rico. I'm not angry with him anymore. I wish him well."

"Good riddance. That's one mistake I'll never make—getting too chummy with that riffraff. Arm's length at all times. I have to be going. Dave. Good luck. If you ever need me, you know where to find me." They shook hands.

"If you can pay the rent, Harry."

Cox was laughing as he went out the door.

PACHANGA RANG THE BUZZER OF THE APARTMENT DOOR. It was opened by Brigante. He and Gail were packing their clothes.

"Entra, Pachanga," Brigante said.

Pachanga stayed by the door.

"Hola, Carlito. Hi ya, Gail. What time do joo gwan me here in the morning?"

"Plane leaves at nine-thirty, Charley," Gail said. "Have him here at eight."

"A las ocho, okay? Listen, where's your car, Pachanga?"

"Double-parked downstairs."

"Drive over with us to Gail's place on 90th Street, off Riverside Drive. With two cars we can do it in one trip. This woman has more clothes—"

"Look who's talking," Gail said.

"I wait for joo downstairs, Carlito. I don gwanna get a ticket," Pachanga said as he started for the elevator.

"Okay, we'll be right down," Brigante said.

Brigante and Gail arrived on the sidewalk to find Pachanga's Pontiac double-parked in front of the building. Pachanga turned the corner of West End Avenue hurriedly and walked toward them. It was dark.

"I gotta call Elena ebry half hour. That was the ten o'clock call. Drive me crazy, that gwoman," Pachanga apologized.

Brigante and Gail laughed. They drove up Riverside Drive in Brigante's Cougar followed by Pachanga in his car. On 90th Street they made a right turn and both cars double-parked on the north side of the street, one behind the other. Pachanga alighted quickly to the street and held the passenger door for Gail as she stepped out.

"Carlito, stay here," Pachanga said, "we take turns. I left my keys in my car. C'mon, Gail," as he lowered the window on the door, "how we suppose to get the clothes in the car if joo got the window op? Ave Maria, Carlito."

Brigante chuckled as Gail led Pachanga toward the steps of the brownstone. A Camaro turned the corner slowly from Riverside Drive and proceeded east into the block. It braked gently alongside Brigante's car as if having difficulty passing. Brigante glanced to his right.

"Hey, Carlito, look what I got for you—"

He saw the white face with the long nose just as a blunt object landed on the seat next to him. Benny Blanco.

Brigante hit the door with his left shoulder. He was halfway out when the grenade exploded, blowing the roof up from the car. Brigante was lifted in the air, his back riddled with metal. He fell face down across a parked car at the curb, rolling his smoking body from side to side and banging the hood with his open hand as the shrapnel chunks seared him like so many burning spits.

The Camaro burst forward toward West End Avenue, where it cut right on screeching tires and was gone.

Gail and Pachanga screamed, then bounded down the steps. Brigante lay on the hood covered with blood and soot, his tattered clothes scorched and hanging in strips. They carried him to the backseat of Pachanga's car. Gail jumped in behind the wheel. Pachanga slid into the backseat.

"St. Luke's is the closest one," she shouted, and shot the car east toward Amsterdam Avenue. Pachanga cradled Brigante in his arms.

"Ave Maria, Carlito, ave Maria—" Pachanga said, over and over. He heard Brigante whisper.

"I'm not gonna make it, Pachanga."

"We get to the hospital, Carlito. Hold on."

"Neither are you, cheeba. Look!"

Pachanga saw the gleam of the nickel-plated barrel in Brigante's hand. It was the brightest light he had ever seen. A muffled double impact erupted his chest, even as he was lifted backward and thrown against the frame of the vehicle. Gail slammed the car to a halt.

"Charley, what happened?"

"Pachanga. . . . Pachanga set me up. Get out of the car. I'm through."

She gunned the car forward again.

"Don't try to talk, Charley. The hospital's on 113th Street. We can make it. Charley, hold on. Please, baby, just hold on!"

The dead Pachanga was upright, his gaping eyes and mouth petrified in disbelief. Brigante, his vital organs lacerated and hemorrhaging, slumped against Pachanga's legs.

She sped headlong through the traffic lights, swearing and crying the length of the route. A sudden braking jarred the fading Brigante. She jumped out of the car and ran to open the back door. Brigante extended his hand, it held the Magnum. His voice sinking, he said:

"Here, take it, put it in your pocketbook. Now you have to get outa here. You want me to go to jail for the rest of my life? Get the fuck outa here. I'll start honkin' the horn, they'll come out. I tol' you five years ago, get outa my mess, girl, now split!"

She took the pistol and held it inside her jacket as she backed away from the car, stunned, almost blinded by tears. She crossed to the west side of Amsterdam Avenue. She leaned against the corner building, clutching her sides, suddenly cold.

Brigante leaned over and grasped the steering wheel with both hands and pulled himself up over the horn, pressing down on it with his elbow. A uniformed officer came down the hospital steps and peered into the blood-spattered Pontiac. He ran back toward the emergency entrance as the horn wailed loudly into the night. Passersby gathered around the vehicle. The officer reappeared with two attendants, running, each pulling a wheeled stretcher clattering up the sidewalk.

People ran past Gail as the excitement surrounding the Pontiac mounted. Dazed, cramped with pain, she drifted back to stand in the midst of the gathering crowd. In front of her a short man, wearing an undershirt, suspenders, and sneakers, sipped on a beer can. To no one in particular, he announced, "Them dudes is gone, g-o-n, long gone." Then, turning his head toward Gail with the back of his hand over his mouth, he murmured, "Lady, you best quit this scene. He gave you somethin'. You got blood all over you. Better check out. Know what I mean?" He raised his voice. "Yeah, last call for them guys."

She stared at the stranger, tightening as she fought an urge to scream. She drew back and stepped off the curb, away from the mass of people. Crossing diagonally toward Broadway, she broke into a run. She never turned back.

32

Y EP, I HEAR THE MUSIC ALREADY. LIKE A TRUMPET
solo, mufflin' a long note, far away . . . sounds like Miles.
Maybe that's where people go when they die. . . . Birdland.

Somebody's pullin' me. Close to the ground. I can sense
but I can't see. I ain't panicked . . . been here before. Same
as when I got shot up on 104th street. White, everything
goes bedsheet white. Like one of them spaced-out Italian
flicks where Marcello wanders around on a blank canvas.
Next they gotta beam a big light down on my face, like in
the dentist chair. Yeah, I been here.

No pain. Floatin' easy now. I know people are movin'
around me. Can't help. All the stitches in the world can't
sew me together again. But my heart don't know how to
quit. Still holdin' up. They'll take care of that though.
Fuckin' emergency rooms—don't save nobody. And they
always bag you at midnight when all they got is a Chinese
intern with a dull spoon.

Now I'm hearin' "Moody's Mood For Love." Yeah, King
Pleasure. Man, that's old. "There I go, there I go" . . . You
goin' all right, Carlito. So big deal.

But they're takin' me out to a jazz sound, instead of
salsa. And me an old Palladium man. Story of m'life, torn
twix and tween. Caught on the shuttle again. Can't make it
in PR, don't want me in the U.S.A. Like the landlord said,
"an undesirable tenant." Fuck him too.

What am I bitchin' about? I partied both sides. Made

439

a dollar. Never did no work. Now I want a towel too? Lay down.

Lay down. Ha. Gonna stretch me out in Gonzalez' Funeral Home on 109th Street. Always knew I'd make a stop there. But a lot later than a whole gang of people thought. Hung in, last of the Mohiricans. Yeah.

Maybe not the last. Gail won't take the kid out. Good broad. Best in the west. And I had to mess her up twice. . . . What the hell, she got my money. I did the best I could. She'll be all right. Don't think about her, it's bad enough you're bleedin' to death.

Blossom Dearie's on this vocal too. Forgot about that. "Lemme take you by the hand" . . . musta been '52. Where was I? Elmira. Yeah, with Earl and Rocco. Earl's the only one with any sense. I never had no sense. Only luck got me this far. Run outa that too.

Still cryin', eh, turkey? Ran around in cars and planes, didn't you? Jooged plenty women too. So? That's where I gotta put my mind. "Show me a man believe in the hereafter, I'll show you a man wanna get laid in his coffin." Amen.

Can't make this trip by myself, right? Let's see. Who's gonna be the lucky broad? Like to get some of that stewardess was on the flight when I went to St. Thomas. Yeah, big legs. Sure, why not. By coincidence I get on a plane and there she is. I'm in the money again and ridin' first class, so right away she gotta notice me. But I'm cool. . . .

Cool? I'm freezin. Gettin' the shakes now. . . . Okay, last call for drinks, bar's closin' down. . . . Don't serve no more drinks, Rudy. Send them home, the sun's out. Where we goin' for breakfast? Don't wanna go far. Rough night. Tired, babe, tired . . .